LONG TIME LOST

Chris Ewan is the award-winning author of *The Good Thief's Guide to . . .* series of mystery novels, which are in development for US television. His debut, *The Good Thief's Guide to Amsterdam*, won the Long Barn Books First Novel Award and is published in thirteen countries, and was followed by *The Good Thief's Guide to Paris*, *Vegas*, *Venice* and *Berlin*.

Born in Taunton in 1976, he now lives in Somerset with his wife, Jo, and their daughter. *Safe House*, his first stand-alone thriller, was a number-one bestseller in 2012 and was shortlisted for the Theakston's Old Peculier Crime Novel of the Year Award. *Dead Line* was published in 2013 and is optioned for film. *Dark Tides* was shortlisted for CrimeFest's eDunnit award for the best crime fiction ebook.

www.chrisewan.com
@chrisewan
www.facebook.com/chrisewanauthor

also by Chris Ewan

SAFE HOUSE
DEAD LINE
DARK TIDES

Long Time Lost

CHRIS EWAN

FABER & FABER

First published in 2016
by Faber & Faber Ltd
Bloomsbury House
74–77 Great Russell Street
London WC1B 3DA

Typeset by Faber & Faber Ltd
Printed and bound by CPI Group (UK), Croydon CR0 4YY

A CIP record for this book
is available from the British Library

ISBN 978–0–571–30747–0

2 4 6 8 10 9 7 5 3 1

For Lucy Fawcett, with grateful thanks.

PART I

Isle of Man

Chapter One

The phone call reached Miller two days later, gone two o'clock in the morning. It didn't wake him because he hadn't been sleeping. He was staring at his reflection in the window of his seafront hotel room, smoothing his fingers over a child's drawing of a cowboy on a horse.

He took a deep breath – he'd been waiting four long years for this moment to come – and raised the mobile to his ear. It was a prepaid handset that he'd ditch as soon as the call was finished.

'Tell me,' he said.

'Someone came here. Just like you said.'

'And?'

No answer.

'You have to tell me what happened, Kate.'

'Can't you come? I really think you should come.'

Which pretty much told Miller everything he needed to know.

He folded the drawing away, tucking it into a well-worn pouch in his wallet, then grabbed his backpack and scanned his surroundings for anything he could have missed. He'd registered at the hotel under an alias. He hadn't used the bed or the bathroom since the room had been cleaned at his request late that evening. The only trace of his presence he would leave behind were the remains of the room-service meal on the tray over by the door.

'Don't call anyone else and stay inside the house. Pack a small bag. Just one.'

'You'll come, then?'

'I'll be there soon. But remember, Kate: there's no going back.'

*

Two Days Ago

Miller waited in the darkness. He was sitting on a tiled floor with his back pressed against a towering wall of rain-beaded glass. Behind him, moonlight shimmered on a restless ocean.

The house was high-end, sleek and minimalist. It was cantilevered out over the top of a cliff above Laxey Beach. There were a lot of hard edges. Plenty of steel and glass. There wasn't much furniture but what there was had been carefully chosen and expensively acquired. Miller had seen an article about the design and construction of the house in the airline magazine he'd flicked through during his flight to the island. It was just one more reason why it was a terrible choice.

Kate came in through the door that connected with the garage. She hit the light over the hob and filled a tumbler with chilled water from the dispenser on the fridge. She was short of breath and dressed in running gear: a lightweight windbreaker, three-quarter-length leggings and yellow sports shoes. Her fine red hair was pulled back into a ponytail and dewed over with drizzle. He knew she liked to run. It was part of her routine.

Which was another mistake.

Not so much for her physical conditioning. There was no disputing that she looked fit and toned. Standing with her head tipped back and the tumbler pressed to her full lips, she was every inch the former athlete. But any kind of routine was bad for her short-term health. Especially running alone, at night, in the rain.

That could be deadly.

Miller flipped on the standing lamp next to him. Hard to tell what caught her attention first – the noise of the switch or the pulse of light. But he had to credit her for not dropping the tumbler. She spun towards him and raised it above her head like a club. Smart and fast. He liked that about her.

'Easy,' he told her. 'I'm not here to hurt you.'

'Who are you?' Her voice was pretty steady, considering. 'What are you doing here?'

Her eyes slid to the phone on the kitchen counter. But the phone was no longer there. Miller had thought of that. He thought of a lot of things. It was what had kept him alive this long.

'Easy,' he said again.

But she didn't relax and she didn't lower the glass. She was wired very tight. He guessed she'd been dreading something like this happening. She'd probably lost a lot of sleep over it during the past few months.

He thought of how the situation must look to her. Of how *he* must look. A man she'd never seen before, lurking in the dark and startling her. And not a man who was good at appearing friendly or approachable, on account of his being neither of those things. He was grizzled and craggy-faced. His hair was wild and needed a cut. His XL sweater and shabby jeans felt a size too small and probably were. The last time Hanson had seen him, he'd whistled and said he looked like something out of *Sin City*.

'You need to leave. Right now.'

'Can't do that.'

'Then I'll go.'

She set the tumbler down and backed towards the door.

'And contact your police handler? You could do that. But he lives twenty minutes away. And he's an amateur at this. They all are, over here. And supposing you call him and he comes immediately, or even scrambles a fast response unit. I'll be long gone by then. And you won't have heard what I came here to tell you. Kate.'

She froze.

'That's right, I know your name. Your *real* name. But that's not even the impressive part. And neither was finding you. The part you should be impressed by is the warning I'm about to give you. There's a man coming for you, Kate. He's been hired to kill you.'

'You?'

He shook his head. 'Look at me – I'm not built to sneak up on people. But I am good at providing protection. My name is Nick Miller. I help people who find themselves in your situation. I'm an expert at it.'

'I already have protection.'

'Not from the man who wants you dead. I found you tonight by getting inside the system that's protecting you. He'll do the same thing. He's done it before. But he can't get inside my system because my system is different.'

'Different how?'

She was stalling for time but that was fine by Miller. It was vital that she heard what he'd come here to say.

'My scheme is privately run. Very discreet. Highly bespoke. I identify people at extreme risk and offer them an alternative option.'

A little of the tension eased from Kate's shoulders. She thought she had him sussed now. He was a salesman. An extreme cold caller.

'I'm not interested.'

'You should be. They probably told you their way is safe. And it is, for most people. But not for you, Kate. Your enemy is motivated and resourced far beyond what they're capable of protecting you from. Connor Lane will stop at nothing to get to you. That's why I'm here. I'll stop at nothing to protect you.'

She lifted her chin as though Lane's name had stung her.

'I don't know who you are.'

'Yes you do. I told you already. I'm Nick Miller. Pleased to meet you.'

'This is crazy.'

'No, this is rational. Think of it as a business meeting. I know you've been in plenty of those the last couple of years – a bunch of them with Lane. Ask me about the service I can offer you. Anything at all.'

She hesitated. Too many questions, he guessed. She was a lawyer, after all. Or had been, until recently.

'Why should I listen to you? You could be lying to me. You could be working for Lane yourself.'

'If I was working for Lane you'd be dead already. And you should trust me for the same reason you're still standing here.

You know your current protection isn't good enough. Look at where they have you living. Did they let you pick this place? They might as well have put up a billboard outside. If you come with me, you'll learn to hide my way. It's not easy, but it's secure. I can teach you.'

She shook her head – a fast involuntary jerk – and he saw how skittish he'd made her. He was going to have to offer something more. It was a prospect he'd anticipated, though not one he welcomed. Keeping secrets and dissembling had become a way of life for Miller. It was a habit he found difficult to break.

'Listen, I don't have a brochure for you to flick through or a company website you can visit. And I can't give you a letter of recommendation from one of my clients because I won't compromise their safety. But I'll level with you, Kate. I'm my own best advertisement. We're exactly the same, you and I. We're ghosts. Maybe you don't get that yet. Maybe you still believe you'll be able to go back to your old life, somehow. A few years from now, right? Ten, maximum? That's what you're probably thinking. But it doesn't work that way. Trust me, I know.'

She was concentrating hard, frowning so deeply that the freckles on her forehead merged and blurred. He guessed that she was running through the possibilities in her mind. Was he telling the truth? Or was he a liar or a fantasist?

Or perhaps she was thinking of nothing at all. Miller knew only too well that fear could instil a strange kind of inertia in a person.

'I want you to leave.'

'And you're sure about that?'

'I'm certain.'

He pushed himself to his feet, stooping a little and curling his shoulders, trying to make himself appear smaller than he really was.

'You're not certain – not by a long way – but I understand your predicament. So I'm going to go, but I'm also going to take a chance. I'll stick around on the island for a couple of days. You won't see me but I'll be close by. Tell your police handler if you like, though I wouldn't advise it. You'll be putting Lane's assassin on notice.'

Miller lifted his sweatshirt at the back and removed a clamshell phone from the rear pocket of his jeans.

'I'm leaving you two things. First up is this prepaid mobile. It's programmed with my number, rerouted enough times to protect my security. It's good for two days. Call me on it when you change your mind.'

He set the phone down on the armrest of a leather couch.

'The second item is upstairs on the bed you've been sleeping in. It's an automatic pistol. Keep it close. When Lane's man comes for you – and I promise you he will – don't hesitate to shoot him. Then call me. Understand?'

She didn't nod. Didn't shake her head. She just watched him.

This was the first time Miller had come face to face with Kate Sutherland, but he knew a great deal about her. Far more than he had any legal right to.

He knew, for instance, that she'd competed for Great Britain in the modern pentathlon at the Beijing Olympics, where she'd placed twelfth. He knew that of the five main pentathlon disciplines, pistol shooting was her core strength. He knew that she'd first learned to shoot at just twelve years of age, when her adoptive father introduced her to grouse hunting on his

Cotswolds estate. He knew that a knee injury had ended her athletics career prematurely, at which point she'd trained as a commercial lawyer with a specialism in mergers and acquisitions. He knew that she was left-handed, that her favourite movie was *The Wizard of Oz*, that she'd been chief bridesmaid at three weddings and counting, that she'd spent close to a year searching for her birth family without success.

Most important of all, he knew that she was willing to sacrifice her life as she knew it to testify in a trial that Connor Lane would do everything in his power to prevent her from appearing at.

He said, 'Lock up after me. If you value your life, you'll call me before I get back to my car.'

Miller crossed to the glass door that opened on to the deck and slid it aside. The breeze gusted in, damp and moist, smelling thickly of salt and kelp.

He turned and looked back at Kate, standing half in and half out of her life, and in that moment, with her face slackened and her eyes haunted and lost, he couldn't quite tell which of them was the more afraid for her.

Chapter Two

Two Days Later

Miller hiked up the mud-slicked path from the beach until he was within sight of the house, then veered off the track and trampled through bushes and brambles, the air dank and vaporous, wetting his clothes. The sky was jammed with rain clouds, skimming low over a turbulent sea. There was no moonlight to speak of. No trace of any stars.

He emerged at the edge of a sheer cliff, the rock face tumbling away into darkness and the sound of the waves striking the shore far below. The deck was a metre in front of him. Maybe half a metre up. The timber was greasy with damp, set almost flush against waist-high glass panels topped with rounded aluminium rails. And Miller was a big guy: a heavy, clumsy brute of a man. He was no kind of acrobat.

He leapt out and hooked his forearms over the railing, jamming the toes of his boots against the glass. The panel shuddered. The timber flexed. He experienced a fleeting moment of weightlessness, of terror, before his momentum carried him on, pitching him forwards from the waist, his backpack lurching sideways as he rolled over the rail and slammed down on to his hip.

The wall of glass at the back of the house loomed over him like a dark mirror. Scrambling to his feet, he stalked forwards and cupped his hands, peering in.

At blackness. At nothing.

He was just reaching sideways, poised to try the door handle, when someone grabbed for his arm.

Miller reacted very fast, swinging round and sweeping a leg, pushing down.

'Ow. You're hurting me.'

Kate.

'What are you doing?' She bucked against him. 'Let me go. Get off.'

Miller released his grip and staggered away, his limbs taut with adrenaline rigor, a sour, metallic taste swamping his tongue.

Kate lay on her side on the deck. She was wearing grey jogging pants and a pale vest top. There were spots of blood on the vest.

Miller said, 'I told you to wait in the house.'

'I couldn't. Not with him in there.'

'Where is he?'

'Upstairs.'

'And the gun?'

'I dropped it.'

'OK.' Miller turned and looked back at the house. 'OK,' he said again.

His mind was racing and so was his pulse. He could feel it twitching in his neck.

'Are you sure he's dead?'

'I think so.'

'Why the doubt?'

'I've never killed anyone before.'

'Wait here.' He slid the door open.

'The lights don't work. I think he cut the electricity.'

Miller eased his backpack from his shoulders and removed his torch and his gun. The pistol was a SIG that had been acquired by Hanson, in the way of all contraband that Hanson was able to acquire, without alerting the necessary authorities or troubling with the appropriate paperwork. The SIG was box-fresh, hardly fired.

Miller only hoped he could keep it that way.

*

On the same night, at the same time, a young man called Patrick Leigh was looking out over Manchester. He had a spectacular view. The city was all lit up. He could see office blocks and apartment towers and street lamps and the distant streaked glow of motorway traffic.

But he wasn't enjoying what he was seeing – he was absolutely petrified – because he was upside down, suspended by his ankles, several hundred metres in the air.

Two men had dragged Patrick out from behind the dumpsters at the back of a department store where he'd bedded down for the night. The men had punched and kicked him, then bundled him into the back of a windowless van where one of them had gagged him with a foul-smelling rag and pinned him down while his companion climbed into the cab and accelerated away.

If Patrick was scared during the journey, his fear spiked when the van came to a halt and he was thrown out on to the ground in a fenced-off construction site on the edge of the city.

In the small hours of the morning, the site was completely deserted. There were shadowy diggers and dump trucks abandoned at all kinds of angles. There were concrete mixers, pneumatic drills and I-shaped metal girders everywhere he looked.

Without saying a word, the two men bound Patrick's ankles together, wrapping them over and over, first with bandages and then with metal chains. After that, the older of the two men – the fat, balding one in the crumpled suit and tie who'd driven the van – walked to the tower at the base of a giant crane. The man opened a door and stepped inside a caged elevator, punched a button and straightened his tie, and Patrick watched the elevator zip up into the sky towards the distant operator's cab.

Patrick had begun to moan then. He'd started to thrash and grapple with his ankle bindings until the second man walked over and squatted next to him. He was short and muscular with a thick, square head and mangled boxer's ears. His lightless grey eyes were wide-set, creeping towards the sides of his skull, reminding Patrick of a hammerhead shark.

The man wore a shiny blue tracksuit and pristine white training shoes. He raised a finger to his lips and shook his head in a no-nonsense warning, which, coming from this guy, was enough to make Patrick stay almost completely still as the big metal hook was lowered all the way down from the end of the jib, where it was secured to the chains coiled around his ankles before the mechanism was reversed and the hook was winched up and Patrick was dragged into the air until he was suspended the wrong way round with his blood rushing to his head, just beyond reach of the tower and the cab and any remote chance of safety.

Patrick kept willing himself to pass out but he remained

stubbornly conscious as the little elevator shuttled downwards then whirred back up again, whereupon the man in the track-suit hauled back the caged door and climbed nimbly and confidently between some railings until he was clinging to the outside of the tower, reaching for the flapping hood attached to Patrick's sweater.

Patrick moaned from behind his gag, and kept moaning even as the man yanked him towards him and shook him vigorously, even as the older man in the suit leaned out of a window on the operator's cab and told him to shut the hell up.

'Do you know who we are?' the older man shouted.

Patrick assumed the question was rhetorical. There was no way he could talk around the gag, even supposing his sweater wasn't crushing his throat.

'Do you know who sent us?'

Patrick nodded and swallowed hard, which was a strange sensation, being upside down and half throttled.

'So then you know why we're here. You've probably heard of my colleague. People have probably warned you about him.'

People had warned Patrick about a lot of things. But nothing specific. And certainly not this.

Why hadn't he listened to those people? Why did he never listen to good advice?

'They call my colleague the Hypnotist. Know why? I'll tell you, Patrick. It's because he has this rare ability to persuade anyone he wants to do anything he likes. But there's one big difference between my colleague and a stage hypnotist. He doesn't have a pocket watch to swing before your eyes. But that's OK. He doesn't need one.'

The guy in the tracksuit let go of Patrick's hood and clutched at his face, digging his fingers into the soft flesh of his cheeks. He pulled Patrick close to him – so close that Patrick could see the crazed glimmer in his eyes – then shoved him away fast and hard.

'You're the watch,' the older man shouted, as Patrick swooped through the air.

Chapter Three

Miller found the body in the bedroom. The man was dead, no question. But it almost hadn't turned out that way. He must have gotten very close to fulfilling his contract. He'd fallen on to his back right next to the bed, toppling the lamp on the nearside cabinet.

There was blood on the duvet. Blood on the pillows and the walls. Kate had shot the man through the throat, close quarters, and Miller guessed he must have been leaning over her at the time. Perhaps she'd been keeping the gun under one of her pillows. Maybe she'd faked being asleep and had waited until the very last moment to shoot.

Impressive, if so.

The guy was dressed all in black. Black trousers, a black gilet over a black cable-knit jumper, black gloves and a black balaclava. His automatic pistol was fitted with a suppressor.

Miller shone his torch into the sightless eyes behind the balaclava. Was this the man he'd vowed to kill four years ago?

He squatted and peeled back the ski mask, revealing a male in his early thirties, well-groomed and clean-shaven. He had no scars or signs of a troubled life or distinguishing marks whatsoever.

Aside from the ugly wound that had killed him.

Miller removed a glove and fished his smartphone out of his pocket – his own phone, not the disposable device Kate had contacted him on – and held it low to the man's face. He took a photograph and attached the image in an email to Hanson.

He didn't pat the man down. No killer hired by Connor Lane for this particular assignment would be amateurish enough to carry ID. Besides which, Hanson was capable of finding out more about the dead man from the hasty mug shot Miller had sent him than any trawl through his wallet might reveal.

Straightening now, Miller stalked around the bed, probing left and right with his torch until he found the pistol he'd armed Kate with poking out from just beneath the cotton valance. He stowed it in his backpack and cast his torch around the rest of the room, flinching when the beam was jabbed back at him by a mirrored wardrobe.

He leaned his head to one side, pausing for a moment to consider his reflection – this dishevelled, oversized wanderer, almost a stranger to him now, who was capable of walking into a house where someone had been shot with the intention of concealing evidence and spiriting the killer away. The man Miller had used to be wouldn't have been able to hold his gaze. But the man Miller had used to be hadn't understood how rules and laws could mean nothing to some men. He hadn't known that to beat them you had to become them. Or sometimes, something even worse.

He slid aside the wardrobe doors and scanned the garments in front of him. There were items here that reminded him of the type of clothes Sarah might once have worn. His wife had liked to dress simply. Most days it was jeans and a blouse or a T-shirt, but every now and again, for a special occasion, she would dazzle him with a black cocktail dress like the one his gloved fingers had settled on. He clenched the silky material and could almost conjure up the feel of Sarah's body beneath it. The swell of her hip. The warmth of her skin. He could almost imagine her batting his hand away, smiling over her shoulder, telling him that now really wasn't the time.

Which it expressly wasn't.

Miller released the dress and took out his phone, firing off several flash photographs. When he was done, his eyes settled on a navy fleece jacket on a shelf to the right. He slipped his phone away and tucked the fleece under his arm, thinking how it wouldn't be wise for Kate to be seen with blood on her clothes on the walk down to the beach.

He was just turning to go – the beam from his torch settling over the doorway that connected with the hall, his mind still snagged by those treacherous thoughts of Sarah and the pain and regret that had led him here – when he heard a low insect hum coming from the dead man. A soft blue light pulsed from behind a chest pocket on his gilet: the light fading, then blooming again, like an alien heart.

Miller knelt and dipped his hand inside the man's pocket, removing a mobile phone between his finger and thumb.

CALLER UNKNOWN.

He held the phone in his gloved palm, the buzz passing up his arm, jangling his nerves. He had a sudden urge to answer the call. He could picture himself raising the phone to his ear, listening to the expectant breathing on the other end of the line.

There were so many things he wanted to say.

*

Mike Renner, the balding man in the suit and tie, leaned back from the open window of the crane operator's cab and stared out at the glinting cityscape with his phone pressed to his ear.

Renner hadn't wanted to place this call. He *never* wanted to place these calls. But he'd anticipated receiving an important text message more than twenty minutes ago. The message should have been something short and vaguely cryptic. *Job done. Contract completed.*

Renner had received a number of similar confirmations during the thirty-plus years in which he'd worked for the Lane family, though the method of sending them had changed over time.

Except not tonight. Because no text had reached him. Which meant one of two things: either there'd been an unexpected delay, or the man he'd hired had failed in some way.

Delay seemed the most likely explanation. The intel Renner had paid for on their target's location and security had been comprehensive, and the killer he'd contracted had an excellent track record. But if the alternative scenario was in play and he'd failed, for whatever reason, then Renner needed to know immediately. Because while it was true that Aaron Wade – the borderline psychotic who was at this very moment hanging off the tower of the crane, pawing at his traumatised victim – was highly adept at persuading people not to talk, or to confess absolutely everything to him, depending on Renner's whim, it was also true that whatever was happening right now on the Isle of Man, or had already happened, would determine the fate of the unfortunate young man currently swinging by his ankles below him, no matter how positively he responded to Wade's particular brand of torture.

So Renner listened very hard to the ringing of his phone. He clamped his free hand over his ear in order to block out, as much as possible, the noise of Wade's jeering taunts and the young man's increasingly desperate whines.

But all he heard was the drone of an unanswered call until eventually he gave up and powered down his phone, stripping out the SIM and pocketing the component parts for safe disposal at a suitable time and place in the future.

He leaned out of the cab, his tie flapping in the breeze, and looked down at Wade, gripping the tower in his fist, a crazed grin on his face.

Renner couldn't say he liked Wade. He was always on edge in his company – the same way, he imagined, a lion tamer could never entirely relax when he took the stage with one of his animals. But he absolutely trusted Wade to carry out his instructions, no matter how extreme or unpleasant those instructions might be, and no matter how much Renner wished he didn't have to issue them.

Because despite his experience and his uncompromising reputation, the truth was that Mike Renner didn't like killing people. Not because he felt guilty – if somebody posed a threat to the Lane family, then they also posed a corresponding threat to Renner's livelihood and the well-being of his own wife and two precious daughters – but because killing someone always carried with it the risk of being caught.

Which was why, when he called Wade's name, with a voice that sounded to him oddly strained, and when Wade looked up, eagerly, and Renner shook his head at the young man swinging from the hook, he couldn't escape a feeling of sickly dread as he cleared his throat and said, 'It's over. Kid has to drop.'

Chapter Four

Miller shepherded Kate to the bottom of the cliff path. She'd refused to put on the fleece he'd fetched for her and he was trying hard not to show how much it rankled him.

'How are you feeling?' he asked, from behind. 'It's OK to freak out. You just shot a man.'

'Oh, I am freaking out. But not about that. He came to kill me. Just like you said.'

'What then?'

She stopped and spun to face him. Miller lifted the holdall she'd packed and used it to motion towards the Audi estate he'd parked at the end of the seafront. They needed to keep moving but she wasn't going anywhere yet.

'It's this.' Kate spread her arms. 'It's you.'

'Me?'

'I keep thinking I'm making a terrible mistake.'

'The mistake would have been lying there and getting shot.'

'I should have called the emergency number I was given. I should have dialled my handler instead of you.'

Miller stared at her a moment, her vest clinging to her skin where it was speckled with blood. The nearest street lamp flickered dimly. There was nobody around.

'You just killed someone, Kate. Think about that for a moment.'

'It was self-defence.'

'Fine, so go ahead and call them. Explain what happened. Here.' Miller dropped the holdall and freed his backpack from his shoulders, thrusting a hand inside for the prepaid phone Kate had contacted him on. 'But if you think Lane is done now, you're wrong. He'll just send someone else. He'll find you the same way he found you tonight. Except it'll be even easier the second time round. Because you'll be in custody. The police will hold you until they can clear this mess up.'

Kate looked down at the phone and Miller could tell that she was asking herself if she should make the call. And he could understand why, in so many ways, it might seem like the easier, more rational move to make.

'Listen to me – Lane already knows something went wrong tonight. He'll have been expecting confirmation of the kill, and without it, he'll send someone to find out what happened. Maybe he already has a backup in place on the island. Maybe someone is heading here right now. Come with me. Believe in me.'

'You have to convince me this isn't the craziest thing I'll ever do.'

But how could he persuade her when he had doubts himself? Hanson had told him this wasn't anything he should get involved in. Becca had said the same thing. But Miller had insisted on making the approach anyway. And now? The truth was he didn't know what to think any more, but the part that bothered him most was whether he could still trust his motives. They'd become muddied ever since he'd first set eyes on Kate. Not because she was beautiful – although she was that and more – but because she was fierce and stubborn and committed. She reminded him so much of Sarah in that way. In a lot of ways. None of which helped.

23

'Seriously? Saving your life isn't enough?'

She didn't answer. She didn't need to. She just stared at him, waiting.

Miller glanced away towards the sea. He was going to have to do this. He couldn't see that he had a choice.

'Miller's not my real name. Everyone calls me Miller, nowadays. I prefer it that way. But my real name is Adams. Nick Adams.'

A puff of misted air escaped Kate's mouth. The name meant something to her. More than something, he was sure.

'You and I, we have something more than fake identities in common. We share the same enemy. Four years ago, Connor Lane sent a man to kill my wife and daughter. I couldn't save them.'

'But you saved me.'

Miller's throat had closed up. He turned away again and blinked hard. He'd learned many years ago that tears were not a good look on a big man like him. Especially when you were trying to convince someone how strong and dependable you could be.

'I still have to testify,' Kate said. 'That's non-negotiable.'

'We'll talk about it.'

'No. We find a way or I don't go with you. Helen wasn't just a colleague to me. She was a friend. I want her killer to face justice.'

'Terrific, so you'll testify. Maybe you'll get killed while you're at it, too.' He shook his head, undone by the earnest way she was searching his face. 'Look, we'll try and figure something out. OK?'

He didn't believe it. Not then. But he had no problem lying.

He was prepared to do or say whatever it took to protect Kate. Even if that meant saving her from herself.

And later, when the time came, he'd explain how things really worked. He'd let her know what they could, and couldn't, hope to achieve. If the past few years had taught him anything, it was that a form of justice inside the law wasn't always possible. Not where men like Connor Lane were concerned.

Kate stooped to pick up her holdall and Miller followed her to the Audi, popping the boot. There were two suitcases inside and he threw back both lids so she could see the opening he'd carved out of them where the cases touched.

'For the ferry crossing,' he explained. 'The next boat doesn't leave the island until after 7 a.m. They could be searching for you by then. You'll have a small oxygen canister. Some water. Food, if you like.'

Kate looked down into the boot at the rigged suitcases. Her first taste of life on the run, the way Miller handled things. It wasn't a lifestyle that was comfortable or pretty. It was rudimentary and crude.

But it worked.

Only Kate didn't know that yet. Not for sure. He studied her reaction – the way she was sucking on her bottom lip – and he felt he had a pretty reasonable idea of what she must be asking herself.

Would it be a mistake to climb into the boot, or was this just one small component part of a much bigger, much more catastrophic error she was making by trusting him in the first place?

*

25

Many hours later, Miller leaned against the railings at the stern of the ferry to Liverpool, watching the humped outline of the island blur and fade from view.

The Audi was parked two decks below with Kate inside the doctored suitcases. She was reliant on him now and Miller felt the burden of his responsibility like a spiked weight in the pit of his stomach.

He gazed at the child's sketch of the cowboy on a horse he was clutching – the crayon faded, the surface crinkled and distressed, the edges worn and ruffled by the swirling sea breeze – and he thought about a lot of things. He thought of the hired killer lying dead in Kate's bedroom. He thought of the man's body being discovered, and of the police officers who would be searching for her soon. He thought of how he'd held the man's phone in his hand. Of the call he hadn't answered. Of the men who would come hunting for them both.

Kate hadn't thanked him for any of it. Perhaps she hadn't understood how badly it might cost him or how much he was putting on the line. More likely it was because she understood that no favour this big could come without an obligation to match and she was afraid of what she now owed him. If so, she was probably right to be concerned.

The drinking bar at the stern of the ship was loud and busy behind Miller. But out here on deck, he was alone and un-watched.

He folded the drawing away the same way he always did, the paper collapsing like a perfect origami structure into a tight square that fitted securely in his wallet. Then, reaching inside his jacket, he removed the gun Kate had fired and the dismantled remains of the phone she'd contacted him on. He leaned over the railings and he opened his hands and let go, watching the Irish Sea swallow everything down.

PART II

Weston-super-Mare, England

Chapter Five

Kate woke to the sound of beating wiper blades. She must have fallen asleep some time after they'd joined the M5.

'Where are we?'

'Guess.'

It was dusk and a fine grey drizzle was swirling around them. They were driving along a seaside promenade. Kate could see blocky, crassly functional apartment buildings, Victorian guesthouses, crumbling grand hotels and derelict ice-cream kiosks. She could see a low stone wall, drenched mud flats, and the outline of a pier flickering dimly through the murk.

'Looks like hell.'

'Close. Weston-super-Mare. Play your cards right and maybe you'll have time for a donkey ride on the beach.'

Kate groaned. She was too warm under the fleece Miller had insisted she put on and her head was fuzzy. She couldn't quite shake the sickly, seesaw sensation of the ferry crossing or the tainted air she'd breathed inside the suitcases. Her body felt cramped, contorted, like it sometimes did when she craved a run.

Miller drove away from the entrance to the pier, sweeping past a string of fast-food concessions and amusement arcades, then along a narrow back alley to a gravel parking space behind a terraced house. A sign fitted to the pebble-dashed wall read: PARADISE APARTMENTS. VACANCIES.

'Wow.'

'Problem?'

'I'm starting to think I'd have been better off getting shot.'

Miller stepped out of the Audi and thrust his arms into the air, stretching his back, his plaid shirt hitching up and exposing a midriff laced with fine, dark hairs. He was unkempt and scruffily dressed, on the wrong side of his forties, but there was no pretending he wasn't handsome in a rugged sort of way.

Which was a bad thought to be having right now.

Kate remained seated and listened to his feet crunch gravel as he came round from behind the car and lifted her holdall off the back seat before flinging open her door.

'Paradise awaits.'

She held back a moment, feeling sluggish and leery, then tramped after him into an unlit vestibule smelling of mildew and damp, and on up a cramped staircase to an unfinished door, where he turned a key in the lock and moved to one side, gesturing for her to go in ahead of him.

The holiday apartment reeked of stale cigarette smoke and had a decor straight out of the seventies. It was heavy on the brown striped wallpaper and dense green carpet. There was a lot of teak furniture. A lot of striped rayon upholstery in autumnal shades.

'Paradise,' Kate muttered.

'Problem?'

She turned to Miller.

Who was this man, really? He'd been a stranger to her until two days ago and she still knew very little about him. They'd hardly talked during the five-hour drive they'd taken to get to this place. Kate had so much she needed to ask that she hadn't known where to begin.

Tears stung her eyes. She felt dazed and close to despair. There were times when she'd experienced similar emotions following a big athletics meet. All the training and the build-up, all the pressure, then the mad thrill of competition and, finally, the inevitable comedown afterwards. But this was more extreme.

She'd made a mistake coming here with him. She must have, she reasoned, because why else would she feel so undone?

Miller tipped his head to one side, the salt-and-pepper stubble on his cheek grazing his shirt collar. His dark hair was long and curled, threaded with silver. His chest and arms were massive, like those of a shot-putter.

'Not the type of place you'd come to on holiday?'

'Not in a million years.'

'What about the town? Have you ever been here before?'

She shook her head.

'Which is exactly why I chose it.' He set her holdall down and managed a fleeting smile. 'I'm just across the hall. Get some rest. Take a shower. Come and knock when you're ready.'

'Ready for what?'

'To begin your new life.'

*

Kate burst through the door to the apartment across the hall less than three minutes later.

Then stopped.

'Whoa.' A young black man reared back from behind a bank of computer monitors. 'Looky here, people. We have a new all-time record.'

33

He grinned at Miller, who was pouring himself coffee from a percolator on a tiled kitchen counter, then leaned way back in his desk chair and looked behind him at a plump, attractive woman over by the window.

'Oh, that's brilliant, Nick. You might have wanted to mention that she was stunning.'

Kate recognised the woman right away. Not because she knew her. Or at least, not directly. Back when Kate had been a law student with a mild addiction to daytime TV, Becca Jarvis had starred in *Haymarket Close*, a Manchester-based soap on a lesser terrestrial channel. Since Becca had left the show in a storyline that involved her character fleeing her abusive spouse for a new life in Australia, Kate had occasionally caught her voice on radio dramas and adverts, though she'd never seen her face on television again.

Becca was big, brash and sexy; memorable for her ample bosom as much as her raucous laugh. And now she was standing in the same dingy room as Kate. In Weston-super-Mare.

'You want coffee?' Miller asked her.

'I want to know what's going on.'

'You're tired, Kate. I told you to get some sleep.'

'You're not sleeping.'

Miller toasted her with his mug. 'Hence the caffeine.'

'You never said there'd be anyone else involved. I didn't agree to this.'

But what had she agreed to, really? She barely knew.

'Oh, I like her.' The young man was immaculately groomed with wiry black hair trimmed close to his scalp. He had on a bright pink polo shirt and designer specs with electric blue frames. 'She's feisty.'

'Excuse me?'

'Relax, honey.' Becca pushed off from the windowsill. She had a sinuous walk, all hips and ass. The bold green dress she was wearing featured a blocky geometric print and a plunging neckline. 'We're on your side.'

'And which side is that?'

'The good guys, obviously.' The young man pulled down his spectacles and peered over the frames. 'We're too fun and irreverent to be the bad guys. Apart from Miller, maybe. But he already saved your life, so you can give him a free pass.'

Miller was sipping his coffee and taking his time over it. He seemed to be enjoying Kate's reaction, which just made her madder and more confused.

'Ten seconds.' She jabbed a finger at him. 'And then either you start explaining what's going on here, or I'm leaving.'

He lowered his mug. 'Hanson's my computer whizz.'

'A-mazing,' Hanson said. 'Do you have any idea how old you sound?'

'Don't be fooled by his appearance. I know he looks like he should be in a boy band but he can create the perfect new ID and erase all trace of your old one.'

Hanson spread his arms to take in all the computer equipment around him. 'Miller really needs to work on his intros. Because I am so much more than just that. You're going to be seriously impressed by what I can do.'

'And not at all surprised by what he can't.' Becca winked at Kate and wiggled her little finger in the air. 'Wow, are you going to be something to work with.'

'Becca will handle your physical makeover,' Miller explained.

'My what?'

'Relax, honey. We're just going to refine a few things.'

'I don't need refining.'

'Amen.'

'Easy, kiddo.' Becca clipped the top of Hanson's head, nodding between Miller and Kate. 'This one is spoken for.'

Kate shot Becca a warning look. Miller echoed it.

'Ooh, *OK*. So I guess you guys haven't picked up on the pretty blatant chemistry you have going on just yet.'

'Actresses.' Miller shook his head. 'You're going to need to alter the way you talk, the way you interact with people, your physical mannerisms. Becca will teach you how to do all that.'

'You make it sound like you want to change everything about me.'

'No, not everything. Just enough to keep you alive.'

Chapter Six

Connor Lane watched from the lawn of his private estate on the shores of Lake Windermere as the sailing yacht drifted towards him. The fifty-foot craft was the centrepiece of a charity Connor had set up to assist youngsters with disabilities and learning difficulties. She'd been adapted for wheelchair users and Connor's foundation had employed and trained a specialist crew. The hull and the mainsail were branded with the name of his company: *www.anycashcredit.com*.

'Do you have a name for her yet?'

Connor returned his attention to the pretty blonde journalist sitting opposite him. She was mid-to-late twenties, more than ten years his junior. Not that age was usually an obstacle for Connor. In his experience, extreme wealth compensated for many things.

'How about Samantha?'

She clutched a hand to her breast. Was it Connor's imagination, or had she loosened another button on her blouse?

'But that's my name, Mr Lane.'

'Connor, please. And a beautiful yacht should be named for a beautiful woman, don't you agree?'

The hull of the yacht nudged against the newly installed pontoon, its sails ruffled by the soft evening breeze. Tomorrow, at a lavish garden party Connor was hosting with his wife, Yvonne, eight disabled youngsters would experience the thrill of sailing for the first time. It was a sport that Connor's father, Larry, had lived for – the very reason, in fact, why the Lane family had moved to their sprawling Windermere home when Connor was just seven years old.

'It's a really wonderful thing you're doing . . . Connor. I'm sure the children will be very grateful.'

He flashed her his best grin. He even allowed the smile to reach his eyes.

'But I wonder . . .?'

'Yes, Samantha?'

'Don't you think it's just a little inappropriate, given the charges your brother is facing?'

Connor tried to maintain the grin. He tried very hard. But he could already feel his muscles tightening, jaw tensing, lips morphing into a predatory leer.

It had always been this way when someone attacked Russell. Connor had been just nineteen when their parents disappeared from his father's sailing dinghy, presumed killed in a gangland hit, their bodies rumoured to be weighted down somewhere among the muddy depths of Windermere. Both boys had been orphaned that April night, but Connor had been left with an eleven-year-old brother to raise amid the sudden extreme demands of the criminal enterprise his father had overseen.

From day one, the hyenas of the underworld had probed and tested him. A lesser man would have crumbled. An ordinary man would have walked away. But Connor did neither of those things. He defended what was rightfully his. He dirtied his hands.

And meanwhile, he did everything in his power to shelter Russell from the violent reality of the world that swirled around them. Because Russell was special. He was sensitive and generous and kind. He was pure.

And now, to think that he was in custody, awaiting trial for murder . . .

'My brother is innocent. His legal team will establish that soon enough.'

'Perhaps. But there's also the matter of your own recent conviction, isn't there?'

Samantha gestured with her pen to Connor's left ankle, which was crossed over his right thigh, resting on the ironed pleat of his chinos. She couldn't see it. Nobody could. But there was an electronic tag fitted under Connor's sock. The strap was a constant menace, snagging his skin, itching like hell. But the tag would remain there for the next four to six months while Connor was under curfew, restricted to the grounds of his estate.

'I made a mistake. I was provoked by a journalist asking me offensive questions about my brother.'

'You were convicted of actual bodily harm.'

Connor fixed another smile to his face. Six months ago he could have placed a call to Samantha's editor and had her fired. Now life was more complicated.

Not that Connor was surprised by how rapidly his stock had fallen. He knew better than anyone that he'd never be widely admired. In part, that was because he'd inherited his father's fortune and had multiplied it countless times over by establishing one of the first, and certainly the biggest and therefore most reviled, of the UK's payday-loan companies.

But it was also because the original source of his family's wealth had been even less respectable. Larry Lane had been

39

a notorious loan shark. He'd started his business empire in Manchester, then expanded into Liverpool. And while some of the stories surrounding his activities were wild exaggerations, there was no getting away from the fact that Connor had made his millions – many multiples of millions, in fact – by refining his father's old business model to apply a veneer of legality to the exploitation of those desperate enough to borrow money they couldn't possibly hope to repay.

So now, instead of the vig there were prohibitive rates of APR. And where once Connor's father might have threatened to break someone's legs, these days his company wielded the menace of bankruptcy or the seizure of assets.

Small differences perhaps, but significant where Connor was concerned. Because slowly, patiently, he'd been working to rehabilitate his family's reputation in the same way he'd refashioned their business. A high-profile charitable gesture here, a timely political donation there.

Not that any of it could begin to compensate for the latest scandal Russell had dragged to their door.

A stiff wind skimmed over the lake, rocking the yacht. Connor stood up from his lawn chair and buttoned his linen jacket.

'I believe we're done here, Samantha. Lovely as they are, you can go ahead and pop your breasts away now.'

She glared at him, baring her teeth. 'I still need a portrait shot for the piece.'

But Connor wasn't listening. His attention had been drawn to the south lawn, where a team of men were in the final stages of erecting a giant marquee. Beneath the flapping canvas, a small army of catering staff and a handful of volunteers from the Fresh Start Shelter for teenage runaways (also bankrolled by one of Connor's foundations) were busy setting up tables and fold-out chairs. And there, waddling through the middle of them all, was the shambolic figure of Mike Renner.

'Mr Lane? One picture by the yacht?'

Connor almost shuddered at the thought of being anywhere near the pontoon. He was afraid of very little in life but he was fearful of the steel-blue waters of Windermere.

'You can see yourself out, Samantha. And please, don't ever come back.'

He turned and walked off towards the stone steps leading up to the main house, the arched windows glowing now with the burnished orange light of the dipping sun. There was an ornamental fountain out front and Connor lingered beside it, looking across the wind-streaked lake at the lights coming on in Bowness, the sky stained in shades of purple and ochre, the wind picking up as if it might storm.

Renner was breathing hard by the time he joined him. Physically, he was a mess. Sartorially, he was even worse. But this balding, overweight man in the creased suit with the carelessly knotted tie and the scuffed loafers was Connor's most loyal and trusted lieutenant, just as he had been for his father before him.

'Nice boat.' Renner made a small puffing sound as he caught his breath.

'It's a sail yacht.'

'Yeah? What's the difference?'

'I have no idea.'

'Guess Larry would have been able to tell us.'

The two men watched the blonde journalist stride away across the lawn, a camera bag swinging from her shoulder, bashing her hip.

'He'd be proud, you know? Of what you're doing here.'

Connor knew that Renner was talking about more than just the yacht. He was also referring to the steps Connor was taking to protect Russell.

'I have some news you're not going to like.'

Which was something Connor had anticipated. He hadn't been scheduled to see Renner until tomorrow.

'I sent Wade to the Isle of Man to clear up after the man we hired. I thought it was sensible to sweep the place where he'd been staying before the cops found it. The man we hired was recommended to me. I was very specific about the levels of service we expect.'

'And?'

'And either my instructions weren't sufficiently clear – which I seriously doubt – or this guy had something else in mind. Maybe he was hoping to make a little extra cash on the side.'

Connor had a creeping fear about where this was heading. It got worse when Renner glanced behind him, towards the teams of people buzzing about the marquee, before pulling a smartphone from the inside pocket of his jacket.

'Wade recovered some surveillance equipment during his sweep. Our guy had a long-lens camera adapted for night-vision photography. Wade checked the camera and he found a bunch of surveillance shots of the house where Kate Sutherland was staying. The photograph I'm about to show you is date-stamped three days ago. The man we hired never sent it to me. If he had . . . Well, things would have been different.'

The image was dark and grainy, rendered in shades of green, but it was distinct enough for Connor to identify the man who'd been captured in a pale mint glow, stepping out through a sliding glass door.

His heart clenched and a deep chill spread through his chest.

'You believe he has Kate Sutherland?'

'I think that's what we have to assume.'

'I won't allow this to happen again, Mike. I can't. Find them. Do whatever it takes.'

'And when I find them?'

'You know the answer to that. But handle things yourself this time. No go-betweens.'

Perhaps it was Connor's imagination, but Renner seemed to sag just a touch.

'I'll need Wade on it too,' he said quietly.

'As you wish. But nobody else. And Mike?'

'Yes.'

'No more mistakes.'

Chapter Seven

Kate stared hard at her reflection in the rust-pitted mirror in her bedroom. Clumps of her hair littered the towel draped over her shoulders and the plastic sheet spread on the floor beneath her chair. Becca was standing behind her with a pair of scissors in one hand and a comb in the other. Not ten minutes ago, she'd dumped the remains of Kate's ponytail into a black bin liner, along with the clothes she'd been wearing since she'd left the Isle of Man and the towel she'd used to dry herself with after her shower.

Kate felt picked apart. Unravelled. Her defences stripped away.

'How many people have you done this for?' she asked. 'Before me, I mean.'

'You know I can't tell you that.'

'But I'm not the first?'

'No, honey, you're not the first. You're not an experiment. We're good at this. Nick's the absolute best at what he does.'

'He hasn't told me how any of this is going to work.'

'He will. But it's a lot to take in. He's just looking out for you.'

Becca brushed Kate's new fringe to the left, tipping her head to one side, frowning at the result.

'Why are you involved in this?'

'Why does anyone do anything any more?'

'Money, usually.'

'Well, I've got me enough of that.'

'So then you're a volunteer. I'm sorry, but that doesn't seem very likely. You're famous.'

'Honey, that's sweet, but that show was a long time ago.'

'You have everything to lose.'

'No, not everything. Not any more. And besides, maybe some things are just worth doing.'

'Seriously? That's the best you've got?'

'A cynic, huh? How about if I told you Nick helped me out once.'

'Must have been a serious favour.'

'Oh, it was.' Becca nodded, and for the briefest moment her eyes took on a faraway look. 'But Nick also convinced me that I'd be doing something important here. He knows I have a serious talent for blending in. When you have this face and these babies,' she clutched her breasts, winking, 'you need plenty of tricks to get by unnoticed.'

Kate gave Becca a dubious look. Back in the day, she'd seen her on the television, in tabloid newspapers and on the covers of glossy magazines, and the truth was that she didn't appear very different today. She was always glamorous, always bold; an unmistakable combination of big hair, big make-up and a big body.

'I know what you're thinking. And I get it. I do. But what you're seeing today is just a costume. I can change it any time I want. Just like I can change you. And if you're clever, you'll pay attention to me, because it might just save your life.'

'Did Miller tell you that I killed a man?'

Becca pushed her mouth to one side and snipped at Kate's hair. 'Way he tells it, you had no choice.'

Kate thought about that. She wasn't sure it was true. And even supposing it was, nothing could rid her of the skin-crawl sensation she couldn't quite shake, or help in any way to make her forget that awful moment of silence, of stasis, after the gun jumped in her hand, before the man in the balaclava toppled back.

A killer on the run. That was who she was now, what she'd become.

'Would you put your life in Miller's hands if you were me?'

'Honey, I put my life in his hands every day. If the people who wanted to get at you knew I was involved in any of this . . .' Becca shuddered, leaving the rest unspoken.

'How do you even find the time for this?'

'Worried I won't be there for you?'

'The thought had crossed my mind.'

'Well, Miller's your main guy. Remember that. But also, it just so happens I have plenty of time on my hands right now.'

'How so?'

Becca met her eyes in the mirror. 'I'm in the middle of what my agent calls a "period of career transition".'

'And what do you call it?'

'A screw-up. And I mean that literally, or figuratively, or whatever. That show you liked so much? I didn't leave it to move on to bigger things. I was written out of it because I spent the night with the head of the network. Huge mistake. His wife was *not* a fan. And he was seriously pissed off when she found out. He's an influential guy. More influential than me or my agent, anyway.' She fluffed Kate's hair. 'You like?'

Kate hated it. But she couldn't pretend she wasn't impressed by the outcome. She looked leaner, sharper, tougher. Although not all of that was down to her new hairstyle.

'And we're done.' Becca lifted the towel from Kate's shoulders and guided her to her feet. 'Stay on the sheet. Take off your robe.'

Kate untied the gown and let it fall from her shoulders. She'd shed a lot of weight recently. The stress had killed her appetite. Her whole life, she'd always been fit and healthy, but now she could glimpse the outline of her ribs through her skin, the jut of her clavicle.

The underwear she had on wasn't anything like she would have chosen for herself. It was peach and silky, covered in frills. Becca had run out for it while Kate was in the shower. She felt like a stranger wearing it, which she guessed was the point.

'Girl, you are beautiful.'

But Kate didn't feel beautiful. She felt depleted and vulnerable. Especially under Becca's gaze.

Becca was wide-hipped and voluptuous. She oozed sex appeal. Kate had already caught herself wondering if Miller had slept with her. If maybe he still did.

She crossed her hands in front of her abdomen, the plastic crinkling under her feet as Becca backed off towards a portable clothes rack in the corner of the room. The rail was jammed with garments suspended from plastic hangers. A set of colour photographs had been tacked up on the wall nearby and Kate could see that they were flash shots of the interior of her wardrobe on the Isle of Man.

'You've spent your whole life with people taking notice of how good you look. Now that's something we have to change.'

Chapter Eight

Detective Sergeant Jennifer Lloyd leaned against a wall on the far side of the incident room, squeezing a squash ball in her palm. The blue rubber was dulled and cracked from months of handling. Lloyd gripped it beneath her fourth and fifth fingers, working through a series of rapid compressions. Her routine with the ball had started out as a strengthening exercise to speed her recovery from a broken wrist she'd sustained while apprehending a suspect. But the exercise had proved habit-forming, and now she found that it was a useful way of relieving stress.

Not that it was working so well tonight.

Lloyd looked around the room and saw at least three colleagues she would happily throw the ball at. Hard.

The headquarters of the UK Protected Persons Service was located in the Central Bureau of the National Crime Agency near St James's Park, London. Lloyd had been seconded to the unit four months ago. This was her third time inside the Major Incident Room in the basement of the building. Already, it was by far the most frustrating experience she'd faced.

There were twelve of them in the room. Lloyd's eleven colleagues had significant experience of working with protected persons. They believed in the principles of the service and were committed to shielding the individuals placed under their care.

Lloyd was different. She had no problem with a programme

that offered sanctuary to innocent people at extreme risk. But she'd been parachuted in by a senior officer who shared her concerns about how the scheme was being used to provide known offenders with amnesty in return for their testimony at important trials.

Officially, Lloyd had a watching brief. Unofficially, she was a mole. Everyone on the team understood her function. Everyone distrusted and disliked her. Which was generally fine by Lloyd, because at least they were open about it.

Across from her, beyond the central table and the computer terminals where her colleagues were gathered, three whiteboards were fitted to the wall. The board on the far right was empty. The board in the middle contained a handwritten timeline of known events on the Isle of Man. The board on the left was crammed with key data about Kate Sutherland.

A headshot of Sutherland was tacked up on the board. She had dark red hair, lightly freckled skin and striking green eyes. Several of Lloyd's male colleagues had lingered in front of the image. One of them, DS Quinn, had made a crack about volunteering to 'debrief' her once she was she found.

Lloyd had never had that kind of effect on men. She knew she never would. It wasn't that she was ugly exactly. It was simply that she was plain. She was average height, average weight, an average dresser – average in every physical attribute.

All of which made her an excellent observer because people tended to forget about her. Which was a mistake, because while Lloyd appeared to be entirely average, in reality she was anything but. She was highly intelligent, extremely driven, and ruthless in her ambition to get ahead.

Above the trio of whiteboards a flatscreen television cycled through a sequence of images that had been emailed to the team by a crime-scene officer on the Isle of Man. The photographs showed different angles of the body of the dead intruder. The corpse had been discovered late that morning by a DI Shimmin, who'd responded when Kate had failed to check in with him by phone at the beginning of the day.

The dead man was currently unidentified but it was clear to everyone in the team that he'd accessed the property armed with a suppressed pistol with the objective of killing Kate Sutherland.

So far, Lloyd had remained silent as her colleagues had reacted to the situation and put the established protocols into action. She'd watched them work the phones and the computers as they liaised with the Isle of Man Constabulary and pulled together all the available information. That was part one of the investigation and it had been slick and impressive.

Then part two had begun and Lloyd had bit her tongue as the team analysed the data they'd amassed. They'd speculated about who the dead man might be and debated whether he was a random intruder or, as seemed more likely, a hired killer. They'd settled on Connor Lane as the most likely candidate to have hired him. They'd spoken in concerned tones about Kate Sutherland's welfare, her possible whereabouts and her likely responses to being targeted. They'd talked about how they might contact her without blowing her cover, how best to reassure her and let her know that it was safe to come in.

And then Lloyd had finally had her fill of it. Because there was something fundamental they were overlooking.

She pushed off from the wall and crossed the room, slipped the squash ball into her pocket and snatched up a marker pen.

She scrawled eight words on the empty whiteboard, then thumped her fist so hard against it that everyone in the room turned to stare.

Issue an arrest warrant for Kate Sutherland NOW.

Chapter Nine

The camera flash was startlingly bright. Kate blinked but the flash fired again, and again, and instantly she was transported back to that darkened bedroom, the muzzle flare lighting up the terror-struck eyes of the masked man looming over her.

'That's perfect.' Hanson checked the digital screen on the back of his camera. 'You can relax now.'

Kate drifted away from the white photographic backdrop, a faint whistling in her ears and a taste like aniseed in her mouth. She steadied herself against Hanson's chair as he downloaded the photographs to one of his laptops.

And then there she was. A collection of head-and-shoulder shots. Washed out. Stark. Somehow reduced. Her, but different. The cropped red hair styled into a no-nonsense bob. The peach lipstick, in the same pale tone as the underwear she had on. Like a stranger. Or maybe a long-lost twin sister, one who'd grown up in a completely different environment to Kate, with a look and a bearing all her own.

And a style that positively repelled men, judging by the way Hanson had grimaced, clutching his hands to his head, the first time she'd followed Becca out of the bedroom.

She had on dark blue jeans with a high waist, a baggy pale blue sweatshirt and white trainers over white sports socks.

Next to her, Becca looked glam and effortlessly fabulous, armed with the make-up brushes and foundation she'd used to tailor Kate's appearance, and it occurred to Kate that this was the exact opposite of all the dumb rom-com movies she'd ever seen. This time, the cool girl had worked her magic only to transform Kate into the ultimate dork.

'That works,' was all Miller had to say, from where he was slouched on a high wooden stool over by the kitchen counter, surrounded by wonky cabinets, a stained fridge-freezer and a grotty, fat-smeared cooker.

He hadn't moved or spoken since. He was monitoring events silently and Kate had to fight an urge to go over and shake him. Didn't he get how freaked out she was? Didn't he understand that this was more than just routine for her?

It was different from before, with the police. Back then, she'd been told that she'd come out of protection shortly after Russell's trial. Everything had been officially sanctioned. Everything had been reversible.

Here, there was no safety net.

She wasn't only afraid of what she was getting into. She was scared by everything she was giving up. Not just her life as she knew it, but also the life she'd hoped to have. She was smart enough to know she couldn't walk away from this unscathed.

'Gotcha.'

Hanson had selected the least flattering headshot, opened it in a new window and tweaked a series of parameters. Then he hit a key and a compact black machine started to whir and hum until it spat out a British passport, opened to the laminated page at the back. Hanson removed the document and wafted it in the air. He bent it and crushed it, then handed it to Kate.

'Kate Elizabeth Ryan,' she read.

'It's best you keep your first name,' Miller explained. 'Easier to remember in pressure situations.'

It was the opposite of the advice the police protection officers had given her.

'Why Ryan? Why Elizabeth?'

'Why not?' Becca asked.

'Kate Elizabeth Ryan,' she said again. But the name meant nothing to her.

Hanson eyed her from over the tops of his spectacle frames. 'In case you were wondering, you should be totally impressed by me right now.'

'Will it work?'

'I'm not going to pretend that doesn't hurt.' He took the passport back, wheeling his chair over to another laptop where he tapped a key and typed a password into the dialogue box that appeared onscreen. He flattened the passport and slipped it beneath a scanner.

There was a brief pause before multiple lines of green text appeared over a black background.

'What is this?'

'The main database for the National Passport Office. If you pass through UK border control and an officer scans your passport, this is what they'll see.'

'You mean it'll look like this?'

'No, I mean it *is* this. I have a back door into their system. *That's* how good I am.'

Kate felt a smile tug at her lips. A sudden flush of confidence.

'Hanson, I am *seriously* impressed by you right now.'

'More like it.'

'But I have one question: what else can you do?'

Hanson could do plenty, as it turned out. First he produced a driving licence with Kate's new headshot on it. Then he manufactured credit and debit cards. Everything was in the name Kate Elizabeth Ryan.

'That's the easy part. Now I have to start work on transferring your funds to your new accounts.'

'How long will it take?'

'You don't want to know.'

'Is it dangerous?'

'Only if I get distracted and screw it up. And I probably will, if you keep standing here, watching over me.'

'It's late, honey.' Becca was sitting on the floor with her back against the wall, holding her heeled shoes by their ankle straps. 'Why don't you go across the hall and get some rest? Let the Boy Wonder do his thing.'

Kate peered at the time at the bottom of Hanson's screen. It was nudging past midnight. She'd been awake for almost twenty-four hours. She was wiped, but she was afraid to be alone, and it was unnerving to think of her identity being stripped apart and remodelled while she slept.

Over at the kitchen counter, Miller was still slouched forwards on his crossed forearms, watching in silence. Was he pleased with how things were going? Was she passing his unspoken test?

She kneaded the muscles at the back of her neck and crossed to the nearest window, pulling the net curtain aside. The street below was in darkness, a third-rate amusement arcade closed and shuttered up.

There was no sign of any faceless men lurking in the shadows. No car parked ominously along the street.

But she felt anxious all the same.

'Will you come with me?' she asked Becca.

'I have to stay and keep Hanson awake. Take Miller. You can ignore his strong, silent routine. He could use some rest, too.'

Kate let go of the curtain and faced him directly. He held her gaze without moving, then finally pushed himself up on the heels of his hands, summoning a crumpled smile.

'I'll take the couch. Beats listening to Hanson bang on about how terrific he is.'

Chapter Ten

The office of the deputy governor of Strangeways prison in Manchester was little bigger than an inmate's cell. It contained a cheap L-shaped desk with a dusty computer and a telephone to one side, a bank of metal filing cabinets and a wilting money plant. But the cramped space had one thing going for it – in a building designed to keep Category A prisoners under constant supervision, it was one of the few places where privacy could be guaranteed.

Mike Renner perched on the edge of the desk with an old paperback novel curled into a tube in his hands. By Renner's watch, he'd been waiting a little over eight minutes, which was eight minutes too long.

He could feel a damp chill spreading across his shoulder blades, a constriction in his throat. He'd loosened his tie and collar but somehow it still felt as if an invisible noose had been slipped over his neck.

Three more minutes crawled by before the door was pushed open and Russell was led inside by a guard in uniform. Russell stood slump-shouldered in his dark blue sweater and matching jogging trousers, contemplating his black training shoes as the guard headed for the door.

'Hey,' Renner called after him. 'Take off the cuffs.'

'Cuffs stay on. I'm not authorised to undo them.'

'Not authorised. Really?' Renner reached out a hand and

lifted the desk phone from its cradle. 'What do you think? Will your boss have a problem with me waking him at home to tell him you're being a prick?'

The guard wavered a moment, then let out a heavy sigh as he freed his keys from his belt and walked over to loosen Russell's restraints.

'I'm going to be waiting right outside this door.'

'Sure.' Renner waved him off. 'Whatever makes you feel like you're in control here.'

Russell waited until he was gone before looking up with a slight smile. He rubbed at his wrists, stepping closer to reach for Renner's hand and pull him off the desk into an embrace.

'How are you holding up?' Renner asked, slapping his back, pushing him away so he could search his face.

But Russell didn't answer. He just swiped at his nose with a knuckle, then sniffed and pointed at the book. 'What did you bring me?'

Renner unfurled the paperback. The colours were faded, the pages yellowed, the spine splintered and cracked.

'Think maybe I've read this one before.'

'I think maybe you have, too. But it's a good one.'

The book was a Western, taken from the collection Renner stored in a pile of boxes in the shed at the bottom of his garden. Renner had been loaning the books to Russell since the boy was a teenager. In the years after Larry and Diane had disappeared, he'd often walked the grounds of the Lane estate with Russell, or watched over him as he built dens in the nearby woods, talking through the stories together, sharing which parts they liked most, the characters they admired, the women they lusted after.

Renner missed those days. He'd been blessed with two daughters but the bond he shared with Russell was something beyond that. It felt purer and more profound than his sense of loyalty and responsibility towards Connor. Something more, truth be told, than he'd ever experienced with either of his girls.

Larry's vanishing act had given him the precious gift of his relationship with Russell, and there were times when he was shamed by how happy it made him. But to see him here, now – to look at his pallid skin, his sunken cheeks and the dark whorls around his eyes; to hear the broken quality of his voice – was almost too much for Renner to take.

'Anyone giving you trouble?'

Russell fanned the pages of the book, shaking his head. Connor's money had paid for his brother's safety inside. Renner had made sure that word got around Strangeways fast that Russell Lane was off-limits. But there was always the danger that some young punk looking to build a reputation for himself might decide to have a go.

'Your brother says your legal team are really shaping up.'

Russell gave him a familiar one-eyed squint and tapped the book with his nail. 'There's something about the sheriff, isn't there? A secret in his past?'

So Renner quit trying to have a real conversation, motioned for Russell to hop up next to him on the desk and started talking about the book instead. But as he gave his take on the plot and the characters, saying how he still thought the sheriff was a fool for setting off to hunt down the crew of bank robbers instead of bunking down with the raven-haired rancher's girl, all he could really do was think about Russell.

He thought of Anna Brooks, the teenage runaway who'd

accused him of violent rape four years ago; of how he hadn't believed it then and couldn't believe it still. And he thought of Helen Knight, the young lawyer who'd been found dead not two months ago now, her bloated body washed up on the shores of Lake Windermere, less than a mile from the Lane estate. Russell was the last person known to have seen her alive. Patrick Leigh had watched Helen get into Russell's car on the day she went missing. Kate Sutherland had witnessed them arguing.

Renner sneaked a look at the man sitting beside him, the lost boy he still reminded him of in so many ways, and something in his heart told him that Russell had been unlucky two times over, accused of sickening crimes he didn't have the capacity to commit.

But also, deep down, he couldn't ignore a stirring of unease; the thought that somehow, biologically speaking, the meek lad he knew, the sweet kid who liked to build dens and talk Western stories, might also have inherited Larry's lust for violence and destruction, just as Connor had inherited his ruthless ambition and drive for success.

Right now, sitting so close to Russell that he could have reached out and cupped his neck, kissed his head, whispered to him that he was going to do everything necessary to protect him, the thing that scared Renner most in all the world was the idea that twelve complete strangers, the members of a jury called to pass judgement on Russell, might be able to discern that quality in him, too.

So as Renner talked of the heroes and villains of the Old West, of noble intentions and sacrifice and doomed romantic love, he renewed a vow he'd made to himself and to Connor four years before.

No trial of Russell Lane would ever take place. Renner refused to allow it. During the past four years, Nick Adams had proved highly adept at disappearing. He was entirely capable of teaching Kate Sutherland to live off the grid. So finding them both was never going to be simple. And if that meant taking an unconventional approach – even an unprecedented gamble, for Renner – then it was something he was more than willing to do.

Chapter Eleven

Kate lay in bed, thinking. The last time she'd fallen asleep in a darkened room a man had come to kill her. He'd gotten so close that she'd felt his breath on her face.

And now this.

A new room in a new place. A new look and a new identity. New people watching over her.

Nothing Miller and his team could offer her was legal. She'd have nobody to turn to if things went wrong.

Kate had never been a risk-taker. She'd always been painfully sensible, almost obsessed with being in control, a trait which had given her the discipline to excel as an athlete. She supposed she had her adoptive parents to thank for that. Her upbringing had been loving but strict. She'd been taught to believe in order and justice above all else. It was one reason, among many others, why she'd ultimately become a lawyer.

And yet she'd killed a man. She was in hiding.

So who was she now?

The question was terrifying. So much had changed in such a short space of time that it seemed inconceivable that anything could ever be the same again. Would she recognise herself tomorrow? Or the day after that?

She threw back her bedcovers and crept over to the door of her room. There was no noise on the other side.

She eased it open.

Miller was slouched on the sofa in the light of a fringed standing lamp, looking closely at a slip of paper, rubbing his thumb over the surface.

Was this a good man? Was he someone she could believe in?

He looked up sharply, as if somehow he'd heard her thoughts, and Kate glimpsed a flicker of hurt in his eyes, realising too late that she'd trespassed on something private.

She stepped back to push the door closed but Miller shook his head and beckoned her towards him.

Kate glanced over her shoulder at her bed, at the fears and the loneliness she might have endured, then bit down on the inside of her cheek and came forward in her T-shirt and panties, cringing at how it must look.

'Can't sleep?' he asked. 'It gets easier over time.'

'Does it? Has it for you?'

He smiled, caught in the lie. 'I keep hoping. Here.' He patted the sofa.

She positioned herself at the opposite end of the couch, clutching a patterned cushion in front of her waist. She felt very aware of how close Miller was to her; of the space he was occupying, of the shape and size of his body.

'What do you have there?' she asked him.

Miller pursed his lips, then shrugged and rocked his head and passed the sheet of paper across to her. The stock was thin, the paper creased and wrinkled from years of handling. The edges were dinged and rounded and dirtied.

'My daughter, Melanie, drew that for me when she was eight years old.'

'I'd never have taken you for a horse rider.'

'I'm not. Maybe she knew something I didn't.'

63

The drawing was in faded crayon. In the foreground, Kate could see a blue man in a cowboy hat sitting on a brown horse. The horse was rearing up in the air and the man was waving to a woman and a young girl standing in front of a storybook house. The girl had brown curls and pink dungarees. She was holding hands with a woman in a green dress with long brown hair. Everyone was smiling, even the horse. The figures were labelled 'Daddy', 'Mummy', 'Me'.

'Nice hat.'

Kate handed the drawing back. The paper was so fragile she was afraid it might tear.

Families were fragile, too. She'd known that since she was a kid but she was sorry that Miller shared her heartache.

She wondered how he could bear it – to have had his family taken from him in such harrowing circumstances. She remembered the story being in the papers at the time. His wife and daughter had been shot dead and their home set on fire. There was speculation that the Lane family were involved, but no arrests had followed.

Until now, she'd assumed it was a tragedy that had hardened and transformed Miller, setting him on a mission to save people like her. But perhaps that interpretation was too simplistic. Maybe everything he was doing was just a distraction from his anguish. Perhaps he hadn't healed at all.

Was it harder to have a family that you loved and cherished torn away from you, or, like her, to have never known your real family at all?

'I've carried this drawing with me ever since the day Mel gave it to me. Thirteen years ago.' Miller gave her a sideways look. 'If I ask you a question, will you answer me truthfully?'

'Depends on the question.'

'Tell me what you think – did she draw me riding away or coming home?'

Kate gazed down at the drawing, the paper shaking almost imperceptibly in Miller's hands. She had a sense of the weight of emotion that lay behind his asking and the responsibility her answer bore.

'You don't know? What did she say when she gave it to you?'

'She didn't. I was working so hard back then that I was afraid to ask.'

'Coming home,' Kate said, with confidence.

'What makes you say that?'

'She was your little girl. Why would she draw you going away?'

Miller tilted the sketch, as if considering it from a new angle. He hummed to himself, unconvinced. Then he shifted around on the sofa and removed his wallet from his jeans and tucked the drawing carefully away.

'Do you miss being Nick Adams?'

'Every day. I miss everything about the life I had back then. But that's gone now. Lane took it all from me.'

'And am I to be your revenge?'

'No. You were a pattern repeating itself. I wanted to break the pattern. That's all.'

She plucked at the cushion. She wasn't sure she could believe him. He'd told her that he'd lost his wife and daughter to Connor Lane and now here she was, a weapon in his possession. He'd want more than simply to protect her, wouldn't he? He'd want to hurt Lane, too.

'Listen, you haven't told me how much this is going to cost.

I'm guessing your services aren't cheap. And Hanson has access to my bank accounts. He'll have seen—'

'He has seen. We all have. But that's not why we're helping you, Kate.'

She was silent for a moment, turning over his words, sifting through them for a deeper meaning.

'So how does it work? You can't possibly do all this for free.'

'We have a benefactor.'

'Really? Who? Are they part of the programme?'

'No.'

'Then why the interest?'

'Reasons. This is day one for you, Kate. Trust me, you'll learn more when it's safe.'

He yawned and stretched, reaching above his head towards the switch on the lamp.

'What do you say we turn this light off and sit here pretending either one of us might sleep?'

Darkness.

Miller rearranged himself against the cushions and Kate heard the clump of his shoes being propped on the low coffee table.

She sat quietly beside him, tensed, unmoving, thinking of things lost and never found, waiting for morning to come.

Chapter Twelve

DS Jennifer Lloyd entered the incident room shortly after 7 a.m. with a take-out cup of hot tea with lemon, no milk. She'd planned to get started on her day before the rest of the unit arrived but two of her colleagues had beaten her to it. Detective Sergeants John Young and Nadine Foster were already seated in front of adjoining computer terminals with take-out cups of their own.

Lloyd wished them good morning, trying to mask her disappointment.

Young grunted. Foster nodded. Neither looked up from their screens.

'Anything new?'

'See for yourself.'

Lloyd carried her tea over to the whiteboards. There was additional information on the middle and left-hand boards. Most of the fresh data was about the set-up on the Isle of Man, but there were also several photographs of the house where Kate Sutherland had been living and the dead man had been found.

'What about witnesses?'

There was no reply.

'Hello? Witnesses?'

'One neighbour,' Foster mumbled. 'If you can call him that. His bungalow is almost half a mile away but he thinks he might have heard a shot.'

Foster was a couple of years younger than Lloyd, a few inches taller, with fine blonde hair and endless legs. She had a varied selection of stylish outfits and a taste for fashionable handbags and jewellery. She was well liked and respected by her peers, more likely to have a Kate Sutherland type of impact on her male co-workers than Lloyd ever would. She was going places, no doubt about it.

'Time?'

'Around 1 a.m.'

'That could fit with time of death.'

'*If* the local coroner's initial assessment holds. We're still waiting for her full report.'

Lloyd took a sip from her tea, sneaking a glance at the board on the right. It remained empty aside from the message she'd scrawled in the centre.

'Pretty embarrassing for you.'

Lloyd turned to find Young smirking at her. His hair was slicked to one side with wet-look gel and he was wearing a dark grey tie over a shirt the same colour. He looked like he should be selling mobile phones in a high-street shop.

Young was the only member of the team Lloyd had history with. Bad history, inevitably.

'So dramatic,' he continued. 'But so embarrassing.'

'I stand by it.'

'That's a shock. You're full of terrible suggestions.' He pushed up from his desk, grabbing a cigarette packet and waggling it at Foster. 'You coming?'

'Not right now.'

'Suit yourself.' He sniffed. 'I could use some clean air.'

Lloyd let him go, waiting until his footsteps had faded along the corridor before toasting Foster with her cup. 'Not my biggest fan.'

'Oh, he *really* hates you.' Foster paused, fingers hovering above her keyboard. 'Care to explain why?'

'I'm pretty sure he's already told you. And the rest of the team, for that matter.'

'Maybe I want to hear your side of it.'

'An open mind? Really?'

'So make the most of it. Just know that I probably won't agree with anything you have to say.'

Chapter Thirteen

Kate woke to find herself curled under a blanket, alone. She levered herself up on her elbow and peered at the note that had been left on the coffee table.

Breakfast next door when you feel like it. Take your time.

Throwing back the blanket, she stumbled through to the bathroom and took a fast shower. The cubicle was cramped and mouldy, the water came out in a frothing dribble, but it was hot and there was complimentary soap in a chalk-paper wrapper and a small tube of shampoo. She washed her hair, so short now that it took barely any time to lather and rinse, and then she stepped out and dried herself with a thin, crusty towel, dressing in fresh underwear and yesterday's new clothes.

Hanson and Becca were waiting for her across the hall. Kate helped herself to a breakfast roll and a mug of black coffee, then perched on one of the kitchen stools and watched Hanson approach.

His hair was matted and flattened down, his polo shirt creased. He'd propped his spectacles up on top of his head and his eyes were puffy, pupils blown.

He smiled blearily as he laid her new banking cards, driver's licence and passport on the counter in front of her like he was spreading a deck of playing cards. He added an embossed card containing a National Insurance number as well as a birth certificate. Everything was in the name Kate Elizabeth Ryan.

'Disappearance 101. Consider this your starter pack.'

'What about money?'

'I've placed a small amount of funds in a current account for you. Your own cash is shuttling between banks and jurisdictions. Once it's stable, I'll send you more details.'

Becca leaned a hip against the kitchen counter. She was freshly made up and dressed in a scooped pink blouse and Capri pants, her hair kinking out in lush brown coils.

'How are you feeling, honey?'

'Groggy.'

She winked. 'And how was last night?'

Kate got what she was really asking but she wasn't about to play the game. She tore off a chunk of breakfast roll and popped it in her mouth.

'I slept OK.'

'Uh-huh. Well, once you're done eating, I've picked out some contact lenses for you to try. Brown tint. Right now, your eyes are kind of a pow. We have to dial them down a couple of notches.'

Kate felt the breakfast roll bulge in her throat. She washed it back with coffee, wondering if there was going to be anything of her left before the day was through.

A door swung back at the far side of the room and Miller stepped out of the bathroom. He had on a blue shirt with white stripes over faded blue jeans. There was a towel coiled round his neck, his hair was damp and his head was tilted to one side as he patted his ear dry.

Kate found herself wondering what he'd look like clean-shaven, with his hair clipped short, dressed in a fitted suit. Then she was struck by the realisation that perhaps he used to groom himself that way. He'd told her that he was in hiding, too, so it stood to reason that he'd need his own disguise. Maybe the mountain-man aesthetic was something Becca was responsible for.

'Hey, you're up.'

'Mm-hmm.' Kate looked down into her coffee. She could feel a burn in her cheeks.

'Hanson, do you have the information I asked for?'

'Hey, Hanson,' Hanson said, in a pretty good imitation of Miller's gruff baritone. '*Great* job on Kate's new ID. I know you haven't slept, and I'm being totally unreasonable, but why don't you show me what else you have?'

He circled behind his tables of computers and tapped a key to wake a desktop, then swivelled the monitor for them all to see. Displayed onscreen was a washed-out photograph of the man Kate had shot. She could tell by the gory hole in the man's throat and the black balaclava rolled up on his forehead.

She set her breakfast to one side.

'If I'd had a little longer, I'd have more to go on. But this is definitely our guy.'

Hanson hit another button and a fresh image appeared in a new window. He lined the photographs up next to one another. The second image was a side profile of the same man, showing him in a suit and tie, opening the rear door of a dark saloon car in the middle of a city street. It was fuzzy and looked like it had been cropped from surveillance-camera footage.

'Ooh, he's cute,' Becca said, and when everyone turned to

her, she added, 'What? I'm talking about the *before* image, obviously.'

'Keep going,' Miller told Hanson, 'before she says something distasteful.'

'His name is Ivan Pavlenko. Russian KGB. An active field agent with multiple kills against his name.'

Kate felt herself teeter on her stool.

'Nah, just messing with you, Kate.' Hanson grinned at her stupidly. 'His real name was Duncan North, an ex-squaddie from Peterborough. Low-level scumbag.'

'That's supposed to be funny?'

'North has served time for GBH. This shot was taken from outside Connor Lane's central Manchester HQ. North was working a year or two back as a bodyguard for one of Lane's business associates. Seems he branched out into contract killing. Not very successfully.'

'Did he have any family?'

'Survived by a mother and an older brother. No wife. No kids.'

It made Kate feel a little better to hear it. She'd been worrying about that. But still, a mother without a son. A man without a brother. And she was responsible.

'I checked, by the way.' Hanson glanced at Miller. 'North was serving an eighteen-month sentence four years ago. He was locked up when Sarah and Melanie were killed.'

Miller closed his eyes and was silent for a moment. 'Any concrete link to Lane? Something provable?'

'I'll keep looking but it's unlikely they'll have been that stupid.'

'Do it anyway.'

Kate was still reeling but she couldn't miss the hurt in Miller's voice. She guessed he was probably haunted by the idea that the man who'd stolen his family from him was still out there, somewhere. She knew she would be.

'Tell me the rules,' she blurted, acting on a sudden impulse to distract him from his pain. 'I'm ready for them now. I have to know what this is going to take.'

Chapter Fourteen

DS Jennifer Lloyd shunted the rusted bolt aside with the heel of her hand and shouldered the ill-fitting door, stepping out on to the flat roof of the National Crime Agency. It offered a spectacular view of St James's Park and The Mall, but Lloyd headed in the opposite direction, leaning her forearms against the sooty masonry, looking over office buildings and rooftops towards the Thames, Waterloo station and beyond. London was a collision of murky greys and browns, splintered by the mirror-gleam flare of distant skyscrapers.

'So this is where you sneak off to.' Foster cupped a hand round her lighter and sparked a cigarette. 'Young has a pool going. My money was on Commissioner Bennett's office.'

'Bad bet.'

'Except your route up here takes you past Bennett's office. Perfect for telling tales.'

Lloyd let the barb go, mostly because it was accurate.

'About Young . . .' she began. 'There's a reason he's pushing the theory that Connor Lane is behind whatever just happened on the Isle of Man.'

'Uh-huh.' Foster took a draw on her cigarette. 'It's because it's the obvious theory to push.'

'Maybe. Maybe not.'

'Seriously? Lane has form for this. The only question is whether we can prove the link.'

'Which we won't.'

'Way to build morale, Lloyd.'

'I'm just saying what we all already know. Lane wouldn't take a risk like this unless he was insulated from it.'

'Just like four years ago.'

Lloyd hummed noncommittally and looked down twelve storeys to where a red double-decker was pulling into a bus stop. Commuters weaved along the pavements, checking phones, carrying coffee cups.

'I read the file,' Foster continued. 'Think what you like about this team but I don't just rely on hearsay. Young had his version. I wanted to make up my own mind.'

'And did you?'

'I did. And I agree with him.'

'Based on the file.'

'That's right.'

Foster's smoke was getting in Lloyd's eyes. It was hard to tell if it was deliberate or not.

'The thing is, the file was incomplete.'

'I don't think so. The name Nick Adams cropped up more than once.'

'But not in one crucial respect.'

The file Foster was referring to was a report compiled by an outside investigation team that Lloyd had been part of four years ago. The team had been tasked with evaluating what, if any, mistakes had been made by the witness protection unit of Greater Manchester Police that might have contributed to the murders of Sarah and Melanie Adams. Nick Adams and his wife and daughter had been scheduled to be taken into witness protection on a temporary basis the morning after Sarah and Melanie were killed.

The plan had been to relocate them to a safe house until the conclusion of the rape trial against Russell Lane.

At the time of the family's planned inclusion in the scheme, Nick Adams had been second-in-command of the witness protection unit run by Greater Manchester Police. This was in the era prior to the co-ordinated, UK-wide approach to witness protection now being undertaken by the National Crime Agency.

DS Young had also been part of the Greater Manchester team, though he'd been a detective constable back then. He'd stayed loyal to his boss, even when Nick Adams had disappeared in the wake of the killings.

'So what was missing?' Foster asked.

'Arguments. Lots of disagreements.'

'Between you and Young?'

'Between Nick Adams and his wife. She didn't want her daughter to testify against Russell Lane. She didn't want the family to enter witness protection. Adams insisted.'

'And you know this how, exactly?'

'By interviewing witnesses. Their neighbours. And I had a handwriting expert take a look at the consent document the family signed. He agreed, on the balance of probabilities, that Nick Adams faked his wife's signature.'

'So why wasn't this in the file?'

'Good question.'

'And the answer is?'

'Sometimes evidence can be unwelcome if it doesn't tally with an accepted theory. Even if we're talking about a report by an outside investigative unit.'

'And you accepted that?'

'Not for one second.'

'So what happened?'

'My additions to the file were excised. And I was exiled. All very neat. Until Commissioner Bennett gave me another chance.'

Foster closed one eye and gestured at Lloyd with her cigarette. 'You seriously believe there was a cover-up? Isn't it more likely that Adams vanished because he was broken? That he blamed himself for placing his family in danger? Maybe he began to see that his wife had been right and his daughter shouldn't have agreed to testify. Or maybe he knew he should have got them protection sooner.'

'Look, I'm no conspiracy theorist. I get that Connor Lane had plenty of motivation. He had the means. And everyone – including Young – was at pains to tell me that Adams was a good man, that I was crazy for even suggesting he might have cracked and murdered his wife and daughter before using all the skills he'd acquired, and maybe even certain loyal members of his team, to arrange his own disappearance.'

'But you still believe that's what happened, don't you?'

Lloyd pursed her lips and moved her head from side to side, as if there were other arguments to be weighed up. Which, as far as she was concerned, there really weren't.

'Doesn't mean I want to believe it. That's the part Young doesn't get.'

Foster took a final hit on her cigarette. 'So what do you want from me?'

'I want you to think some more about Kate Sutherland. I want you to consider that issuing an arrest warrant for her might be the way to go.'

'And if I don't agree with you?'

'You will. Eventually. Because I'm going to prove to you that I'm right.'

Chapter Fifteen

'You're ready?' Miller asked.

Kate nodded, watching as he fixed himself a coffee and slid on to the stool next to her. His shirt was damp at the collar and twisted a little. Kate fought the impulse to reach out and straighten it.

'OK, we let you keep your first name, right?'

'Right.'

'Well, that's about all you get to hold on to. That's rule number one.'

'That's a pretty sweeping rule.'

'Lawyers. Nearly as bad as actresses.' He tried a smile that didn't seem to fit him quite right. 'Rule two is you don't contact anyone from your old life. You sever all ties. Family. Friends. Passing acquaintances. They're all gone. Like they never existed for you.'

'My family are gone anyway.'

Miller raised an eyebrow and Kate worried that she'd sounded flippant and crass. Then he looked at her some more and she began to sense something behind it. There was a queasy turning in her stomach.

'We know you've been looking, honey.' Becca stepped closer. 'We know what we're asking you to give up.'

'You were getting close,' Hanson added.

Kate felt the room begin to tilt and spin. They couldn't

know. Nobody did. She hadn't told anyone about the search for her birth family – not even the police who'd hidden her before.

'We're sorry for you,' Miller told her. 'Truly. If there was any other option, we'd offer it to you, Kate. We understand how badly you want to find them.'

She closed her eyes.

'How do you know?'

'We're careful. We know everything there is to know.'

No, not everything, Kate thought. No one but her could know how much it hurt.

Kate had been abandoned by her birth parents outside Cheltenham General Hospital when she was almost nine months old. Soon after, she was taken in by her foster parents, James and Caroline. When Kate turned five, they adopted her, and she grew up happy and privileged in the idyllic setting of their Cotswolds farm estate, but from the day they first told her the truth, shortly after her thirteenth birthday, she'd been plagued by questions about who her real parents might be and why they'd left her. Then, when her adoptive parents were killed in a small-plane crash two years back, she discovered that she'd been willed half their fortune.

Suddenly, Kate was wealthy beyond all reason, but she was grief-struck and rootless. It was only in the past year that she'd summoned the courage to begin searching for her birth parents. Until recently, her attempts had proved fruitless. Then the specialist agency she'd hired had given her one fragment of information to hold on to. Kate had a brother who'd been left at the same time as her. His name was Richard and he was three years older than Kate. But Richard hadn't been so fortunate. He'd grown up inside the care system, shuttled between a succession of foster parents and children's homes until, at the age of sixteen, he became a blank. As far as the records were concerned, Richard simply ceased to exist.

Where had he gone? What had become of him? Did he even remember Kate?

She'd spent countless hours thinking about him, speculating about what he might be like, wondering if he knew of her existence, and if he didn't, whether he somehow sensed her absence from his life, in the same way, she believed, she'd always known that a piece of her was lacking; a hole she couldn't fill.

Finding her parents had been one thing. There was always the possibility they wouldn't want to meet with her if she tracked them down because they'd abandoned her once before. But Richard hadn't made that choice. Neither of them had.

She wanted so much to find him. She had ample money to throw at the problem, and yet a solution had so far eluded her. Now, she was being asked to walk away from the search before she had the answers she craved. She was being asked to walk away from Richard.

'I'm sorry,' Miller said again.

And damn if she wasn't starting to cry.

'You said I was getting close to finding them?' She looked up at Hanson.

'I think so, yes. To your brother, anyway.'

'Well, that could be dangerous, couldn't it? Connor Lane could get to him. He could threaten him to get to me.'

'We don't think that will happen,' Miller told her.

'Lane doesn't know about Richard,' Hanson put in. 'I had to do some serious digging to find out myself. The agency you hired have a first-rate security system. But I'll monitor the situation. If a crack appears, I'll fill it. And you should know that I haven't been able to locate your brother. I've tried. If I can't find him, then Lane can't either.'

Becca put an arm around her and Hanson smiled awkwardly, looking very young all of a sudden. Kate blinked at Miller, pressing the heels of her hands to her eyes.

'Where will I live?'

'Europe.'

'Do I get to pick a place?'

'That's rule number three. I choose. At least to begin with.'

'But not England?'

'No.'

'You don't ask much, do you?'

'You'll also need to work. We can't allow you to access the majority of your funds for the first year. And then we'll drip feed them. We have to make sure the money's not being followed. That's how Hanson found you in the Isle of Man, by the way.'

'So place me somewhere with an international law firm.'

'Not an option. You can't work as a lawyer. You'd be too easy to track. Menial jobs are best. But not anything where you'll meet lots of people. Being a waitress is bad. Working in a bar or a coffee shop is worse. We've had clients work as late-night cleaners in factories or stockrooms. Data input is OK. Basically anything that keeps you away from the public or your face behind a computer terminal.'

Hanson glanced up from behind his laptop. 'I'm going to choose not to take offence at that.'

Kate had excelled as a lawyer. She'd been on the partnership track at her firm. And now she was being told she had to turn her back on eight years of hard work. To become a cleaner. Or a factory worker. To live in a strange place that was not of her choosing, leaving without saying goodbye to any of her friends or colleagues, giving up the search for her brother and her birth parents.

'When this is over, I'm going to find Richard. You can help me to do that, can't you?'

'Kate,' Miller told her gently, a look of regret on his face, 'this will never be over. Not for you. Not like that.'

'But I still testify. Right? I'm going to give my evidence against Russell Lane. You agreed to it.'

'Whoa.' Becca stepped back. 'You did not tell her that.'

Kate looked between them, bewildered.

'You promised me I'd testify. I told you that was non-negotiable.'

'It's complicated, Kate.' Miller was looking down now; at his coffee, at his hands, anywhere but at her.

'Then forget it. Forget all of it.' She jumped off her stool. 'Richard is my brother. Understand? And Helen was my friend. She was a good person. She didn't need to volunteer at that shelter but she did it because she wanted to help people. And now I'm going to help her. I'll walk out of here into the nearest police station in order to testify if I have to.'

'Er, Kate.' Hanson had gathered up his laptop in a hurry and was hustling over to the kitchen counter, angling the screen for them all to see. 'You might want to reconsider.'

Despite herself, Kate looked, then immediately wished she hadn't.

Hanson had called up a news article from the BBC website. The report concerned the discovery of a man's body among the foundations of a building site in Greater Manchester. Early indications were that he'd been killed in unexplained circumstances, possibly involving a fall. The dead man had been identified as a Patrick Martin Leigh.

'This can't be real. Tell me this isn't real.'

'Oh, it's real,' Miller said. 'It's like I told you at the beginning – there's no going back.'

Chapter Sixteen

Kate was still staring at Miller, speechless, when Becca grabbed the laptop and took her by the hand to the apartment across the hall. She guided her on to the sofa and sat beside her with the laptop on her knees.

Kate looked blindly about the room. This situation wasn't just bigger than her, it was swallowing her.

A man had plummeted to his death. He'd been murdered, Kate was sure. And all because, like her, he'd been willing to testify in the trial of Russell Lane.

'Listen to me,' Becca was saying. 'You're hurting. You're scared. And I'm sorry for you, I am, but I think maybe you needed this. Your situation is real, Kate. It's terrible but it's happening. Now is the time to commit to it.'

But Kate didn't feel capable of committing to anything. She felt powerless and disconnected, as if all of this was happening to someone else. Even the room around her had an unreal quality to it – the decor so dated it might have been a museum exhibit.

'I have something to show you. Look.'

Becca circled her fingers over the laptop's trackpad and clicked several times until a video began to play.

Kate took a moment before gazing down, then did a double-take. The video featured colour footage of the apartment next door, shot from an angle that suggested a camera had been fitted to the corner of the ceiling. It showed Kate sitting down to eat breakfast, talking with Hanson and Becca.

'You've been filming me? You didn't ask.'

'Honey, until we know that you're safe, you have absolutely no privacy. You'd better get used to it.' She tapped a nail against the screen. 'See what you're doing here? The way you tilt your head? How you bite your lip? You do it all the time when you're listening. Especially when you're about to disagree with something.'

The Kate in the footage seemed oddly fake, as if she was watching an impostor. Her movements had an abrupt, doll-like quality.

'When you argue, you lead with your chin. You scratch your temple when you're flustered. And you constantly tuck your hair behind your ear. It's a habit from when your hair was longer. If you can't break the cycle, we'll use clips or a hairband.'

Kate drew a fast breath and looked away but Becca cupped her chin and turned her face back to the screen. Another thirty seconds of footage elapsed and Kate saw herself push her hair back twice.

'It's the small tics that define you. You have to find new habits. And we really have to work on your walk. You spring forwards from your toes. It's an athlete thing, but it's distinct-ive. I have insoles for you to try.'

'You're kidding.'

'You're kidding.' Becca frowned, mimicking her. 'We'll soften your accent. Shift the emphasis you place on certain words. We'll change all your markers.' She tapped the screen with her nail again. 'Some juicy stuff coming up.'

Kate studied her onscreen responses as Miller appeared and

stepped around behind the breakfast counter, his hair tousled, the top two buttons of his shirt undone.

'Girl, you have it all going on. There's the hair-touching, the raised eyebrows, the fidgety lips. And the way you lean in. Do you even know how many times you almost touched him?'

'That's not true.'

'Oh, relax, honey. Most of this stuff is instinctive. There's not a lot we can change or really need to. Mostly we're watching this for my own titillation. Besides, so much of what we're seeing depends on the other person's responses.'

Kate hated herself for it, but she couldn't help glancing at Becca for more.

'Mirroring.' She nudged her. 'He likes you, too. I haven't seen him look at anyone that way in a very long time.'

*

Lloyd and Foster rode the elevator down to the NCA basement in an awkward silence. Lloyd was embarrassed and frustrated. She'd still been working on Foster up on the roof when Young had telephoned her mobile to say that a street kid called Patrick Leigh had decided to go high diving without a swimming pool in Manchester on the same night Kate Sutherland had been targeted. In itself, it might have meant nothing, except that Patrick had also been due to give evidence in the trial of Russell Lane. Aside from Kate, he was the last person to have seen Helen Knight alive – he'd been due to testify that he'd watched her climb into Russell's BMW on the day she disappeared in the alley behind the Fresh Start Shelter. Coincidence was one thing, but this had to be something more.

Worse, there'd been a breakdown in communication with Greater Manchester Police and the news had hit local media before it reached the NCA. So far, the national press hadn't made the link to the Lane family, though Lloyd guessed it was only a matter of time.

The elevator pinged, the doors parted, and Lloyd followed Foster along the basement corridor, already dreading the smug look on Young's face when they entered the incident room. But they were intercepted before they got there by a uniformed officer.

'DS Lloyd?' The officer was flushed and out of breath. 'This came in for you upstairs.'

He handed Lloyd a padded brown envelope. The words URGENT: FAO DS JENNIFER LLOYD ONLY were printed in marker pen across the front. There was no postage stamp and no delivery details.

'Who gave this to you?'

The officer winced. 'He had a bike helmet on. I'm sorry. There was a queue at the front desk and he just sort of walked up and dumped it. I didn't see what it said until he was gone.'

Lloyd shot a look at Foster, then tore open the envelope. There was only one item inside. It was a glossy photographic print that looked as if it had been taken with some kind of night-vision equipment. There was a blurred, blackish corona around the edges while the details in the middle were picked out in varying shades of green.

Lloyd recognised the glass-fronted exterior of the clifftop house where Kate Sutherland had been living. The image showed a man stepping out through a sliding door.

'Tell me I'm not going nuts,' Foster said, 'but isn't that Nick Adams?'

'You're not going nuts. And be honest now – do you really still believe he has no questions to answer?'

Chapter Seventeen

Kate walked with Miller along the seafront promenade, keeping her head down against the driving wind. It was raining steadily, the tide a long way out beyond the sodden beach and slickened mud flats.

They trudged by a derelict outdoor swimming pool, the word TROPICANA picked out in bas-relief on stonework that was discoloured and crumbling. The lights of the Grand Pier shone gaudily through the drizzle; forlorn streaks of neon in search of absent tourists.

'Hungry?' Miller asked, pointing ahead through the rain in the direction of the Winter Gardens, where a grinning cartoon whale was suspended above a fish-and-chip cafe.

'Like you wouldn't believe.'

The cafe was close to empty, the windows all steamed up. Stepping inside and standing in front of the heated counter, smelling the hot frying oil, water dripping from her hair and clothes, Kate had a sudden sensation of the world around her being too vibrant – overloaded with colour and sounds and smells.

Miller, sensing her unease, stepped up and ordered cod, chips and mushy peas twice, then asked for two mugs of hot tea that he carried over to a window booth with leatherette seats.

Kate drifted after him, sliding in opposite. She dabbed at her face with paper towels plucked from the metal dispenser at the end of the Formica table. There was a boxy television high in the corner of the room, above the service counter. It was screening Sky News, the volume on low.

'Hey, you're smiling.' Miller shed his jacket and began rolling his shirtsleeves up his forearms.

'I used to beg my parents to bring me to places like this. They thought they were slumming it but I loved the smell, the atmosphere. There's a romance to a place like this, don't you think?'

She curled her hands around her mug, looking down into her tea. *Romance*. What had she said that for?

'How's it going with Becca?'

'You tell me.'

She was using the new voice Becca had been working on with her. It wasn't dramatically different. Just a slight change in tone and pronunciation and emphasis. It was going to be difficult to maintain and already she was wondering if she'd stick with it.

'It's a good start. How about being in here? You feel OK?'

Kate did a one-shoulder shrug, reaching for the sugar dispenser, pouring a stream of granules into her tea. She didn't take sugar normally, but maybe it was something the new Kate should try.

'Because a lot of our clients feel threatened once they're in the real world again. That's why I thought it would be good to get out of the apartment. See how you cope.'

'I'm OK.'

Miller leaned back, stretching his arms along the top of the bench, water leaking from his hair. He looked tired and dishevelled, his fingers tapping restlessly on the faux-leather upholstery.

'Thank you,' Kate told him.

'Hey, it's only a chip dinner.'

'No. For saving my life. I should have said something before.'

He smiled, a real slow-burn number, and Kate had to will herself not to look down, touch her hair, do any of the hundred and one other things Becca had mentioned.

'Sure you're all right? You look like you've just had a stroke.'

'It's Becca.' Kate shook her head. 'She's got me questioning everything I do.'

'You'll get used to it eventually. I did.'

She tipped her head on an angle and stared at him, only now aware that she had no idea how much of what she was seeing was genuine. Were any of his reactions really his, or where they all part of an act? Was everything he said and did filtered and distorted?

'Messes with your head, doesn't it? But if you want to see something authentic, watch me eat this.'

He pointed towards the heaped plate of food that was being slid in front of him by a pretty waitress, no more than sixteen years old. The girl passed Kate her own meal, then smiled shyly, almost bowing, before backing away.

Kate popped a chip in her mouth and bit down. It was hot and soft, dowsed in vinegar. She prodded the battered cod with her fork and found it to be crisp on the outside, fleshy in the middle. The peas were, well . . . they were just like most other mushy peas, but they tasted wonderful.

'Good?' Miller dunked a chip in ketchup, folding it into his mouth.

'The best.'

'I only take my clients to the very finest restaurants.'

'Do you meet all of your clients?'

'That's the way it works.'

'Hanson and Becca, too?'

'I couldn't do any of this without them.'

'What's Becca's story? She said you did some kind of favour for her. A big one.'

Miller chewed, watching her. He didn't answer right away and she wasn't sure he was going to. Then he reached for a napkin and dabbed at the corner of his mouth.

'She didn't tell you?'

'I didn't like to press her.'

'But you're willing to press me?'

'I'm curious is all. You're asking me to trust her. She's kind of high-profile.'

'And you're worried she might be unreliable? Don't be. She had an ardent fan who got much too ardent. I warned him off.'

'How?'

'That's the part you probably don't want to know and I'll probably never tell you. The guy was scary, Kate. He had prior convictions.'

'And you took justice into your own hands.'

'I told you before – I'm good at providing protection. I protected Becca. Just like I'll protect you.'

'And Hanson? Shouldn't he be in Silicon Valley making obscene amounts of money instead of breaking the law on your behalf?'

'Probably. And one day I guess he will be. But for now, he works with me.'

'So what did you do for him? More vigilante justice?'

'Isn't it possible he might just believe in helping save people like you?'

'Oh, please. Becca tried that one on me already.'

Miller held her gaze, smiling tightly.

'The truth? OK. Hanson works with me because of Sarah.'

'Your wife Sarah?'

'Yes. But if you want to know more about it, I suggest you ask him.'

'Maybe I will.' She speared a bite of fish with her fork and popped it into her mouth. 'So what else do I need to know about how all this is going to work?'

'Lots, probably. But the main thing we should talk about is the system you'll use to check in.'

'Here? Is that safe?'

Miller made a show of glancing around the cafe and Kate turned in her seat to track his gaze. The waitress was busy wiping down the counter with a dishcloth while an overweight guy in a white tunic and checked trousers poured a basket of uncooked chips into the deep fat fryer. An elderly couple were seated at a booth towards the back, chomping through pie and chips.

'I think we can risk it. I gave you a phone to call me on before. Remember?'

'I remember.'

'Well, we can't do that when you're out in the field.'

The field. As if she was some kind of spy now.

'Why not?'

'It's complicated. Hanson-level complicated. He changes my phone all the time for a bunch of reasons I don't pretend to understand, but the bottom line is that a phone is out for you.'

'So what do I use instead?'

'Have you ever heard of Dungeon Creeper?'

'I think I may have dated him once.'

Miller reached into his jacket and removed an iPad Mini from the inside pocket. He switched the tablet on and swiped a greased finger over the screen, tapping it multiple times before turning it for Kate to see.

'Dungeon Creeper is an online role-playing game. It has a big following in Europe. Germany, mostly.'

Kate stared at the home page. There was a lot of flashing text, some spooky music, plenty of cartoon-style graphics. She could see dragons, dwarves and scantily clad damsels.

'And you can communicate via this?'

'There's a message board with thousands of members. People use it to pass on tips or to trade weapons and other stuff.'

'Power-ups.'

'No wonder Hanson likes you.'

Kate took hold of the iPad and muted the sound. She clicked on a button marked ENTER and a new screen opened up. She saw more dwarves, more dragons and more busty girls in fur bikinis.

'So what do I do?'

'Hanson will give you some login details. Every Tuesday, between seven and eight o'clock in the evening, GMT, you'll send a private message to the username Hanson will provide you with.'

'And what will I say?'

'If everything is good, and you're safe, you type "Green Flag".'

'Green Flag. That's it?'

'Assuming everything's OK.'

'And if it's not?'

'Then you type "Red Flag".'

'Wow, Miller, that's a pretty complex code. I really hope I can remember it.'

'None of our clients have ever had to send us a Red Flag. If you follow the rules, you won't have to, either. I'll be checking in with you in person every three weeks or so. You won't know exactly when but I'm not trying to catch you out. It's just that I never know when I'll be with a particular client. Take what happened with you. I had to respond very fast once we knew you were under threat.'

'What if I have a problem on a day other than a Tuesday?'

'You can send a Red Flag at any time. Hanson has an automatic alert set up.'

Kate powered off the iPad and slid it back across the table.

'What if I can't get to a computer?'

'You have to.'

'And if I can't check in on a Tuesday?'

'You have to do that, too. It's your first and only priority every week. If we don't hear from you between 7 and 8 p.m., we come for you right away. We'll be with you within twenty-four hours. Faster, if we can make it.'

'By which time it could be too late.'

Miller gathered in the iPad and butted it up against the table edge, pursing his lips.

'Like I said, nobody has ever sent us a Red Flag.'

'Today is Tuesday.'

She made a point of looking over towards the clock above the serving counter. The time read 6.20 p.m.

'Yes, and the reason I'm telling you all this now is that I want you to watch tonight. I want you to see all those Green Flags popping up. We do it with everyone we introduce to the system.'

'How many Green Flags am I going to see?'

She half expected Miller to duck the question, or to tell her she wouldn't be able to watch every message. But he didn't flinch.

'Five.'

So there were five other individuals being protected by Miller. Six, now, including her. Not a big scheme. Not a huge operation by any stretch of the imagination. Which she supposed was a good thing.

She remembered what he'd told her right at the beginning. He'd talked about a discreet, highly bespoke service. And yet it was one that required all of his time. He had to be on call at a moment's notice, twenty-four hours a day, seven days a week. What kind of life was that? What kind of drive would sustain someone to live it?

Then she thought of something else.

There weren't just six of them in the system. There were seven, in reality, if you included Miller himself. He was the hub, no question, but he was in hiding, too. From the same man as Kate. Which brought everything full circle. And was probably a risk. Possibly a sizeable one.

'Are you hiding any of the others from Connor Lane?'

Miller looked away from her, towards the rain-drenched seafront. But all there was to see was the steam on the glass.

'I can't tell you that.'

'But it's possible?'

'Anything is possible, Kate. But the other people in the system aren't your concern. We have your back. That's all you need to know.'

Kate pushed her plate aside. She reached for her mug and leaned back from the table, glancing up at the television in the corner of the room.

And almost dropped her tea.

She was looking at a picture of herself. The photograph had been taken four years ago, when the law firm she was working for refreshed all the staff profiles on their website. The word MISSING was stamped across a BREAKING NEWS banner at the bottom of the screen.

Kate set her mug down too hard, drawing the waitress's attention. She knew that she should smile, act casual, roll her eyes at her klutziness. Maybe then she could stand and lead Miller outside.

But she could do none of those things.

'What is it? Kate?' Miller's phone started to buzz inside his jacket. 'Damn.' He fished it out, turning at the same time to see the television for himself, letting go of a low groan.

'Stay calm. We've got this.' He put his phone to his ear, grabbing his jacket and the iPad, sliding out of the booth. 'We've seen it,' he said, into the phone. 'We're on our way back.'

But Miller hadn't seen everything. Not by a long way. Because as he'd started talking, another image had appeared on screen. It was a picture of Miller. Younger, smarter, neatly groomed in a suit and tie.

And scrolling across the bottom of the television was a ticker-tape message.

POLICE ARE SEARCHING FOR NICK ADAMS, FORMER DETECTIVE WITH GREATER MANCHESTER POLICE, IN CONNECTION WITH A BODY FOUND ON THE ISLE OF MAN. ADAMS HAS ALSO BEEN NAMED AS A SUSPECT IN THE UNSOLVED MURDER OF HIS WIFE AND DAUGHTER FOUR YEARS AGO. HE IS CONSIDERED DANGEROUS AND MEMBERS OF THE PUBLIC ARE WARNED NOT TO APPROACH HIM.

Chapter Eighteen

Connor Lane raised the television remote from the corner of his desk and paused the live news feed, freezing the image of Nick Adams on the wall-mounted screen.

'You still think this was a good idea?'

He pointed the remote at Mike Renner. The two men were sitting in Connor's study, which had been his father's study before him and was furnished like a gentleman's den. His desk chair and the club chair Renner was slouched in were upholstered in green leather with brass studs. Nearby was a globe that doubled as a drinks cabinet.

Not that Connor felt like offering Renner a drink anytime soon.

'You wanted him found.' Renner's shirt was greying at the cuffs and collar, his tie tight as a ligature around his jowly neck.

'By you, Mike. Not by the police.'

'He knows how to hide. I had to try something big to flush him out.'

Connor's gaze slid back to the television.

'He's changed his appearance.'

'But not his size. He's still huge. Practically an ape. Someone will notice.'

'And when they do?'

'We'll have a lock on him.'

'Most likely inside a police station.'

'Which is going to be an uncomfortable situation for him to be in with Lloyd involved.'

'You're placing an awful lot of faith in her, Mike.'

'One thing Larry taught me is when the stakes are high, you play your strongest hand.'

Connor turned his head slowly, lips pressed thin. Both men knew that Connor hated it when Renner alluded to the way his father would have handled a particular situation.

'Even if your strongest hand is a bluff?'

'Especially then.'

'Has it occurred to you that now he's come back, the girl may do, too?'

Renner knew the girl Connor was referring to. Anna Brooks had disappeared four years ago, only days before she was due to testify in court that Russell had raped her. Russell had admitted to having sex with Anna, although he claimed it had been consensual.

Anna had vanished on the same night Nick Adams had gone underground. The same night his wife and daughter were killed. The same night, to all practical purposes, that the prosecution case against Russell had collapsed.

Both men were convinced that Adams had hidden Anna Brooks from them.

'That's highly unlikely.'

'I want her found, Mike. She can't become an issue again. Not now.'

'And I'm working on it. I've *been* working on it. But the first step is Adams. We find him and it unlocks everything else.'

Connor was about to respond when he was interrupted by a knock at the door. His PA, Stacey, ventured inside.

Stacey was, without question, Connor's least competent employee. Several times a day she revealed herself to be painfully dim. But she was also physically desirable and unashamedly awed by Connor's wealth, and she more than compensated for her many shortcomings by certain tasks she regularly performed against, on top of and beneath his desk.

'I told you I wanted privacy.'

Stacey wrung her hands. Her skirt was still a little rucked up from a pleasing, if all too brief, interlude in Connor's day a half-hour earlier.

'I have a call for you. He says it's urgent.'

'Then take a name.'

'He won't give me a name. He says you'll definitely want to talk to him. Says it has to do with an item on the evening news.'

Her eyes strayed to the image of Nick Adams on the television, then dropped to her hands.

Connor shared a look with Renner.

'Put him through. Close the door.'

The two men waited in the sudden charged silence, the only noise the fading percussion of Stacey's heels and the static hum of the television screen.

Then the phone on Connor's desk started to buzz. He answered the call on speaker.

'Mr Lane?'

The voice was drawn and wheezy. Not someone Connor recognised. Renner's shake of the head signalled it wasn't anyone he knew either.

'Who is this?'

'Who I am doesn't matter. It's what I can do for you that matters.'

'This number is unlisted.'

The man's laboured wheezing filled the room. Connor could hear the faint beat of dance music in the background and the yobbish chanting of a group of men. Was that German they were shouting?

The whispery voice said, 'We have mutual acquaintances.'

'None of my acquaintances would pass on this number to a stranger who won't give me his name.'

'Somebody did, or we wouldn't be having this conversation. But let's not get sidetracked. How about we focus on what I *can* give you, Mr Lane?'

'And what is that exactly?'

'The man on television. The man I'm guessing you'd especially like to find right now.'

Lane hitched an eyebrow at Renner, who pursed his lips for a moment, then nodded that he should proceed.

'Supposing I know the man you mean. Why would you do that for me?'

'You're rich, Mr Lane. Why don't you go ahead and take a wild guess?'

Chapter Nineteen

Kate rushed back inside the apartment, Miller following close behind. He snatched for her arm, calling her name, but Kate wrenched herself free, knocking into a suitcase on the floor.

She steadied herself on the kitchen counter, sweeping her hair from her eyes. She was angry and confused. She had a strong urge to lash out.

The apartment was a mess. There were suitcases and laptop bags open on every available surface, loaded with computer equipment and clothes.

Hanson clambered up from behind a table, wrapping a cable around his elbow and hand, just as Becca hurried out of the bedroom with an armful of clothes.

'You OK, sweetie?'

'Not even close. I want to know what's going on.'

'If it helps any, you're not the only one.'

Kate flung a hand at Miller. 'How do the police know I'm with you?'

'Someone must have been watching your place on the Isle of Man. They must have seen me warn you.'

'The police?'

'I don't think so. Not unless they said something to you?'

Kate's jaw was tensed. She shook her head in a fast, irritated jerk.

'So then it was the man Lane sent to kill you. He

must have had you under surveillance.'

Hanson blew air through his lips. 'Doesn't explain how the cops know about it.'

'They must have found where he was based. They must have searched his things.'

'This fast?'

Miller shrugged, checking the time on his watch.

'So what's the play?'

'I have you booked on separate flights out of Bristol airport. Your flights depart at 21.00 and 21.20. Kate's headed to Lisbon. You're set for Madrid.'

'How long until we're out of here?'

'Give me another ten minutes and I'm good to go.'

'Becca?'

'I can make that.'

'Good.' Miller raised an eyebrow at Kate. 'How's your Portuguese?'

'Are you insane?' She sliced her hands through the air. 'I'm not going anywhere yet. That news report said you're wanted for murder.'

The room fell silent.

'Not cool,' Hanson told her.

'Sweetie, really,' Becca warned.

Miller looked at Kate for several long seconds. He didn't blink or alter his expression. But Kate could tell he was angry. It was there in his eyes.

'Are you really asking me if I killed my family? Because you know better than anyone what Lane is capable of, Kate.'

'Maybe. But right now what I'm interested in is what you're capable of.'

Becca moved as if to intervene but Miller raised both palms, warning her off. He didn't break eye contact.

'You need to hear me say it? Fine. I didn't kill my wife and daughter. I did everything in my power to protect them. Lane sent a man to shoot them dead. The same man set fire to their bodies and our house when he was done. He burned them, Kate. He burned them right up.'

Kate swallowed hard, trying not to let his intensity deflect her. 'So why does it say otherwise on the news?'

'Honestly? I have no idea. But there was a line of enquiry put forward by one investigating officer. Sarah and I argued before she was killed. This particular detective got it in her head that an argument might have turned violent. She was wrong. You're wrong.'

'We don't hang with killers,' Hanson put in.

'You *hang* with me.'

'Yeah, but you're the good kind of killer. There's a difference.'

'There is?'

'There is to us.' Becca took a step forwards. Then another. She approached Kate like she was a bomb she intended to defuse. 'We're short on time here, honey. You can trust us now or you can go it alone. Without Miller, I'd give you two days tops, but it's your call.'

Kate looked between them. She was cautious by nature. She liked to weigh the pros and cons of any given situation before reaching a decision. But this situation was so far beyond anything she'd ever had to contend with that the only thing she had to go on was her gut.

'We're safe here for now, right?' Her attention was locked on Miller. 'You wouldn't have booked these apartments under your own name. You probably dealt with the owner over the phone, or maybe you had Hanson or Becca do it. So nobody knows we're here, even supposing someone in that cafe recognised us after we left. Which means we have longer than fifteen minutes to play with.'

Miller didn't say anything.

'I want to see those Green Flags you were telling me about. I want to see them before I go with you, or I don't go with you at all.'

Miller looked at Hanson, then gauged Becca's response. But Kate already knew that she'd won. He needed her just as she needed him. She didn't know quite why yet, or what it was he hoped to achieve, but somehow, she was the key to it all.

'Five Green Flags,' he said finally. 'Then we're out of here. *All* of us.'

*

But they didn't get five Green Flags. They got four instead. They popped up in rapid succession, a series of bland, two-word private messages sent between 7.02 and 7.10 p.m. The usernames of Miller's clients comprised short random words and long numerical sequences. The process was fast and slick and wholly depersonalised, and Kate got the impression it had become simple routine for the individuals checking in, almost as if it was just another weekly chore, like taking out the rubbish or shopping for groceries.

Kate was sitting in front of the only laptop Hanson hadn't packed away, with Hanson, Becca and Miller standing over her. It was a little over a thirty-minute drive to Bristol airport. Time enough – just – to make their flights.

Except that the fifth Green Flag stubbornly refused to come through.

They waited past 7.20 p.m. Then seven-thirty. Then a quarter to eight.

Nobody spoke and the silence between them grew more fraught with every passing second.

Then something happened. Something so unusual that, according to Miller at least, it was completely unprecedented.

The time was 7.48 p.m. and the message that blipped up on-screen consisted of just two words.

RED FLAG.

The group drew a collective breath and crowded in around Kate.

'Where's it from?' Miller asked.

'Hamburg,' Hanson told him. 'Client number three.'

PART III

Hamburg, Germany

Chapter Twenty

Clive Benson shovelled takeout currywurst into his mouth and looked through his apartment window at the plane trees and shop awnings of Schanzenstrasse, searching for a sign that he hadn't screwed up.

Clive didn't know exactly what he was looking for. He never did. But he wasn't only searching for strangers hurrying towards his building or unfamiliar vehicles. He was also hunting for meaningful numbers in the scramble of graffiti on the wall of the *apotheke* opposite, in the telephone number listed at the end of a letting agent's sign, among the prices of the fruit and vegetables displayed outside the late-night corner shop.

In nearly every way, Clive was entirely, even painfully, ordinary. He was in his early forties with too little hair, a too-big paunch and a too-fatty diet. But in one crucial respect, Clive was exceptional. Wherever he was, whatever he was doing, numbers would speak to him. They might, for example, leap out of a newspaper advertisement to reassemble themselves into a combination that triggered pleasing childhood memories. Or perhaps he'd be strolling along the street and the digits on a series of car licence plates would rearrange themselves into the postcode of his first home, or the telephone number of an old girlfriend who'd cheated on him.

Numbers worked with Clive. They *co-operated* with him.

He'd always been able to rely on them, even when nothing else in his life made sense.

Clive wasn't a crackpot. Licking now at the curry powder he'd sprinkled over his wurst, he knew he didn't possess some kind of extraordinary superpower. (And anyway, what kind of superhero would that make him? Acutely Aware Man?) It was just that he noticed things, analysed sequences and saw patterns, that would pass most people by. Probably he was on some kind of spectrum. Not that the thought bothered him a great deal. After all, there was a time when numbers had made him a lot of money.

Clive had started his own betting empire straight out of school. At first, he'd operated an unofficial book for a handful of friends, but within a few years he'd gone legit. Business was good and the profits were encouraging, but as his outfit matured and the stakes grew higher, one thing never altered: the numbers always remained on his side.

Until, that is, he began taking bets that weren't really bets at all. Until a certain criminal gang in Manchester with a sideline in recreational pharmaceuticals made him an offer he couldn't possibly refuse. Until, in short, he laundered drug money through his three high-street betting outlets in return for not being beaten, or stabbed, or, ultimately, killed.

At the bidding of a series of increasingly scary men, Clive had attempted to manipulate his precious numbers and the numbers hadn't liked it. So they'd rebelled.

Two years ago, the police had come calling with a warrant to take a look at Clive's business records. They had forensic accountants at their disposal who were able to see exactly where the numbers were giving him away.

Clive was presented with a choice: testify against the drug gang and spend a lifetime in witness protection, fearing constant reprisals, or spend eight to twelve years behind bars, locked up with the same men who would be convicted on the basis of his skewed record-keeping.

The odds weren't good either way. The numbers looked very bad indeed. Until a third, previously unheard of opportunity presented itself.

Which had led Clive to Hamburg, courtesy of the man who called himself Nick Miller, but who, it now turned out – by virtue of the Sky News channel on the cable TV in the laundrette below his apartment – wasn't called Miller at all.

Life in Hamburg had been tough from day one. Clive spent his days lonely and isolated, afraid to make any meaningful connections in case he somehow gave himself away. He existed in a constant state of anxiety, terrified in one moment that the British police would somehow locate and deport him, and in the next that a member of the gang he'd betrayed, and whose assets had been seized along with the rest of Clive's business, would track him down and take revenge.

In the early weeks of his stay, Clive had sought refuge among the tawdry distractions of the nearby Reeperbahn – the all-day nightclubs, the live sex shows, the dive bars and prostitute booths – but soon, even those had lost their appeal. Now, he ventured out as little as possible, spending long days in his miserable flat, which had a major damp problem courtesy of all the steam from the laundrette, and which, in turn, aggravated his asthma.

But the real problem was that Clive's precious numbers had been forbidden to him. Nick had said that he couldn't get back into the betting game because he had to lead a different life now. And though Clive could appreciate the logic of it, could even, deep down, acknowledge that it would be close to impossible to get a piece of the Hamburg numbers action anyway, he also couldn't deny the need that was bubbling inside of him.

The numbers had been calling to him, whispering in his ear. They'd been telling him to go somewhere else. Somewhere hotter. A place with an expat British population. Spain, or maybe Portugal. But some place, anyway, where he could start small, test the water, build anew.

And now, he was sure, he'd found a way to get there. A number would be his salvation.

Two hundred and fifty thousand.

That was the sum he'd specified to Connor Lane. That was the amount that would fund his escape.

The only problem had been how to collect, since a bank transfer was definitely out. Nick had Hanson monitoring all Clive's accounts. So cash on delivery was the only option. And anyway, Lane had wanted someone there when Nick showed up.

Another betrayal. Clive felt a twinge of guilt. Nick had helped him to begin with, there was no denying it, but his rules were suffocating him. He lived on a few measly euros a day, earned by cleaning the offices of an international consultancy firm two bus rides away. It was demeaning. This evening, Clive had finished his final shift and he didn't believe any of the late-working execs would notice when he failed to show the following day.

A knock on the door.

Clive peered down from his window at the entrance to the

laundrette. The street was deserted. He hadn't seen anyone approach.

Setting his currywurst aside, he shuffled through his living room to his front door, wiped his hands on his vest and undid the three security bolts Nick had insisted on fitting.

The man standing before him was short and muscular, with grey lidless eyes set wide in his head. He was wearing a blue-and-white tracksuit and carrying a weighted holdall. The number 26 was printed on the front of his tracksuit top.

Which, to Clive's mind, could mean one of two things.

It could be a simple 26, or a 2 and a 6, or a 6 and a 2, all of which were harmless.

But if you took that 2 and you divided the 26 by it then you got 13. And 13 was always bad.

Clive wheezed as he opened his mouth and asked, 'Do you have the money?'

'No money, Clive. There's been a change of plan.'

Chapter Twenty-One

Late morning the following day, Miller stood among the pyramids of fruit outside the corner shop across from Clive Benson's apartment. There was a police van and a patrol car parked in front of the laundrette. An officer in a blue uniform and high-lace boots guarded the door.

It was obvious to Miller that something had gone badly wrong. The Red Flag was no hoax. But it was also clear that whatever had happened here had taken place many hours ago. The uniformed officer looked complacent, almost bored, and there were no emergency lights or rubberneckers gathered on the street.

Kate leaned towards him. 'What do you think?'

'Hard to say.'

'Do you think your client is up there?'

Miller didn't reply. It was possible, he supposed, but if Clive was inside his apartment, it was because he was dead. That would explain the presence of the police and it would account for the stutter of camera flashes that kept lighting up the window above the laundrette sign. Miller had seen the work of enough forensics units during his years with Manchester CID to have a reasonable idea of the procedures the German force would be following.

Kate leaned closer. 'What are we going to do?'

'*We're* not going to do anything. You shouldn't even be here right now.'

Which had to be the understatement of the year. Miller was breaking all his rules by allowing Kate to accompany him to Hamburg, let alone to the street where one of his clients was based. But then it wasn't as if she'd left him with a lot of choice. As soon as the Red Flag had blipped up, she'd insisted on coming with him. She needed to know his system was still secure. She had to see it functioning with her own eyes before she could commit to it for good.

Miller could understand where she was coming from but he'd had to decline. He had no idea what he'd find when he reached Germany because Clive hadn't responded to any of Hanson's attempts to contact him. So he'd refused Kate's request point blank, only for her to up the stakes.

'I'll go to the police. I'll give them your alias and tell them about everything you're involved in here. I'll give them Hanson's name. Becca's, too.'

Becca had looked like she might slap her. 'You wouldn't dare.'

'Try me.'

'That would be a really bad idea, Kate.'

'Without us, Lane will find you,' Hanson added.

'Maybe.'

'No "maybe" about it. He'll track you in days.'

'You told me you were the best.' Kate looked at each of them in turn. 'All I'm asking is for you to prove it.'

'You're blackmailing us.'

'I'm seeking assurances. You'd do the same thing if you were in my shoes.'

Miller doubted that. Not after everything they'd done for Kate already. But her threat was explosive enough to be treated as genuine. They both had to get out of the UK before the police appeal gained momentum. And Clive needed his help.

So now here they were, standing together in the middle of Hamburg, the scent of ripe fruit hanging in the air and an unknown situation confronting them from across the street.

Miller said, 'Stay here. Try to look inconspicuous.'

Kate blinked up at him and he knew right away what a dumb thing that had been to say. She was wearing some of the clothes Becca had picked out for her – tan chinos, a green fleece and a blue baseball cap – but she still looked terrific.

Miller had on beat-up jeans over his scuffed desert boots, a flannel shirt and a blue nylon jacket. He also had a small rucksack fitted over his shoulders.

'Where are you going?' Kate asked him.

'I need cigarettes.'

'You don't smoke.'

'Maybe now's the time to start.'

The corner store was the size of a cramped studio flat and stocked as if it was a supermarket. Everything anyone in the neighbourhood could possibly desire was jammed inside. The way Miller saw it, a corner store was the lifeblood of any neighbourhood. It guaranteed gossip.

He worked his way towards a counter that seemed to have been hollowed out from cascading rows of confectionery. A guy in his early twenties was sitting behind the cash register, flicking through a magazine.

'A pack of Lucky Strike.' Miller's German was good, close to fluent. He'd spent a lot of time in the country these past few years. 'And a box of matches.'

The guy had on heavy eyeliner and he wore multiple studs

in one ear. He reached behind himself without looking up and his fingers landed on the cigarettes, then crabbed along to the matches. His nails were painted black, the same tone as his hair.

'Eighteen euros.'

Miller smiled. Tourist rates.

He removed a fifty from his wallet and laid it on top of the cigarette packet.

'The apartment opposite. The police outside. What have you heard?'

The guy looked up blearily. He didn't smack gum, but he got close.

'You're screwing me on the cigarettes, friend. But that's OK. You can keep the fifty. Just tell me what you know.'

The guy smirked sleepily as he reached out and took the cash.

'The man who lives there is English. Like you.'

'What happened to him?'

'People tell me different things.'

'Such as?'

'Some say he was stabbed. Others that he was shot. One customer told me they found him hanging from a noose.'

Miller's stomach plummeted.

'He's dead?'

'It's what I hear.'

'Who found him?'

'The woman who runs the laundrette called the police. The lock on her door was broken. She's had trouble with junkies busting in. We all have, round here. She was afraid to go in alone.'

Miller thanked the man and scooped up his cigarettes and matches, drifting outside without another word, at which point his phone buzzed and he fumbled it to his ear.

He heard Hanson say, 'I got a hit for our client's name in a hospital database. He's in intensive care.'

'You're telling me he's alive?'

'As of two minutes ago, although his medical notes haven't been uploaded yet. I guess they're still reacting to the situation. According to the records, he wasn't admitted until ten o'clock this morning.'

Miller gazed blindly ahead. If what Hanson was telling him was really true, then it was a reprieve, in a way. So why was he finding it so hard to believe? Why did the hearsay from the goth behind the shop counter seem more credible?

All too slowly, he became aware of Kate tugging on his arm, calling his name.

'Miller, we have a problem.'

And that was when he snapped out of it and saw that she was right. He'd been staring blankly at the uniformed officer on the other side of the street. The officer was peering back at him and now he was lowering his mouth to the radio clipped to his jacket.

'We need to get out of here,' Miller said. 'Right away.'

'Huh?' Hanson asked, over the phone.

'Not talking to you.'

He switched his mobile to his other hand and raised his right arm in the air. A cream Mercedes taxi swooped towards them and Miller snatched open a door at the rear, bundling Kate inside.

'Which hospital?' he asked Hanson, ducking in next to Kate.

'The University Medical Center. You need an address?'

'No, no address. I'll call you back.'

Chapter Twenty-Two

Jennifer Lloyd sat on a thinly upholstered chair with her shoulders back, one hand clasped loosely over the other. Her left hand was on top of her right, functioning as a shield. Her right hand concealed her squash ball. She was squeezing the ball rhythmically. Not all that frequently. Not terribly fast. A lot slower, certainly, than the runaway beat of her heart.

Commissioner Bennett looked down on her from the opposite side of his desk. He was standing and clutching the backrest of his office chair so hard that she was tempted to ask if he could use a squash ball of his own.

Bennett was early fifties, medium height, very trim and very lean, never seen inside the NCA building, to Lloyd's knowledge, in anything other than his full dress uniform. His face was drawn, his skin pulled tight against the prominent bones beneath. Lloyd had heard other officers refer to him as Skeletor, though never the ones with any interest in long and fruitful careers.

'Quite the turnaround, DS Lloyd.'

It was the second time Bennett had used the phrase. The first had been when Lloyd had entered his office. He'd motioned for her to sit and then he'd closed the door to his glassed-in corner unit and spread the Venetian privacy blinds to peer out at the secretarial pool beyond. He couldn't have made the situation look more illicit if he'd tried. Lloyd didn't know whether to believe he was unaware of the rumours concerning their relationship or whether he preferred others to gossip about an improbable affair rather than the true purpose of her visits.

Which was to inform and betray and subvert.

Except not today, maybe. Because even for a man with a fearful reputation, Bennett was clearly agitated.

'So, DS Lloyd, you have an awful lot of our people, and most of the British public, searching for one of our own. Your nemesis, I suppose we might call him.'

'We followed the facts, sir. They led us to Adams.'

'And the evidence?'

'That too.'

'By which, of course, we mean an unverified, indistinct image, provided to us by an anonymous source.'

'The image is authentic, sir. Our tech team are confident of that.'

'Well, that's reassuring, Lloyd. Because it's not as if our tech team have ever been wrong before, is it?'

Bennett yanked back his chair and dropped into it hard. He braced his elbows on his desk and steepled his fingers. He remained completely still for several long seconds, during which Lloyd squeezed her squash ball extra hard.

'Are you really confident about this? How far do you believe in it?'

'All the way, sir.'

'Good.' He nodded definitively. 'Because I believe in you, Lloyd. In my opinion you raised some valid concerns about Nick Adams four years ago and you have grounds to be concerned again now. So I want to know where he's been and what he's up to. I want to know why. We have a mess on our hands. Tell me what exactly is being done about it.'

Lloyd eased off on the ball and drew a fast breath.

'The team are functioning well, sir. We already have a series of hits from a number of surveillance cameras at Bristol airport. They show a woman matching Kate Sutherland's description boarding a flight to Hamburg, Germany.'

'I know where Hamburg is, DS Lloyd. You can dispense with the geography lesson.'

'The techs are working with facial-recognition software to prove that it's her. She's changed her appearance quite effectively but there's no doubt in my mind after seeing the images. We already have provisional calls in to the German police. We believe she's travelling with fake ID, possibly in the name Kate Ryan. We're working on confirming that.'

'And Adams?'

'No hits yet. We're still looking.'

'So they may not be together.'

'We still have a great deal of information to sift through, sir. And there have been a lot of calls from the public. We'll find something.'

'What else?'

Lloyd hesitated.

'The team are eager to talk to Connor Lane. His likely role in this situation is impossible to ignore, particularly in light of the discovery of Patrick Leigh's remains. Young and Foster are planning to drive to the Lake District to interview him.'

'He's agreed to speak with them?'

'Only on condition that his lawyer is present.'

'Then they're wasting their time. Lane's lawyer will hedge and delay and generally prove what a fine and expensive pain in the arse he is.'

Lloyd happened to agree. She happened to have said the exact same thing. But Young was persuasive. And the general attitude of the unit was resentful about the hunt for Nick Adams. Resentful of her. Even Foster was giving her the stink-eye, as if it was her fault the evidence pointed towards Adams having some level of involvement. The simple fact was they *wanted* Connor Lane to be solely responsible for what had happened on the Isle of Man. They wanted to go after him.

'I'm intrigued, DS Lloyd. You keep telling me what the team are doing.'

'With respect, sir, reporting on the activities of the unit was the brief you asked me to fulfil.'

'But I picked you for that role precisely because you're not a team player, Lloyd. You never have been and you never will be. So what I'd like to know is what are *you* doing?'

'Sir?'

'Here's the thing about witch-hunts, Lloyd. Eventually, the witch gets found. But times have moved on a little since the Dark Ages. These days, you need hard evidence before you can burn them at the stake.'

'I'm not sure I follow.'

Bennett gave her a withering look and lowered his right hand below his desk. He opened a drawer and removed a bulging Manila folder held together by frayed elastic bands.

'Is that what I think it is? I thought it had been destroyed.'

'Then you were mistaken.' He tossed the folder on to the desk. 'I've had this in safekeeping. And now, I'm returning it to you.'

Lloyd reached out for the folder. The file was heavy and the cardboard had wilted and started to tear where the rubber bands were cutting into it.

The paperwork inside contained all of Lloyd's original notes on the murders of Sarah and Melanie Adams. Lloyd had found enough circumstantial evidence to make her believe Nick Adams could have been responsible for their deaths, but no concrete proof.

'I'm confused, sir. What is it you expect me to do with this?'

'What you do best, Lloyd. Identify the mistakes and oversights of one of your fellow officers in order to build a flawless case against Nick Adams for the unsolved murder of his wife and daughter. And while you're at it, see if you can uncover anything that might help us to locate him. The only difference this time is that the officer you need to outperform is you.'

Chapter Twenty-Three

Hamburg's University Medical Center was a state-of-the-art teaching hospital with an enviable research record, more beds and patients than any of the other hospitals in the city, and a glossy, modern finish inside and out.

Unfortunately for Miller, it also had excellent security.

He hustled Kate across the gleaming white entrance foyer and on through a network of pristine corridors to the intensive care unit, but that was as far as they could get. A pair of doors with wired glass inserts barred their way. The doors could only be opened by swiping a magnetic card through an electronic reader on the wall, or by buzzing the internal nurses' station and waving up at a surveillance camera for admittance.

None of which would have been a problem, necessarily, if it weren't for the female police officer Miller could spy, who was sitting on a chair outside a private room at the beginning of the ward.

Kate pressed her face to the glass. 'Do you think she's guarding the room your client is in?'

'Makes sense to me.'

'Can't you just go in and tell the nurses you know him?'

'Hardly. The police will want to talk to me. Imagine if you were in that bed. Would you want me to tell them what you were hiding from?'

'Then maybe I should go. I can pretend I'm a friend.'

'You don't even know his name.'

'So tell me.'

Miller shook his head. He was trying to think what his next move should be. He was asking himself if he was just wasting valuable time that could be better spent elsewhere. But he needed to know Clive's condition. If he was able to talk, he could tell Miller what had happened.

'You don't get it, do you? This started yesterday, Kate. The only Red Flag we've ever received and it comes three days after my first contact with you.'

'You think what happened to this man is connected to me?'

'I don't know. I don't know anything for certain right now. That's the problem.'

The female police officer was showing excellent discipline. She wasn't checking her phone or reading a magazine or engaging passers-by in conversation. She was sitting upright on her chair, her eyes fixed dead ahead, giving no sign that she'd vacate her post anytime soon.

She didn't even glance up as a young orderly in a white button-down shirt, blue trousers and white rubber shoes pushed a metal trolley towards her. The orderly wheeled the trolley past the nurses' station and on towards the security doors. Miller dragged Kate aside as the orderly thumbed a switch, then butted his trolley through and pushed it off along the corridor.

He was wearing a set of in-ear headphones. Maybe that was why he didn't react as Miller fell into step behind him.

*

129

Miller returned shortly after the orderly had re-entered the ward with a roll of yellow dustbin bags tucked under his arm.

'Did you speak to him?' Kate asked.

'He didn't know anything. He only came on shift half an hour ago.'

'Maybe we should leave. He might tell someone about you.'

'He won't.'

'He might.'

Miller inclined his head towards the wired glass panels as the orderly showed his ID to the female police officer stationed outside the private room. The officer scanned his credentials, then waved him through.

'What's happening?'

'Patience.'

Three minutes later, the orderly was back, banging through the double doors with a weighted yellow rubbish bag, his forehead speckled with perspiration. He gave Miller a quick, wild-eyed look, then walked briskly off along the corridor.

Miller ushered Kate after him, following the orderly around a corner and through a door that opened into a cleaning-supply room. The orderly stood with his back pressed to the scarred porcelain sink where he'd dumped the refuse bag. The air was thick with the smell of chemicals. A bank of metal shelves were jammed with cleaning cloths and packs of paper towels and bottles of bleach.

'Who are you?' The orderly's voice trembled. A plastic ID was clipped to his shirt that said his name was Ralf. 'What do you want with this man?'

Miller pulled the door closed behind Kate and took a step towards him.

'Did you do what I asked?'

Ralf was sweating so badly that one of his headphones slipped out of his ear and dangled in front of his chest. He wet his lip.

'You already took half my money, so let's not pretend you want to know more about this than you already do. Now, hand it over.'

Miller made a 'gimme' gesture and Ralf exhaled hard, shaking his head, before lifting his shirt to dig a hand into the waistband of his trousers. He removed Miller's smartphone and passed it across.

Miller angled the screen so that Kate could watch as he hit play on some video footage.

The camera work was shaky. The angle was bad. A few seconds in, Ralf had been spooked by a thud somewhere off-screen and had turned abruptly, as if he'd been afraid somebody was coming into the room. But his fear had proved baseless and he'd jerked the camera back around again, taking in the tiled ceiling and part of the privacy curtain before settling in on what Miller needed to see.

Clive lay inert and unconscious in a raised hospital bed, his head swathed in bandages, his belly swelling the sheets that had been pulled up to the mass of dark hair around his chest. His left eye was covered by a gauze patch. The right was grossly swollen and discoloured, closed almost to a slit. His lips were flattened and bloodied, parted around the ventilator tube that had been inserted into his throat.

The audio feed was dominated by the pant and rasp of Ralf's breathing, but Miller could also hear the background beep of a heartbeat monitor.

'Oh my God.'

Miller ignored Kate's reaction, waiting until the video was finished before asking Ralf, 'Did you look at the chart?'

'I took photos. Like you said.'

Miller checked his phone. The focus on the stills wasn't great, but he had enough to send on to Hanson.

'What do the notes say?'

'I told you already, I don't understand most of that stuff.'

Miller took a half-step back and reached into his pocket. He removed the rest of the cash he'd rolled into a tight tube.

'Tell me about the parts you did understand.'

Ralf swiped at his nose, eyeing the cash. He glanced nervously at the door behind Miller.

'There was one thing.'

'Go on.'

'It was a note on the first page of the chart. It said that when they found him, he was hanging upside down from his ankles. He'd been beaten that way.'

Chapter Twenty-Four

They left the hospital in another Mercedes taxi. There was plenty of space in the back and Miller and Kate made the most of it, sitting far apart, looking out through the dirt-streaked glass.

Miller waited until their driver became uncomfortable with the silence and cranked his radio before he pulled out his phone and dialled Hanson. He listened to the long international dial tone, then got right into it when Hanson picked up, asking him if he'd received his email. When Hanson confirmed that he had and that he was about to start work on translating Clive's medical charts, Miller moved on and told him they were going be staying in Hamburg for at least one night, possibly longer, and he needed him to book two hotel rooms in two separate hotels that fronted on to the small plaza in Altstadt where Miller had based himself on previous visits.

Miller sensed Kate glancing across at him, as if she expected an explanation, but he didn't feel any need to provide one. He wanted to avoid the impression that he and Kate were travelling as a pair because he was concerned by the possibility that a British tourist staying in the same hotel might have seen the televised police appeal before coming to Hamburg. Likewise, even though they'd taken separate flights into Germany – Kate from Bristol and Miller from Gatwick – there was the danger that one, or both, of them might have been spotted on airport-surveillance footage by now. If so, the Hamburg police could have been asked to put them on some kind of watch list, which might have involved hotels across the city being issued with recent images. Not likely, perhaps, but it was a risk Miller wanted to manage as best he could.

And besides, there were other reasons why he wanted Kate based in a separate hotel. Like their plans for later that night, for example.

Which was all very prudent, and all very neat, and all a little naive. Especially since he'd made the mistake of telling Hanson what he needed him to do without noticing that Hanson had placed him on speakerphone.

'Oh, puh-lease,' Becca cut in. 'Why go to all this trouble when the two of you will only end up sharing the same room anyway?'

'That's not going to happen.'

Kate peered harder at Miller, intrigued by the change in his tone. He switched his phone to his other ear.

Becca said, 'Trust me, Nick. There are some things I just know. It's time, OK? You're allowed to enjoy life a little.'

'Text me when you have our bookings. And Hanson, let me know the moment you decipher those charts. I want that information.'

He cut the connection and rested the phone against his lip, staring through his window at the rows of plane trees blipping past. He saw strikingly modern architecture and grand old buildings with turquoise copper roofs; saw the dingy entrance of a U-Bahn station; saw pedestrians and cyclists and a chic young woman riding by on a pastel-coloured scooter.

You're allowed to enjoy life a little.

But he wasn't. Not any more. Not until all of this was over and he'd made amends.

Their driver was taking them east towards the Hauptbahnhof to collect their luggage from a train-station locker. After that, they'd check into their respective hotels and get some food and rest in preparation for the night ahead.

The taxi blew across a box junction, then over a bridge that offered up a view of the ruptured waters of the Binnenalster, the spray from the fountain in the middle of the lake blown astray by the wind.

Miller had visited the city eight times in the past twelve months. Clive had been made aware of his presence on six of those occasions. Twice, Miller had watched him from afar.

Until Kate, Clive had been the client who'd bothered Miller the most. Nobody found the life easy. Nobody ever could. But Clive had rarely stopped complaining. From the very beginning, he'd harked after his old life, and when it was denied to him time and again, he'd turned in on himself, shunning the outside world. As far as Miller knew, Clive didn't have a single friend in the city, which on the face of it was good for his safety, but had always worried Miller, because how long could the guy be expected to last with only his thoughts and regrets for company?

So it stood to reason that if any of his clients were unstable, if any of them would screw up, it would be Clive.

And yet, he'd been attacked just days after Miller had saved Kate. Which could be coincidence, or plain bad luck, but Miller had a hunch it was something worse than that. He'd tempted fate by crossing Connor Lane's path again.

All of which made him think of Sarah and Melanie, and of

how much he wished he could be with them right now. If he kept his back turned on Kate, if he concentrated hard, he could almost make himself believe they were sitting next to him, close enough to touch.

He would like to have known what Melanie would have made of Hamburg. For her sixteenth birthday, in that final year they'd spent together, she'd asked for a writing journal and an annual subscription to a travel magazine. She'd said that she wanted to become a travel journalist. She hoped to see the world and be paid to write about it, too.

Where had that instinct come from? It had struck him as so peculiar at the time. To think, the kid of a police officer and a charity worker aspiring to a life like that.

But perhaps, somehow, he'd taken on his own warped version of Mel's dream. Perhaps that was how he was able to live the life he lived now; always moving on, his every possession fitted inside a holdall and a small backpack, rarely connecting with anyone he met, not even his clients, in anything more than a fleeting way. Perhaps, unwittingly, it was an impulse he and Melanie had shared.

He wished he could ask her about it. He wondered what she'd say.

But Kate interrupted his thoughts, asking him, 'Does your client have family? Is there someone we should contact?'

'Just his mother. She has dementia. She wouldn't understand.'

'How about you? You know all about my family situation. Are your parents still alive?'

'Mum was taken by cancer years ago. We lost Dad to a heart attack not long after.'

'Any brothers or sisters?'

He shook his head. 'Sarah had a sister. They were pretty much inseparable. I envied them that.'

'Are you still in touch with her?'

'You know the rules, Kate. Sever all ties.'

She was quiet for a beat. He hoped she wouldn't push it. He hoped his tone had been enough.

'What time will we go? Later, I mean?'

She made it sound as if they had plans for a dinner date. But the reality was very different. Clive was in no position to talk with him, so Miller was going to have to find answers another way.

'Two a.m.'

'And you'll come by my hotel?'

'I'll meet you outside. There's a kiosk in the middle of the square. If I'm late for any reason, go back to your room. Wait to be contacted.'

'I can't stop thinking about him lying there all alone.' Kate bit down on her thumbnail. 'I can't help wondering if the sound of a familiar voice would be comforting to him.'

But if she was seeking insight from Miller, she'd come to the wrong guy. Miller didn't respond, looking down at his phone instead, making out as though he was waiting impatiently for Hanson's summary of Clive's medical chart to come through.

Chapter Twenty-Five

Lloyd pulled her car over in a residential cul-de-sac in Manchester. The weather was warm for late April, the evening sun shimmering through the splayed branches of a nearby oak. At the end of the street, a haze of midges swarmed above the lawn of a 1930s semi with tile-hung walls. A child's bike had been abandoned in the driveway, its back wheel spinning lazily.

Lloyd contemplated the suburban scene for several long moments, then turned her head and looked towards a square of weed-strewn land that was hemmed in tight behind temporary metal fencing. It was all that remained of the family home of Nick Adams and his wife and daughter.

Lloyd slumped with the same weight of emotions she always experienced when she came here: saddened because of the lives that had been lost; frustrated because the barren plot seemed so much a symbol of how badly the investigation into the murders of Sarah and Melanie had withered and died; ashamed because she'd failed to prove that Nick Adams was to blame.

The fire that had been set following the shootings of Sarah and Melanie had taken hold rapidly. It had raged through the property, collapsing the roof, tearing down walls. By the time the fire brigade had gained control of the inferno, the structure was so unstable that the house had to be levelled, but not before Sarah's remains were recovered from the charred kitchen, where fire investigators believed the blaze had been started, and

Melanie's body had been carried out under a blanket from the hallway outside her first-floor bedroom.

The clearance work had taken place without the owner's consent. Nick Adams had vanished on the night of the fire, his car abandoned outside the front of the house with the keys in the ignition. Based on a neighbour's sighting of a blurred figure darting away from behind the property, Lloyd had always believed that he'd fled the scene by bolting through the tangled area of woodland that backed on to the rear garden.

The woodland was creeping closer now. Lloyd knew the neighbours were unhappy with the situation, but without owner consent, the land couldn't be built on or sold to a developer, and until a few days ago, nobody had seen the current owner for nearly four years.

All anyone knew was that six months after the council had stepped in to tear down the blackened husk of Nick Adams's home, a single lump-sum payment had been made against his mortgage. The amount had been sufficient to clear all debts. Some of Lloyd's colleagues had attempted to trace the source of the money but had drawn a blank at a shell company based out of the Caymans. No insurance claim was ever lodged.

Popping her door, Lloyd stepped out on to the street, leaving her folder of notes behind in the car, then circled around the ruptured concrete plinth and tramped into the woods beyond.

The trees were straggly and sparse, the vegetation dry as tinder. After no more than thirty metres, the land fell away into a shallow compression that might once have been a stream but was now little more than a bramble-choked trough. Then the bank rose up again, the trees began to clear and Lloyd pushed aside branches and briars until she found herself on a neat lawn that led towards the rear of another 1930s semi.

A half-glazed door swung open and a slim, dark-haired woman leaned her hip against the frame. Fiona Grainger was early forties, barefooted, dressed in leggings and a denim smock that was flecked with dried paint, as were her hands and cheeks. Lloyd had been invited into her studio once. It was a white, light-filled space in a converted room in the attic, filled with easels and canvases and the reek of oils and turps.

Fiona waited until Lloyd had stepped on to her patio before saying, 'I was wondering when you'd come. I saw the television.'

'Has he contacted you?'

'No. But I wouldn't tell you if he had.'

'I'd like to come inside.'

Fiona looked away from her towards the trees, as though she was searching for something among them that would tell her how best to respond.

'Would it make any difference if I told you to go away?'

'Not a lot.'

'If you're planning on carrying out some kind of search, you're wasting your time. He's not here.'

'I just want to talk. That's all.'

'Right. Because look at all the good it did me last time.'

But Fiona backed away and gestured for Lloyd to come past her into a kitchen that looked just the way Lloyd remembered it. The units were solid but uninspiring, finished with dark veneer fronts that contrasted with beige countertops. There was a lot of earthenware crockery, all of it crooked and warped, given to Fiona as cast-offs by an artist friend.

Lloyd drifted towards the window above the sink and found herself wondering, as she often had in the past, how similar it all was to the kitchen where Sarah had been killed. Instinct told her it would have been close to a mirror image, though she knew she was swayed by how alike Sarah and Fiona looked, which wasn't the least surprising, given that Fiona was Sarah's twin sister and sole surviving relative.

The twins hadn't been identical – at least not in strictly biological terms – but they'd always been close. Which was the reason why, Fiona had told Lloyd the first time they'd met, she'd moved to a house that backed on to Sarah's place following a messy divorce.

In the years before Sarah's murder, the sisters had often walked through the woods to call on one another at all times of the day. Now that Sarah was gone, Lloyd found it hard to decide if Fiona had stayed because she had no place better to go, or because she sometimes looked out of this window and imagined Sarah walking towards her through the trees again; the ghost of a memory she couldn't bear to leave behind.

'You won't find Nick, you know. Not if he doesn't want you to.'

Lloyd turned to see that Fiona was leaning her forearms across the breakfast bar, picking at the paint on her fingernails. She hadn't offered Lloyd a drink or closed the door to the garden. It was clear she wanted her to leave as soon as possible and Lloyd tried not to show how much she was stung by it. In the days following the fire, it had felt as if the two of them had become close. It was Fiona who first confided in Lloyd about the arguments Sarah had been having with Nick.

But as the months and years had passed, Fiona's judgement of Nick had mellowed. She'd told Lloyd more than once that she regretted speaking about him in the way she had.

All of which was suspicious, of course. And then the fact that the two sisters looked so alike . . . Well, Lloyd had sometimes wondered if perhaps there had been an affair. Maybe *that* was the reason Nick had come running through the woods after the fire. And maybe, once it was clear that her sister and niece were dead, it was guilt and regret that had made Fiona criticise Nick so savagely.

Lloyd said, 'You do understand why I'm here.'

'Not in the slightest. Do you?'

'If Nick contacts you, you must call me. We need to talk with him. We can help him.'

'Right. Because helping Nick is your number-one priority. Anyone who's seen the news appeals can tell that.'

Lloyd could remember when she was welcomed here. She could remember when Fiona had clung to her and wept.

'What are you working on these days? Do you have a show coming up?'

'Don't play nice with me.'

'Where's that?' Lloyd had spotted a picture that was stuck to the fridge-freezer with a magnetised frame. It was a mountain scene. There were snowy peaks in the far distance and a meadow of spring flowers in the foreground. 'Are you planning a trip?'

'Only in my head. It was a freebie with a travel magazine. Every morning when I come down for breakfast I stare at it for a few minutes. It calms me.'

Lloyd stepped closer. She could understand why someone would want to transport themselves to that flower-filled meadow with its view of raking mountaintops and dazzling glaciers and azure skies. She could understand the need to escape there, if only for a minute or two each day.

'He won't hurt her, you know. If that's what you're worried about.'

Fiona had moved to the far side of the kitchen. She had one hand on the open door, a signal that she expected Lloyd to leave soon.

'Hurt who?'

'The redhead. Nick is protecting her.'

'That's one interpretation.'

'But not the one you favour?'

'I honestly don't have a preference either way.'

And that was when Fiona's face twisted and Lloyd knew that she'd lost her trust for good.

'I miss my sister every day. I miss my niece very badly.'

'I know you do. I was here for you. I tried to help. Don't forget that.'

'I betrayed them once before. I let my grief get the better of me. But the truth is I know Nick loved them. Deep down I *always* knew that. And I know he's out there now doing the best he can for them. I know that's what he's dedicated his life towards.'

'You know it how?'

'Because I know that's the kind of man my sister would have wanted to spend the rest of her life with. And now, if you wouldn't mind, I'd really like you to leave.'

Chapter Twenty-Six

At just before 1 a.m., a full hour before he was scheduled to meet Kate, Miller walked towards the revolving doors at the front of his hotel. He was wearing black cargo pants, a light-weight black fleece and his small black rucksack, and feeling awkward about it, because the outfit reminded him of the dead assassin on the Isle of Man.

The doors were locked due to security concerns. But there was a night porter on duty and he flicked a switch below the reception counter so that Miller could exit, whereupon Miller offered him a quick salute and a glum smile and said, 'Can't sleep.'

Which was a lie, and almost certainly one the porter could see clean through, though possibly not for the reasons he had in mind. The porter probably assumed Miller was yet another middle-aged tourist heading off in search of the dubious comfort available to lonely men in the Reeperbahn, and if so, his suspicions would only have been confirmed had he been able to listen in as Miller ducked inside a taxi parked out front and asked to be taken to the fringes of St Pauli.

The driver was a middle-aged Turk with a receding hairline and way too much aftershave. He showed a lot of teeth in re-sponse to Miller's request, then cranked the engine, punched the meter and swooped out on to the sodium-lit street, all the while grinning back over his shoulder.

'You want girl? What kind do you like? I know great place.'

Miller told him he wasn't interested in anything like that.

'What about live sex show? I know best in the city. Best girls, easy. I take you there. We drink lots of beer, yes?'

Miller guessed the driver was on some kind of commission, and when he declined again, the guy frowned and his mood darkened, as if Miller was trying to bilk him out of his fee based on some misplaced sense of propriety.

So he tried a third time, at which point Miller switched to German and told him to shut the hell up and just drive him to where he'd asked to go, and the guy took clear offence, which he communicated via the manner of his driving, which featured a lot of abrupt acceleration and snappy gear changes and heavy braking.

All of which was fine by Miller, because he was perfectly willing to get to his destination as fast as possible and more than content to be left to his own thoughts.

His thoughts were of Clive. Hanson had emailed through a summary of Clive's hospital notes not long after Miller and Kate had fetched their luggage from the train station. Like the orderly had said, he'd been discovered hanging upside down. There was bruising to his stomach and kidneys, broken ribs, a collapsed lung, and abrasions to his shins and ankles, one of which had been dislocated, but most of the violence had been concentrated on Clive's head. He'd been beaten over and over. It was thought that a chair leg had been used as an improvised bat.

He was still alive, according to the update Hanson had texted through within the last hour, but his prognosis was dire. His doctors had inserted a shunt to relieve pressure from his skull, but if he emerged from his coma, it was likely he'd show signs of brain damage.

There'd been related news in a call Hanson had placed once Miller was alone in his hotel room.

'Patrick Leigh,' Hanson had said. 'I hacked into his autopsy report.'

'And?'

'He was killed by multiple injuries consistent with a fall from a very tall building. Blunt force trauma to the head and chest. Severe fractures to just about every bone in his body.'

'Sounds painful.'

'But get this: there were extensive abrasions on his shins and ankles. The pathologist spends a couple of paragraphs on them. She concludes that metal wire or chains were wrapped around his lower legs and he was hung upside down for a long time before he was dropped, possibly from a construction crane on the building site where he was found.'

'Hung upside down like Clive, you mean.'

'I thought you should know right away.'

'So Lane is behind both attacks.'

'Looks that way. And whoever he has working for him has a thing for stringing people up by their ankles.'

Miller hadn't told Kate about the connection and he felt bad about that. He also felt bad about tricking her tonight, and he hated to think of how she'd react when she realised she'd been stood up. He was sure she'd be mad. She'd suspect that he'd deceived her. Eventually, though, he hoped she'd remember to return to her room, where Becca was prepped to phone her promptly at 2.30 a.m. and tell her that something had come up. She'd explain that she couldn't provide details over an open line but that Miller would be in touch later in the morning.

Which was all good in theory, until Miller's driver slammed on his brakes at the cross street where he'd asked to be dropped and Miller stepped out on to the pavement only to see another taxi swoop into the kerb directly behind him.

Kate jumped out.

'Funny,' she told him, 'I could swear you told me we were meeting at *two* o'clock.'

Miller opened his mouth to reply but Kate rushed towards him and jabbed a finger into his chest before he could summon an excuse.

'Don't lie to me again. And don't underestimate me. I'm coming with you, no arguments. So deal with it. OK?'

The taxis were idling at the kerb, both drivers bending low and peering out, paying more attention to their spat than Miller would have liked. He considered opening the door on the second cab and forcing Kate back inside. But she knew where he was going. She knew what he had planned. He couldn't guarantee she wouldn't interfere.

And at least she'd gone to some effort with her appearance. She had on dark blue jeans, a black turtleneck sweater and the baseball cap she'd worn earlier in the day.

Miller stared at her, weighing up the alternatives. But in reality, she'd already made the decision for him. Again.

Grabbing a fistful of euros from his pocket, he paid both drivers, then turned and walked on, feeding his arms through the shoulder straps of his rucksack, texting Becca not to stay up to make the call.

'That was not smart,' he said, when Kate caught up to him.

They were a block behind Schanzenstrasse, the night pulsing

with the blur of dance music from a late-night bar. A huddle of people stood smoking beneath the coloured bulbs strung up around a makeshift terrace.

'Neither was sneaking out of your hotel to come here without me.'

'The police will have the place under surveillance. Any slip-ups and we could easily get caught.'

'Then let's not slip up.'

Miller looked across at her. 'If you're coming with me, you'll do everything I say and nothing I don't. Those are the rules. Understand?'

'More rules. You're a real stickler for them, aren't you?'

He had been, Miller thought ruefully. So what had changed? What was it about Kate that was making him act this way? She was stubborn, no question, but he'd had stubborn clients before.

But of course, he already knew the answer to that question, even if it wasn't one he was prepared to confront. It was tied up with the insinuations Becca had made; a creeping truth lodged deep inside him.

He liked Kate. A lot. And the thought of it scared him on a far deeper level than the risks they were about to take.

Chapter Twenty-Seven

Miller was right. There was surveillance in place. Down the street from the laundrette, just beyond the pool of light being cast by a street lamp, a grey Volkswagen Transporter van was parked beneath an overhanging tree.

Two men were slouched in the darkened cab, one of them pouring steaming liquid from a flask into a cup, the other with his head propped against the driver's window. Miller had no doubt that they were police.

He took Kate's hand – the signal they'd agreed on – and they hurried along the opposite side of the street.

'Stumble a little,' Miller told her. 'Act tipsy.'

'Where are they?'

He told her. 'But don't look. Focus on your feet. Lean into me, as if I'm holding you up.'

'Why can't I be the sober one?'

'Just do it. Please.'

Kate did as he asked and he wrapped his arm around her, supporting her weight.

'You're hurting me,' she whispered. 'Ease off a little.'

It was his size. His strength. But also his nerves.

'Better?'

'Much.'

They walked beyond the van to the next cross street, then turned a corner and doubled-back along an unlit alley that smelt of rotting litter. Kate's footfall echoed off the concrete, her pace picking up as she skipped clear of Miller's embrace.

'Will they be watching the back, do you think?'

'I doubt it.' He was a little thrown by how quickly she'd darted away from him. 'Clive's attacker gained access through the front. If he comes back, they'll be betting he enters the same way.'

Kate was quiet for a few seconds. Perhaps she thought Miller had slipped up by mentioning Clive's name. But he hadn't. Kate had seen the pictures of Clive's medical chart and he credited her with enough intelligence to have sneaked a look at his name.

'What do we do if they spot us?'

'You're the athlete, Kate. I'd say running would be a great idea.'

There was a high garage behind the laundrette with a roll-up metal door. Miller slid his rucksack off his shoulders, unzipped a compartment on the front and removed a pair of latex gloves. He snapped the gloves on over his wrists, then tried the door handle. It didn't budge.

'What now?' Kate asked.

'How much can you lift?'

'Excuse me?'

'You weigh what, one hundred and twenty, hundred and twenty-five pounds?'

'I'm not going to answer that.'

'Fine. Call it an even one-twenty. I'm a lot heavier than that. Think you can boost me?'

Miller took her hands and formed them into a bowl shape below her knees.

'Size fifteen,' he said, resting the sole of his boot in her palms and propping his hands on her shoulders. 'Sometimes I wish I was a little more spry.'

'Newsflash,' she grunted, 'you're not any kind of spry.'

He bounced up, stretching his arms above his head, and grasped the tarred lip of the flat roof above the garage. One handhold was good. The other was bad. Something pierced his glove, breaking his skin. He snatched his hand free, then hooked his elbow over the ledge and heaved himself forwards as Kate pushed at his tangled legs from below.

He rolled on to his back, panting up at the starless sky tinted green by the light spill from all the street lamps and neon in the neighbourhood. Pushing on to his elbow, he looked down to where Kate was gazing up at him, her face very pale in the darkness of the alley. The thought of leaving her behind crossed his mind and he guessed she must have sensed it from the way she jumped and flapped her hands.

'Come on, Miller. We had a deal.'

And before he thought better of it, he found that he was leaning down and grasping her wrist, lifting her, the sudden weight digging his wedding band hard against the bones of his ring finger. She twisted around, kicking a foot off the garage door, scrabbling for something to hold on to.

'Crap.' She scraped her knee, banging her shin, before stumbling on to the roof.

'OK?'

She sucked air through her teeth, clutching her leg.

'Take your shoes off,' Miller told her.

'What? Why?'

'I only have one pair of gloves. You'll need to use your socks.'

'Seriously?'

'Does this look like a time for practical jokes?'

Miller peeled back his own glove and sucked at the trickle of blood oozing from the heel of his hand as Kate leaned on his shoulder and worked her feet out of her trainers. She removed her socks and slipped her shoes back on to her bare feet.

'What now?' she asked, in a squeaky voice, and Miller turned to find that she was using one of her socks like a hand puppet.

'White socks? Really?'

He moved away from her, shaking his head, and began to pick a route across the roof.

'That's our entry point.' He nodded one floor above them to a pair of glass French doors set back from a concrete balcony ringed by bowed metal railings.

'And how do you propose we get up there? It's pretty high, Miller. If I boost you again, I'm not sure you'll be able to reach down for me. Or is that your big idea?'

'The big idea is that I'm going to grab hold of the bottom of the railing and hang there. You can climb me like a ladder.'

'A ladder?'

'That's right.'

'Sure you can handle all a hundred and twenty pounds of me?'

'I apologise. It felt more like one-fifteen a moment ago.'

Kate punched him on the arm.

'Supposing this even works, how are you intending to get in? Are you secretly a burglar, Miller? Do you have some lock picks hidden in that backpack of yours?'

'Better. I chose this place for Clive. We rent it for him. I have spare keys.'

Chapter Twenty-Eight

Miller could tell immediately that the living room was where the attack on Clive had taken place. Stepping in through the French doors from the balcony, he didn't need his torch to see the bloody residue on the laminate flooring. He flicked the torch beam upwards and spotted a patch of bare plaster and four drill holes in the ceiling directly above. It looked like a metal plate had been fixed in place with a bolt gun. Must have been where Clive's attacker had suspended him from.

He flashed his torch quickly around the rest of the room. The apartment was small – little more than a studio flat – and it was sparsely furnished. The sofabed and television stand had already been here when Miller had signed off on the rental agreement. So had the shelving unit along the opposite wall. Clive hadn't added to the place with any of his own decorative touches, unless you included the materials the police forensics team had left behind.

There were numerical tabs next to the blood spills on the floor, the holes in the ceiling, a missing door handle and the switch for the main light. Maybe the German forensics team had found fingerprints belonging to Clive's attacker, though Miller thought it unlikely.

He stepped out into the hallway, ducked his head into the bathroom, then went to assess the locks on the front door. There was no sign of tampering. Carefully now, he rotated the only lock the German police had secured behind them and peeked out. There was no evidence of scarring or scraping. Two lengths of yellow police tape criss-crossed the door frame.

Miller closed the door, turned the lock and walked back through the apartment to the balcony.

'You can come in now. It's safe.'

Kate stepped inside, her hands tucked up beneath her armpits in her socks.

Miller could still feel the sensation of her touch from when she'd climbed him to reach the balcony. It had been more intimate than he'd intended. He'd smelt the hotel shampoo she'd used and had felt the contours of her body pressing into his own. An image had flashed through his mind – one he'd fought hard to forget – of her standing before him in the dismal apartment in Weston-super-Mare, wearing only a T-shirt and panties.

'This is where he lived? It's tiny.'

'It had everything he needed. Nothing he didn't.'

But even Miller had to admit that it was pretty bleak, and it certainly wasn't as luxurious as the place where Kate had been living on the Isle of Man.

'What do we do now? What are we looking for?'

'Anything the police may have missed. Anything that could tell us what the people who did this were after.'

He wasn't about to tell Kate that he had a pretty reasonable idea already. Miller guessed it was Connor Lane's way of applying pressure to him. It was his way of signalling that he wanted Miller to give Kate up. Just possibly, it was also something more than that.

'Where do I start?'

'You take the bathroom. I'll begin in here.'

He showed Kate the way with his torch, pulling on the light cord when she entered the room. There was no window and no extractor fan. The walls were damp-stained and furred with mildew.

'Take your time. Call me if you find anything.'

He returned to the living room and gazed back up at the ceiling. Clive was a big guy, at least two hundred pounds based on the records Becca had taken when he'd first joined the programme. He'd spent close to nineteen months on his own since then, eating takeaway food. Chances were he was heavier now. And even allowing for a pulley system, it would have taken someone strong to hoist him. Maybe more than one man.

Miller let his eyes wander, following the torch beam around, and after a few seconds they settled on an empty charging cradle for a cordless phone. Which was something Clive was not supposed to have.

Staring at the charging cradle, trying to quell his anger, Miller was reminded of how he'd hidden Kate's phone in a kitchen drawer when he'd first broken into her place. Maybe Clive's attacker or attackers had done the same thing. Maybe they'd been lying in wait for him when he got home.

But ten minutes later, Miller decided that scenario didn't fit. Clive's locks had shown no sign of having been forced, which suggested he'd invited his attacker inside his home, or had been obliged to. Miller also couldn't find the missing handset, no matter how hard he looked, and he reasoned that was because it had probably been taken by the German police for forensics analysis.

But the most compelling reason of all was that Miller had

found a second handset in a second charging cradle in Clive's bedroom, half concealed by a pile of dirty laundry. The phone had a digital screen and Miller was able to scroll through the information it contained until he discovered that the last call placed from the phone had been to a UK number the day before yesterday.

'Miller, I think I've found something.'

He spun to find Kate standing behind him, wrinkling her nose as she took in the funky grey sheets twisted on the bed and the discarded Y-fronts and socks down on the floor.

She was holding a small piece of white card in the mouth of the sock puppet on her right hand.

'Where did you find this?'

'He had a paperback next to the toilet. This was keeping his place.'

The card was a ticket stub in Clive's assumed name for an AlItalia flight to Rome Ciampino, date stamped just over three weeks ago. He'd occupied seat 14A.

'Is it important?'

Miller's chest contracted painfully. His mouth had gone dry.

'I didn't think you allowed people to travel. I thought it was one of your rules.'

'I don't,' he muttered. 'And it is.'

'But this Clive – he went anyway?'

'Seems that way.'

'Why do you look so freaked out? Miller? I know you like your rules, but maybe he just needed a holiday.'

'I don't think so.'

He pinched the bridge of his nose, squeezing his eyes shut, as if he had a sudden pain in his sinuses.

'Oh, you have a client in Rome, don't you?'

Miller knew he should be contacting Hanson and instigating some kind of emergency response. But he felt leaden. This couldn't be real. There was no way this was real.

Clive had travelled *three weeks ago* and he was only learning of this *now*.

'Who's in Rome?' Kate asked him.

'Client number two.'

'Are they in danger?'

'I think we all are.'

*

Outside on the street, a few hundred metres back from the plainclothes officers in the grey VW Transporter, Aaron Wade lay across the darkened rear bench of a black Renault Clio, his knees bent, legs folded, his neck crushed and contorted. Wade's hand was cupped to the side of his face, shielding a radio earpiece. He was listening to the feedback from the transmitter he'd stashed behind the light switch in Clive Benson's living room as Nick Adams ended the phone call he'd just placed.

Once Wade had heard enough, he raised his mobile and made a call of his own.

'They're in the apartment,' Wade said, when Renner picked up. 'Both of them. They know Benson was in Rome.'

Silence.

'Adams is talking about flying there. She doesn't use his real name, by the way. She keeps calling him Miller.'

'I'll have someone look into it. What else?'

'He's figured out that Benson telephoned someone in the UK before he was attacked. I missed a second phone. He's getting his crew to put a trace on the call. He knows the number is unlisted and he's guessing Benson contacted Mr Lane. It won't take them long to know it for sure.'

'No names. Jesus.'

Wade supposed he should apologise for the slip, but he didn't much feel like it. He'd been cramped up in the car for hours now. He was hungry and dehydrated. He wanted to stand on the street and stretch, find some place where he could get a late meal and some good German beer. Maybe even a girl.

There was no way he was going to mention the part before the phone call, where Adams had told Kate that they could link the style of his assault on Clive Benson with the murder of that Patrick kid back in Manchester. Renner was already pissed off with him. He wasn't going to make it worse.

'What do you want me to do? They went in around the back. They'll come out the same way.'

'Follow them. But keep your distance.'

'And then?'

'Call me when you know more.'

It was Wade's turn not to saying anything. He hated this softly-softly stuff.

'How about you?' he asked. 'Anything new?'

'Not much,' Renner told him. 'It's raining in Rome.'

Chapter Twenty-Nine

Becca was right. Miller did end up in Kate's hotel room. But only while she grabbed her belongings. She was lifting her carry-on suitcase off the bed and turning towards him when his phone chirped in his hand. It was Hanson.

'You're booked together on the first available flight out of Hamburg. Seven-forty a.m. departure to Rome Fiumicino. Promise me you won't miss it.'

'Why? Are you worried about cash?'

'I'm worried about Kate. There's a border-control flag against her ID. The police know she flew into Hamburg and they'll be watching for any Kate Ryan on a flight out of the city. I've hacked in and deleted the flag for now. But if you face any kind of delay, best let me know.'

'What about Rome?'

'They'll track her there. Eventually. But Rome's a big place. And you won't be staying long. Right?'

Miller shook his head, trying not to be thrown by the glitch. He had no choice but to trust in Hanson's temporary fix.

'How about the telephone number?'

A pause. 'You were right. Clive called Connor Lane, or someone at Lane's Windermere house, at least.'

'He gave us up.'

'Looks that way. Seems he applied for the phone using the details of the guy in the flat above. Maybe he paid him off.

The line was installed three months ago.'

'And client two?'

'She's safe. Becca just spoke to her. She's on her way to the back-up location.'

'Did she say how Clive contacted her?'

'In part. But you're not going to like it.'

And he didn't. When Hanson explained what had happened, Miller began to see just how complacent they'd been. How foolish.

'Look at it this way,' Hanson told him. 'Every system has a bug in it. At least now we've identified ours.'

'That's your silver lining?'

'Best I can do.'

'I'm going to need you and Becca in Hamburg. If Clive shows any improvement, you have to be ready to step in. Who knows what he'll remember or say?'

'Already booked our flights. Becca's packing as we speak. But don't worry, his alias is sound. I'll make sure it stays that way.'

Miller ended the call and hit himself on the side of the head with the heel of his hand. He did it again. And again.

'You know,' Kate told him, 'you're not going to be a whole lot of help to me if you beat yourself senseless.'

She was staring at him with big doleful eyes, holding the suitcase double-handed in front of her waist. She was faring pretty well, considering. He hadn't liked telling her that Connor Lane was behind the attack on Clive and on his system. He hadn't liked watching what it had done to her. First, she'd been angry. Then she'd been scared. The worst part had been seeing the guilt and self-blame grip hold of her. He was experiencing it himself and it was affecting his thinking. He needed to stay calm, be detached, but visions of what had been done to Clive kept filling his mind.

'I have a question.' Kate said.

'Only one this time?'

She set the suitcase down, somehow managing a broken smile.

'Your theory is that Clive saw the police appeal and gave you up in return for a big pay-out from Lane.'

'That's not a question, Kate.'

'I'm getting to it. You also believe Lane sent some kind of heavy to meet Clive.'

'Lane has a right-hand thug called Mike Renner. He's more than capable of putting together a small team for something like this. He's the guy who hired the hitman Lane sent to kill you. Did you ever meet him?'

'Once. I think.'

'Be grateful it wasn't more than that.'

'So here's my question: why did this Renner, or whoever it was he sent to Hamburg, beat Clive like they did? They had a deal. Why not just pay Clive and wait for you to arrive?'

'Cost-saving.'

'I don't think so. That's pretty much the definition of false economy. Because while they didn't pay Clive any money, they didn't get you, either. Or me. Which suggests they had another priority. A whole other objective.'

'They did.' Miller nodded. 'And they do. Because they're not primarily interested in me. At least, not exclusively. And the same goes for you.'

'Should I be insulted by that?'

'You should be grateful.'

'So who are they primarily interested in?'

'A girl.'

'A girl in your system?'

Miller held her gaze. 'Yes.'

'In Rome?'

'Not in Rome. The client we have there isn't someone Lane would ordinarily be concerned with.'

'So why are you worried about her?'

'Because she could be a link to the girl Lane *is* interested in. It all depends.'

'On?'

'I don't know for sure. We built the system so our clients couldn't communicate with one another. But there was a flaw. We didn't allow for human error. We didn't anticipate how incredibly able and incredibly self-destructive our clients could be.'

'You'd better explain.'

So Miller did. He reminded Kate that the username she'd been given for the message board where she'd been supposed to check in each week was made up of a short word and a long, random collection of digits. In her case the word was 'royal' and it was bookended by thirteen numbers.

He said, 'Remember Tuesday evening, watching all those Green Flags pop up?'

'It's a hard thing to forget.'

'How many were there?'

'Four. A total of five messages altogether, if you include the Red Flag that Clive sent.'

'Can you remember any of the usernames?'

'I was watching for the messages, not the senders. There was one called Solo-something, I think?'

'Not bad. But that's the point. The names are there to snag your attention. They're simple enough to remember. Your eyes go to them. You ignore the numbers. Because of that, you can't recall the full username.'

'So?'

'Clive was our third client. When we demonstrated the system to him, he only had two Green Flags to watch for.'

'But still. Those are very long numbers.'

'For most people, sure. Maybe even for 99.9 per cent of the population.'

'So what's special about Clive?'

'Numbers. They were always his thing. I should have thought of that. I should have known what he was capable of.'

'You really think he memorised the usernames? In such a short space of time?'

'It's the best explanation we have. But he didn't contact our client in Rome on the Dungeon Creeper message board. Hanson monitors its use. He would have known.'

'So how, then?'

'We don't know exactly. That's what we're going to Rome to find out. I have to know if Clive has contacted anyone else.'

'What about Lane's men? Do you think they're in Rome too? Do you think that's the information they beat out of Clive?'

'I think that's what we have to assume. In which case, they're twenty-four hours ahead of us. And we have a lot of catching up to do.'

Miller grabbed the door handle, holding the door open with his arm raised so that Kate could pass through underneath. But Kate didn't move right away.

'And the girl? The one you think Lane is really interested in? Who is she, Miller?'

'Later.' He reached over for her suitcase. 'First, we have a plane to catch.'

PART IV

Rome, Italy

Chapter Thirty

Christine closed the door to Nicoli's bathroom and fumbled for the light switch. The bulb stuttered on and settled into a rapid, migraine-inducing flicker. One day the filament would finally give out. But not today, probably. The light had been like this for weeks already. It was entirely possible it had been blinking away for years, since Nicoli lived like a slob and a faulty bulb wasn't the type of thing he would fix in a hurry, but Christine had no way of knowing because it was only in the past couple of months that she'd become a regular guest in his home.

She was a little embarrassed to be sleeping with the guy across the hall from her apartment. It was such a cliché. But it was also safe and uncomplicated and it gave her a degree of comfort, a connection, in this hot and alien city.

Besides, she wasn't looking for a serious relationship in Rome with Nicoli, who she was pretty sure was a lot younger than he claimed. Not that Christine could tell for certain. Nicoli's English was patchy, her Italian wasn't even basic, and there were a lot of things he hadn't been exactly forthcoming about. Like his girlfriend, for instance. All of which was fine with Christine, since she was keeping secrets of her own.

They'd fallen into the habit of sleeping together three, maybe four times a week, often in the middle of the day when Nicoli returned from a night shift, though sometimes, like tonight, in the early hours of the morning. To begin with, it had been purely about the sex, which was rarely more than mediocre. But in the last six weeks or so, it had also become about something else.

It had turned out that Nicoli worked as a nurse at a sanatorium in the heart of the city. It had also turned out that Nicoli had a habit of taking things that didn't belong to him. Like cash from Christine's purse, for example. And like drugs from the sanatorium.

The first time Nicoli had shown Christine the pill stash he kept in his bedside drawer, he'd popped some blue capsules out of a foil pack and offered them to her with a laconic shrug and no attempt at an explanation. Christine didn't normally stay over but that afternoon she'd swallowed the blue pills and had drifted away into a deep, stress-free slumber which had lasted until she found herself alone and disorientated in Nicoli's apartment the following day.

Since then, Nicoli had introduced Christine to a spectrum of pills of differing colours and shapes, some of which did things that Christine didn't particularly like, and others that made her feel a whole lot better. Lately, she'd developed an appreciation for a lozenge-shaped yellow pill with a name she'd looked up online using Nicoli's laptop. The pills dulled Christine's anxiety, muted her emotions and generally made her life much easier to cope with. They were also mildly addictive. So she'd followed Nicoli's habit and had started taking some things of her own – namely, a key to his apartment and a steady supply of the yellow antidepressants.

Christine guessed that Nicoli knew she was helping herself to his stash. In the last week, the yellow pills in his bedside drawer had been regularly topped up. But she also knew that if he woke now and caught her with his entire supply stuffed inside the pockets of her jeans, things might turn bad.

But then, judging by the message Becca had just given her, things were bad already. Becca had told her to leave immediately for the prearranged back-up location Miller had shown her. She'd told Christine that she shouldn't go back to her apartment, that she had no time to pack and that she probably wouldn't be returning.

Which meant she wouldn't be seeing Nicoli again and she wouldn't have any more access to the yellow pills.

Staring now at her reflection in the smeared mirror above the bathroom sink, her hair coarse and straw-like, her skin waxy, the light twitching away, Christine palmed two more of the pills and washed them down with a handful of water.

Was it simple insomnia that had made her stir and creep out of bed to fetch Nicoli's laptop and begin surfing the Web? Or was it some profound but impossible-to-explain instinct for survival? The same instinct, perhaps, that had led to her being in Rome in the first place?

Whatever the answer, Christine had woken a little under an hour ago and padded through to the living room, where she'd spent some time scanning websites for titbits on the British soaps she could no longer watch, until she'd grown bored and had logged into the Dungeon Creeper message forum, as she'd done so many times in the past before clearing her search history and closing down the laptop.

Only this time was different, because there was a message waiting for her, flagged as urgent, telling her to call a UK number as soon as she could.

Christine didn't have a phone in her apartment. She had nobody to call and there was nobody who might call her. Miller hadn't allowed her to keep a mobile. So she'd nudged the door to Nicoli's bedroom closed, her hands trembling, her pulse jumping in her throat, and she'd picked up his phone to dial the number on the message, then whispered a few hoarse words before listening to what Becca had to say and feeling her legs give way from under her.

For the second time in her life, Christine's whole world seemed to contract and collapse in an instant.

Even through the yellow-pill haze, she could still feel the stinging jolt of it now, staring deep into her dilated pupils, her heart seeming to skip and falter in keeping with the flickering bulb overhead.

She backed away from the sink and her reflection, and floated out past Nicoli's bed, barely pausing to glance at his sleep-mushed face and loosely curled fist, then she stalked on through the living room and out into the stairwell, resisting the throb and lure of the door to her own place, gliding down the stairs, out the front of her building and along the street.

She never once glanced up to see the balding man in the crumpled shirt who was watching her from her bedroom window.

Chapter Thirty-One

Take-off was smooth and the plane half empty. The carrier was German, a low-cost outfit that Miller figured had to be losing plenty of money on this particular flight. There were spare seats either side of him, the row behind was vacant and only a teenage boy wearing a pair of oversized headphones occupied the row in front.

Miller could have used some time to relax but he was tense and uneasy. They'd boarded the flight without being challenged but he was afraid the flag against Kate's ID might be restored before they landed in Rome.

Needing a distraction, he removed Melanie's drawing from his wallet, flipped down his tray table and spread the paper flat. He stared at the storybook house Melanie had sketched, taking comfort, as he always did, in the way she'd drawn herself holding Sarah's hand. Then his eyes drifted to the brown horse with its stubby legs and its too-long tail, and to the man in the cowboy hat sitting on the horse's back. He looked at the stick man's raised hand. Waving goodbye or hello? Leaving or returning?

'Sir, would you like something to drink?'

A stewardess was smiling down at him. He ordered coffee, tucking the drawing away, avoiding her kindly eyes as she set his cup on a paper napkin. She lingered, wreathed in hairspray, then inclined her head and asked if he wouldn't prefer to move to the window or the aisle? But Miller told her he was fine where he was. The flight was only an hour and forty minutes long. Hanson had reserved him a seat in the emergency-exit row, so he had ample legroom, and he had no use for a view because his thoughts were distraction enough.

Or they had been, until a few minutes later when Kate veered sideways on her return from the toilet cubicle and swooped in next to him.

'Oh, relax, Miller. Nobody on this flight is interested in us.'

'You don't know that.'

'Really?' She turned in her seat. 'Where's the threat coming from? Is it that cute old couple with the guidebooks and maps? Or the girl who's had her face in her phone since before we boarded?'

'I had Hanson book us separate seats for a reason.'

'And that reason made sense before we got on this plane. But right now we're just two strangers in a cigar tube in the sky. Nobody cares if we talk for a little while.'

Miller took a sip from his coffee. He hadn't told her about the hiccup with her ID. Why worry her more than necessary?

'No risks. I told you that.'

'And I'll return to my seat when we're coming in to land. I'll ignore you at passport control. But I have to talk to you first. I want to know about the girl you say Lane is looking for.'

Miller shut his eyes and leaned his head back against the square of tissue paper attached to his seat. It was warm in the cabin and the constant droning of the jet engines was making him drowsy. He hadn't slept properly for days. For years, it felt like.

'Tell me about her, Miller.'

'You know, you make an awful lot of demands.'

'You already told me she exists. And I'm only asking because I'm pretty sure I know who she is. I just need you to confirm it for me.'

Miller rolled his head towards Kate and opened one eye.

'Pretty please?'

'She's a client, Kate.'

'How about I say her initials? If I'm right, you can just nod.'

'It's not a game.'

'So talk to me. *Include* me. I know about Clive. I'm flying with you to meet client two. We're basically a team here.'

'I already have a team.'

'Right. And Becca and Hanson know who this girl is. So do Lane and his goons, if your assumption is correct. Doesn't it make sense to keep me in the loop?'

'Go back to your seat. Read the in-flight magazine. Order some duty-free.'

'Look, I'll write it down for you.'

She tugged the paper napkin out from beneath Miller's coffee cup and reached for the little plastic spoon he'd used to stir in his creamer. She dunked the spoon in his coffee and dabbed at the napkin. The result, when she was finished, was clumsy and blurred, but legible all the same.

AB.

'Am I right? I am, aren't I? You'd tell me if I was wrong.'

Miller looked down at the paper napkin and the coffee stains swelling and spreading.

'Huh.' Kate leaned across and raised her lips to his ear. 'Anna Brooks,' she whispered.

Miller stayed very still, acutely aware of the weight of her breath on his skin.

He clenched his jaw.

Then he nodded, almost imperceptibly.

'I knew it.' Kate backed away. 'But I still can't quite believe it. Everyone thought she'd just run away after the fire.'

'She did.'

'But not with you. No one knew that.'

'Well at least one person suspected it. And now he wants her found.'

When Miller had first heard the name Anna Brooks, he had no inkling that she'd be any different to so many of the other teen runaways Sarah had helped over the years. He had no idea that she'd be the trigger for everything bad that was to come.

Sarah had managed the Lane Shelter for Runaway Teens on behalf of the Lane Foundation since it was first opened in the mid-2000s. Put simply, the Lane Shelter was a safe haven for homeless kids. It was also Sarah's passion.

Sarah had never lived on the streets. She'd never suffered abuse or been witness to domestic violence or become addicted to drugs or to alcohol. But her role at the Shelter had always been far more than just a job for her – it had been a calling.

Miller was busy himself. His role with the Protected Persons Service of Greater Manchester Police wasn't nine-to-five, either. But although he was professional and diligent, he'd never had anything like Sarah's fervour.

The needs of the Shelter came to shape their family life. Whenever Miller had time off, he'd invariably end up spending it there, carrying out odd jobs and chores. It was the same for Melanie. She was around the place so much that she became friends with lots of the Shelter kids. Sometimes, she'd invite a few of the girls home for dinner or to watch movies.

And naturally, Melanie had wanted to please her mother, she'd been keen to impress, but she'd also shared her belief in the innate goodness of people, in the potential of the kids at the Shelter to overcome the obstacles that had been placed in their way and move on to better lives.

So it was no surprise, ultimately, that Melanie was the one Anna confided in, even though what she had to say rocked the Shelter and everything Sarah had built to its core.

'All those rumours,' Kate was saying now, shaking her head. 'About Russell. About how he'd got to Anna and that was why the trial collapsed. That he'd killed her, even. Him or his brother.'

'They would have done, if they'd had the opportunity.'

'You don't know that.'

Miller stared at the back of the seat in front of him, not quite believing what she'd said. A fierce rage swirled inside him and he gripped very hard to the tray table, as though he might rip it free.

'Tell that to my wife and daughter.'

Kate was quiet for a long moment. He could tell she was searching his face but he couldn't bring himself to look at her.

'I'm sorry. I didn't mean—'

'Go back to your seat, Kate.'

'I shouldn't have said that.'

'It's done. Go back to your seat. We'll be landing soon.'

She reached for his hand, his bunched fist, but when he pulled away she finally backed off and left him alone once more.

Miller couldn't help thinking of Melanie, of the way she'd come to him very late one night, tears staining her face.

'It's all right,' he'd told her, once she'd finally got through what she'd had to tell him, once the halting sobs had stolen away her words. 'Everything is going to be all right. You'll see. I'm glad you told me. We'll fix this. We'll figure it out. You and me, together. Mum will understand.'

But Sarah wouldn't. He knew that then and he sure as hell knew it afterwards. It had killed him to tell her, to see everything she'd worked so hard for crumble with his words.

They'd liked Russell. All of them had. Miller had talked with Sarah many times about how Russell really did seem to be sincere and honest, so unlike his older brother or his father. There were times, even – and Miller felt a flood of shame whenever he thought of this now – when he'd speculated with Sarah about Melanie's fledgling relationship with Russell, about whether she'd end up marrying the guy, end up rich.

Russell had volunteered at the Shelter, too. He was there almost as often as Melanie. There, Sarah often claimed, *because* of Melanie.

He'd never made a big deal out of who he was. He hadn't ever pointed out that it was his family's money that funded the Shelter's work. He'd pitched in like anyone else. Cleaning rooms, serving meals, folding laundry.

But he'd also been doing something else, something none of them were aware of. He'd been sneaking into Anna's room, slipping into her bed. He'd been touching her when they were alone. Touching her in ways she'd asked him not to. And then he'd done much worse than that, and Melanie had found Anna afterwards, had seen with her own eyes the rage and hurt Russell had unleashed.

It was Miller who'd insisted there had to be an investigation.

Miller who'd contacted the rape unit. Miller who'd pushed for Russell's arrest. And later, as the trial drew nearer, as Connor began to exert his influence, as he even, once, sent Mike Renner to Sarah's office with veiled threats, it was Miller who'd tried to persuade Sarah that she and Melanie should enter witness protection and move to a safe house – at least for a little while, until the trial was concluded one way or another.

But Sarah had refused and they'd argued repeatedly.

'I just don't believe it,' she'd said. 'I'm sorry, but I don't think Russell is capable of it. He's always been good around us, Nick. Always. I don't think he's guilty.'

And then, on that very last night, just a few short hours before Lane's hired killer would come, before he would stalk inside their home, shoot for the head and set fire to Miller's world, he'd finally had his fill of it.

'It's not that you don't believe it,' he'd snapped. 'It's that you choose not to believe it. Because the truth is you'd rather sacrifice one girl if it means you can keep your precious Shelter open for a hundred more potential victims.'

The words finally uttered, he'd stormed out of the house and driven away in a fury, undone by the terrible thing he'd said to the only woman he'd ever loved, by how stricken she'd looked as he'd left her, by the fear she might never forgive him.

And the most painful thing of all – the thing Connor Lane had made sure of – was that he couldn't ever take it back.

Chapter Thirty-Two

After touchdown and taxi, Miller was one of the first to stand and fetch his backpack from the overhead bin and begin the awkward sideways shuffle to exit the plane. He emerged into fierce heat and white light and the smell of jet fuel and scorched rubber, tramping down the wheel-away steps, pacing towards the terminal building.

Then there came the long, air-conditioned walk to passport control, the anxious wait to queue and pass through, and afterwards, Customs and the chaos of Arrivals, and finally a trek along a chain of rubber travelators to the platform for the Leonardo Express. A train was waiting to depart, its sleek, bullet-shaped engine compartment branded with swirls of red, white and green. Miller fed some euros into a ticket machine and stepped aboard a few minutes before the doors slid closed and the train pulled away.

He wasn't certain Kate had made it. He'd been reluctant to look back and check. But five minutes later, with the express gliding alongside a multilane *autostrada* choked with dusty European city cars and delivery trucks, he'd felt a tap on his shoulder and had looked up to see her standing in the aisle, gripping hold of the handle to her suitcase.

'I don't have a ticket. I didn't have time.'

'I bought two.'

'Does that mean I'm forgiven?'

'It means you can travel on this train without fear of being fined. Sit down.'

She clambered into a seat on the opposite side of the table from Miller, her suitcase next to her, her back to the direction of travel.

'Listen, about what I said on the plane . . .'

'Doesn't matter. It's forgotten.'

'It matters to me. What happened to your family was terrible. I know that.'

'But . . .'

'But I stand by what I said. About Anna.' She bit her lip, looking up from beneath lidded eyes. 'The way you helped her to disappear cast doubt on Russell. A lot of people said that he'd killed her. Or that his brother had arranged for her to be killed.'

'So?'

'So part of the reason I agreed to testify against Russell for Helen's murder, and part of the reason I agreed to accept the consequences that came with that decision, was because of what so many people believed had been done to Anna. Because it made me even more sure that he killed Helen, too.'

'You were afraid.'

'Very.'

'And you were right to be. You know that now. You've seen what his brother is capable of.'

'But that's my point. His *brother* is capable of it.'

Miller grunted and gazed out the window at banks of arid earth and yellowing grass and the looping, cyclical patterns of overhead cables zipping by.

He could see industrial warehouses, haulage depots, factories, gleaming office complexes and sports grounds. It looked like the hinterland of most major European cities. Looked like a hundred other places Miller had been these past four years.

'You're forgetting something,' he told Kate. 'You're in this situation because of what you saw. You're sitting here right now because you were the last person to see Helen Knight alive, with Russell, close to where her body washed up. They were arguing. She was distressed. *You* saw that. It was going to be your testimony.'

'I know.'

'And he has form, Kate. Anna is evidence of that. The fact I helped her to rebuild her life in the wake of what was done to my family doesn't change anything.'

'It does for me.'

Miller's head rocked on his shoulders, jostled by the shuffle of wheels on track, by the jerk of changing points.

'You should go straight to the hotel and wait for me there. It'll be safer for you. Lane's people could be watching my client. They could have followed her to the meeting point.'

'I'd rather we stick together.'

'Suit yourself. But we'll need to stow our bags first. I don't want anything slowing us down when we get into the city. Keep your passport and some cash on you. Everything else goes in your suitcase.'

'Whatever you think is best.'

The train was slowing now, coasting between high-rise apartment buildings, through tunnels and underpasses. Miller looked at the dusty concrete, at the graffiti and litter, and there, in the curved tint of the thickened windowpane, he caught a glimpse his own reflection and looked quickly away.

Wade's phone buzzed in the pocket of his tracksuit bottoms just as the train's brakes bit and hissed.

'Where are you?' Renner asked.

'Rome.'

'Be exact.'

He flicked his eyes up to the flatscreen monitor at the end of the carriage.

'Just coming in to Roma Termini.'

'Do you have a visual?'

He pulled the phone away from his ear. What did Renner think this was? A Bourne movie?

'They're in the next carriage along.'

Which was a way of fudging the issue. Because in truth, Wade couldn't see either of them right now. But then, he didn't need to. The Leonardo Express was a direct service from the airport into the city centre with no intermediary stops. And it was clear where Adams was headed, ultimately, because he had to meet with his client.

'Where are you?' Wade asked.

'A cafe. Not far from the Trevi Fountain.'

It meant nothing to Wade. He'd never been to Rome before.

'So I guess we'll be with you soon.'

'Don't guess. Call me when you know more.'

Chapter Thirty-Three

The Lane Shelter for Runaway Teens occupied a redbrick Victorian building close to the centre of Manchester. Little had changed in the years since Jennifer Lloyd had last approached it. She could see the same smoked-glass entrance doors, with the same security cameras angled down over them, and the same blend of dishevelled adolescents sprawled on the stone steps outside.

But one thing was different. The sign above the entrance had been taken down and replaced with another, more discreet plaque. Officially, the institution was no longer called the Lane Shelter for Runaway Teens, even if Lloyd still thought of it that way, and even if the Lane Foundation still funded it. Now it was known as the Fresh Start Shelter.

Fresh Start. The rebranding so obviously fulfilled a dual purpose. Yes, the street kids who came here were looking for a new beginning, but so too was the Shelter itself and the family that bankrolled it. The Anna Brooks affair had tainted them both, but the murder of Helen Knight threatened to destroy them.

Lloyd weaved through the kids on the steps and pressed a button on the intercom fitted next to the entrance. She heard a brash buzz and a sudden clunk, followed by speaker crackle as someone barked, 'Come in. Make sure the door locks behind you.'

She entered a deserted foyer, the door clicking shut after

her. The kids who bedded down at the Shelter weren't allowed inside during the day. The hours between ten in the morning and four in the afternoon were when a small army of volunteers stripped mattresses, scrubbed toilets and prepared the evening meal. It was also when the manager of the Shelter could catch up on emails and phone calls and, with a little persuasion, spare twenty precious minutes to talk with a police detective who wouldn't take no for an answer.

'I'm back here.'

Lloyd tracked the voice to a small office located beyond a cluster of brightly coloured couches and chairs.

'Take a seat.'

But there was nowhere to sit, which was something Lloyd guessed the man with his back to her knew only too well. There were documents and files stacked high on the desk in the middle of the room, on the floor, on the windowsill, on the visitor chairs.

The man was sorting through the bottom draw of a metal filing cabinet. His hair was long and brown, tied into a ponytail, and the small of his back was exposed above the waistband of his corduroy trousers and his checked boxer shorts.

'One minute.'

He didn't take one minute. He took two. And if he planned on subtracting them from the twenty he'd promised Lloyd, she'd make sure he regretted it.

Finally, he turned and extended a hand to shake. 'Sorry about that. Call me Sean.'

'No need to introduce yourself, Mr Ellis. We've met before.'

Lloyd kept her arms folded across her chest and waited until he lowered his hand a little awkwardly.

'It was four years ago. After Sarah Adams was killed. You really don't remember?'

'No offence, but I spoke to a lot of police around then. It was a tough time for all of us at the Shelter. Sarah was very much loved here.'

Lloyd hitched an eyebrow at the nametag screwed to the front of the office door.

'So you're the manager now, Mr Ellis.'

'Sean, please. And believe me, I was much happier being Sarah's assistant. The money was almost the same and the admin was a lot less painful. I took the job because nobody else would. Especially since I don't have an assistant of my own any more. Funding cuts, you know?'

'Connor Lane fell out of love with the place? You surprise me.'

Ellis made a humming noise and faked a sudden need to consult one of the papers on his desk. He was early thirties, tall and lean, with a wispy goatee beard and frameless spectacles.

'Why are you here, Officer?'

'*Detective Sergeant*,' Lloyd corrected him. 'And I'm here because of the news appeal. I'm assuming you've seen it?'

'About Nick, you mean? What does that have to do with us?'

'I'd like you to tell me about Anna Brooks.'

Ellis blinked. 'Anna? Why?'

'Because I asked. Because you promised to talk with me for twenty minutes and by my count we have at least eighteen minutes left.'

'But why now all of a sudden?'

'Start with the basics. What was Anna like? Was she popular here?'

'I wouldn't say popular, no. She was troubled.'

'Wow. And there I was thinking she ended up here because her life was all pony rides and debutante balls.'

'*More* troubled than most.'

'How so?'

He shrugged, looking about him for a distraction he couldn't quite find. 'She complained a lot. All the time, really.'

'About?'

'Her room-mates. The food. You name it, she complained.'

'About being harassed by Russell Lane?'

'Not at first.'

'But that changed?'

He sighed and fussed with a yellow charity bracelet on his wrist. 'She came to me once. About a fortnight before the alleged incident.'

Alleged incident. Now wasn't that a phrase loaded with connotations?

'And what did you do?'

'I told Sarah, of course.'

'Did she report it?'

'She spoke with Anna directly.'

'And?'

'And nothing.'

'Did Sarah confront Russell to your knowledge?'

'I don't think so.'

'What about you? Did you speak with him?'

'I decided it wasn't my place to.'

'And why was that?'

He sighed again, louder this time, dropping his hands to his sides. 'Because neither Sarah nor I believed Anna. Once she

185

was challenged on a few simple facts, she took back what she'd said. She admitted she just wanted the attention.'

'She told you this?'

'Sarah did.'

'What about Helen Knight? Did she mention anything to you about Russell before she was killed?'

'No, but then she wouldn't have. She was here in a professional capacity. The law firm she worked for handles all Mr Lane's legal work. He arranged it so that some of their trainees would help us out on a pro bono basis.'

'Doing what, exactly?'

'Sometimes it was legal stuff to do with the Shelter itself. Our rental agreement, say. Other times the trainees might talk with some of our kids if they needed legal advice.'

'Could any of the kids have approached Helen with some concerns about Russell? Do you think she could have confronted him about something?'

'Look, I've answered these questions already. I've given prepared statements. I'm really not sure I should say anything else.'

'I know this is upsetting for you, Mr Ellis. I know it's not something you want to think about. But a young woman is dead and the brother of your benefactor is facing serious charges. Again. Then there's Patrick Leigh. He stayed here, didn't he? He was due to tell a jury that he watched Helen climb into Russell's car outside this place on the day she was killed. Kind of careless, wouldn't you say? Two deaths linked to the Shelter you manage in less than a year.'

'I'm sorry, but is that some kind of accusation?'

'It's a question. One you haven't answered so far.'

Ellis exhaled and shook his head, exasperated.

'Helen would never have *confronted* Russell.'

'Why not?'

'Because she liked him.'

'Liked him?'

'She was attracted to him. Anyone could see that.'

And some people, Lloyd got the impression, were a little disappointed by it, too.

'How did Russell respond?'

'How do you think he responded? Helen was very attractive.'

'Did you tell Helen about Anna Brooks? Did you warn her?'

'Why would I do that?'

Because you were jealous, Lloyd thought. Because you wanted Helen for yourself, probably, or at least wanted to make sure the rich hotshot who dipped in and out of Shelter life, bringing scandal to its doors, didn't get her instead.

'Russell admitted to having sex with Anna,' she pressed. 'Here, at the Shelter.'

Ellis paused before responding, as if sensing a trap. 'He could hardly deny it. I understand there was DNA evidence.'

'That's more than a little inappropriate, isn't it?'

'These things happen. We all know that.'

'Really? A millionaire falling for a street kid?'

'Please. Nobody said they were in love.'

'No, nobody did say that, did they?' Lloyd turned from him. 'Thank you for talking with me, Mr Ellis. It's been . . . helpful.'

'What about Nick? You haven't asked me anything about him.'

She was already on her way out the door. She hadn't planned to stop and she wouldn't have done if Ellis hadn't called after her with quite such urgency.

'*They* argued, you know. Nick and Sarah. They argued all the time towards the end.'

*

Wade hung back after the train pulled in to Roma Termini, waiting until Adams and Kate walked by his window. He counted off thirty seconds, then made his way on to the platform and fell into step with the passengers moving towards the ticket barriers and the main concourse.

Adams towered over everybody else. He was moving with pace and purpose. It was clear that he knew exactly where he was going.

For a moment, Wade was pretty sure he was making for the taxi rank, which could have been problematic, but his destination turned out to be a down escalator near the wall of glass at the front of the station. Wade scanned the signs above.

USCITA/EXIT.

SERVIZI/TOILETS.

DEPOSITO BAGAGLI/LEFT LUGGAGE.

He waited until they'd stepped off the escalator before hopping aboard, descending into a vast underground space lit by coloured fluorescents and filled with shops and food concessions. Adams and Kate had joined a long line of tourists snaking out from the left-luggage department.

Wade was hungry. He'd snacked on crisps and chocolate on the flight and he could have used a proper meal. But he had no time for that now, so he veered towards a takeout counter and grabbed a salted pretzel before joining the queue himself, maybe fifteen people back.

Ten minutes later and the pretzel long gone, Adams reached the counter and Wade watched him exchange a suitcase and a backpack for a pair of ticket receipts. Then Adams turned and marched away fast with Kate rushing to keep up.

Eight minutes after that, Wade reached the counter himself and nodded at a young guy in a faded blue uniform shirt.

'Speak English?' he asked.

'A little.'

'I have two bags to collect. A green suitcase and a black backpack.'

'You have ticket?'

Wade reached into the zipped pocket on his tracksuit top and removed a tight roll of hundred-euro notes. He tapped the roll on the counter, his massive upper body shielding the bribe from the line of tourists waiting behind.

'Absolutely. It's right here.'

Chapter Thirty-Four

Miller and Kate took an orange city bus west into the bustle of the Trevi district, where Miller jumped off and led the rest of the way on foot through narrow cobbled streets, the heat close to suffocating, Kate struggling to keep up.

He threw in extra turns, doubled-back on himself and paused in front of shop windows. But he couldn't spot a tail. He didn't think they'd been followed.

The back-up location was a dismal two-star hotel inside a thin wedge of a building, the reception located one floor up, above a failing *gelateria* where the flies buzzing on the tubs of ice cream vastly outnumbered the customers.

The old guy working the hotel reception was thin and scrawny, his back bowed, his collarless shirt badly stained.

Miller felt like a giant standing before him, grit crunching under his shoes, the stench of blocked drains filling his nostrils. He asked the old man if he spoke English, and the man gazed up with yellowed, rheumy eyes and replied that he did, which was a relief, since Miller's Italian didn't extend much beyond *ciao* and *per favore* and a series of elaborate hand gestures. So Miller gave him Christine's name and said she was a guest in the hotel and that she was expecting them.

The old man peered at him closely, then past him at Kate. He spent some time consulting a guest ledger.

'What is your name?'

Miller swallowed his irritation and introduced himself. The man nodded and studied Kate a second time. Her presence seemed to confuse him.

'She's also a friend,' Miller explained.

'She waits for you.' The man pointed a crooked finger out the door. 'There is a cafe.'

'She left here?'

He nodded.

'Was she alone?'

'*Si*. But another Englishman is looking for her. He came here not so long ago. An hour, maybe. He also said he was a friend.'

'And what did you tell him?'

'Nothing.' His lips peeled back to reveal a set of discoloured dentures. 'I no speak good English, understand?'

'Can you describe this man to me?'

He did, and his description was detailed. He told Miller the man was white, mid-fifties, fat, badly dressed – which was something, coming from this guy – and wearing a straw sun hat.

Which made the man Mike Renner, Miller thought. Had to be.

'Thank you,' he said, and turned to go, following Kate towards the door.

'Your friend,' the man called after them. 'She's very afraid, I think.'

But Miller didn't turn back or acknowledge him. He just placed his hands on Kate's back and hurried her down the stair- case, his heart pumping hard in his chest, his mind taunting him with the dangers Christine had exposed herself to.

Outside, the street was crammed with people. Tourists,

mostly, though there were some Italians in tailored business attire and a cleaner in orange overalls pushing a rubbish cart along. Miller waded into the crowds. He saw plenty of cafes. Plenty of people. But he couldn't see Christine.

'What does she look like?' Kate asked.

But Miller didn't answer. He was busy asking himself if they'd just been played. He was wondering if the old man in the hotel hadn't been just a little bit *too* helpful. Maybe he'd sent them out on a fool's errand. Maybe Renner had been lurking in the back office.

But no, he was being paranoid, because finally he spotted Christine sitting beneath a sun-faded parasol at a pavement cafe.

She looked pensive and fearful, her face angled down, her eyes flitting left to right. She stubbed out a cigarette in a glass ashtray, stabbing it repeatedly until the filter was crushed. She was still tamping away when Miller surged forwards and grabbed for her wrist.

'Get up. Let's go.'

Miller had already snatched up her handbag before she'd seen it was him. The handbag was tangled in her arm and her hand flew up with it.

'Move,' he said, quietly but firmly.

'Miller? What are you doing? I haven't paid.'

'Here.'

He threw some money on to the table and pressed the handbag into her chest, steering her away from the cafe, smiling tersely at the other patrons.

'What's happening? What's wrong?'

'Keep walking.'

'You're scaring me.'

'Everything will be OK.'

'Who's she?' Which told Miller that Kate was keeping up with them. 'What's going on?'

Christine's dishwater-blonde hair was a tangled mess, her skin jaundiced, and there were dark circles around her eyes. Miller had suspected for a while now that she was self-medicating. He hated to think where she was getting the drugs.

'Be calm.' Miller scanned the faces that surrounded them. There was nobody he recognised. No obvious threat.

'Is it Danny? Please tell me it's not Danny.'

'Danny's fine. But we have to go, OK?'

'Go where?'

'This way.'

He picked a path through the tourists, urging Christine ahead of him, closing in on the Trevi Fountain.

The crowds swelled. The crush got worse. A thousand cameras and smartphones were pointed their way. Miller saw tour groups and holidaymakers, backpackers and street artists. Beyond them all, he saw the great Baroque fountain and the flash of sunlight reflecting off the coins being flicked into the pool.

He jumped up on to a stone plinth at the fountain's base and looked all around until a shrill whistle pierced the backbeat of chatter and he turned to see a policewoman in a starched white uniform motioning wildly at him to get down off the stonework.

Christine tugged on his arm. 'Is someone following me? Miller? Is that why you're here?'

'You should have stayed in the hotel. That's what we agreed.'

'I had to get out. I had to. It was smothering me in there. I was scared.'

'It's OK,' Kate told her.

But it wasn't. Not really. Not yet.

'This way. Hurry.'

He led them towards Piazza di Spagna, his arm on Christine's back, Kate skipping along at her side. He stopped and looked back three times and didn't spot anyone suspicious. Certainly nobody he recognised. He didn't think they'd been tracked.

But he was wrong.

*

Mike Renner was a long way back. Adams was moving faster than he'd anticipated, but his height and size made him easy to spot, and Renner was able to hide his face whenever Adams stopped suddenly and looked around. It didn't hurt that Renner had been in Rome a day now, long enough to concede to the pounding heat and invest in new clothes. He had on khaki shorts with canvas boat shoes, a blue polo shirt and a straw hat. He looked like a hundred other sunburnt Brits abroad. He looked about a thousand degrees cooler than Adams right now.

The big man was sweating prodigiously. His plaid shirt was pasted to his back and his hair was slicked down against his face.

For the hundredth time that day, Renner asked himself if he should have moved sooner, if there'd been more to be gained by cornering the sad-eyed blonde outside her hotel than waiting for Adams to show.

And for the first time that day, Renner was about to receive a definitive answer.

His phone buzzed in his clenched fist and he snatched it to his ear.

'Where are you?'

'At the train station,' Wade replied.

'Well, they're here, with me. You've left me with three of them to track. What am I supposed to do if they split up?'

'Relax. I have something better.'

Renner crabbed sideways to peer around an overweight American in shin-length shorts and a hockey jersey. Adams was moving on a diagonal trajectory towards the far right of the piazza.

'Better how?'

'They stowed their luggage. I have it now.'

'And?'

'I have ticket stubs from their flight, other documents, too. They're travelling under false names. She's Kate Ryan. He's using the Nick Miller alias I already told you about.'

'How does that help us?'

'First up, if you lose them, we know they're going to come back here. They'll want to collect their stuff.'

Renner was silent for a moment, thinking it through. Wade was right, although he wasn't inclined to acknowledge it.

'I also have Adams's iPad.'

Renner faltered as a group of Japanese tourists converged on him, following a woman who was holding a yellow umbrella above her head.

'So?'

'So I switched it on and there's some weird security system guarding this thing. I'm thinking there has to be something important on here.'

'Can you bypass it?'

'Oh, sure, because I've kept my talent for hacking computers secret from you until now.'

'Then it's of no use to us.'

'Maybe it can be. I just need some time.'

'How much time?'

'A few hours. Maybe three or four. It's hard to say exactly.'

Four hours.

'Fine.' Renner shook his head. 'Let me see what I can do. But I want updates, Wade. *Regular* updates.'

Chapter Thirty-Five

Jennifer Lloyd accompanied Sean Ellis to a wooden bench on the banks of the Bridgewater Canal. Ellis had said that he was hungry and needed something to eat. He'd asked if she'd like to join him. Lloyd wasn't flattered, and she wasn't fooled. She knew the food and the walk were an excuse to get them both out of the Shelter. Maybe it felt like less of a betrayal for Ellis to talk with her away from the place.

'The real tragedy', Ellis said, tearing open his sandwich bag and lifting a limp cheese-and-pickle-on-granary towards his mouth, 'is that we didn't just lose two people on the night of the fire, we lost three.'

Lloyd waited for him to chew, her sandwich bag unopened in her lap.

'Melanie perished, of course. And Sarah. And that was awful, obviously. But I was beginning to think Anna had turned a corner. She seemed positive about the trial.'

'Even though you didn't believe her.'

'It wasn't for me to determine the truth. That was for the jury to decide.'

Which sounded like a platitude he'd comforted himself with before.

'But the jury didn't get to decide, did they?'

'Anna ran, Detective Sergeant. Things got very serious very quickly. Running was what she knew.'

'Did you talk with her before she left?'

'No. It was several weeks since I'd seen her last.'

'Because she was kicked out of the Shelter.'

Ellis took another mouthful of sandwich, a gob of pickle clinging to the corner of his mouth. 'We found her a place in another shelter that seemed more suitable to her at the time.'

'Because Connor Lane made you evict her?'

'No.' He swallowed. 'Mr Lane never *made* us do anything. He still doesn't.'

'But you knew he'd want her gone. So who told her? Was it you?'

Ellis stared at the opposite bank of the canal, his gaze becoming unfocussed. Eventually he nodded.

'Why not Sarah? She was the manager.'

'Sarah asked me to do it.'

'You sound like you resent her for that.'

'Sarah was a remarkable woman. An inspiration to me. But I admit I was a little disappointed in her. Asking Anna to move on was the right decision to make, politically speaking.'

'And ethically?'

'Ethically I'm not so sure.'

'I took another look at the file. A witness claimed that Anna was seen talking with Sarah on the afternoon of the fire. With Melanie, too. On the steps outside the Shelter. She seemed agitated.'

'I was told the same thing.'

'Do you know what they discussed?'

'No. I didn't hear about it until afterwards.'

'And what about since then? Has Anna contacted you?'

Ellis shook his head and took an even bigger bite from his sandwich.

'It's not so unusual,' he said, his mouth full. 'The kids at the Shelter are grateful for what we do. I know they are. But they feel no obligation to explain themselves when they choose to move on. And Anna would have heard about the fire and how Melanie and Sarah were killed. She would have run into other kids from the Shelter, on the streets.'

'You're saying she was scared?'

'Perhaps. But we still don't know what caused that fire. Or who. There's never been any proof it had anything to do with the Lane family, if that's what you're suggesting. I wouldn't work at the Shelter if I believed for one moment that was possible. Who knows? Maybe it was Anna herself.'

But it wasn't. It couldn't have been. The fire, maybe, but the fatal gunshots? It didn't fit.

'What about Nick?' she asked. 'What about his arguments with Sarah?'

Ellis grimaced, as though reluctant to spill. Before Lloyd could press him, her mobile began to vibrate. The call was from Foster.

'Curious thing,' Foster began, before she could speak. 'We got a hit on the Kate Ryan passport. A notification came in from Italian border control at Rome Fiumicino airport.'

'Rome?'

'But here's the strange part – the notification was sent automatically, close to an hour ago. I just called for more details. It doesn't exist any more.'

'I don't understand.'

'Frankly, neither do I. It could be a system error.'

'What about passenger manifests for flights out of Hamburg to Rome? Can you get access to those?'

'I already did. There's no record of Kate Ryan on any flight. No flag against Nick Adams, either.'

'I think we can assume he has a fake ID of his own. How often do false flags crop up?'

'I asked the guy I spoke to the same thing. He said never.'

'So the Ryan passport triggers a blip, then the blip disappears. Could it have been deleted somehow?'

'The guy I spoke to says not.'

'But—'

'I'm keeping an open mind about it. Just like you asked me to.'

She hung up, leaving Lloyd to lower the phone, trying to assimilate the new information. Ellis was staring at her, waiting.

'The arguments.' She nodded at him. 'Tell me about them. Did they focus on Melanie's decision to testify?'

'Mostly, yes. And about Sarah wanting to continue her work at the Shelter. Nick never really got comfortable with the idea of her working for Mr Lane. She didn't, of course. Not directly. But he couldn't get his head around that.'

Because he wasn't stupid, Lloyd thought. Because all the foundations and board members in the world couldn't disguise who made the real funding decisions that would be the life or death of the charity.

'To your knowledge, was Nick ever violent towards Sarah?'

Ellis's throat bulged, as though he'd tasted something foul in his sandwich.

'Once. Perhaps. She came to work with a bruise on her face. Another on her wrist. She was cradling her arm. But she wouldn't talk about it.'

'When was this?'

'Two, three weeks before she died?'

'Could Nick have killed her, do you think?'

'Honestly? I don't know. Don't they say that anyone is capable of killing, given the right circumstances? Or the wrong ones, I suppose.'

'Including Nick?'

Ellis set down his sandwich.

'If he was in a complete rage, I guess I couldn't rule it out completely. They were in love. I believe that. But their relationship wasn't perfect. They both worked so hard. That created some conflict. But Melanie?' He shook his head. 'Nick doted on her. She was everything to him. And to shoot her? To burn her body? I think it's inconceivable.'

Ellis scrunched up the paper bag from his sandwich, then stood abruptly and kicked a toe into the ground.

'I really have to be getting back.'

Lloyd stayed seated. She was thinking about everything he'd said, looking for weak points and for flaws. There were plenty she could identify, but none she felt the need to challenge him on quite yet. And she was thinking about the phone call from Foster. Thinking about Rome.

'Just one more thing: if you had to guess, where do you think Anna is now?'

Ellis blew air through his lips, crushing his paper bag between his hands.

'Truthfully? She could be anywhere.'

Which was exactly what was beginning to concern Lloyd. Because what if Fiona was right about Nick and she'd been wrong all along? What if he hadn't run because he was a killer but because he was protecting someone? Had he spirited Anna away somewhere? Was that what he was doing with Kate Sutherland, too?

Chapter Thirty-Six

The Spanish Steps were a cascade of crumbling stone, blood-red azaleas and sun-dazed tourists. Miller found a spot towards the top of the steps, in an oblong of false shade being cast by the ochre facade of the church of Trinità dei Monti. He lowered himself on to the baking stone as Christine and Kate perched on the step below.

Rome shimmered before him; a clash of terracotta rooftops, teetering buildings and wayward alleyways. The city hummed with life, with noise, with the plaintive bleat of car horns and the jammer of voices.

He looked towards the knot of people clustered around the boat-shaped fountain at the base of the steps. He couldn't see anyone climbing towards them, paying them too much attention, scoping them out.

Christine bunched her hands in her lap, rocking slightly. 'I want to know about Danny.'

'He's safe. I told you that.'

'Is it Steve? Is he here?'

Miller shook his head, still scanning the crowd. Christine fumbled for a cigarette, stabbing it between her lips, flicking a lighter.

'Do I have to leave this place?'

'Yes, Christine. You have to leave Rome.'

'Where am I going?'

'I don't know.'

She inhaled raggedly. 'Who's she?'

'This is Kate.'

Miller didn't elaborate and Christine seemed to assume that Kate was another part of his team. A new member at her beck and call.

'Did he tell you about Steve?' She turned to Kate. 'About my Danny?'

'Should we be talking like this?' Kate shielded her eyes and gazed up at Miller. 'Isn't it dangerous?'

'It's fine.'

And it was. There were people all around them, sitting and admiring the view, eating ice cream, reading. People with their own lives and cares to worry about.

'Steve's my husband,' Christine was saying. '*Was*, I guess I should say, although I couldn't exactly hang around for a divorce, could I? He killed a kid. Hit and run. I was in the car. I reported it, afterwards. Had to, didn't I? But my Steve is a scary guy. All kinds of scary. He heads up a big gang in Liverpool, see? So Miller here told me I had to get away. I kind of figured I was *dead* anyway. What did I have to lose?'

'And Danny?'

Her eyes dimmed, as if she was shying away from looking at something within herself.

'Danny's my son. I wanted to take him with me but the afternoon I was leaving he was playing at a friend's place. I went to pick him up but when I got there he was already gone. Steve beat me to it. Steve *knew*.'

But the truth was Steve hadn't known. It had been coincidence. Sheer bad luck. Miller had told Christine this a hundred times, though he'd long ago come to realise that she'd never accept it. He still couldn't tell if it was because she honestly thought her thug of a husband had some kind of all-knowing power, or because it eased her conscience to tell herself she could never have got away without leaving Danny behind.

'So now Miller keeps a watch on him for me. And Hanson sends me updates. Photos, videos, that kind of thing. One day, when it's safe, Becca's going to get word to him. Then he'll come and join me. We'll be together again.'

There was a toneless, robotic quality to her voice, as if she repeated the scenario to herself several times a day. Maybe she'd even believed it. Once.

Miller ached when he heard her talk this way because he knew the hard reality of Christine's situation, even if she wasn't ready to confront it quite yet.

Danny's eighth birthday had been a month ago and Hanson had managed to clip some photographs from Steve's Facebook page for Christine to pore over. She'd cried when Miller had shown her – she was often crying – and he hadn't dared tell her how in awe of his father Danny had become. Steve had poisoned his son's mind, telling Danny his mother had abandoned them both. Miller doubted there could be a reversal. He was pretty sure Danny was lost to Christine for good. And now, she'd lost Miller and his team, too.

'Tell me about Clive Benson.'

'Who?'

'Don't do that, Christine. We know he contacted you. We know he came to Rome. You two met. Why? What did you say to each other?'

'I don't know what you're talking about. Honestly. I don't.'

'He's in hospital,' Kate told her. 'He was attacked. He was beaten very badly inside his apartment.'

'Well, that sounds shitty for . . . What did you say his name was again? Colin?'

Miller clutched his face in his hands. It was all he could do not to reach out and shake her.

'Christine,' Kate said, 'the men who beat Clive, the men who put him in hospital, we think he could have told them about you. They could be here looking for you.'

'*Here?*'

Christine turned her head wildly, half standing. Miller pulled her back down again.

'We can't help you until we know what you talked about. So tell us now. What did he come here to say?'

She cast her cigarette around in careless loops, looking up at Miller with a familiar pleading in her eyes. She'd often looked at him that way whenever she'd asked him about Danny, and sometimes when she'd asked him for other things, a form of comfort he couldn't possibly provide.

'I'm sorry, Miller. Really, I am.'

'Forget sorry. I need answers. I have to know what you talked about.'

'Just . . . nothing.' Her lip trembled. 'The life, you know. We understood each other, I guess.'

'Did you talk about me?'

'A little.'

'And Hanson? Becca?'

'I don't remember too well.'

'Try, Christine. What else?'

'I don't know. I've been pretty messed up. Look, I've been

taking some stuff. I don't think it's been good for me.'

The tears were starting. They might have been genuine, though Miller doubted it. She wiped at her face with the hand holding the cigarette.

'Your personal stories?'

She shook her head. 'I wouldn't tell him that. Why would I tell him that?'

Because you just told Kate, he thought. You just opened up to her right away. As if your story was there to be shared. As if the secret wasn't keeping you alive.

'How did Clive contact you? It wasn't in the Dungeon Creeper forum. We'd have seen.'

'That was stupid. I should never have replied to him.'

'Replied to him how?'

'Look, I was dumb, OK? I get that now. But there was this one time I used my username on another site. A chat site, for soap fans.'

Miller groaned and pounded his fist into the stone step.

'I *know*. I screwed up. I'm sorry.'

'And Clive found you there how?'

'He said he googled my username. It came up, so he sent me a message.'

'And you just replied? Do you have any idea how dangerous that was?'

Her shoulders bunched and she curled in on herself, crocodile tears rolling down her cheeks. She stubbed her cigarette out on the stone steps.

'I was lonely, OK? And he sounded nice. He knew all about you. I could tell he was one of us. I could just tell.'

'Jesus.'

'I wouldn't have replied otherwise.'

'What about the others? Did he try and contact any of them? Did you?'

'Not me.' She snivelled and wiped at her face again. 'I wouldn't know how. I deleted my account from that other website after I met him. He told me to do that. He was careful, see?'

'And Clive? Did he say if he'd contacted anyone else?'

'I don't know. Why don't you ask him instead of me?'

'Because he can't speak, Christine. He's in a coma. He's probably going to die.'

He was being aggressive but he didn't particularly care. She'd risked her life. Risked all of their lives. And for what? A chat. A moan. Maybe even a quick, sad tumble with a sad and lonely man.

'Please, Christine,' Kate cut in. 'If Clive told you *anything* you have to tell us so we can stop this before anyone else gets hurt.'

Christine looked between them, lifting her face to stare up at Miller, then bowing her head and reaching for her shoe, tugging idly at the laces.

'I haven't spoken to anyone else. I don't *know* anyone else. I don't think Clive did, either. Nobody else had used their username online. You're right. I'm probably the only one daft enough to do it.'

So maybe the rot hadn't spread as far as Miller had feared. Maybe the rest of the system really was safe. For now.

But Hanson would need to fix things. He'd have to sweep the Web for their usernames. He'd have to change all their logins. Find a new forum, too, probably.

'What happens now?' Christine asked. 'Where am I moving to?'

'I honestly have no clue.'

'When will you know?'

Miller shook his head, scanning the shimmering rooftops, lifting his eyes to the piercing white sun that was burning down and pinning him there.

'I'll never know, Christine. You're on your own now. I can't help you any more.'

Only her eyes moved, growing wide in her head.

'You made it so that I can't trust you, Christine. And if I can't trust you, I can't work with you. None of us can. You broke the rules. You're out.'

'But . . . you can't do that.'

'It's already done. You did it yourself.'

She looked at Kate for help.

'I don't understand. What am I supposed to do?'

'I taught you the life, Christine. Now you have to live it for yourself. I won't be around any more. There'll be no Hanson. No Becca.'

And no photos of Danny. No updates on her son's life. He saw the brutal reality of it hit her then. The stupidity and the absoluteness of what she'd done. She started to cry again and this time he had no doubt the tears were real.

'No. No.' She was shaking her head over and over, shaking it like she had when Miller had told her they couldn't get Danny out, that she had to leave the UK without him. 'Don't do this to me. You can't do this to me.'

Miller didn't respond.

'You *can't*. I'll die without Danny. You won't do it. You won't.'

But he already had, and she saw that now. Saw it in his face. In the way he glanced away from her.

She sobbed and flailed her arms, batting his legs.

People were beginning to look. A lot of people.

'Stop it, Christine. Stop. Listen to me.'

But she wasn't listening and the audience were getting restless. Men and women were murmuring, shaping up to approach.

'Christine,' Kate told her. 'Christine, it's OK. He doesn't mean it. He's just angry. We'll help you. We will.'

Miller fixed his jaw and glared at Kate but she leaned over and took Christine in her arms, stroking her hair.

'You're not alone. We're here for you. You're not alone.'

'Your life is in her hands,' Miller reminded Kate. 'Think about that.'

'You'll help her. I know that you will.'

'I'll just stay here.' Christine wiped her nose with the back of her hand. 'I don't care any more. I'll just stay where I am.'

'You can't. Clive compromised you. There's a man here looking for you. He's already been to the hotel. He could be watching us right now.'

'So help her,' Kate urged. 'One more move, Miller. Set her up somewhere new. A new name, new identity, all of it. *Then* you walk away. That's fair, isn't it? That's reasonable.'

Miller knew he shouldn't have looked at Kate in that moment. He knew he shouldn't have let himself see how badly she wanted to believe in him. Probably, on some level, she was comparing Christine's situation with Danny to her own aborted search for her brother. Perhaps, because of that, she couldn't stand to see Christine cut off from her old life completely.

But what did Kate know about reasonable? What did anyone?

'One more move.' He grunted and pushed up to his feet, dusting off his hands. 'But that's it, Christine. That's all I can do for you. You've chosen your own path.'

Chapter Thirty-Seven

The Galleria Porta di Roma, located just off the A90 ring road to the north of the city, looked like most of the shopping malls Wade had visited back home. The complex was a low-level concrete box surrounded by austere landscaping, acres of tarmac, and thousands of parked cars.

It was just as familiar inside. About the only thing that told Wade he was outside the UK were the Italian signs on the shops that surrounded him. But the store he was interested in had a sign that didn't rely on any language. It was a symbol of an apple with a bite taken out of it, and he found it on the first floor of the mall.

Wade didn't own many Apple products but he'd been in plenty of their stores over the years and this one looked much the same as all the others. There was a lot of glass at the front, then a series of pale wooden tables loaded with iMacs and iPhones and iPads and i-Whatevers. There was a scrum of customers hanging about. Some were testing products, some were making use of the free wifi. And some were gathered at the back of the store where the Genius Bar was located.

Wade was no Luddite. He was familiar with the standard four-digit security code that protected most handheld Apple products, so he was aware that the system blocking his access to the stolen iPad was something more specialised. And no matter how clever some of the nerds working in this particular Apple Store might be,

Wade was pretty sure that classing them as geniuses was playing fast and loose with the term. So he had no intention of queuing up for the supposed expertise of some pimple-faced kid.

But there was one thing Wade was relying on, and that was simple human nature. In his experience, like-minded people tended to stick together. Wade was a thug and a crook, and because of that, he knew lots of thugs and crooks back home. So it stood to reason that geeks in Rome would know other geeks. And somewhere in the city, just waiting for Wade to come find him, there had to be a kid who was so good with computers that working in an Apple Store for him would be like Ronaldo selling football boots in Foot Locker. And just like Ronaldo, this kid would have fans. He'd have admirers who'd recognise that he was the absolute best at what he did. And some of those admirers would be working here, for Apple, masquerading as geniuses while the real genius lurked in the shadows.

'Can I help you?'

A chubby teenager who didn't look quite old enough to shave was smiling at Wade. He had on thick-frame glasses, a bulging blue T-shirt and a lanyard hanging from his neck. Maybe Wade should have been insulted that the kid could tell he was English just from his appearance, but right at that moment, he was grateful for it.

'I'm looking for someone.'

'Someone who works here?'

'I doubt it.'

'I don't understand.' The teen blinked. 'Who are you looking for?'

'See,' Wade said, pressing a hand down on his shoulder, 'that's what I'm hoping you can tell me.'

Chapter Thirty-Eight

Renner waited until Adams had made his way to the bottom of the steps – the two women tracking his movements precisely, as if following him through a minefield – then stood up from behind a screen of carnations, brushed the dirt off his shorts and set off in pursuit.

He couldn't tell for sure why Christine was so distraught because he hadn't been close enough to hear what was being said. He guessed Adams had told her she could be being watched and he'd probably let her know some of what Wade had done to Clive Benson in Hamburg. Maybe the two of them had been closer than Clive had let on, or maybe she was afraid of the same thing happening to her. But on balance, Renner suspected it was something more – some kind of fight or disagreement with Adams. There was a tension between them. A physical distancing they seemed unable to bridge.

Not that Adams appeared inclined to try. He was busy forging a route across the piazza into a cobbled shopping lane. The street was narrow to begin with but it was made narrower still by the displays of postcards, T-shirts and baseball caps outside a series of souvenir shops; by the pavement seating for a line of restaurants; by the congealed mass of tourists lurching on.

Just ahead of Adams, a white taxi nosed out from a concealed side street, the driver beeping his horn, gesticulating at people to get out of his way. The crowds swelled and parted, separating Adams from the two women. Renner saw Adams signal at them to head down the alley the taxi had emerged from, and when they failed to move right away, he lost patience and clambered over the bonnet of the taxi, the driver blasting his horn, yelling out of his window.

Renner shoved and elbowed his way forwards, but by the time he entered the side street, he'd lost a lot of ground. The alley was empty aside from a line of dusty city cars parked bumper to bumper. There were no shops or restaurants, and by extension, no people. Without the pedestrian congestion, Adams and the two women had raced ahead.

I just need some time.

Renner thought of Wade. He thought of the iPad he'd taken and the information it might contain. It was possible it could give them a lead on Anna Brooks; a surer lead, perhaps, than trying to force the information out of Adams or taking a chance that either of the women knew where he'd hidden her.

The rapid click of a pair of high heels approached from close behind and Renner turned to see a chicly dressed woman skip by, trailing a cloud of perfume. The woman aimed a set of car keys at a red Fiat 500 nestled against a fire hydrant. The Fiat's indicators blinked and the doors unlocked in a fast shuffle.

By the time the woman was reaching for the driver's door, Renner was already moving towards her. He didn't pause or think or analyse the situation. He reacted on instinct.

His instinct was to reach out and yank her backwards by her ponytail.

*

Miller heard a yelp, like a small dog's bark, from somewhere far behind. He didn't look back. He was focussed on the way ahead, preoccupied by his next move and the move after that. He was trying to decide if he should head to Christine's apartment to grab her things, whether it was worth the risk, and how best to get there. He was asking himself if he should relocate Christine within Italy or introduce her to a new country altogether. He was contemplating the steps that Hanson and Becca would need to put in place to reinvent her once more. And he was trying to block out the yammer of Christine's constant apologies.

'I'm sorry,' she was saying again. 'I messed up. I'm an idiot. Will you forgive me? You have to forgive me.'

Would he? Miller wasn't sure that he could. But he did know that it was too soon for her to ask, his anger too raw. Because the truth was that despite everything he'd experienced and seen in the last several years, despite the way his heart had callused and scarred, Christine wasn't the only one who'd hoped that someday, no matter how improbably, Danny could be reunited with her again.

And yes, part of that was for the boy and for Christine, but the truth was that Miller had wanted it for himself much more than that. He'd wanted to be able to identify one clear and positive sign that the people he'd helped to hide and survive could do more than simply exist, that their lives could be rebuilt, that the fractured relationship between a child and a parent could be salvaged and renewed against all odds.

So Miller was hurting. He was upset. And because he was distracted he didn't pause and turn back to investigate the source of that yelping noise or engage with the muffled whump of a car door closing, or the muted squeal of tyres, or the high-pitched whine of an engine during a snatched gear change.

But eventually, something did get through to him – a delayed awareness of the sequence of noises overcoming his sensory lag – and he spun around to see a red Fiat 500 bearing down on them, zeroing in, the driver in the straw sun hat hunched forwards over the steering wheel, his eyes locked on Kate to the exclusion of everything else.

Miller didn't have time to shout out a warning. He didn't have time to think through his response. He'd stopped so abruptly that Christine had moved ahead of him but Kate was much closer, just to his right, and he dived for her, thrusting his shoulder into her midriff, her upper body folding and collapsing as his hands clasped for the backs of her thighs and he leapt for the cover of a brown Peugeot estate.

Something clipped his left foot – the wing mirror of the Fiat, maybe – and the force of it twisted him sideways. He landed on the bonnet of the Peugeot, striking his hip and knee and elbow. He lost hold of Kate who flew out of his arms, smacking into the dusty wall ahead.

Miller didn't see the Fiat strike Christine but he heard the awful thud, the crack of glass, the slap and crunch of her limbs hitting the deck.

He whipped his head round as he was sliding across the Peugeot's bonnet, and he saw the Fiat veer left, throwing up sparks as it scraped the wall of a building. His skull glanced off the Peugeot's windscreen as the Fiat jinked right, the driver overcompensating, heaving the wheel too hard and slamming into a parked Lancia, the light cluster popping, the wing mirror shearing off. The Fiat slewed left again, then fishtailed and straightened, and finally sped away.

There was a brief moment of silence and then the first of many doors and windows opened along the street, followed by the shrieks and shouts of unknown voices, the wails of shock and dismay.

Miller pushed himself up on to his elbow, clutching at his side, his knee giving way as he dropped down and hobbled towards Christine. She was lying on her front, her face towards him, her legs bent and splayed. There was blood on the cobblestones. More blood trickling out of her mouth and her ear. She blinked at Miller, lips quivering.

'Ambulance,' he hollered, looking wildly at the faces that were watching them. 'Somebody call an ambulance.'

The chant was taken up, repeated in Italian, rebounding off the walls that hemmed them in. Kate staggered out from behind the Peugeot, bent at the hip, bleeding from a cut on her head. And now Miller was down on his knees, squeezing Christine's hand, brushing her hair from her face, telling her that everything would be OK, that help was coming, that she had to hold on because he would find a way to bring Danny back to her soon.

Chapter Thirty-Nine

It turned out the chubby kid in the Apple Store wasn't able to provide Wade with the contact he needed, at least not directly, but he'd spoken with one of his colleagues who'd given Wade a long, sideways look, then made a call and written down an address on a scrap of paper that he traded with Wade for a crisp hundred-euro note.

Wade had left the mall immediately and climbed into another taxi, where he'd shown the driver the address on the shred of paper and watched as he frowned and shook his head and began to gesture at him to get out of his cab until two hundred euros changed his mind.

The journey took almost an hour through heavy traffic and then they arrived at their destination where Wade understood the real cause of the driver's concern.

Decrepit high-rise apartment buildings towered over them, marred by dirt and blight, nestled up close to a raised stretch of *autostrada* that teemed with traffic.

A group of boys in dirtied tracksuits, not unlike the outfit Wade was wearing, watched the taxi from the remains of a collapsed bus shelter. Two of them were straddling BMXs. All of them had restless, baleful eyes.

Wade got out and marched over to the group as the taxi turned in a tight circle and roared away.

Thugs know other thugs.

Wade flattened the square of paper in his palm and showed it to the group like he was a cop flashing a badge. No reaction, so he opened his other hand to reveal a one-hundred-euro note. The tallest boy, a lean and stringy black kid with a thick gold chain around his neck, muttered something to a younger white kid on a BMX. The kid sniffed and shrugged, then dropped his bike to the floor and motioned with his head for Wade to follow him.

He led the way through a sunken concrete underpass, scriptured in graffiti, towards a pair of twin apartment towers that looked like the final outpost of some long-ago collapsed communist regime.

The entrance to the tower on the right was ankle-deep in litter and when the dented elevator doors shuffled apart they released a fetid stench. Wade pulled the sleeve of his tracksuit over his hand and covered his nose and mouth as the kid punched a button and they rode the elevator to the twenty-third floor, where the doors parted again and Wade stepped out.

There was a plain plywood door opposite the lift, the frame splintered and scratched from being jimmied multiple times. Wade's guide barely gestured to it before snatching the cash from his hand as the elevator doors stuttered closed and the carriage began to descend.

Wade checked the address on his paper but there was nothing to indicate he was in the right place. He stepped up and knocked, then listened to silence, followed by footsteps, followed by the slide and clunk of multiple locks and bolts being withdrawn.

A slim girl of East Asian origin stood before him, aged about fifteen. She was wearing a grey school dress over a navy blue blouse and knee-high blue socks.

'Show it to me,' she said, in perfect English.

Wade unzipped his tracksuit top and removed the stolen iPad. He watched as the girl flipped back the magnetic cover and hummed in surprise and delight as the security screen flashed up.

'Can you crack it?'

'Of course,' the girl replied. 'How much money do you have?'

Chapter Forty

Another city, another hospital, but this time Miller found himself sitting in the waiting area of the casualty department of Ospedale Fatebenefratelli, one hand clamped to the bruising on his hip, a sterile patch covering a graze on his thigh. Kate was next to him with her head resting on his shoulder. A line of four stitches curved across her forehead. There were adhesive patches on her elbow and wrist.

Three hours had rushed by in a blur of sirens and police officers and paramedics, of hospital paperwork and triage questions and medical treatment. Miller knew they'd been lucky. Their injuries were minor. It was much worse for Christine. She'd been loaded on to a spinal board and driven away in the first ambulance. Right now, surgeons were working on her in an operating theatre somewhere. Miller hadn't been able to obtain an update on her condition from the nurses rushing by. He took that as a bad sign.

Just an hour ago, a female police officer had sat across from Miller and written down his preliminary statement in a pocket notebook, then gone through the same process with Kate. The officer had confiscated their passports and told them to report to a central police station within the next twenty-four hours to sign off on full witness accounts and reclaim their IDs. Not that that would happen. Miller couldn't contemplate the risk. And besides, it was largely irrelevant, because he was confident the police would never catch the driver of the red Fiat 500.

He'd been able to provide an accurate description of the man, largely because he'd recognised him, but he hadn't provided a name. What was the point? Mike Renner was experienced enough to get out of Italy without being caught. And if he identified Renner, Miller would have to explain how he knew him and why they'd been targeted.

But that didn't mean he could forget what had happened. It didn't mean he wouldn't try to make amends. First, though, he had to wonder what Renner's intentions had been. Had he been aiming to kill Kate? Was Christine just collateral damage? Or was something else going on?

'How much longer until we get some news, do you think?'

Miller stirred and looked down at Kate, nestled against his arm. All around them was speed and bluster and noise, the banging of doors, the shuttling to and fro of trolleys and patients and staff.

'Could be a while.'

Kate hadn't said anything before snuggling up to him and she hadn't said much since. She'd treated it as a perfectly normal thing to do. And perhaps it was. For her.

But it was different for Miller. He'd tensed at first, then relaxed in degrees, and now he was leaning into her just a little.

What would Becca say if she saw them? Something that didn't need to be said any more.

'What is it?' She rested the flat of her hand on his chest. 'Your heart is racing.'

'It's the stress.'

He straightened until she had to lift her head away from him, then feigned a stretch and a yawn, trying to make it seem like a natural response. Which obviously didn't work, because Kate frowned at him, one eye closed in a squint.

'You want coffee?' he asked her. 'I know a great little vending machine.'

But she tugged at his shirtsleeve, not willing to let him escape just yet.

'Promise me something, Miller. I don't want to be like Clive or Christine. I don't want to end up alone in a foreign hospital. I don't want to die without anyone knowing who I really am.'

'Christine's not by herself. We're right here for her.'

'I couldn't bear it, Miller. Truly. If something happens to me, I want you to find my brother. Find Richard. I want you to tell him about me. Tell him I was looking for him.'

She bit down on her lip and he knew right away what it was that she expected him to say. She wanted him to tell her that it wouldn't be necessary because he wouldn't allow anything bad to happen to her. That he was strong and smart and could protect her from every kind of danger.

But he couldn't bring himself to tell her that because he wasn't sure he believed it any more. Look at how he'd failed Sarah and Melanie. Look at Clive. Look at Christine.

'*Signor* Miller?'

A doctor was standing before them. He had on crumpled blue scrubs, white plimsolls and a day's worth of stubble and eye-strain. He reached up and scratched at his head, then took a deep breath and gave them the news.

Miller didn't listen to the details. The doctor's sombre expression and regretful tone had told him everything he needed to know.

Chapter Forty-One

'Something occurred to me,' Jennifer Lloyd said, when Foster eventually answered her mobile. It had already rung out twice before. 'There's something we haven't focussed on nearly enough.'

'Sorry? Who is this?' A pause. 'Lloyd? Is that you?'

'Something is bothering me.'

'Something is bothering *me*. I'm off duty, Lloyd. I'm on a *date*.'

A date, yes. Women like Foster did things like that. They socialised. They had a life outside of work.

Lloyd backed into the pillows she'd propped behind her on her hotel bed, the notes from her file scattered around her. She was staying in a Travelodge and her room was almost entirely bland. The only exception was the cheap, abstract piece of art on the wall across from her. She didn't care for it.

'Can't this wait until tomorrow?' Foster continued.

'Think about this for a second – Sarah and Melanie Adams were killed the night before they were due to go into a protection programme. That suggests their killer had foreknowledge of their situation. Nick Adams had that knowledge.'

'We're really doing this, are we?'

'Same thing applies on the Isle of Man with Kate Sutherland. Nick Adams shows up again. He finds her when she's already in the programme.'

'So you've basically just called to tell me you still think your theory holds water. That's great.'

'It does. I'm not worried about that.'

'So then what *are* you worried about?'

Lloyd's stomach rumbled. The radio alarm clock beside her bed told her it was just after 8 p.m. She supposed she should eat soon. She'd bought a cold pasty and a bottle of Lucozade from the petrol station linked to the Travelodge. She even had a bruised banana for dessert. Fine dining, for her.

'How did Adams know? That's what bothers me. How did he find out where Kate Sutherland was in hiding?'

'We don't know that.'

'Or suppose you're right. Suppose Connor Lane sent the dead guy to that house on the same night. How did he know where Sutherland was living?'

Foster sighed. 'What's your point?'

'We could have a leak. If Nick Adams didn't kill his family, we had a leak four years ago, too. But either way, we sure as hell have a security problem now. Somebody could be selling information.'

'Come on.'

'You come on. Unless you have another explanation?'

Foster fell silent for several long seconds and Lloyd glanced down to consider the yellow legal pad she'd been doodling on. There was one other alternative explanation. Possibly. But she wasn't about to lay it out just yet.

'*One minute,*' she heard Foster whisper, presumably to whoever she was on her date with. There was the clink of a glass and the sound of liquid being poured.

'You need to look into this,' Lloyd told her.

'Me?'

'I'm outside of London. And now is the perfect time. It's out of hours. It's quiet. You need to get back to the incident room and check records. Check logins. See if anyone has been accessing Kate Sutherland's file who shouldn't have been.'

'You expect me to do this now?'

Lloyd didn't say anything. There was no need to push too hard. Foster already knew she had the ear of Commissioner Bennett.

'OK, *fine*,' Foster said. 'But only because this date was never going to work out anyway.'

Lloyd heard the wounded plea of a male voice from somewhere close by.

'Oh, please,' Foster said, sotto voce. 'You're wearing a pork-pie hat. To a restaurant. Where do you think we are? The 1940s?'

Chapter Forty-Two

Miller had the middle-aged guy behind the luggage counter at Roma Termini go back and check for their bags a second time. The guy was a jaded type who'd seen it all before, so he puffed out his cheeks and rolled his eyes, and then he did as he was asked, or maybe he just went around behind the partition wall that screened off the storage area from paying customers and pretended to do what he was asked, before returning empty-handed once more.

Miller was tired and irritable and emotionally wrung out – he'd drifted around the city in a daze with Kate in the hours since they'd left the hospital – and he barely listened to what the guy was trying to say before he told him that he wanted to take a look for himself. The guy refused. He said it wasn't possible. And anyway, he'd already checked twice and their things were definitely gone.

Miller slapped a palm on the counter and asked to speak to the guy's younger colleague, the one they'd dealt with earlier that day. Miller was told that wasn't possible either, and when he swore and planted both hands on the counter as if he might vault over it, the guy backed off and told him in a hurry that his colleague had gone home sick.

'What time did he leave?'

The guy exhaled and told him it had been around ten or eleven o'clock in the morning.

'Which one? Ten, or eleven?'

'Ten. I think.'

Miller looked down at the ticket stub in his hand. They'd deposited their luggage at 9.38 a.m.

'I want to speak to your manager. Now.'

But they couldn't talk to the manager right away because she was on her break and she didn't return for another twenty minutes, even though Miller made the guy behind the counter radio her. Twice.

Miller was in a fury by then. He was pacing the floor, cursing loudly. So when the young woman finally appeared, strolling across the station concourse with a two-way radio clipped to her belt and a can of Diet Coke in her hand, Kate stepped in front of him and apologised for calling her back from her break a little early.

The manager looked to be only five or six years out of school, but she was smartly dressed in a grey trouser suit with a crisp white blouse and an identity lanyard around her neck, and it was clear from both her appearance and her attitude that she took her job very seriously. She seemed genuinely concerned when Kate told her that their luggage appeared to be missing, and when Kate added that a good friend of theirs had been killed in a car accident just a few hours earlier and that they were drained and upset and really just wanted to collect their things and go to a hotel, the manager framed an expression of deep compassion and invited them to follow her through the hatch in the counter.

The luggage storage area was vast and well organised. There was row upon row of metal bins and wooden cubbyholes and clothes hooks, all of them numbered sequentially, many of them empty now that the day was nearly through. But there was no sign of Kate's suitcase or Miller's rucksack in any of the cubbyholes or bins close to where their numbered tags said they should be. There was no sign of them anywhere.

'You have surveillance cameras.' Miller pointed at the ceiling. It was a statement, not a question.

The manager winced. 'But you leave your bags this morning. I'm sorry, this is a long time ago. I cannot go through it all now.'

'Then let me look.' Miller showed her the receipts for their bags. 'We know the time we left our things. We know that one of your staff went home sick shortly afterwards. I don't think that's a coincidence.'

'Please just let him,' Kate added. 'Believe me, he won't let this go otherwise.'

The manager eyed Miller, gauging his resolve.

'Thirty minutes of footage,' he told her. 'That's all we need to see. And if I'm right about your luggage guy, you need to know about it. Think what else he might take.'

But Miller wasn't right. At least not completely. Eight minutes into the footage, they saw something worse than he'd feared. The young guy behind the counter hadn't taken the bags for himself. He'd exchanged them in return for a cash payment from a stocky blonde man in a blue tracksuit.

The manager propped her hands on her hips, holding back the tails of her suit jacket. 'I will call the police. Tomorrow, I can speak with him. I will find out—'

'Forget it,' Miller told her. He was already removing his smartphone from his pocket, opening the camera app, snapping an image of the blonde man on screen. He grasped for Kate's hand and pulled her out through the fold-up hatch in the middle of the counter.

'We have insurance,' the manager called after them. 'You can fill in the forms. We will pay for your things.'

But Miller just shook his head without looking back, his thumbs tapping away at his phone, attaching the image to an email to Hanson.

'That man,' Kate was saying. 'Miller, he was sitting behind me on the plane.'

'He followed us from Hamburg.'

'For Lane?'

'Of course for Lane.'

'But why? What does it mean?'

'It means Christine wasn't a target. And neither were we. At least not directly. Christine was a distraction. It could have been any of one of us.'

Which was not entirely true. Renner had been aiming for Kate, Miller was sure. But the repercussions would have been much the same.

He put his phone to his ear, scanning the area all around. The food outlets were almost empty and most of the shops in the underground section of the train station were shuttered and in darkness. The only person close to them was a maintenance guy in a blue jumpsuit, up on a ladder, pulling on a tangle of cables hanging from the ceiling.

The call connected and Hanson picked up.

He said, 'We're still so upset about Christine. Becca wanted to call you but she's been kind of a mess. We both have, to tell the truth.'

'No time for that now. We have a problem. One of Lane's men got hold of our bags. He has our aliases.'

Hanson whistled.

'He also has my iPad.'

'It's security protected.'

'This was more than ten hours ago.'

Silence.

'Can you wipe the iPad remotely?'

'No problem. I've got this. Oh, and by the way, I just opened your email, and yikes – that guy's eyes are so far apart he must have to walk sideways to see where he's going. And check out his arms. He's like a human crab. Relax, Miller, there's no way this steroid-abuser could bypass my security patch.'

'Just wipe it, OK? I want to be sure.'

Miller heard the rapid clatter of computer keys followed, seconds later, by a muted, 'Huh.'

'What?'

'Minor issue. Somebody did get through my security. They're blocking me.'

'Can you get round it?'

'Eventually.' Miller heard more keystrokes. 'But whoever they are, they're good. I think we have to assume that the first thing they'll have done is to copy all the data from the iPad on to another device.'

'You're telling me they have everything?'

'That would be my guess.'

Miller hung up and covered his eyes with his hand.

'What is it? Miller? What's wrong?'

He told Kate.

'So? It's just an iPad.'

'The details of my clients are on there.'

'*All* of them?'

Miller lowered his hand from his eyes. 'Nearly all. We're

talking real names, assumed names, locations, medical records, bank accounts. Pretty much everything except an exact address and recent headshots.'

'Including Anna?'

'Not her. But there are two others.'

'And you think Lane's men will go after them?'

'Why not? Anna might be their goal now, but they must think my other clients are potentially valuable to them, too. They probably think they can get to Anna through them. Just like with Clive and Christine.'

'Why not come for one of us? For you?'

'Because they gambled. They took a chance on my iPad. They thought Anna's details might be on there.'

'And now they don't know where we are.'

Miller spun round, checking to see if they were being watched. There was nobody near them except the maintenance guy. He looked legit.

'They know we had to come back here. But more importantly, they know where I'm *going* to be. They know I have to go and protect my clients.'

'Where are your clients?'

'Prague. And Arles, in the South of France.'

'So have Hanson contact them. Tell them to run.'

Miller phoned Hanson again, on speaker this time. But Hanson had more bad news.

'I just tried sending them both private messages on the forum. I couldn't do it. Our mystery computer expert has their usernames. Their accounts have been deleted. I'll post a public message but I have no idea if they'll see it.'

Miller shared a look with Kate. Maybe he should have kept

some of this from her, but after Christine, he felt she deserved to know what was going on.

'Keep at it. And speak to Becca. Maybe she can think of something else we can try.'

'Speak to her yourself. She wants to talk to you.'

There was a moment of silence, then a series of muffled, shuffling noises as Hanson passed his phone across.

'Hey,' Becca said, and Miller could hear the torn quality in her voice. 'About Christine—' she began.

'I know,' he cut in. 'Us too.'

Becca fell quiet. Miller hated to rush her but there were steps he should be taking.

'Was there something, Becca? Things have gone a little crazy.'

'Don't be mad, OK?'

'What do I have to be mad about?'

'I couldn't stand Clive being alone. I couldn't stand just waiting. So I had Hanson make me an ID. Not his fault, OK? It was all my idea. I've been Clive's sister, Rebecca Benson, for the last couple of hours. I've spoken with Clive's doctors. I've been by his bed.'

Miller was silent for a moment.

'I'm not mad,' he told her. 'I should have suggested it myself.'

'He's deteriorating pretty fast. I thought you should know.'

'How long does he have?'

'His doctor didn't exactly say.'

'You can tell me. Kate's listening, too. She needs to hear it.'

'The next twenty-four hours are crucial. That's all I know. But I'm talking to him. I'm holding his hand. And . . . oh, wait, Hanson wants you back.'

Miller heard the clunk and the shuffling noises again, then Hanson was on the line once more.

'Our friend in the picture – Crab Man – I ran a check on my database of Connor's known associates. Nothing came up. Then I tried Mike Renner and got a hit. His name is Aaron Wade.'

'What do we know about him?'

'Not much. He has a record, naturally. Served eighteen months for GBH. But get this: it seems he had a disagreement with the manager of his boxing club. Guess how he resolved it?'

'Violence?'

'Specific violence. He took down a punchbag and strung the manager up in its place. He hung him *upside down* before he beat him.'

Miller caught Kate's eye and she nodded. She'd made the same connection. It was just like Clive. Just like Patrick Leigh.

'It hit the tabloids in a minor way,' Hanson continued. 'Seems to have earned him a nickname, too. The Hypnotist. How lame is that?'

'Lame,' Miller agreed. 'Until you're the punchbag. Keep working.'

He cut the call and cradled the mobile to his chest, staring at Kate, shaking his head, feeling foolish and vulnerable, more powerless than he had in years.

'It's OK,' Kate told him. 'You'll come up with something.'

'These people have a head start on me, Kate. They could be closing on my clients already. And I need to find them. I have to stop them. Stop this.'

'So think: which witness will they go for first? Is one of them more vulnerable, or more likely to be in contact with Anna?'

'Doesn't matter. They don't *have* to choose. There are two of them. There's Renner and then there's this Aaron Wade guy. They can split up.'

'Maybe. But you're forgetting something – there are also two of us. So tell me, where do you want me to go? The Czech Republic, or France?'

'I can't ask you to do that.'

'Then ask Hanson or Becca instead.'

'I need them in Hamburg. Clive needs them. And besides, they work the backroom. They're not equipped to be front and centre.'

'Which is why I'm volunteering.'

'It's a bad idea.'

'Yeah, well, maybe all you have left to you now is bad ideas.'

'You don't have a passport any more.' And also, he was thinking, the Kate Ryan alias was blown anyway. They couldn't risk Kate travelling under the same name again. Eventually, Hanson would miss something. There'd be a gap he'd fail to plug. 'You can't fly.'

'Neither can you.'

Which wasn't strictly true.

Miller didn't say anything. But then, he didn't need to. He could see from the look in Kate's eyes that she understood there was something he was keeping from her. Not that it mattered. He checked the station clock above her head. It was gone 9 p.m., and even if he could leave for the airport immediately, he doubted he'd make a flight to the Czech Republic or France in time.

Kate took his mobile from him and hit redial.

'We're calling Hanson back. We're going to ask him to make

me a new passport. And you're going to tell him to find a way to get it to me as soon as possible.'

So Miller did. Because she'd asked him to. And because all he had left to him now were bad ideas.

*

Miller had been right about being stuck in Rome. There was no way he could have made a flight.

It was different for Renner and Wade. They were already at Fiumicino, staring up at the electronic departure boards. There were no flights to the South of France until early the following morning, but Czech Airlines had a direct flight to Prague, departing at 21.45. Check-in closed in ten minutes.

Wade said, 'One of us should get on that plane. We should keep up the momentum. We should start looking right away.'

He was thinking the person to go should be Renner. This was his gig. He answered to Mr Lane directly. Wade was sub-contracted. And besides, he was wiped out. He wanted a night in an airport hotel. He wanted a hot shower and a room-service meal. After his breakthrough with the iPad, he *deserved* to lie flat on a sprung mattress and sleep for six or seven hours straight.

'I agree.' Renner gave him an uncompromising look. 'One of us definitely should go.'

Chapter Forty-Three

The three-star hotel Miller selected was one of many similar places only a few streets away from the train station, on the corner of a doglegged alley. He pulled his wallet from his pocket and removed enough cash to cover a couple of rooms for the night.

'Here,' he said, pressing the cash into Kate's hand. 'Check us in, get some rest, take a shower. Do whatever you need to do. Oh, and do me a favour. Check yourself in under a different surname, OK?'

'Why?'

'Variety. Try Grant.'

'Why Grant?'

'Because it's not Ryan and it's not Sutherland and I can remember it. Grant was my old headmaster.'

'How long will you be?'

'Not long. Don't go out before I'm back. Lock your room and don't let anyone else inside. I'll bring food with me.'

Kate peered in through the yellowed glass in the door to the hotel reception.

'What if they've followed us here?'

'They haven't.'

'But you're worried about my name, which suggests you're worried that they could track me down. And what if they find you?'

'They won't. They're on their way to Prague or Arles already. They have no idea where I'm going.'

'Neither do I.'

Miller stepped closer, lifting her chin. 'I'll be back soon, I promise. OK?'

Kate held his gaze, then fixed a wry smile on her face and shrugged her shoulders before stepping away and entering the hotel.

Miller waited across the street next to a pavement restaurant, faking interest in a menu board that featured aged colour photographs of the meals on offer. He counted off four minutes and declined two attempts by a waiter eager to get him to sit.

When he was finally satisfied that Kate wasn't going to reappear, and that nobody had followed her in, he turned and broke into a jog.

*

He was back in under an hour, by which time darkness had fallen and trade at the restaurant had picked up. The terrace was filled with sunburnt English couples, overweight men in football shirts and teenage backpackers. The night was humid, the air perfumed with the scent of charred pizza dough and sun lotion.

Miller walked into the hotel and approached the woman on duty at reception. She was late fifties or early sixties, short and stocky, with a swollen, pouched face and a matted wig that looked about as tired as her attitude.

Miller told her a friend had arranged a room for him and she scanned his duplicate passport without a great deal of interest before using a biro to enter his name and passport number into a form on a carbon-copy pad, having him sign it and passing him his tear-off receipt along with a room key. Letting the receptionist note down his passport details was a risk, but not a big one. The hotel facilities were basic and Miller didn't get the impression she was likely to upload his information to a computer database that could jeopardise his stay.

His room was on the second floor of the hotel, immediately opposite an antique caged elevator, and when he let himself in, he found that it was already occupied.

Kate was sitting on the end of the bed. She switched the television off with the remote in her hand and turned to face him. The room was brightly lit. Every available lamp and bulb seemed to be on.

'You made it,' she said. 'Got your passport?'

He lifted it in the air, feeling suddenly awkward and self-conscious. He took a step inside and let the door fall closed behind him. He didn't know how to stand, where to move.

What was she doing in his room?

'I suppose I could ask how you got that so fast, but I suspect I'd rather not know. Did you show it to the woman on reception? It's still in the name Miller, right?'

He nodded.

'She was giving me a hard time about not having ID myself. She almost wouldn't let me check in. I told her we'd been mugged. Did she ask you about it?'

He shook his head. 'I'm pretty sure she hears all kinds of stories from people wanting a room here on short notice.'

'I guess she does. It's kind of interesting that you asked me to check in under a different name when you're still going by

Miller. Care to explain why?' Kate hitched an eyebrow and held his eye for a beat too long before he feigned a sudden intense interest in his new passport. 'Well, maybe it's better I don't know. So, anyway . . . Kate Grant is going to take that shower now.'

She stood and passed through an open doorway on the far side of the room without looking back. Miller heard the squeal of taps being turned on worn washers, the splatter of water, the creaking and banging of the pipes running under the floorboards beneath his feet. He waited for Kate to close the bathroom door but the door remained open.

He looked about the room. It could have been any one of a hundred other cheap European hotel rooms he'd stayed in these past few years. The bed was a queen, sagging in the middle, the pillows lumpy, the mattress soft, all of it concealed beneath a dark green throw. The dressing table and the wardrobe were cheap self-assembly items, the laminate peeling and scratched. There were plastic drinking cups wrapped in cellophane on a tray by the bed, along with a dusty bottle of sparkling water and a rotary-dial telephone. And, apparently, there was an en suite with a working shower and a door that wouldn't close.

Miller crossed the room to a fabric armchair positioned beneath a window. He rested a knee on the chair, pushed open the window and looked out at the view. The view was of the grimy plaster of the wall opposite and a corroded drainpipe with a Vespa locked to the bottom of it, but if he craned his neck he could glimpse the pavement restaurant. He could hear the restless noise of the city, and he could feel wisps of shower steam drifting out the window past his head.

He turned and dropped into the chair, gripping hold of the armrests. He thought of Kate standing in the shower. He thought of the water cascading down over her body.

What was it about that door?

Had she left it open as an invitation, and if so, was it one he dared accept?

Or was it an indication of how secure she felt in his company, or of how scared she'd been by what had happened to Christine?

He heard laughter from the restaurant and the faint, caterwauling strain of guitar music.

He crossed his legs. Uncrossed them again. Kate had arranged for the receptionist to hand him a key to this room in particular. There was only one bed. There was the open door and the shower steam and then there was the wrench of taps being turned and the fading hiss and slow drumming of water and finally there was Kate coming through the doorway, wrapped in a white bath towel, her hair swept to one side in a dark red curl, the line of stitches a little raised on her forehead.

The towel wasn't all that big. The material was thin and it was wrapped very tightly around her body, extending from the tops of her breasts to the tops of her thighs. Miller could see a whole bunch of contours and dimensions, all of them good. No way of avoiding it. She was breathtaking.

She padded across the room, her feet leaving dark prints on the carpet, and sat down on the end of the bed, next to the television remote. She stroked the bedspread, then her hands came together on her thighs, fingers entwined, and she plucked absently at the frayed hem of the towel.

Looking up at him, she said, 'You're probably asking yourself about the room situation. You're probably wondering if I have a key to another room.'

'Do you?'

'Do you want one?'

He didn't say anything to that.

'It wasn't like in Hamburg. You didn't say we'd be staying in separate hotels. You could walk fifty metres in any direction from the front of this place and find fifty other hotels to stay in.'

Still Miller didn't speak. He was looking at her eyes, the way they were slightly downcast, the lids half closed. But his gaze wasn't focussed. His pupils were fully relaxed. He was taking in more than just her face. He was letting his gaze blur and cloud around the entirety of her. He couldn't look away.

She said, 'I thought that you wanted this. I thought you knew that I wanted it, too.'

Miller kept sitting. He kept staring. He didn't trust himself to move just yet.

'I don't normally shower for that long, Miller. Nobody showers for that long.'

An invitation. An open door.

Finally he stood and moved closer, standing before her at the end of the bed. He lingered a moment before reaching out his big hand and cupping her chin, tilting her face. He smiled and then he lowered his hand and he hooked a finger into the top of the towel, where the cotton rested snug against her breasts. He pulled her to her feet.

'I do,' he said. 'When I have company.'

*

Later, lying together in the muggy dark, the soft mattress caving in under Miller's weight, rolling them together, their legs and arms entangled, a warm, gritty breeze drifting in through the window, Miller stared up at the ceiling, thinking about the woman he was holding now and the woman he used to hold, asking himself if he deserved this, if he was allowed it, if he could be trusted to care for another person again.

'You forgot to bring food,' Kate whispered. 'You said you'd bring dinner back with you. That's when I knew for sure.'

He touched his nose to hers. He could feel a strand of her hair on his cheek. Her hand low down on his abdomen.

'I thought we could go out,' he said. 'There's a restaurant opposite the hotel.'

'It's gone midnight, Miller.'

'If you're hungry, I could fetch a takeaway.'

'No,' she said, her hand sliding round to the back of his thigh, pulling him towards her. 'I wouldn't like that at all.'

PART V

Arles, France

Chapter Forty-Four

Peter Kent, as he was now known, stood in his pyjamas at the bottom of the stairs with a bowl of breakfast cereal in each hand, listening to his daughter, Emily, sing a nursery rhyme in her bedroom. She was singing in French, which mesmerised and confounded him. His daughter's adjustment to their life in France had been much better than his own.

It wasn't long now until Emily would start as a pupil at the local primary school. She'd be taught in French and her friends would be French. With every day that went by, a little more of the Emily he knew would fade from him, and he feared the process of letting go.

There were important arrangements to be put in place before then, of course; contingencies to be planned, responses to be rehearsed. And there were the smaller, more ordinary matters to be taken care of. Like buying Emily a new bag for school.

The bag would have to look different to the Peppa Pig knapsack on the hook behind the front door. They couldn't ever be confused. The knapsack was there for emergencies only. It contained everything Emily needed if they ever had to leave in a hurry – her passport (as well as Pete's), spare clothes, a double of her favourite teddy bear, a photograph of her mother. It was the last thing Pete saw whenever they left the house and the first thing he checked when they got home.

It was a constant reminder of their very particular situation. As if he could ever forget.

He'd been lonely to begin with. Life in Arles had been tougher than he could have believed. But in the past year, things had begun to improve. They'd made friends, so there were people he could talk to. His broken French was getting better and he was starting to find that he could even think in French sometimes, without that awkward delay while he translated in his own mind what it was he needed to say.

He still missed home and family. He still missed talking with his friends back in England and he didn't imagine that would change. There were no phones in the house whatsoever. Not a landline. Not a mobile. It was a safety precaution insisted on by Miller, but one he was more than willing to comply with, since it was a mobile phone that had led them to their life here in Arles in the first place.

You'll never guess who I've just seen on this flight. Seriously weird! Will call soon x.

That was the last text Pete ever received from his wife, Zoe. As far as he knew, it was the last message Emily's mother sent out into the world.

Zoe had worked as a stewardess for a company that leased executive jets. Over the years, she'd flown with pop stars, with movie stars, with high-profile businessmen and wealthy families.

Normally, there were only three staff on any flight – Zoe, the pilot and the co-pilot. Zoe handled everything inside the passenger cabin. She served the drinks and the meals. She chatted with the clients if it seemed appropriate to do so or kept her distance if not. She was good at her job. She was professional and charming and she was always beautifully dressed and made up.

Perhaps too beautifully. That had bothered Pete a little. They'd married young, when Zoe had worked as cabin crew for a long-haul carrier and Pete had been starting out in air traffic control. He knew she loved her new job, that she was caught up in the glamour of it, and he'd been nervous about how she might react if one of her rich clients made a move.

Which should have been the least of his concerns. Because it turned out it wasn't only famous or wealthy people who hired executive jets. It was also people who needed to travel from country to country without ever being seen.

Pete never did guess who was on that flight. Zoe never had the chance to tell him. And he was certain it wasn't anything he ever wanted to know.

Zoe had been found in the toilet compartment of the jet by a ground crew at a remote airport on the eastern fringes of Ukraine. Her throat had been cut. The pilot and co-pilot had been shot through the back of the head, still strapped in their chairs.

Wallets, ID, jewellery and phones had been taken from all three of them. The phones included the mobile Zoe had texted Pete on shortly after they'd landed, in all likelihood just moments before she was killed.

The first he knew of her death was when the police showed up at the airport control tower in Manchester and ushered him into a side room. Later that night, when Emily was finally asleep and the family liaison officer had hugged him and left with a promise to return first thing in the morning, there was a knock on his back door and he met Nick Miller for the first time. Miller knew about Zoe and he knew about the text. He said he even knew who her mystery passenger had been.

The text was a big problem, he told Pete. It was as good as a death sentence for him and anyone he might have spoken to that day. Miller claimed that the British security services had colluded in the flight out of Manchester. He had images on an iPad that proved to Pete that the family liaison officer he'd just hugged wasn't a police officer at all. Miller said that he and Emily were in great danger and that there wasn't anyone Pete could turn to. Except for him.

And so Pete had. Because he believed what Miller had told him. Because he was afraid for himself and for Emily. Emily had lost one parent in bizarre circumstances already and he couldn't handle the idea that she might lose them both.

So now here they were, coming up for a year later, living in Arles; alive, adjusting, about to begin a new day.

Chapter Forty-Five

Kate's plane landed at Marseilles in the flat blue light of late afternoon, her nerves shaken by the unscheduled delay to her flight and too much bitter airline coffee. Inside the terminal building, she stood in line and waited to be beckoned forwards by a bored-looking passport official behind a scratched glass cubicle, where she handed over her new passport (now in the name Kate Edwards) and waited for what felt like several seconds too long as her face and her credentials were studied before she was finally acknowledged and waved on through.

She had no luggage to collect and no time to waste, so once she'd exited the airport building she veered away from the lines of dawdling tourists and shuffling taxis to hop on a transit bus out to the vast hire car collection point. The white Hyundai saloon that Hanson had reserved for her was parked out front of the Avis building with a child-safety seat already fitted in the back. Kate signed for it with her fake signature, handing over her false passport and driving licence for verification and copying. Then she scooped up the Hyundai's keys and sped away from the depot, rejoining the slip road to the airport and swooping into the drop-off zone outside of Departures.

Hanson and Becca were waiting for her there, standing together beside a revolving glass door, looking tired and frazzled. Hanson clambered into the rear of the Hyundai, dragging his laptop bag and cloth satchel behind him, while Becca popped the boot and stowed her carry-on suitcase before hurrying round and joining Kate in the front.

'Any problems?' she asked.

'None. You?'

'Only the embarrassment of watching Hanson try to charm the stewardess. Let's go.'

Kate pulled out from the kerb and accelerated away, watching her mirrors even though logic told her they couldn't have been followed because they were the ones playing catch-up.

She noticed that Hanson had opened his laptop and was poring over the screen.

'Anything?' she asked.

'Still nothing. I've posted a new message on the forum. Maybe that'll help.'

He didn't sound like he believed it, which wasn't surprising, because Kate didn't believe it either. The way their day was going, it felt like everything was against them. Kate had been forced to wait at the airport in Rome until Becca and Hanson had arrived with her new ID documents shortly before mid-morning. They'd had an hour to kill before the next available flight to Marseilles, but that hour had soon become three because of a problem with the landing gear on their plane. They'd investigated other flights, talked of splitting up and trying alternative routes, but none of the options were simple or fast. So they'd waited, all the while asking themselves if they were too late already, if one of Lane's men had beaten them to Pete and Emily.

At one point, in desperation, Kate had suggested contacting the local police in Arles, but Hanson had ruled it out. He said they had no credible way of explaining the threat Pete and Emily were facing without exposing them to even greater danger. Waiting was safer. They had to hold their nerve.

Tell that to Pete and Emily, Kate thought now, speeding north along the A7 *autoroute*, her window low, the warm wind ruffling her T-shirt and hair. Tell it to Clive.

Becca had called Miller's mobile with the news at three in the morning. Clive hadn't pulled through.

Miller had been silent for a long time, breathing heavily down the line, sitting up in bed, clutching his head, staring through the dark blue light towards the open window. Then he'd composed himself and told Becca to leave the hospital as soon as she could. Clive's death was a murder investigation now, he'd said, and as his self-declared sister, the police would want to speak with her in detail. It would be better for Becca to come to Rome with Hanson. Better for both of them to support Kate in Arles.

Then Miller had said how sorry he was, that Becca had made a difference to Clive in his last moments, and that because of that she'd also made a difference to him, too. He'd thanked her for it sincerely, and told her to stay strong, and then he'd hung up and walked through into the bathroom without another word.

Kate had stayed in bed, clutching the sheets around her, feeling a bewildering sense of loss and loneliness that had only grown worse when Miller had returned to the room and dressed quickly, pulling on his jeans and a shirt, sitting down on the side of the bed, resting a hand on her leg, telling her to be careful if she went ahead and travelled to Arles. He'd said she could still back out if she wanted. She didn't have to go. But if she chose to commit to helping Pete and Emily, then she should drive directly to their house and only park up and approach if it seemed safe from the outside. If she spotted Renner or Wade, if she felt threatened or at risk, she should turn and go.

But of course, if she saw one of Lane's men then in all likelihood they would have seen her, too. And even supposing she was able to get away, how could she run and abandon someone else to the terrible things that had been done to Clive and Christine?

Kate glanced over her shoulder at the child seat in the rear. A kid was caught up in this situation now and that made it so much worse than before. Without Miller she felt cast adrift and untethered, left to speed towards a situation that seemed too big and complex for her to handle.

She missed having him beside her. She missed the connection they shared, something genuine and kinetic that she'd experienced from the very first night he'd broken into her life. She'd trusted him because of what had happened afterwards, but she also knew that, deep down, part of her had wanted to believe in him from that very first encounter.

So was she driving to Arles to impress him, to act on some kind of dumb infatuation? Or was her motivation more noble than that?

Hard to tell. Impossible to know. But it seemed that she was doing it all the same. It seemed that she wouldn't back out.

'Something on your mind?' Becca asked.

'Just nervous. And feeling sad about Clive.'

'Uh-huh. Because if it's something else, Gadget Boy isn't listening to us right now. He gets this way when he's working on his laptop. It's like he's plugged into the Matrix or something. We can talk girl-to-girl.'

Kate kept her gaze on the asphalt and the traffic.

'You got a piece of Miller, didn't you? You guys finally hooked up.'

Kate didn't respond.

'Was it good? I bet it was hot. Last night, right? Rome. A strange hotel. Lots of emotions rolling around.'

'Just so you know,' Hanson spoke up, from the back, 'I *can* hear you.'

'Exactly how many times did you guys do it? More than once, right?'

'Don't answer that,' Hanson said. 'I don't want images of Miller like that in my head. Seriously, if you answer that question I'm opening this door right now and rolling out.'

'Relax,' Kate told him. 'Becca's just fishing. And I'm not going to bite.'

She slowed and glided towards the toll station that lay ahead of them, Becca squinting at her forensically as she squirmed in her seat and dug in her pocket for some loose euro coins to toss into the machine. The barrier lifted and she pulled away, sliding up her window, her eyes flicking to Hanson in her mirror.

'Miller's wife,' she said. 'Sarah. He told me you help him because of her.'

'He said that to you?'

'He said I should ask you about it if I want to know more. So that's what this is. I'm asking.'

Hanson blinked, the whites of his eyes red-tinged and magnified by the lenses of his spectacles. He tipped his head from side to side, weighing it up. Then he sucked on his lips and nodded.

'Anna Brooks. I was like her once. Except I was one of the

253

first kids Sarah helped at the Shelter. She took me in off the street. She talked with me, listened to me.'

'I had no idea. I'd never have guessed.'

'Because Sarah saved me, just like she saved hundreds of other kids. She set me straight. Gave me security, stability. She got me access to computers, even set me up with some advanced programming experience at local companies.'

'And you feel like you owe her because of that.'

'I do owe her. But honestly? I also owe the thousands of other kids who'll never get to have what I had because of what Connor Lane took from them. The ones who'll never meet Sarah.'

'But Connor funded the Shelter. He still does.'

'Sure. And he got a neat tax break from doing it, maybe some slaps on the back from politicians, people with influence. But Sarah was the one who made a real difference. To me, and to lots of kids like me. Russell Lane dishonoured that, but his brother? By killing Sarah he ripped the heart right out of that place.'

Becca reached back, touching Hanson's leg, and he looked away for a moment, leaving Kate to stare ahead at the road, absorbing his words. She was closing fast on a line of trucks, getting ready to indicate and swing out to overtake. When she glanced at her mirror again, Hanson was waiting for her.

'That's why I understand what you gave up to be a part of this,' he told her. 'The search for your brother? Walking away from that link to your family? I get it, Kate. I do. I walked away from the same thing myself. But only because Sarah gave me a future. Because of her, Miller and Becca are the only family I need right now.'

Kate understood what he meant, but it wasn't the same thing. Not really. She hadn't chosen to leave her birth family behind. Her parents had left her. And as for Richard, she still hoped, deep down, to find her way to him some day. She wasn't prepared to let go of that particular dream just yet. She doubted she ever would.

Chapter Forty-Six

Jennifer Lloyd got out of her car in front of a pebble-dashed bungalow in Lancaster, stepped over a garden hose and approached a balding man in a blue jumpsuit and rubber boots who was washing a small car.

'Mr Brooks?'

Suds dripped from the sponge in his hand, splatting on the ground.

'I'm DS Lloyd. I spoke with your wife. It's about Anna.'

'You'd best come in. Have some tea.'

The tea was as weak and lifeless as Mr and Mrs Brooks. Lloyd found herself sitting opposite them in a chintzy living room, snared by a silence as complete as any she'd ever known.

'This is lovely, thank you.' She raised her cup in the air.

The Brookses were almost completely still; their mouths tightly closed, skin puckered and drawn. A carriage clock ticked quietly on the mantelpiece, flanked by two framed photos of Anna in school uniform. She looked ten or eleven in one of the photographs. Perhaps a year or two older in the next. Her hair was frizzy, her chin speckled with pimples, her smile hesitant and gap-toothed.

'You're probably wondering why I'm here.'

Lloyd's hosts didn't say a word.

'I know this might be painful but I hoped you might tell me

about Anna. I'd like to try and find her.'

Their heads twitched and they looked at one another, eyes vague.

'We don't understand.' Mrs Brooks's voice was tight and waspish. 'Is she in trouble?'

'That's not why I'm here. I'd just like to find her and make sure that she's safe.'

And I'd like to know if Nick Adams is hiding her. I'd like to know if she could tell me where I might find *him*.

'We haven't seen Anna since the day after her fifteenth birthday.' Mr Brooks's tone was neutral, his gaze unfocussed. 'Not since she ran away.'

'When was the last time you heard from her?'

'She never got in touch. We only know what happened in Manchester because of the papers. And because of the police officers who came to talk to us afterwards.'

'We tried speaking to her before then,' Mrs Brooks added quietly. 'We visited the shelter where she was staying before the trial, but she wouldn't see us.'

'What about the police officers who spoke with you after she left the shelter?'

'They didn't stay long. They told us there wasn't much they could do. Anna was sixteen by then. She could go where she liked.'

Lloyd felt reduced by their words, shamed by their fatalism. Because the truth was that in the wake of the deaths of Sarah and Melanie Adams, none of her colleagues had made a concerted, co-ordinated effort to find Anna. Not even Lloyd.

And why? Because she was a runaway. Nobody had cared enough to wonder where she might have gone.

Except for her parents, probably. She guessed they worried about it every day.

'I'm sorry.' Lloyd set her cup aside, shuffling forwards in her chair and pressing her hands together. 'But that was wrong. *We* were wrong. And I'd like to fix things, if I can. I'd like to be the one to help you find Anna. I'd like to try and make it so that you can talk to her again. But to do that, I need to ask you questions about her.'

Mr Brooks reached across for his wife's hand.

'Ask us then,' he said. 'Ask us anything you need to know.'

Chapter Forty-Seven

The plan changed when they reached Arles. It was evening, twilight fading rapidly, and Kate found that she couldn't drive to Pete and Emily's house because the walled town was closed to traffic, shut off by an endless sequence of metal barriers, plastic cones and uniformed police. She circled the outskirts, finding no way through, until eventually she pulled over by the banks of the Rhône river, cut the engine and cracked her window.

She could hear music – a fast, percussive beating of drums – mixed with boisterous clapping and shouts. On the far side of the patch of sandy earth where she'd parked, people were queuing in front of food vans serving pizza, paella, burgers and frites. Gaseous generators spewed noxious fumes into the warm dusk.

'Uh-oh.' Hanson looked up from his phone. 'There's a bull-fighting festival going on. Pedestrian access only.'

'So what do we do?'

'We walk in,' Becca said.

'All of us? Isn't that a bit risky?'

Kate was thinking of Miller's instructions. He'd been very clear about only getting out of the car if she was sure it was safe.

'Hanson can stay here. If we need to leave in a hurry, he can pick us up.'

'I'll guide you in.' He pecked at his laptop keyboard. 'I've called up a map. Stay on your mobile and I can track your movements.'

'Neat idea.' Becca plucked the satnav from its cradle on the dash and shoved open her door. 'But I think somebody already invented just the tool we need. Sit tight, kiddo. Leave this one to us.'

*

Mike Renner's legs ached and his feet were hot and swollen inside his loafers. He'd spent hours already going from bar to bar, shop to shop, growing sweatier, more frustrated. He was carrying a photograph he'd printed from one of the few news articles he'd been able to find online about the killings of the crew of an executive jet in Ukraine. He'd shown the photograph to hundreds of people, shouting over music, being jostled and pushed, asking if anyone recognised the man and the little girl being hugged by the smiling stewardess.

Nobody did. Nobody cared. And now Renner had an overwhelming need for space, for air. He wanted to be in a place where he wasn't being bumped into constantly, where people didn't dance around him or spill beer on his clothes.

Arles wasn't a big place, yet Renner felt like he'd walked every inch of it twice already. Surely an Englishman and his daughter would stand out. They'd be memorable. Which worried him. Because what if he'd screwed up by running with Wade's plan? What if the information on the iPad had been a plant and Adams had sent them off on a fool's errand?

From what Renner had come to know of Adams these past few years, it was the type of stunt he was capable of pulling off.

But was it likely? He had no way of telling. The only thing he was sure of was that his patience was running low, his persistence dwindling. He was almost ready to quit. He wanted out of this cramped town, the whole place feeling to him like one big closed fist, squeezing and crushing him.

A street stall lay ahead, selling freshly squeezed lemonade in plastic cups burrowed deep in trays of chipped ice. There was no queue. Everyone else seemed too busy getting drunk.

Renner removed his sun hat as he approached, longing to grab a handful of ice and clamp it to his neck. He nodded at one of the young men running the stall – a muscular guy with curly brown hair and a deep tan who looked like a surfer or a climber – and set his hat to one side, propping the photograph on its brim.

The young man glanced at the image, then glanced again. His face brightened and he asked Renner in broken English how he knew Peter and Emily.

'Pete's a friend of mine,' Renner said, smiling himself now. 'Emily's precious, isn't she?'

The young man nodded eagerly and smiled some more as Renner reached into his back pocket to remove the crumpled map of Arles he'd picked up at the bus station.

'Maybe you can help me? We're meant to be meeting, but I've lost their address. Can you show me where they live?'

Chapter Forty-Eight

Kate ducked beneath an archway running through the old town walls and joined a throng of people hemmed in tight between the jumble of tilted houses. Above her, more people were leaning out of windows, drinking, smoking and laughing. Dusk had fallen.

Becca bumped into her from behind, turning the satnav in her hands, the screen glowing brightly in the dim. She'd muted the voice instructions but the device still drew attention to them in a way Kate didn't like.

'OK,' Becca said, beginning to move. 'So we basically need to head the same way as everyone else.'

'It's massively crowded.'

'Good for cover.'

Kate skipped after her. 'I really wish we'd heard from Miller.'

'Don't worry. He gets this way sometimes. He'll be in touch.'

Would he? When? Kate wanted to hear his voice and felt foolish for it. What could he possibly say to reassure her? He was hundreds of miles away, and he had other concerns that were more pressing than her.

The confined street was alive with people and talk and laughter. The crowds thickened and slowed, the street widening into a cramped square where a makeshift bodega had been constructed amid some lime trees and a brightly lit fountain.

'Head for the hotel,' Becca shouted.

'What hotel?'

'Over there.'

She pointed towards a canvas awning outside a hotel terrace on the far side of the square, gas lamps flickering around it, and Kate wrestled her way forwards.

By the time she got close, Becca was moving again, waving towards a distant street, and Kate floundered after her until they were within sight of the central Roman amphitheatre, its dun stone walls being strafed by the coloured beams of a son et lumière.

Blood-red banners were draped from stone buttresses and street lamps, all of them featuring snarling black bulls. The queue to get inside the arena was closer to a scrum and Kate, who'd lost sight of Becca, twirled madly around before she finally glimpsed her standing on tip-toes and waving from beneath a stone colonnade.

'This is nuts,' she said, pushing her way through to her.

'It's not far now. See for yourself.'

Kate took the satnav until she could see the circular icon that was tracking their progress and the checked black-and-white flag that marked their destination. Becca was right, they were close, but it took another twenty minutes of shoving and weaving to force their way through to the correct street, by which time it was almost full dark.

The alleyway was thin and forgotten, the sandstone walls of the buildings that pressed in and towered over them scuffed from the bumpers of passing vehicles, reminding Kate sickeningly of Rome and of Christine. The way ahead seemed strangely hushed and they walked forwards in silence, scanning the blown-plaster walls and paint-flaked doors, until Becca spotted the right address.

The house was a terraced building faced in pale, unfinished stone, the front wall bulging in the middle, supported by a metal brace. The number 17 had been drawn over the hardwood door in marker pen.

Kate stepped back and looked up. The windows were in darkness, the wooden shutters pulled closed upstairs. She checked the street both ways but the only movement was the play of coloured lights from the direction of the amphitheatre.

'Should I knock?' she asked Becca.

'It's why we're here, isn't it?'

So Kate rapped her fist on the timber. No response. She looked at Becca, then beyond her at the empty alley again. She knocked a second time, a little quieter.

'Maybe they're asleep,' Becca whispered.

Kate nodded, but a bolus of fear was rising in her throat. She didn't like the unnatural silence in this lonely street. She didn't like the darkness. And she especially didn't like the memory that flashed through her mind, unbidden, of stepping inside Clive's apartment back in Hamburg, of the dread she'd experienced, knowing that something terrible had occurred within those walls.

Miller had told her that Emily was only four years old, so it was possible she was asleep in bed. But that didn't account for Pete not answering.

Could one of Lane's men be on the other side of the door, listening? Or had he been and gone already? Was that why there was no answer?

A crooked sash window was fitted into the wall to the side of the door and Kate swallowed dryly as she took a step towards it. She peered inside, seeing nothing but blackness, and tapped a nail on the glass.

'Try opening it,' Becca said.

Which Kate thought was a fine suggestion to make, coming from someone who was safely off to one side. But she braced the heels of both hands under the frame, took a breath, and pushed. And . . . nothing.

'OK. Stand aside.'

Becca barged her out of the way, hopping on one foot, removing her shoe. She held the shoe by the toe, the heel jutting outwards, and then she covered her face with her free arm and whipped the shoe back behind her shoulder.

'*Je peux vous aider?*'

Becca shortened her swing just in time, bringing her shoe up shy of the glass. She whirled round and stared up with Kate to where a middle-aged woman was hanging out of a neighbouring window, her hair wet and knotted, a towel draped over her shoulders.

'We're looking for our friends,' Kate said. 'They told us to meet them here.'

'*Là-bas.*' The woman smiled, perhaps thinking they were tipsy, and pointed down the street. '*Dans le parc.*' And, when Kate hesitated, she repeated the instruction. '*Le parc.*'

Still Kate didn't move. She was thinking about asking the woman for more information. It was possible that she'd seen one of Lane's men come here before them. It was possible she'd talked to them or offered them directions, too. But Becca had already slipped her shoe back on and was tottering off down the lane, so Kate waved her thanks and rushed to catch up.

The alley followed a long, tight curve, and Kate glanced

back over her shoulder before the house was completely out of sight. There was no sign of anybody tracking them but she couldn't escape the sensation of being watched. Paranoia, she told herself. It was an understandable reaction to everything she'd been through.

It struck her then, with sudden force, that this would be her life from now on. A life of constant anxiety and nerves, of being watchful and cautious, of having to always choose doubt instead of trust. Connor Lane had done this to her, just as he'd done the same and worse to Miller, and just as someone unknown to her had scared Peter Kent so badly that he'd been forced to sweep up his daughter and flee.

She quickened her pace, feet skipping over the cobblestones, Becca cursing her heels as she fell behind. And then there Kate was, abruptly and without warning, bursting in upon a scene of such simple beauty that she stopped on the spot.

A park, the woman had called it, but this was something far more magical. Kate could see a roundabout and a swing, a rusted old climbing frame and a wooden bench on a square of dusty soil. Fairy lights and paper lanterns had been strung up around the area, dangling from walls and laundry lines, twirled around the frame of the climbing equipment and laced through the umbrella branches of a lone Aleppo pine. The glow was soft and welcoming, the air laced with the sweet, smoky scent of barbecue.

Twenty or so people were gathered together; a collection of adults and children of various ages.

Miller had shown Kate a photograph of Pete and Emily on his phone the previous night. If she closed her eyes, she could still conjure up the image. In it Pete was sunburnt with chapped lips. He had a broad build, black curly hair and a startled look in his eyes. His daughter, Emily, was sitting on his shoulders. She had a gapped-tooth smile and a head of corkscrew blonde locks and she was wearing a Peppa Pig T-shirt over pink shorts, her knees skinned and grimy. Kate had studied the shot for a long time. She'd absorbed every detail of it.

But she didn't need it now.

Pete must have sensed something in Kate's bearing, or perhaps the way she stopped short and stared, because he reacted right away, swooping down to hoist Emily from the picnic blanket she was sitting on, cradling her in his arms, even before Becca had caught up to them, raising her hand, out of breath.

Kate found that she couldn't move or look away. She was transfixed by Pete's darkly gleaming eyes, by the worry and the knowing brimming over in them.

She shook her head and whispered, 'You don't know who I am.'

'It's OK.' Pete swallowed hard as Emily burrowed her face into his chest. 'Tonight was too perfect, anyway. I should have known.'

'We're so sorry,' Becca told him.

'How long do we have?'

'No time at all. You need to come with us right now.'

Chapter Forty-Nine

Jennifer Lloyd waited in the car park of a motorway services just south of Lancaster. There was still no sign of Young or Foster, and no missed calls or messages on her phone. Squeezing hard on the squash ball in her hand, she flipped open the Manila file on the passenger seat and dialled a number she'd scrawled at the bottom of the inside cover.

Lloyd was prepared to leave a message. It was mid-evening and she didn't expect anyone to pick up. But to her surprise a woman answered in a tired, end-of-the-day tone.

'Manchester Coroner's Office.'

Lloyd gave the woman her name and rank and told her that she'd like to make an appointment to speak with Thomas McGuintyre, Her Majesty's Senior Coroner, early the following morning. She kept an eye out of the windscreen as she spoke, wondering if Young and Foster had decided to skip their meeting altogether, feeling her resentment fester and build.

'So would I, Detective Sergeant, believe me. But I'm afraid Tom's no longer with us. He suffered a stroke last year and died a month later. I certified his death myself. I'm Julia Summerhayes, Tom's replacement.'

Lloyd muttered condolences, thrown for a moment. 'Perhaps you can help me? I have a question related to an old file he signed off on. Sarah and Melanie Adams. They were a mother and daughter who were shot inside their home just over four years ago. Their bodies were burned.'

'I remember. Tom was very affected by it. I was an assistant coroner at the time. What is it you wanted to know?'

Lloyd paused, trying to decide on her best approach.

'Am I right in thinking that the relatives of a victim have the right to request a copy of the coroner's findings, if they so wish?'

'They can, in theory. But in my experience it's not very often that anybody does.'

'Did anybody in this case?'

'Forgive me,' the coroner said, 'but am I to assume this is related to the police appeal that's been in the news? If you're wondering if Nick Adams requested the file because it might somehow lead you to him, I have to tell you that's highly unlikely.'

It was precisely what Lloyd had been hoping, though it bothered her to have the idea shot down so fast.

'It's one of several avenues we'd like to explore.'

'I see. And no doubt you'll tell me this is urgent.'

'Top priority.'

'Then let me try to catch my assistant before he leaves for the day. Is this the best number to call you back on?'

Lloyd said that it was, then lowered her phone and scanned the car park once more, looking towards the lighted canopy of the petrol station and a Travelodge where she felt pretty sure she'd be spending the night. Her eyes swept back again and this time she caught sight of John Young holding open a door at the entrance of the services for Nadine Foster to pass through.

Lloyd shut the file, locked her car and caught up to them at a table in the buffet cafeteria. Young was sprinkling salt over a plate of pie and chips, his silk tie dangling towards a smear of ketchup. Foster was clutching a mug of mint tea.

Lloyd searched Foster's face as she dropped into a seat across from her but Foster kept her expression neutral, waiting until Young was shovelling chips into his mouth before scowling in warning and shaking her head. Lloyd took the gesture to mean that Foster hadn't yet found anything to suggest that Kate Sutherland's file had been accessed in a suspicious manner, nor that the information on her whereabouts in the Isle of Man had been sold by a member of the team. She also took it to mean that Foster didn't want her to mention her suspicions in front of Young.

So maybe, Lloyd thought, their system had been hacked by somebody on the *outside* – the same somebody, possibly, with the ability to erase border-control flags and doctor the passenger manifests of international airlines.

'Nice place, Lloyd,' Foster muttered, tucking her elbows into her body as if she feared contamination.

Young looked up from his plate. 'The food's OK. You should eat. We won't be back in London until late.'

'Was this even necessary?'

Lloyd shrugged. 'We were all in the same area and I'm going to be stuck here for another couple of days, at least. How did it go with Lane?'

Foster pushed her mouth to one side without saying anything. Young grunted.

'That well, huh?'

'His lawyer was a right pain in the arse.'

'Did Lane answer *any* questions?'

'He told us his only connection to the Isle of Man is some offshore accounts he holds. Rich bastard. You should see his house.'

'And what about hired help? Have any of them taken a trip to the island recently?'

'That was one of the questions he couldn't answer.'

'Shocking.'

Young and Foster shared a look. It was the kind of look Lloyd was used to people sharing around her. She imagined they were going to devote quite some time to bitching about her on their drive back south.

'I may have something,' she said, feeling suddenly nervous. 'Anna Brooks. I think it's possible Nick Adams could have helped her to hide from Lane.'

Young stared at her, a forkful of pie halfway to his lips. 'And this is the same Nick Adams you think is a killer.'

'If I'm right and we can find Anna—'

'Then maybe we can find Adams, too,' Foster said.

Lloyd nodded, waiting in silence as Foster looked at Young again. Finally, Young sighed and set his knife and fork down on the table.

'All right.' He wiped his lips with his fingers. 'I'll bite. How do we find Anna Brooks? Another media appeal? I can't see that going over too well with Commissioner Bennett.'

'Epilepsy,' Lloyd replied.

And then she explained how Anna's parents had told her that they believed their daughter's medical condition had been the trigger for many of her problems. She'd had her first seizure at the age of eleven, two weeks into life at her new secondary school. She'd been bullied because of it. She'd been isolated.

Her self-confidence had taken a knock and her resentment had grown.

Three years later, Anna had accused her physics teacher of inappropriate sexual behaviour. Her parents were dubious and the charges hadn't stuck. Ultimately, her accusations were proved false. The episode was chalked up as a plea for attention – ADHD was a corollary of her condition – and it triggered a fresh onslaught of bullying. Before Anna's parents could look at moving her to a different school, she ran away, leaving behind a note that blamed them for her decision.

Young whistled. 'So Anna Brooks had a history of false accusations of sexual assault. That could have seriously hurt her credibility if her case against Russell had come to court.'

'And you can bet Russell's lawyers would have been all over it when they were preparing his defence. Not that it came to that.'

'So how does Anna's epilepsy help us to find her?'

'These are the drugs she was taking.' Lloyd passed over a scrap of paper on which Mrs Brooks had printed the information in slanted biro. 'It's not a typical combination. And it was an ongoing treatment. Chances are, she'll still be on these meds today.'

Foster shook her head. 'Talk about a long shot.'

'We can contact the suppliers. Contact health authorities. We can narrow the field by asking them to notify us of any female patients in their early twenties prescribed this exact drug combination.'

'*We?* This is a crazy amount of work.'

'So let's get some uniforms to run with it. We put two or three of them on it for—'

Lloyd raised a finger. Her mobile phone was ringing. She lifted it to her ear.

'DS Lloyd? Julia Summerhayes. I had my assistant call up the files for Sarah and Melanie Adams.'

'And?'

'Can I ask where you are you right now?'

Lloyd felt a prickle of excitement. A flutter in her belly.

'I'm outside Lancaster. Close to the motorway. Why do you ask?'

'Because this really isn't something I'm keen to discuss over the phone. Could you drop by my offices? I'll be working late this evening. There's something I think you should see.'

Chapter Fifty

The first thing Pete said as he carried Emily away from the park was, 'We have to go back to the house.'

'You can't,' Kate told him.

'Five minutes. That's all I need.'

'We have a car waiting for you down by the river.'

'And we have a whole life to walk away from here. Five minutes isn't much to ask.'

But it was. And Kate knew that Miller would never have allowed it.

'We have a go-bag all ready and packed. It contains our ID, plus a few of Emily's things. Her favourite teddy. Stuff we can't leave behind.' He turned to Becca. 'Please. For Emily.'

Kate said, 'Someone will come back for your stuff. Miller, maybe.'

Emily had been crying softly since they'd left the park but she was becoming more distressed as the discussion continued. Pete shushed her, cupping her head.

'No, we get it now.' He stopped dead in the alley. 'We won't go otherwise.'

Kate stared at him, disbelieving. He was holding Emily tight, his chin propped on the top of her head, a determined look on his face. It was already clear to her that he was willing to break Miller's rules. The hurried farewells he'd said to their friends in the park – the whispered conversations and the solemn hugs and the tears – suggested that he'd confided in people about their situation.

'Have you seen anyone hanging round outside your house? Anyone you haven't seen before?'

'There's a festival going on. I've been seeing strangers for days.'

'Has anyone threatened you? Has anyone suspicious approached you in any way?'

'Do you really think we'd still be here if they had?'

'Easy, Miss Marple.' Becca raised her hand. 'You're scaring the little one. And don't look at me that way,' she told Pete. 'Kate's right. It's dangerous. We can't all go.'

'Then how about you go into the house and grab the bag for us? I have a car just down the street. I can get it and drive us all out of here.'

Kate shook her head. 'The roads are closed.'

'Trust me, I know a way. I've planned for this. I'm *always* planning for this. Five minutes maximum. I promise.'

Kate stared through the dark towards the bend in the alley. She could hear the pulse of distant flamenco music and the hum of crowd noise from inside the amphitheatre. If Lane's men were really coming, surely they should have arrived by now. Unless they were waiting. And watching.

Becca stepped close to Pete. She caressed Emily's face. 'It's OK, baby girl,' she said. 'Becca's going to fetch your things.'

'You don't have to do this,' Kate told her.

'Here, you take her.'

Pete thrust the girl towards Kate before she was ready. Emily screamed and tried to hold on to Pete but Kate grappled with her, wrapping an arm around her tiny waist, the girl bucking against her, reaching for her father, shouting 'no' over and over.

'Be good.' Pete blew her a kiss. 'Daddy will be back soon.'

'I'll wait five minutes,' Kate told Becca, struggling to look past Emily. 'If you're not back by then, I'm taking her to Hanson.'

Becca nodded, turning to go. She broke into a jog, chasing after Pete, her wide hips swaying, backside juddering, her plump arms swinging.

Kate watched the darkness swallow them, their footsteps thumping off the cobblestones, echoing off the close-packed buildings, the noise fading to nothing as first Pete then Becca rounded the bend.

Emily squealed and bucked but the worst of the fight had gone out of her now that her dad was out of sight. Kate hushed her and held her. She whispered in her ear.

'Emily, your daddy's going to be back soon. Please be still. He won't be long.'

She lowered her to the ground, keeping a tight hold of her arm as she dropped to one knee and swept her hair back from her eyes. The girl sniffed and shied away, her face a damp, pink mush, snot glistening on her cheek.

'Everything's going to be OK. I promise.'

Emily gave her a wary, sideways look. 'Who are you?'

'My name is Kate. I'm a friend of your daddy's. I'm here to keep you safe.'

'Are the bad men coming?'

'No, sweetheart. No. Look.' She pulled back her sleeve and showed Emily her watch. 'Your daddy and Becca will be with us again before the big hand hits fifteen. OK?'

Emily gripped Kate's wrist and pressed her nose to her

watch. Kate could smell the barbecue smoke in her hair and clothes.

'Come over here with me. Sit down, OK?'

Kate led her to an alcove beneath a dim street lamp where a metal shutter was drawn across a half-glazed door. It looked like the entrance to some kind of workshop.

They huddled together on the stoop, the girl fixated on Kate's watch while Kate did her best to ignore the whispers and murmured conversation from a group of Pete's friends who were edging towards them from the park. It was obvious they were concerned for Emily. It sounded as if they were asking one another if they should intervene.

Kate willed them not to. She didn't want Emily getting any more upset.

'Will Miller be here?' Emily asked, frowning up at the stitches on Kate's forehead.

'You'll see him soon.'

'I like Miller. He's nice.'

Kate forced a smile, conscious of the perspiration that was breaking out on her face and upper lip. Her pulse was racing. Fear churned in her stomach.

Then a male voice called out to them. One of Pete's friends, a man in his late fifties or early sixties, had broken away from the others. He was crouched at the waist, extending a hand towards Emily. He called her name and Emily sniffed and smiled. He beckoned some more and she strained against Kate's grip, ready to go to him, but Kate tugged her back.

The group from the park didn't like it.

The man grew bolder, stepping closer. Kate fixed her jaw, shaking her head, warning him off. She wasn't sure what she might do exactly. It was hard to know how best to handle the situation.

She never had the chance to find out.

The quiet of the street was torn through by the brash note of an engine and the patter of tyres on cobblestones. Kate turned her head and saw a slanted yellow light climb the walls along the alley, then a pair of headlamps swept round. She shielded her eyes from the glare and pulled Emily to her feet, pushing her behind her. She couldn't see what type of vehicle it was. She couldn't see anything at all.

The headlamps sped closer, then the vehicle braked hard, bearing down at the front, brake lights blooming at the rear. It was a dusty Citroën estate.

'Daddy,' Emily squealed. 'That's Daddy's car.'

She yanked on Kate's arm, dragging her through the head-lamp beams, twisting sideways to fit between the car and the wall. She reached for a handle on a rear door, opening it against brickwork as a dome light came on at the front, shining down over Pete and Becca and a dark, hunched figure crouched low in the back.

Kate only glimpsed Mike Renner for a fraction of a second. It was barely enough time for her to comprehend what she'd seen. Renner had a gun pressed to the back of Becca's head. Her hands were in the air.

'Run!' Pete yelled, and the car shot forwards, Renner's head rocking back. The open door knocked Emily into Kate before slamming shut as the vehicle sped on.

'Daddy!'

The car kept going, accelerating towards Pete's friends. They scattered and ducked, diving for cover, the man who'd called

278

out to Emily flattening himself against the wall of a house. The car veered away from him and raced on until Kate saw a flash of light inside the cabin and heard a double pop followed by the shattering of glass. Her legs flexed. Her stomach dropped. The car slewed right, slamming into a wall, scraping to a halt as a terrible, high-pitched scream escaped from the front.

There was stillness for an instant, then another stutter of light and a loud pop, and the screaming stopped altogether.

A rear door was thrown open, butting into the wall, and Kate saw the dark, hunched figure of Mike Renner force his way out.

She didn't wait any longer.

Pushing off from her standing foot, she lifted Emily from the ground and hoisted her over her shoulder, covering a good fifteen metres before she looked back to see Renner bumping off the wall, staggering towards the rear of the car, his dark form backlit by the scarlet brake lights. He was listing to one side, limping heavily. He had a pistol in his hand.

'Daddy!' Emily screamed. 'My Daddy!'

She reached backwards over Kate's shoulder, clawing at the air.

'Stay still,' Kate said.

'Daddy!'

Kate ran on, tussling with the girl, aware she was hurting her but unable to let go.

She looked back a second time, almost falling, and saw Renner hobbling through drifts of steam and smoke, his left leg dragging behind him.

The man who'd approached Emily shouted loudly, then leapt forwards, lunging for Renner's gun.

Which was a bad idea.

Renner batted him away and raised his pistol in a two-handed grip, firing a single round into the man's lower leg. The man dropped and yelped and squirmed on the floor as a chorus of screams and cries rose up, varying in pitch and volume and duration, bounding after Kate as she whipped her head forwards and pumped her knees hard and kicked for the curve in the alley ahead.

Chapter Fifty-One

Take Emily out of the equation and Kate could have outrun a man half Renner's age. Factor in the way he was limping heavily, swinging his left leg from his hip, and Kate would have been confident of sprinting clear. But Emily was weighing her down, fighting against her, flailing and writhing so unpredictably that Kate lost her balance and bashed into a wall.

'Stay still,' she yelled, but Emily dug a knee into Kate's chest and tried clambering over her shoulder, almost toppling them both.

'Daddy!' Emily screamed again.

'Stop it,' Kate told her. 'Get down.'

Kate pinched her on the flank. But it was no good. The girl just fought even harder.

They'd barely covered two hundred metres and already Kate was struggling. The added weight was jarring her bad knee. The pain was sharp and gnarly, hot needles in the joint.

'You have to be still. Emily, you have to be.'

The girl was getting in her face, blocking her airways, obscuring her view. The festival crowds weren't far away. Five hundred metres, maybe less. But there was only a straight, downhill gradient ahead of them, and while the alley was getting blacker every moment, once Renner lumbered round the corner, he'd have a clear shot.

The house where Emily had been living was coming up fast

on the left and for a second Kate thought of stopping to try the door. But if it was locked, she'd have lost momentum and time, and if it was open, she had no way of knowing what she might find inside. Renner appeared to be alone but perhaps Wade was here, too.

Sweat sheeted Kate's brow, stinging her eyes. Walls and doors whipped by in a jolting blur.

And that was when she saw an opening in the wall ahead. Make that two openings.

First was a narrow passageway carved into the street between two tall buildings, a street lamp shining weakly just inside the entrance.

The second opening was a garage in the ground floor of the next building along. Kate thought back to what Pete had said about having his car parked nearby. She guessed this was where it had been stored.

She could hide in the garage, but not while Emily was fighting her. And if Renner found them there, they'd be trapped.

The alley then.

She wheeled right, into the passage, streaking through the lamplight and on into the funnelling black.

She ran on instinct, on trust, unable to see if there were obstacles in her way. Her arms and hips smashed into brick and pipework as Emily lurched from side to side, reaching outwards, clawing her fingers into the powdery render.

Kate ran harder, kicking on, until she felt a sharp pain in her upper arm. Emily was biting her. She swore and released her and Emily fell to the ground, Kate clattering into her, losing her footing, starting to tumble.

Her knees struck stone, followed by her hands and her chin.

Emily cried out, then pushed up and turned to run in the direction they'd come from. Kate grabbed her wrist. She yanked her back and spun her round, clutching her to her chest.

A shadow sliced through the light at the end of the passageway and Kate saw Renner hobble towards them, his body twisted at the hip, his left shoulder lifting in time with his gimpy leg. One arm cradled his flank, as if he'd sustained a blow to his kidney, his gun held low at his side.

He peered at them, jutting his chin forwards, then straightened his arm and lifted his gun. There was a flash of light, an explosion of noise, the ping and ricochet of a bullet skipping over Kate's head.

'Run.' She shoved Emily. 'Faster. Move.'

How many shots had Renner fired now? Was it five?

He was using an automatic pistol but Kate had no way of telling how many rounds it held. He most likely had a spare magazine with him as well. Maybe more than one.

She tripped over Emily's heels, grasping her slim hips, using her momentum to drive her on. Emily screamed and streaked ahead – running from Kate as much as from Renner – and when, all of a sudden, they emerged from the darkness into a dimly lit cross street, they were sprinting so hard they rammed into a shutter that had been pulled down in front of a shop.

Emily bounced off the gridded metal and fell to her side. Kate clung on, winded, then pushed away, her chest aching, arm stinging.

She heard the clunk and scrape of Renner's footsteps in the passageway, followed by the droning squeals of emergency sirens; rising and falling, overlapping and out of sequence. The police response would target the scene of the shooting and spread out from there. They'd be searching for Kate. For Emily, too.

Stumbling forwards, fighting for breath, Kate picked Emily up in her arms.

'It's OK,' she told her. 'I've got you. It's OK.'

This time, Emily didn't fight.

Kate strode on, the sirens getting louder, closer. Perhaps she was being foolish. Perhaps the police could help. But no, Hanson's warnings came back to her again. If she made it to the police ahead of Renner, they'd want to question her. And what would she tell them? That Emily's father had been on the run? That she herself was part of an illegal operation that was helping to hide them both?

'You're hurting me,' Emily whined.

'I'm sorry.'

She eased her grip, cradling the girl's head, beginning to jog on down the street to where a group of men in shirts and jeans were smoking and drinking beneath a eucalyptus tree. Stereo speakers suspended from the tree's branches crackled with rapid-fire commentary about the bullfight in the arena.

Kate spun and saw Renner stagger out of the darkened passageway, looking wildly in all directions. He locked on to her and lurched into movement again, grimacing as he dragged his bad leg in a wide arc.

The street ahead was choked with market stalls and tourists. Kate embraced the crush, spying a stall selling kitchen equipment to her right. She reached out a hand as she passed, snatching up a boning knife, cupping the wooden handle in her palm and resting the blade against her inner wrist.

She barged through a young couple holding hands, breaking their grip, not troubling to apologise. In the distance, she could glimpse floodlights skimming off the crumbling stonework of the Roman amphitheatre. The arena promised more people and more confusion; a chance of losing Renner.

But there was a problem.

A uniformed police officer was standing on a raised platform up ahead, scanning the flood of people moving towards him, his eyes sweeping from left to right. Before Kate could think to duck or to swerve, his gaze found her, then fixed on Emily. He grabbed for the radio clipped to his flak jacket and jumped down from his vantage point into the street.

Kate slowed, conflicted. She couldn't go forwards. She couldn't go back. She raised herself up on her toes, searching for alternatives, clutching the knife. There was a packed restaurant bar on her left and a tiny supermarket alongside it. Further ahead on her right was the turning for a small street, about halfway between her current position and the police officer.

She put her lips to Emily's ear. 'Sweetheart, I need you to walk. You have to be brave.'

She lowered Emily to the ground, steering her to the right, between a market stall selling handbags and one stocked with cheeses. She flattened Emily against the glass of a florist's shop, pausing a moment, then leading her on past a *boulangerie*. She pushed people aside, slinking through, pulling Emily after her, turning the corner.

The street was rammed with people, none of them moving. Everyone was standing with their backs towards Kate, craning their necks, shouting and hollering.

'Follow me. Stick close.'

But Emily had already ducked and wriggled free, dropping to her hands and knees, crawling between the legs of a man standing in front of them. The man raised his foot, annoyed, and Kate swooped in front of him.

She could see Emily scurrying across the ground, darting into gaps, charting her own zigzagging path forwards, and she had to push and shove to keep up until, almost before she knew it, she reached the very front of the crowd just as Emily sprung up beside her, grasping her hand.

A set of waist-high metal barriers blocked their way, penning them, sealing off a curved cross street. More barriers hemmed in a knot of bystanders on the opposite side. People were waving flags and drinking beer, standing with smartphones and cameras held high, screens glowing in the dark.

A carnival procession, Kate thought. She could hear drums from further along the street. There were whoops and catcalls, the bleat of a whistle, the urgent cicada click of football rattles.

She glanced back and could just see the flushed face of the uniformed officer, reaching forwards into the crowds, pulling people back by their shoulders. She couldn't spot Renner. Perhaps he'd been spooked by the policeman. Or perhaps he was keeping low and out of sight, creeping closer. The knife wouldn't be much use if he got to her undetected.

They had to keep moving.

Kate grabbed Emily under her arms, hoisting her high, her feet tangling with the top of the barrier until she kicked and her legs came free and Kate set her down on the other side.

People yelled at Kate, tugged at her, as if she was breaking some kind of rule. Kate didn't care. She used her elbows to clear space and threw a leg over the barrier, gripping the top rail with both hands and swinging her trailing leg after her.

Her trailing leg didn't move. Someone was holding on to her

ankle, yanking her back. Her first thought was that it must be the policeman, but as she fought to wrench herself free, she saw that it was two middle-aged men working together. They raged at her in urgent French, spittle flying from their lips, but their words were swallowed by the roar of the crowd, by the sudden pressing need she had to get away. She sliced the knife through the air, driving them back, their palms held high, their faces flushed, then paling as the barrier tipped and gave way, toppling forwards, crashing down.

Kate slammed on to her hip, trapping her leg, the crowd stumbling and surging towards her, then seeming to be sucked back by some unknown force. She wriggled free and staggered to her feet, turning just as Emily screamed in her ear.

A bull was thundering towards them.

It was big and it was brown, its legs seeming to blur as its hooves scrabbled for grip on the weathered cobblestones, its tail flicking the air. A stringy guy in a bright red T-shirt leapt out of the bull's way, scaling a hay bale, clinging on hard.

Not a carnival procession.

A bull run.

Emily was frozen. The bull seemed to have fixed its sights on her.

Kate dropped the knife and scooped Emily up, carrying her crossways in front of her chest, running hard for the barriers on the opposite side of the street, her legs leaden, as though she was wading through sand, the bull lowering its head, its horns, wheeling round in a clumsy arc.

It seemed to double in size as it pounded close.

Kate arched her back, clattering into the barriers, throwing Emily forwards into the waiting arms of the terrified spectators.

The beast skimmed by in a blur of heat and movement, of terrible friction and a hot animal stink. Kate's knees gave out but unknown hands grabbed for her, yanking her forwards, heaving her up and over the barriers and dropping her to the ground.

She crashed to her knees, her hair getting in her eyes, then more hands lifted her up, brushing her down, pushing her, prodding her. She could hear the cursing of the people all around.

Across the street, the police officer was caught up in the confusion as people rushed to lift the fallen barrier and secure it before the bull returned. He saw her and shouted, gesturing wildly, but the crowd was distracted and Kate snatched for Emily's hand and walked her away.

There was space in the street beyond. There was air. Kate's heart was beating erratically. Her lungs were tight and cramped. She felt weightless, aimless, as though she might faint.

Emily was sobbing, her mouth opening and closing, a cascade of mumbled words tumbling out.

'The bad man. The bad man. I want my daddy.'

'It's OK.' Kate fought a sudden tide of nausea and the pressing desire she had to sit down and place her head between her knees. 'We're just going to find my car. Hanson is there. He'll look after you. We just need to find my car.'

She pointed to a road that wound down and away to the right, having no idea if it was the correct route to take.

'It's by the river. We'll find it soon. OK?'

But as it happened, the car found them, pulling up sharply as Kate led Emily by the hand through an archway carved into the city wall, the Hyundai's suspension bearing down at the front, tyres grinding to a halt.

Hanson threw open the driver's door and leapt out on to the street and Kate met his eyes, lips trembling, shaking her head. She opened her mouth to speak, to tell him what had happened, but he smiled and raised a hand and yanked open a door at the rear. Becca was there, extending an arm to Emily, gripping a soiled, limp teddy bear in her fist.

'Hiya, sweetheart.' Becca smiled. 'There's someone who wants to see you back here.'

Emily burst forwards, clutching the bear, clambering over Becca's lap. There was blood on Becca's blouse and her free hand was clamped to her ear. Kate ducked and looked past her and saw Emily embracing Pete, her body crushed into his. Pete had some kind of temporary dressing on his shoulder, the wadded bandage dark with blood. He was wincing, baring his teeth, crying, smiling, crying some more. A Peppa Pig knapsack was unzipped on the rear bench between them.

Kate stared at Becca. 'I thought you were dead.'

'Honey, it's gonna take a lot more than that to bring me down.' She was talking very loud, almost shouting. 'But those shots messed with my hearing. You're gonna have to tell me if I start yelling, OK?'

'Get in,' Hanson told her.

'Where are we going?'

'These two need medical care. You too, by the looks of it. Miller has a private doctor lined up not far from here.'

'And the police?'

'Leave me to worry about that.'

He guided Kate round the front of the car and into the

passenger seat, closing her door. Her throat was dry and gritty, her ears ringing, her body vibrating with the flush of adrenaline and fear.

'Take this.' Hanson had climbed behind the wheel and was thrusting a mobile at her. 'Someone wants to talk to you.'

*

Renner watched the white Hyundai streak away into the night, crossing the river, blitzing past the vapour-lit forecourt of a petrol station.

The young black kid was driving fast, getting far away while the going was good. Which was fine by Renner.

He lifted his Beretta in his right hand and ejected the magazine, catching it in his free palm. He had one round left. Blank, like all the others. Not capable of killing, but enough to scare Kate and to set her running. Which was all that Renner wanted right now.

He clutched his left thigh and heaved it up until his foot was propped on the low wall in front of him. His shin throbbed. It was deeply gashed and beginning to swell. The front passenger seat had deformed in the collision, crushing him badly.

Gently, he lifted his trouser leg and loosened his ankle holster from his drenched sock, sucking air through his teeth as his bloodied fingers slipped on the Velcro straps, more blood oozing out as he pulled the holster away, slipping the Beretta into it, tucking it under his jacket.

He grimaced as he set a little weight on his foot, then limped off in search of the vehicle he'd hired.

PART VI

Prague, Czech Republic

Chapter Fifty-Two

You will never guess who I've just seen on this flight. Clue: he's been in the news and he's supposed to be dead! Z xxx

Darren often thought of that text. He hadn't asked his sister to send it to him, and if she could take it back now and prevent everything that had followed, he had no doubt that she would.

Sometimes, the tragedies we face in life can take a brutal but familiar enough form. Take what had happened to Darren and Zoe's parents, for example. The motorway coach crash that had claimed their lives had been savage and abrupt but it had been something Darren could almost accept over time because it was the type of unfortunate incident that appears in the news all too often. What had happened to his sister in a lonely airfield in Ukraine hadn't been like that at all. And what had happened to him afterwards, the dangers and the transformation to his way of life that had come from receiving a simple text message, could never have been anticipated.

Not that everything since that day had been bad. Darren had always dreamed of travelling and he'd come to love living in Prague. He'd had no family other than his brother-in-law and his niece to leave behind, and had only worked a temporary job after leaving university, so in many ways it was easier for him to disappear and start again than it might have been. Plus he had Miller and his team looking out for him. He had their friendship and support.

And he had Agata.

Maybe.

Secrets. That was the problem. Agata believed that the strongest relationships were built on openness; on trust and intimacy. Her previous boyfriend had been a cheater. The guy she'd been seeing before that had turned out to be married. So she was nervous, flighty, in constant need of reassurance. And Darren had tried to give it to her, despite being compromised by those truths he couldn't begin to share. His background story was a lie. Even his name was a distortion. And Agata had sensed it in him. She was highly attuned to bullshit. She'd begun to pull back.

Which was why she'd suggested that they should take some time apart, and why Darren had gone along with it, and why he'd just endured three of the dullest and most miserable days of his life in Kutná Hora, a two-hour train journey from Prague.

Their time apart hadn't changed anything for Darren. The soul-searching hadn't either. But there remained one question he couldn't get past, and as a maths graduate, there was one sum he couldn't square.

How do you build a future for yourself when you can't use all the foundations of your past? And how do you let someone into your life when keeping them safe means shutting them out?

Darren didn't know. He didn't believe he ever would. Perhaps, in the end, he would have to leave Prague altogether. Maybe it was best for him to start somewhere fresh.

But before all that, he wanted to return to Agata and hold her in his arms one last time. Because if there was only one truth he could tell her, it should be that she was the woman he loved.

Chapter Fifty-Three

Miller clenched his phone to his ear, struggling to think how to begin. 'It's me,' he said finally, hopelessly. 'How are you holding up?'

'Not so good.'

'I'm sorry for what I put you through. I'm sorry for what it took.'

Kate's breathing was a faint rasp on the end of the line. Miller could picture her fighting back tears, and it made him think of the way she'd looked that first time he'd allowed her to see him, with her pale, bloodless complexion and her eyes big and tremulous.

He pinched the bridge of his nose between his forefinger and thumb. The alley he was standing in was dark and deserted, barely lit by the wash of pale light from the windows at the side of the hostel. He could hear faint guitar music from high above, the murmur of conversation and laughter.

'I wish I could have been there for you. I wish I could be with you right now.'

No response.

What had he meant by that exactly? What would she take it to imply?

'You're safe,' he told her. 'Remember that. Once you get Pete and Becca patched up, Hanson will take you somewhere you can rest.'

Still nothing. Just the buzz and crackle on the line, the droning of a car engine, the murmur of Emily's voice. It would be better to leave it at that, he supposed. Better for her, and for him. And normally he might have stopped there. But not tonight.

'Listen, there's something I have to know. Something I have to ask. Was there more than just one man?'

Silence.

He waited.

'I only saw one,' she said, haltingly. 'It was Renner.'

'Not Wade?'

'I didn't see anyone else. I think he was alone. We lost him, but he could be looking for us still. He could be heading your way.'

'Then I'd better get on.' He paused. There was more he wanted to tell her – more he felt she needed to hear – but he couldn't bring himself to say any of it. He wasn't sure he knew how. 'We'll talk soon,' he told her. 'I promise.'

He waited a beat before hanging up, then stuffed the phone into the back pocket of his jeans, thinking of all the words left unspoken, all the things left unsaid.

He cursed himself for his weakness, for the foolishness of believing he could care for someone again without hurting them deeply, and then he slunk off with his hands in his pockets, kicking the ground, steering his thoughts back to the unlit apartment above the pet shop in Malá Strana and the trouble that might be waiting for him there.

*

Many hours earlier, shortly before noon, Miller had crossed the tram tracks running along Karmelitská, the drizzle clinging to his face, his shirt limp with damp. He'd hustled inside the pet shop, a bell ringing above his head.

Darren wasn't behind the counter. He didn't appear to be anywhere.

Which was no great surprise, because Hanson had been calling the shop telephone, trying to contact him, since just after ten the previous night.

A girl Miller had never seen before turned away from a birdcage she was peering into. She was eighteen or nineteen, kind of dowdy-looking, with coarse brown hair and spectacles with round metal frames. She glanced at the floor, murmuring something in Czech, but Miller walked straight past her and blasted through a door at the back.

Darren had taken a job in the pet shop more than nine months ago. The pay was terrible but the job came with a free apartment one floor up. He hadn't consulted Miller before moving in. He hadn't listened to his protests or his safety concerns. He'd said he needed some freedom and that he wanted to pay his own way. He'd said he'd enjoy the company of the animals. But Miller soon found out that wasn't the only attraction.

The pet shop connected with a stockroom and then a veterinary surgery out back. It was a solo operation, owned and operated by a female vet.

Agata was up on a stepladder when Miller burst into the stockroom. She was delving a hand into a box of medical supplies, bracing an elbow on a metal shelf.

'You,' she said, as if she might spit.

297

Agata was short and slight with a bob of fine blonde hair. She was dressed in a green fleece top over grey corduroy trousers.

'Where is he?'

She turned her back on him, plucking a foil pack of pills from the box, then leaned sideways, reaching for something else.

'Is he upstairs?'

'He's not here.'

'Where can I find him?'

'You can't.'

Miller growled and started for the door leading up to Darren's apartment.

'I'll call the police,' Agata shouted after him.

But Miller ignored her, pounding up the near-vertical staircase, hammering on the bare wooden door at the top. He got no answer so he tried the handle and found that it was locked.

He slapped his palm on the wood, bowing his head, then turned back towards the stairs. Agata was right behind him. She bumped off his chest, losing her balance, falling.

Miller snatched for her arm and pulled her towards him, leaning right in her face.

'Where is he?'

'You're hurting me.'

'He could be in danger, Agata.'

'From you?'

Miller held her gaze for a long moment, fingers digging into her flesh. Then he swore and let go.

'You scare him,' she said, rubbing her wrist.

'I help him.'

'You make him anxious. Afraid.' She rolled back her sleeve, lifting her arm, showing him the red welts on her skin. 'You scare me, too.'

She turned to leave, to head back downstairs, maybe to carry out her threat to call the police.

'Agata, please. I need your help. So does Darren.'

She paused, looking away from him towards the wedge of gauzy light at the bottom of the stairs.

'There are people coming for him. People who *will* hurt him. Here. This man.' He hurried after her, pulling his phone from his pocket, jabbing it in front of her face so that she could see the grainy picture of Wade he'd taken from the surveillance footage of the luggage counter in Rome. 'Have you seen him? Has he been here?'

'No.' She barely looked.

'Tell me where Darren is. Tell me where I can find him.'

'He's in Kutná Hora. He won't be home until tonight.'

'Then let me wait in his apartment.'

'I don't have a key.'

She did, and Miller knew it. But she'd started moving again, treading downstairs, nursing her wrist.

'I can wait in the storeroom,' he told her. 'I can protect you both.'

'No, you leave. Or I call the police.'

'What time will he be back? Agata? Tell me that, at least.'

'Late,' she said, and swerved into her surgery, locking the door behind her.

*

Miller didn't go far. He crossed over the street to a chain coffee outlet with a specialism in doughnuts. He was so wired from his encounter with Agata that the last thing he needed was a hit of caffeine and sugar, but the location was good, so he ordered a selection box of six doughnuts and a large black coffee from the spotty kid in a peaked cap working behind the till, then took up position on a moulded plastic stool that faced the plate-glass window. He braced his elbows on the raised Formica counter-top and stared out through the beads of streaking rain at the pet shop across the street.

One p.m. Many hours to go.

Miller sipped his coffee, pushing the box of doughnuts to one side.

He was worried about the rear entrance to the veterinary surgery. He was concerned that Wade could approach from the dingy alley out back. But he was on his own in the city and low on angles and options, so he played the odds and kept his eyes on the front of the pet shop, staring past the scramble of pedestrians, the bob and weave of umbrellas, the rush of taxis and scooters and trams.

He waited for Wade to show himself. Waited for Darren to return home. He waited to find out what his next move should be.

*

But he was already too late. Because up in that first-floor apartment, slumped in a wilting couch, Aaron Wade was sitting very still and highly alert, his body tensed and poised, ready to spring forwards and attack, just as he'd been ready a few minutes earlier when Miller had beat on the thin plywood door that had separated them both.

Chapter Fifty-Four

It was clear to Miller that the kid with the acne didn't know how to handle his ongoing presence in the coffee shop. He obviously wasn't used to having customers spend long hours sheltering from the rain, staring across the road. Every hour or so, the confusion and the frustration would get too much for him, and the kid would wait for a break in customers, circle round from behind the counter and linger for a moment until Miller glanced up. Then he'd ask in broken English if there was anything Miller needed. And Miller would say yes, a matter of fact there was, and he'd order a coffee refill and another box of doughnuts.

By ten to six, Miller had five greasy cardboard boxes stacked on the counter in front of him. He flipped open the top box and ate a raspberry cream. Then he wiped his lips with a paper napkin, sipped a little more coffee and gazed back across the rain-blown street.

The kid was getting antsy again. He'd switched off the coffee percolator, wiped down the counter and had started clearing out trays of unsold doughnuts. It wouldn't be long until he finally summoned the courage to come over and tell Miller to get out. But that was OK with Miller, because he'd just watched the mousy girl in the glasses step out through the front door of the pet shop and hurry away along the street. Two minutes after that, Agata emerged and locked the business behind her.

The shop alarm was primed and it bleated shrilly for several seconds as she put up an umbrella and looked anxiously around before striding away in the opposite direction.

Miller waited until the alarm had fallen silent, then slid off his stool and stretched. He gathered together his boxes of doughnuts and his stained coffee mug and he carried them over to the kid behind the counter.

'We close now,' the kid told him. 'You leave, OK?'

'No problem.' Miller patted his gut. 'But I need to use your bathroom first. There's a chance I may have drunk a little too much coffee.'

*

Miller took a cab across the city to a modern hostel located behind a grand rococo building in the Old Town, where he walked into the entrance foyer and brushed the rain out of his hair. He didn't have any luggage with him, though he supposed that wasn't altogether unusual for someone looking for a cheap bed for the night. Besides, Miller was a familiar face. He'd stayed here many times before.

He recognised the girl sitting on the stool behind the reception counter and from the lazy smile she summoned he could tell that she recognised him. She was late teens, early twenties, with a stud in her nose and her hair tied back in dreadlocks.

'Hey, you're back.'

Her English was good, marked with a slight American drawl. She'd told Miller once that she'd spent a season working at a ski chalet in Vermont. She'd told him many things about herself, in fact, but if she'd expected Miller to reciprocate, he never had.

He sometimes got the impression she liked that about him.

'Just for one night. Do you have a bunk free?'

'For you, always.'

She placed a locker key, a bed sheet and a pillowcase down on the counter.

Miller was already parting his wallet, thumbing through some koruna, trying not to catch the amused, mildly flirtatious look she was giving him. He had no intention of using the bed. He didn't anticipate coming back. But he didn't want to cheat the hostel on the bill, either.

'And I'll take a six-pack of beer.'

'No problem.'

The girl's stool was on castors and she rolled over to a discoloured fridge set against the back wall, grabbed a carton of Budvar and glided back again.

'Which dorm?' he asked, setting his cash down, hefting the beers.

'You decide. It's not so busy.'

Miller nodded his thanks and scooped up the bedding, backing off towards the stairs. He passed a line of public computers that had seen better days and a noticeboard layered in handwritten notes asking for lifts to Vienna or Budapest, for places to stay, for companions to travel with.

The dorm Miller chose was on the second floor, at the back of the building, beyond the communal showers. He punched a timer switch on the wall as he stepped inside and a series of ceiling lights stuttered to life, revealing a bare wooden floor, eight bunk beds and sixteen metal lockers. Most of the beds were empty. One was draped with drying laundry. Another had a guy laid out on it, barechested, who grunted and rolled on to his side, clamping a pillow over his face.

Miller tossed his bedding on to a low bunk on his right and crossed to the open window next to the dozing guy. He climbed out over the sill, first one leg, then the other, setting his boots down on to the gridded platform of a metal fire escape. A rust-flaked ladder was bolted to the wall and Miller began to climb.

By the time he neared the top, three storeys up, he could hear music and singing, and when he stuck his head over the parapet he saw a gaunt teenager with a shaved head and sleeve tattoos sitting cross-legged on the flat roof, his back resting against a dilapidated timber shed, plucking at the strings of a guitar. Two girls in raincoats were slumped in frayed camping chairs close by, humming along self-consciously.

There was nobody else around and Miller guessed he had the light rain to thank for that. He pulled a Budvar from the six-pack, popped the cap with one of several corroded bottle openers that had been abandoned on the roof, then took a long pull and set the rest of the beers down by the trio of teens, waving aside their offers to come join them as he paced behind the shed.

The night-time view was spectacular, but to Miller it felt strangely mournful, too. There were pinpricks of light everywhere he looked and countless buildings jostling for space. There were a whole bunch of church towers and spikes and domes jabbing upwards, and he could see the graceful sweep of the Vltava river, its blackened waters shimmering beneath the illuminated spans of an arched bridge. But no matter how hard he looked, he couldn't spot a single identifiable person.

Crouching now, he scraped back a scree of cigarette butts

and crushed reefers from the ankle-high parapet until his fingers settled on a loose brick towards the bottom. He dug his nails into powdery mortar, working the brick free, bringing with it a shower of dust and debris and the smell of dead air.

Behind the brick, deep in the cavity, lay a nylon washbag. Miller extracted the bag and unzipped it, removing a clear plastic ziplock bag from within.

The bag contained a number of items. First up was a micro penlight, the kind that came with a key ring fitted to it. Miller clicked it on and aimed the blue-white beam at one thousand euros in cash, rolled into a tight tube, with another ten thousand Czech koruna rolled inside that. Next up was a duplicate British passport bearing the name Nick Miller, as well as a spare passport for Darren. There was also a Swiss Army Knife, the main blade still coated with dust and grit from when he'd used it to carve the brick free more than a year before, as well as a key to the pet shop and another to Darren's apartment. Miller kept a similar back-up stash in every city where his clients were based.

Checking over his shoulder, he quickly pocketed the knife, peeled off six hundred koruna to replace the cash he'd already spent, and looped both keys on to the ring attached to the penlight. Then he tucked the remaining money and the passports back inside the plastic bag and the washbag, stuffed the package into the cavity again, replaced the brick and packed fresh handfuls of dirt and gravel around it. Finally, he poured the remainder of his beer away before stepping out from behind the shed, waggling his empty bottle at one of the girls, throwing a salute to the guy with the guitar, and starting back down the ladder.

It was only a few minutes later, after he'd climbed through the open window to the unlit dorm and had waved goodbye to the girl on reception as he made his way outside, that his mobile had chirped and he'd answered Hanson's call, listening carefully as Hanson updated him on events in Arles before, quite suddenly, there was a pause until Kate came on the line and he heard her broken voice for the first time since he'd left her in Rome that morning.

Chapter Fifty-Five

Connor Lane leaned back in his leather desk chair, pinching his lips between his finger and thumb. He felt apprehensive and powerless, and didn't like it one bit.

His feet were on the corner of his desk, his legs crossed at the ankle, and he was contemplating the bulge of the electronic tag beneath his Argyle socks. He wanted very badly to tear the tag away.

Instead, he reached forwards and put his desk phone on speaker, hitting a number on speed-dial. He was cradling his forehead as Renner picked up.

Renner sounded a long way away, his breathing pinched and ragged, and Connor could hear shouting and live music behind him.

'I just talked with Russell,' Connor said. 'He's not doing so good. They're talking about pushing his trial back until they can locate Kate Sutherland. It could mean months of uncertainty. I'm not sure he can take it.'

'You want me to talk to him?'

'No, Mike. I want you to tell me this is going to be over soon. I want to be able to tell *him* that.'

'We're making progress.'

'Progress.' Connor lowered his hands and mimed squeezing something with his fingers and thumbs. Renner's throat, perhaps. 'You do understand what's at stake here, don't you, Mike?'

'I understand.'

'Well, let me lay it out for you all the same. Let me eradicate any doubt you might be experiencing.'

'I don't have any—'

'Mike, listen to me. Here's the problem: if Adams can get Kate Sutherland on that witness stand, that's bad, no question. But if he can get Anna Brooks there, too – if she's asked to give evidence about Russell and she stands in a courtroom shouting rape, no matter how much we work to discredit her – it's going to be worse than bad. It's going to end with a guilty verdict.'

Silence on the other end of the line.

Connor hated waiting. His approach to anything he wanted in life, and especially in business, was to push forwards relentlessly until he secured the outcome he desired.

'Do you get it, Mike? This is about more than just money to me.'

'I already said I understand.'

Connor pulled his feet down from the desk and lowered his mouth to the speaker. 'You're sure?'

'Wade's in Prague now. I'm waiting to hear from him.'

'See, Mike? This is what I'm talking about. Stop waiting. I want results.'

'But—'

'Results, Mike. Russell needs them. I need them. And believe me, you and Wade need them, too. Because I think you know by now how much I hate to be disappointed.'

Chapter Fifty-Six

Miller walked beneath the towering spikes of the Tyn Church and on into the Old Town Square, his shoulders hunched, his hands buried deep in his pockets. Prague felt hostile tonight, the winding streets and Gothic architecture seeming to crowd in on him, mutating into something unpredictable and predatory.

He'd never felt threatened here before. Or watched. On previous visits to check on Darren, Prague had held a bitter-sweet charm because it was the last place where he'd taken a holiday with Sarah and Melanie before all their troubles began. It had been a spontaneous trip, which was pretty much unheard of for them. Sarah was a planner – the Control Freak, as Melanie had called her – and Miller was away from home so often with work that he disliked travelling when he took time off. But Melanie had just finished her GCSEs and Sarah had spotted a cheap deal with a low-cost airline, and he'd arrived home late one evening, worn down and wrung out, to find a suitcase on his bed, his clothes neatly packed and his passport resting on top.

They flew from Manchester early the following morning. Back then – though it seemed almost impossible to believe it now – he wasn't widely travelled in Europe, and it had shown. He'd been bewildered by Prague from the moment of their arrival. He'd been ripped off by taxi drivers, insulted by waiters, left disorientated and confused when he'd misread a tourist map on a family outing to Wenceslas Square.

Sarah had taken control before he lost his temper completely. Melanie was sulking by then, caught up in a deep teenage funk, but Sarah had guided them towards a bar overlooking the river, where she'd ordered cold Czech lager and they'd found themselves sitting on a terrace in the sunshine, finally relaxing and beginning to smile. Melanie, high on beer buzz and the uncharted novelty of drinking in front of her parents, had started to goof off about Miller's gormless tourist routine. They'd laughed, and had kept laughing the rest of the weekend.

He could almost hear the drifting echo of their laughter now as he paced towards the Astronomical Clock where they'd stood so many times because Melanie had begged to watch the mechanical show over and over, an indulgence for the child she'd once been and the adult she was yet to become.

Tonight, he skirted the group of tourists gathered in front of the tower, reluctant to look up at the patterned dial or the ghoulish, skeletal figure of Death, who lurked and waited to begin his next display by jerkily upending the hourglass gripped in his bony fingers.

Miller didn't want to think about time. He didn't want to concern himself with its cruel trickery. So he lowered his head and tried to ignore the sensation of the buildings creeping towards him, stretching above him, hemming him in.

At the Charles Bridge, where a dank breeze skimmed off the surface of the lamp-lit waters, he came close to running through the gauntlet of blackened statues that lined the parapets. He couldn't stand to look at them – couldn't stand to be seen by anyone at all – and kept his face averted as he dodged between buskers and portrait painters and young lovers holding hands.

The district of Malá Strana loomed ahead: a raggedy, tumbledown knot of buildings, domes and spires. He swept left, along Hroznová, then over a small bridge where the railings were covered in thousands of locked padlocks, couples leaving them here as a symbol of their everlasting love. Miller had shaken his head at the tradition the first time he'd seen it, waiting impatiently for Sarah and Melanie to catch up to him, bemused at why Sarah felt the need to trace her fingers over the coloured spectrum of rusted and corroded locks.

Then he'd noticed the wistful expression on her face, the faraway gaze that took hold of her as she spun the locks with a dull clatter. And so, very early the following morning, Miller had slipped out of bed and fetched the lock from his own suitcase and walked down to fasten it to the bridge.

He'd experienced a sense of euphoria on his return to their hotel room, but by the time he'd shed his clothes and crept back into bed, with Sarah stirring and murmuring beneath twisted sheets, he felt suddenly embarrassed by the gesture and pretended to be asleep. Only now did he realise what a fool he'd been not to tell her and it stung him anew to think that he could never bring her here to show her what she'd meant to him that day, and every day since.

If he'd felt inclined to linger, perhaps he could have found the very same lock. But the idea of searching for it seemed improper, somehow, after what had happened with Kate in Rome.

He still loved Sarah. He always would. And yet he felt an undeniable pull towards Kate. How much simpler it would be to ignore the attraction, to bury it deep. There was a twisted solace in the hurt that still rankled inside him, in the guilt and fear that walked with him each day. But four years had gone by. Four years to honour the memory of Sarah, to cherish the time they'd had together with Melanie. Four years to find a way to move on with his life.

And today, for the first time, despite everything that had gone against them, he could begin to see a way to believe that four years might be enough. Provided, that was, he could end this latest threat for good. Supposing, also, that with Kate's help he could find some form of redemption for failing to protect his family by saving those clients he'd unwittingly placed in harm's way.

He hurried on through alleyways and passageways, pursued by his grief and regrets, making his way back to the wide, charmless boulevard of Karmelitská, where a tram teetered towards him, blue sparks arcing from the web of overhead lines. Across the street, the light spill from the pet-shop window was a lurid, chemical green, similar to the water in the fish tanks at the back of the store. He looked up at Darren's unlit apartment, at the deserted pavements and the shuttered businesses, then finally turned his head, his gaze sweeping past the closed doughnut shop and settling on the entrance to a three-star hotel.

The hotel was where he'd stayed with Sarah and Melanie. It was the main reason why he hadn't wanted Darren moving here, to the same street. Whenever he visited Darren, he found himself gaping at the slowly revolving glass doors, remembering passing through them back then, thinking of walking through them once more, as if, somehow, he might be magically whisked back to a time before everything fell apart.

But not tonight – not ever – and so tugging the penlight and keys from his pocket, his fingers bloated with wetness and cold, he crossed to the pet shop and popped the lock and swept inside.

And noticed something.

The alarm didn't sound.

Was Darren back early? Or was Wade waiting for him here?

He stood very still, listening to the burble of aquarium pumps, the squeak of a hamster on a wheel. There was a strong odour of sawdust and animal hair and meat paste. Spilt nuggets of dried cat food crunched under his boots as he crept past the counter towards a spinning rack loaded with squeaky toys and a low animal pen in which a rabbit thumped its hind leg fitfully.

He drifted by the wall of aquariums at the rear and on into the darkened stockroom, where he shone his penlight over the alarm control panel and could find no obvious signs of tampering.

His anxiety dampening down a little, he climbed the stairs to Darren's apartment, aiming the beam of his penlight ahead of him, the disc of light skimming over the treads.

As he reached the top, he saw that the door was partway open, tapping against the jamb. His penknife was in his trouser pocket and he fumbled it out, tearing a nail as he tugged a blade free. He gripped the knife in his right fist down by his waist, the penlight held overhand by his left shoulder.

The door bounced off the frame once more, then started to swing back, and Miller moved with it, barging it aside, striding into the unlit room, his senses heightened to such a degree that he felt the slightest breeze against his face.

There was a faint shimmer to his right; the play of moon-light on net curtains. The nets drifted inwards, billowing and lifting, revealing a pair of glass French doors flung wide open.

Miller crept nearer, pushing the curtains aside, stepping through on to a balcony that looked down over the alley running behind the building and the entrance to the veterinary surgery below. The door to the surgery was thrown back, spilling a wedge of light on the ground.

Something cracked beneath his feet. Not cat food this time, but glass. He turned and saw that a door panel had smashed. Dropping to his haunches, he cast his torch around, catching the oily reflection from a slick of blood amid the glitter of shattered beads.

Leaning forwards, gripping the iron railings, he peered down into the alley and spotted a dumpster toppled on to its side, its wheels in the air, spewing yellow plastic bags branded with some kind of medical hazard symbol.

Something grazed the back of his neck and he spun fast, knife raised, into a tangle of curtain.

Nobody there.

Batting the fabric away, he looked down again and spied an abandoned shoe just beyond the dumpster. It was a Converse trainer, dirtied and worn, exactly the type Darren might wear. Miller pictured him limping away, his foot twisted, his ankle broken or sprained, after leaping off the balcony into the dumpster.

He must have been seriously scared to risk a fall like that. Which made all kinds of sense where a man like Aaron Wade was concerned.

Miller rocked back and raised his eyes to the blur of rain clouds overhead, asking himself if Darren could have got away, and if he hadn't, where Wade might have taken him. And right then he was struck by a terrible thought.

Patrick Leigh. The construction crane in Manchester. Wade had strung Patrick up from the tallest structure he could find, and the highest point anywhere close to him now was the giant green cupola of St Nicholas Church, rising in a great swell just beyond the roofline of the buildings he was looking towards.

Chapter Fifty-Seven

The church was undergoing renovation and was surrounded by scaffolding concealed behind a tarpaulin shroud. The tarpaulin was pale brown in colour and featured an outline drawing of the Baroque exterior of the landmark beneath.

At ground level, the perimeter of the building was shielded by temporary metal fencing set several metres back into the street, secured with industrial padlocks. The site was unlit and appeared to be empty and unguarded. Miller paused at the mouth of an alley near the rear of the church, scanning his surroundings. There was nobody behind him, nobody ahead, darkness all around.

He picked up his pace, breaking into a run, and lunged for a fence panel, grabbing hold of the top edge, springing from his toes. Which turned out to be a bad move. The metal was sharp and Miller was heavy. The panel cut his left hand. He hooked an elbow over the top, hoping to spread the load, and felt his skin break as the panel shook and flexed beneath him, threatening to tip until he heaved a leg over and dropped down on to grit and sand.

His palm was bleeding. The wounds weren't deep, but blood was creeping through his shirtsleeve from where the ragged metal had sliced into his arm. He flexed his fingers, testing his movement, wincing at the stretch and sting.

There was a cement mixer near to him with a shovel resting

against it. Beyond the mixer, a wooden ladder had been lashed to the scaffold.

Miller craned his neck and looked up. He couldn't see any movement or hear any signs of a struggle. But the tarpaulin was thick and the scaffolding very high, and if Wade had forced Darren to climb to the top, they could be concealed from view.

He stepped forwards and grasped a sand-crusted rung, then climbed as far as the first floor of scaffold, where he switched to another ladder.

The cuts on his hand were sucking in grit and sand. On the next level of scaffold, he found a ratty piece of fabric tied loosely around a horizontal pole. It was a vest top. Perhaps it had once been white but now it was grimy with dirt and sweat.

Miller used his penknife to slice the vest in two, wrapping the fabric around his palm and tying it off with his teeth. When he was done, he flexed his fingers again. His movement was restricted but the pain was muffled. Tucking the knife away, he stepped over to the next ladder and climbed on.

The light wind that had buffeted him at ground level built steadily the higher he climbed. Strong gusts blasted the tarpaulin, making the scaffolding shake and rattle.

He passed stained-glass windows and carved masonry and gargoyles. He didn't see or hear Wade, and he couldn't spot Darren. Eventually he found himself on the very top deck, the rain spitting in his face, the wind blustering. He could see right across the night-time city, far beyond the roof of the hostel where he'd gazed from earlier. Stepping forwards and seizing hold of a scaffold pole, he leaned out and looked down over the cobbled square at the front of the church, where a few pedestrians scurried to and fro.

Miller had never liked heights, and certainly not on this scale. Maybe it had something to with his size, his bulk. He was big and rangy, prone to tripping.

A gust of wind slammed into him and he backed off from the edge, moving round the turquoise cupola, beneath the twin bell towers, craning his neck, searching out threats.

He was beginning to think he'd been mistaken. He seemed to be alone and forgotten up here. None of the passers-by down below were stopping and pointing. Nobody was standing back or screaming or giving any indication that they could see someone in trouble.

And yet somebody was in trouble, out of sight, at the very rear of the cupola, where Miller found Darren strung up by his ankles, his hands tied behind his back, suspended from a metal chain and dangling way above the spiked roof of the main church building.

Chapter Fifty-Eight

Darren's shins were bound with duct tape and the metal chain had been coiled around them, stretching up to be wrapped once around the horizontal pole Miller was leaning against, then tied off multiple times on an upright pole several metres back that was clustered with knots and tangled with drooping chain loops.

Miller couldn't reach Darren. The length of chain was too long, the distance down to him too far. He leaned out further over the abyss, stretching his arm and shouting Darren's name, the horizontal pole digging into his gut. He thought of trying to hoist Darren up but he doubted he could do it. Darren was thirteen, maybe fourteen stone. Factor in the way Miller's hand was shredded and the strong possibility that Wade was close by, and he decided on a different approach.

He hurried down a trio of ladders to a lower deck. The tarpaulin masked his view but he could see an indent where Darren's body was pressing against the material. Folding out the blade on his penknife, he pierced the canvas and began carving a long, ragged slit to Darren's right. Which was easier said than done because the blade wasn't particularly sharp and the tarpaulin was damp. Miller pulled the blade out and stabbed a line of holes, ripping at the material in between with his hands. Then he switched to a saw-toothed attachment on the penknife and worked it to and fro until the gap was big enough to force his head and shoulders through.

Darren was facing away from him, wriggling against his restraints, his movements fast and desperate.

Miller stuffed his knife into his back pocket and reached for Darren's knees, triggering a muffled howl and some furious bucking, then spun him towards him, grabbing him by the belt and raising him up until he could look in his inverted face.

His eyes were bloodshot, his nose was broken and he was bleeding from an ugly cut on his temple. Two strips of duct tape covered his mouth in an X shape and his cheeks bulged as he tried to shout.

'I'm going to get you out of here.' Miller hauled him closer, trying to ignore the mighty drop to the peaked church roof below.

But Darren kept moaning, kept nodding his head.

'I'm going to pull you through. Stop fighting. Stay still. Hey!' Miller reached out with his free hand and balled Darren's sweater in his fist, glaring into his fear-blown eyes. 'Work with me.'

For just a moment, he relaxed. The muscles in his face slackened off. His pupils seemed to clear.

But just as rapidly, a new stimulus altered his response.

The fear returned. It spiked. Darren moaned and flailed, jerking his head. Miller barely had time to process the warning before he felt one hand thump against his back and another dig into his hair.

There was no real pause and certainly no reprieve, and before he could defend himself or even turn, he was pitched forwards and thrust out.

He fell hard and heavy, flipping right over, his legs

cartwheeling around, the light-streaked cityscape rotating with him.

His wrists flexed and extended, fingers digging in to Darren's belt and sweatshirt. Then his weight bore down and he tightened every muscle and tendon, wrists smarting, fingers loosening as he slammed against Darren's upturned body, his knee crunching off his jaw.

He clung on and looked up. Above him was only wind and whirling darkness and the fluttering tear in the tarpaulin until, many fearful seconds later, he heard a whoop and saw Wade lean his upper body out over the top deck of the scaffolding, his big, square head slashed by a frenzied grin.

Wade ducked out of sight again and Miller eyed the split he'd carved in the tarpaulin, asking himself if he could climb up to it, when there was a sudden clunk and a slackening of the chain and the two men plummeted a fast and terrifying ten metres.

The chain tightened off, almost jerking Miller loose. The metal was so taut it seemed to hum. The links cut in to Darren's shins and he screamed from behind his gag, wriggling in an attempt to get Miller off him.

But Miller wouldn't let go. He couldn't.

He looked down and around, searching for a way out, but Darren's writhing was becoming wilder and more unpredictable, the chain spinning and swinging. He stuck out a leg, failing to hook a foot around a pole behind the canvas. Wade was shouting at him, taunting him, and Miller looked up into his flat, wide-apart eyes, his gaze almost bovine, blissed out, amused, only to see him clench the chain and begin to shake it some more.

Miller loosened his grip on Darren's sweater and grabbed for the bunched chains between his legs, then above his ankles. Darren screamed harder. Miller gritted his teeth and freed his other hand from Darren's belt and planted one foot on his chest as he leapt up, the metal links carving into the cuts on his hand through the padding around his palm.

His grip failed on the rain-greased links and he slipped, but reached up and kept scrambling, kept climbing, heaving his upper body clear of Darren until only their feet were entangled below.

Wade tipped his head to one side. 'Where do you think you're going?'

He jolted the chain.

Miller clung on, the wind and rain whipping against him.

'This won't hold much longer,' Wade shouted. 'Or maybe your strength will fail first.'

Miller pressed his face against the fragile metal, intensely aware of the tension running through it, of the thin air that surrounded him, of his own lumpen weight and the give in his arms and the gaping hole in the canvas high above.

'You want Anna,' he shouted back. 'You need Anna.'

'Not me.'

'Lane does.'

'Mr Lane isn't here. And I'd like to see what kind of a mess you make when you hit that church roof.'

Wade jangled the chain. Darren whined forlornly through his busted nose and taped mouth.

'What do you think Lane's going to do to you if I fall?' Miller shouted. 'How will you find Anna then? I have a team behind me. They'll carry this on.'

Wade stilled for just a second. Maybe he really did think about it. And a second was all it took.

Miller lowered a hand and plucked his knife from his back pocket, opening a blade with his teeth, springing off the chain, holding on with his feet and ankles as he stabbed the blade into the tarpaulin. It popped the canvas, slipped, tipped back, the knife beginning to loosen just as Miller forced his free arm through the frayed gap up to the elbow and grasped for the pole behind.

He stabbed at the canvas again and again, punching furiously, then forced his head through, and afterwards his shoulder and his other arm, clutching the pole in both hands, heaving with the last of his strength, his hips snagging, the tarpaulin puckering round him, dropping on to a dusty scaffold deck.

His arms were numbed and aching, his fingers so stiff with muscle strain that they'd curled into claws. He levered himself on to an elbow, his entire body seeming to buzz and convulse.

Then he heard the fast shuffle-zip of the metal chain unravelling and he whipped his head round to see Darren drop once more.

Chapter Fifty-Nine

Julia Summerhayes unlocked the rear door to Manchester Town Hall, took a detailed look at Lloyd's warrant card, then led her through the dark and echoing building to an office in a far corner of the fourth floor.

The coroner was dressed stylishly in a black pencil skirt and a beige silk blouse. Sliding into her office chair, she swept aside a half-eaten packet of crisps and an open drinks can that bore all the hallmarks of a vending-machine dinner, and invited Lloyd to take a seat across from her.

'It's good of you to see me so late.'

Lloyd felt suddenly nervous and out of her depth, though she wasn't sure why exactly. Perhaps it was because she didn't know quite what she was looking for or hoping to hear, whereas the coroner had an air of professional certainty about her. Then again, she was the only one who knew what she was about to say.

'Oh, I had paperwork to catch up on anyway. And now,' she added, ducking for something on the floor by her feet, 'it seems I have even more.'

She lifted two box files and placed them carefully on her desk with their spines pointed towards Lloyd. The name Sarah Adams was written on one of the files, together with the date of her death and what Lloyd took to be the number of her case file. Lloyd could see the same information about Melanie on the second file.

'You said there was something you wanted to show me?'

'"Want" is a strong word.' The coroner tapped a nail against the file on the left. 'These are Sarah's records.'

She pushed the file across the desk and Lloyd reached for it. The box was heavy. A stack of papers slid around inside.

The coroner said, 'On a quick inspection, the records for Sarah are full and complete. My assistant checked, and according to our system, nobody has requested access to them.'

'That sounds like something you could have told me over the phone.'

'And I would have done, if it weren't for this.'

Now she slid over Melanie's file. Lloyd weighed it in her free hand. It was much lighter.

'I'm not sure I understand.'

'Frankly, neither do I. The death certificate is in there, signed by my predecessor. There's also a top sheet confirming that a forensic autopsy was carried out by one of our senior pathologists who retired only a few months ago. He has a place somewhere in France, I believe.'

Lloyd flipped open the box and leafed through the few sheets of paperwork the coroner had referred to. The autopsy form was signed and dated by the pathologist. Stapled to it was a summary page that confirmed Melanie's gender and listed brief details of her weight, height, eye colour, hair colour and ethnicity, with an additional note about the extensive burns to her body. After that came the formal death certificate, then the cardboard base of the file.

'What else should there be?'

'Notes and photographs. Transcripts of the recording the

pathologist made during the autopsy. Various forms my predecessor would have signed off on.'

'So where is it all?'

'I have no idea. I checked Sarah's file, on the off chance that
somehow the papers got bundled together. That's not the case.'

'Could they have been misfiled somewhere else?'

'That's a possibility.'

'How about electronic records?'

'I had my assistant take a look. There's nothing on the
system.'

Lloyd was silent for a moment, listening to the gathering
quiet of the building all around them. She could feel an icy cool
at the base of her neck. A clenching in her gut.

'My assistant is going to investigate this further in the
morning,' the coroner told her. 'He'll be able to get help from
our IT department. It *could* be a simple glitch in our computer
systems.'

'You wouldn't have called me here if you believed that was
true. What is it you're not telling me?'

'You asked me if anyone had requested access to the files.
We keep details of all requests in a separate database. It seems
that somebody did apply, but only for Melanie's records. The
request was logged shortly after we released the body for
cremation.'

'Who made the application?'

'A Fiona Grainger. The note on our system lists her as
Melanie's aunt.'

Chapter Sixty

Darren fell fast – much further this time – then the chain tightened off again, wrenching him to a halt. Miller heard moaning from below and cursing from above. Clutching his knife, he pushed to his feet and teetered towards a ladder, stumbling in his haste, grasping for the rungs, climbing to the top deck, where he swayed drunkenly for a moment, fixing on Wade, then lowered his head in a charge.

Wade had his back to him. He was busy fighting with the last loops of chain that had been tied off around the upright pole. The chain was stretched taut across the deck and the upright was creaking. The metal was under a lot of strain.

So was Wade's body. He had part of the chain under his armpit and he was leaning all his weight on it, trying to work enough slack to slip his fingers beneath the tangled links so he could free the final knots. He kept fumbling even as he turned his head and saw Miller advancing on him with the knife in his hand. He smiled stupidly, perhaps believing another second or two was all it would take to undo the tangle.

But the chain was too taut, Darren was too heavy, and Miller was faster and angrier than he'd anticipated.

He slammed into Wade, grappling with his arms, driving with his shoulder, forcing Wade back so hard and so fast that his temple smacked off the upright scaffold.

The impact made a dull, hollow noise, like a golf club swung at a fridge door.

An average man would have collapsed and lost consciousness. But Wade just grunted through his teeth, eyes dimming for the briefest instant. Then he blinked and swung a massive arm at Miller, clubbing him behind the ear.

A fast follow-up blow slammed into Miller's stomach – a closed fist, driven high, that forced the air from his lungs. He jackknifed on instinct, just as Wade lifted his squat thigh in the air and drove his knee into Miller's face.

Wade was probably hoping for the nose or the jaw but he clipped Miller's eye socket. Miller stumbled back, pressing his bandaged palm to his face, and Wade took the opportunity to grab his free arm and slam his wrist down against a scaffold pole until he dropped the knife in his hand.

The knife tumbled away, but Wade wasn't done with his arm just yet. He pulled and twisted it, turning Miller round, contorting his wrist until he slumped to his knees, at which point Wade grabbed a fistful of his hair and forced Miller's throat down against the chain that was stretched crossways in front of him.

He was going to break Miller's arm or choke him out, whichever came first.

Throat bulging, his pulse thumping in his ears, Miller fumbled with his trouser cuff, digging his fingers beneath the hem of his sock. He ripped free a syringe that he'd taken from the veterinary surgery, trailing the swatch of sterile tape he'd used to secure it in place, then flicked the plastic cover off the needle point with his thumb and stabbed down to his side, plunging the sharpened point through the toe of Wade's training shoe, striking bone.

Wade yelled and let go, withdrawing his foot, and Miller felt the syringe snap as he freed his throat from the chain, unravelled his wrist and probed at his neck. He squinted through tears and saw that the needle of the syringe had sheared off close to the top. And now Wade was lurching towards him, the rest of the needle sticking out through his shoe, embedded in his toe.

He looked furious, and for the first time in Miller's life he experienced something he'd never truly known before. He'd always been bigger than most thugs he encountered. He'd always been stronger and smarter. But he was beaten here and he knew it. Wade was shorter, he was slighter, but he was ruthless. A killing machine, pure and simple.

He leapt forwards, springing off his good foot, diving with his arms extended and his fingers hooked into claws. He clutched at Miller's ears and slammed his head back against the tensioned chain. Slammed it again and again, harder and harder, the links stabbing into his skull, every impact shaking loose a little more of Miller's resolve.

He didn't have long. A few seconds only. He waited for Wade to yank his head forwards once more and then he thrust his left arm up, aiming for Wade's mouth. But he didn't punch him. Didn't strike him at all. Wade's jaw was parted, his teeth bared in a wild-eyed, nostril-flared snarl, and Miller slipped his fingers in, then his balled hand.

Wade's teeth gnashed against the wadded material protecting Miller's flesh. He shook his head, trying to shake Miller loose. But Miller was already lifting the syringe in his right hand, already lining the shattered point of the needle up with the opening in Wade's mouth.

He squeezed the plunger and a jet of murky yellow liquid spurted out, wetting his fingers, pooling on Wade's tongue.

Wade gagged and reared back. He spat and retched.

But it wouldn't help. Miller had been very careful to take his time and select the most potent drug he could find in the medical lockers at the veterinary surgery. He'd called Hanson on his mobile, asking him to google the meds on offer.

The vial he'd settled on contained a combination of Domitor and Torbugesic that resulted in a powerful horse tranquiliser. The drug didn't need to be fully ingested. It just needed to spend a second or two in the mouth to be absorbed through the tongue or the cheeks.

And it was clearly working, because Wade was swaying and clawing at his throat, croaking hoarsely. He dropped to his knees and his lightless grey eyes blinked once, twice, then roved wildly around. His face sagged, his muscles slackened and he slumped down on to his side.

Chapter Sixty-One

Miller braced a hand against the scaffold. His throat felt swollen, his Adam's apple crushed. His eye was already starting to puff up, restricting his vision. He probed at it with his finger. His skin felt tight and rubbery, and there was a deep ache in the back of his head from where Wade had clubbed him. A dull ringing in his ears.

He looked at Wade and had a sudden urge to kick him hard in the ribs. But something stopped him. Not decency, exactly. It was more a fear that once he started he might not be able to stop.

Hanson had said that the tranquiliser would knock a racehorse cold for a minimum of two hours. Miller guessed it would be at least double that, and very possibly longer, before Wade came round.

Pushing off from the scaffold, he weaved towards the nearest ladder and laboured down many more until he could see the outline of Darren's body pushing against the tarpaulin halfway between two levels of decking. He had no way of getting to him. He had no knife. But he had the vague beginnings of an idea, and so he made his way down the rest of the ladders to the ground, where he grabbed for the shovel that was leaning against the cement mixer and started the long climb back up.

He was out of breath and sweating profusely by the time he returned to the deck that was in line with Darren's lower legs and his feet but he didn't pause, lifting the shovel up by his shoulder, jabbing it forwards, the blade barely sharp enough for Miller to puncture the tarp and work a new hole.

Darren was still conscious, just, but he was gripped by terror, moaning and trembling, and Miller had to poke his head and shoulders out and shout several times before he processed his instructions and began to flail his head and upper body, building momentum, generating enough swing so that Miller could grab for his trouser leg and haul him towards him, bracing his heels against the scaffold and heaving him through the split tarpaulin on to the deck.

Darren flipped on his side, digging his head into the splintered planking, fighting his restraints. Miller dug a nail under the tape on his mouth, ripping it away, pinpricks of blood erupting across his skin.

'Easy,' Miller told him. 'Take a moment. Catch your breath.'

He squatted and set about stretching the duct tape coiled around Darren's wrists, nicking at it with the shovel blade, freeing Darren's hands.

Darren cried out, snatching his arms in front of him, his face wracked with pain as the blood began to flow.

'Where is he?' he asked, through the blockage in his nose.

'Don't worry about that now.'

'He'll kill us both. He's a psychopath.'

Miller shook his head.

'Just breathe.' He shuffled down to Darren's ankles. Beneath the chains, his jeans were wet and stiff with blood. 'This is going to hurt.'

It hurt plenty. The chains had bitten deep into Darren's lower legs. There were friction burns around his shins. One gash in his left calf was especially bad, blood gushing between Miller's fingers as he compressed the wound.

'Tell me about Agata. Do you trust her?'

Tears were springing from Darren's eyes. His lips were peeled back, his face contorted with pain.

'Darren, do you trust her?'

Finally he nodded.

'Is she a light sleeper?'

'Why do you ask?'

'Because we need to wake her. She has to come take a look at your legs.'

*

Agata slipped in through the door at the back of the veterinary surgery, an olive raincoat belted around her waist, a leather medical bag at her side. Her blonde hair was mussed from her pillow, dampened down by the misty drizzle outside. Her face was pale and sleep-stung, lips puckered as she took in the scene.

First there was Darren, laid back on the metal treatment table in the middle of the room. He was propped on his elbows, his bare legs covered in a patchwork of sterile pads, his blood-soaked socks and jeans dumped on the floor. And then there was Miller, sitting on the counter with his legs dangling freely, one eye swollen shut, dabbing at the cuts on his hand and arm with pads of cotton wool dipped in a bowl of antiseptic.

Agata set her bag on the counter among the litter of vials Miller had pulled from the cupboards.

'You are not Darren's friend,' she told him. 'A friend would take him to the hospital.'

'That's not an option.' Miller squeezed the cotton wool he was holding over the bowl. Scarlet threads drained down, blooming in the oily liquid.

Agata tutted and grabbed for his wrists, inspecting his hand.

'You're lucky you don't need stitches.'

She glanced at his eye, then released him and approached Darren's legs, pausing a moment before peeling away a corner of a bloody, puss-stained pad.

'Who did this to you?'

'Better you don't know,' Miller told her.

'And if I help?'

'We'll talk about that afterwards.'

'No.' She shook her head. 'You talk now.'

With his good eye, he could see the muscles bunch in her jaw as she reached a finger towards the back of Darren's hand, stroking it lightly, looking up at him, seeing the wretched truth on his face.

'I'm sorry,' he croaked.

'You'll have to leave the city,' Miller told her. 'At least for a few weeks. Possibly longer. The men looking for Darren could come for you. He can never come back.'

'So this is how it is.'

But it wasn't all of it. Not by a long way. Miller had been preoccupied with thinking about what Wade might try when he came round from the sedative, but there was Renner to consider, too. Kate had got Pete and Emily away from him in Arles, but Renner could stick around and try to work some leads. Perhaps he'd threaten Pete and Emily's friends or find a way to search their home before the police got to it. Unlikely, but possible. And Wade would attempt something similar in

Prague. He'd want to know for sure if there was anything that might lead them to Anna Brooks.

Miller didn't think there could be. He'd always been uniquely careful with his very first client. He was cautious by nature but he'd been extra cautious where she was concerned. It was why he hadn't stored any details about her online. It was also why he hadn't needed to. She was the beginning of it all for Miller. He knew everything connected to her safety and security by heart.

Agata touched Darren's face. 'This is what you would not tell me.'

'Some of it.'

'And the rest?'

'We don't have much time,' Miller pressed.

'The rest?'

There was a dignity to her that shamed Miller for what he was asking of her, for what he was making Darren ask of her, too.

'We'll talk,' Darren muttered. 'I promise. After we get away from here.'

And for once, though he was aware of the possible repercussions of that decision, of the unseen risks and future pitfalls, Miller didn't feel any urge to intervene.

*

Later, he stood in the damp chill of the alley and watched the tail lights of Agata's car until they were swallowed up by the rain and the murk, and then he turned and walked away from the surgery, eager to leave Malá Strana and the memories that had ambushed him here.

The wounds to his hand and arm had been swabbed and dressed, wrapped carefully in cotton bandages that smelled of the astringent lotion Agata had applied to his skin. The bruising to his eye was so severe that he could barely see out of it.

Agata had cleaned and stitched Darren's wounds, tearing open more sterile patches and dressings, leaving the wax paper wrappers scattered across the floor. There were yellowing contusions across his ribs and abdomen and abrasive marks around his wrists. His lips were cracked and bloodied, his mouth ringed by a pink crescent-shaped discolouration from the duct-tape gag.

'I didn't tell him much,' Darren had said, as Miller had helped him off the treatment table, Darren's arm draped around his neck, his left leg bent at the knee, too painful to set down. 'You didn't ask, but I wanted you to know. I told him a little about you. About what you'd done for me. That's all.'

'Did he ask you about someone called Anna?'

Darren nodded. 'But I couldn't tell him anything. I kept saying I didn't know about anyone else.'

'Did he believe you?'

'I think so. But I don't think it mattered all that much. I'm not even sure he was really listening. I think he just enjoyed hurting me.'

Together, they'd made their way out to Agata's dated Nissan and Miller had opened the passenger door, easing Darren inside, his face straining beneath the glow of the courtesy light. Agata had clambered into the driver's seat, fingers tapping the steering wheel restlessly as Miller squeezed Darren's shoulder and told him to take care, to be cautious, to heal up and wait for him to get in touch.

Back on Karmelitská, alone once more, Miller paused and stared at the entrance to the three-star hotel across the street, at the revolving doors and the alternative worlds they might once have led to, then he raised an arm and flagged down a cab, the driver contemplating his injuries for a prolonged moment before finally beckoning him in, leaving him to stare out the window in silence as the sad fairy-tale city glided by.

At the train station, Miller hobbled through the hushed late-night calm to a bank of public payphones, where he snatched up a handset and looked out through the scratched bubble of Perspex at a trio of backpackers sprawled on the floor, listening to a platform announcement in Czech, then English, about a sleeper train that was due to depart for Vienna.

'Kate,' he whispered, when his call was connected, and then he had to pause and gather himself, clinging on to the metal cradle, mashing his head against the Perspex dome. 'Darren's OK. I got him out. But I'm calling because there's someone I'd like you to meet. Somewhere I need you to come. Will you do it?'

'Come where?'

He swallowed against the rising lump in his throat – a lump he wasn't sure would ever go away – until finally he said it, letting her all the way in.

'Switzerland, Kate. It's Switzerland. Will you meet me there?'

PART VII

Brienz, Switzerland

Chapter Sixty-Two

Lake Brienz was long and vast, ringed by mountains, surrounded by trees. Miller propped his forearms on a low stone wall and squinted across the windswept waters. He'd heard talk that the lake was as deep as the mountains were high. Glancing up at the jagged tips of the most distant glaciers – ice white against massed banks of low grey cloud – the notion seemed inconceivable to him. But then, many things had appeared almost impossible to Miller just lately. Like, for instance, how to begin to tell Kate what he needed to say.

He heard footsteps on gravel and turned to find her coming towards him, her movements hesitant and unbalanced, her face white as bone beneath whipped tendrils of red hair. She had on a hooded top over faded jeans. Her arms were folded tightly, her shoulders hunched.

'You made it.'

She stopped many metres away and considered him without speaking. She looked cold and worn out and he felt a sudden need to go to her, to hold her, but something in her demeanour, in the awkward way she was standing there, watching him, made him hold back.

'Where are the others?'

'Nearby.' Her voice was cracked and wavering. 'Emily needed to sleep. They're checking in to a hotel. I thought we should talk alone.'

Miller nodded. It was what he had wanted, too.

'What happened to your face?'

He shrugged, and showed her his bandaged hand also. 'Aaron Wade happened to it.'

'Looks painful.'

'I think that was the general idea.'

He half smiled and the sliver of sight in his bad eye blurred and merged. Behind him, yellow storm lights blinked from the villages on the far shores. He could sense a tightening of the air, a friction all around him, and the particular smell he associated with the coming of thunder and lightning – of woodsmoke and metal and match strikes.

He was wearing a flannel shirt and a vest under a corduroy hunting jacket but still he felt chilled.

Kate said, 'It's beautiful here.'

Miller was glad that she was seeing Brienz when the weather was raw and fierce, when the light faded unnaturally fast with the coming of a rainstorm and the mountains pressed in, making the tangle of twee wooden chalets clustered around them seem somehow vital and primitive.

'I missed you,' he told her.

She didn't respond, and Miller could almost have believed that he hadn't spoken at all. For a big man, he felt suddenly small.

'I've been waiting here thinking of what to say to you. Of how to start.'

Kate took a half-step closer.

'There are so many things to talk about. Rome, for one.'

She raised a hand. 'You said there was somebody you wanted me to meet.'

'I'm getting to that.'

'I want to hear it, Miller. I don't want any more secrets between us.'

There was a strained, robotic quality to her speech, almost as if she was repeating lines she'd rehearsed too many times. Miller sensed some kind of disconnect between her eyes and mouth. Did she regret sleeping with him? Was that what he was seeing in her expression? How else to explain the strange way she was holding herself, or the distance she was keeping between them?

'Is she here?'

'Who?'

'Anna. That's who you want me to meet, isn't it?'

There were several answers to that question, but none that were simple.

'Yes,' he said. 'And no.'

'Enough riddles.' She was crying now, shaking her head, the line of dark stitches on her brow contrasting with her bloodless face. 'Tell me the truth.'

'The truth.' He held her gaze. 'The truth is there is somebody here I want you to meet. But it's not Anna.'

'Who then?'

Miller took a deep breath and opened his mouth to begin.

Chapter Sixty-Three

'We need to talk.'

DS Lloyd barged past Fiona Grainger and through the front door of her house, heading for the kitchen.

'Hey!' Fiona called after her. 'You can't just come in here like this.'

'Tell me about the coroner's report into Melanie's death. Tell me why you requested access to the file.'

Fiona rushed to catch up with Lloyd. Her hair was a mess and her clothes were rumpled. An empty bottle of red wine was open on the counter, next to a stained wine glass.

Over by the back door, down on the floor, Lloyd could see a suitcase with a passport resting on top. Fiona caught her looking and dived towards it but Lloyd got there first. She snatched the passport up, flipping it open.

Fiona's image was in the back but the name printed on the document was not her own.

'What is this?' Lloyd asked. 'What's going on?'

But Fiona didn't respond. She was too busy trying to get the passport back.

'Nick's behind this, isn't he?' Lloyd held her away, lifting the passport beyond her reach. 'Nick's behind all of it. He's been in touch with you all along. He asked you to get access to that file.'

Fiona stretched until the frustration became too much for her and she stepped back, glaring.

'You might as well tell me now. I can't let you leave. You understand that, don't you?'

Fiona didn't say anything.

'Where are the records from the coroner's file? Why did you take them?'

'I didn't.'

'Then who did?'

She shook her head, breathing hard.

'I'm not talking to you about this. I can't. Just go. Please.'

'I can arrest you. Obstruction of justice.'

'Then do it.' Fiona looked at her with defiance in her eyes. 'Do it and end this for me. The hope has been killing me, anyway.'

'Hope for what? Fiona? Hope for what?'

But before she could reply, Lloyd's mobile began to ring, the bright electronic tune sounding crass and misplaced in the charged silence of the room.

Lloyd fixed a warning look on her face as she answered the call.

'DS Lloyd? It's Julia Summerhayes. I have some news for you, though I'm afraid I'm not sure what to make of it just yet.'

Lloyd maintained watchful eye contact with Fiona.

'Go on.'

'My assistant managed to track down the missing documents from the Melanie Adams file. Not directly. The records have been wiped from our master system entirely. IT couldn't retrieve them at all. But my assistant thought to check email correspondence. The electronic file was attached as a PDF to an email my predecessor sent to himself. He sent it to his private email address.'

'And that's unusual?'

'It's not something that has ever been allowed. I took a quick look at the records before calling you.'

'And?'

'At first glance everything seemed to be in order.'

'But at second glance?'

'I noticed something. Something I can't explain. A mix-up of some kind.'

'Yes?'

'The path lab ran a tox screen on Melanie. The results don't make any logical sense. There were traces of drugs in her system that shouldn't have been there.'

Lloyd's heart was banging in her chest. Fiona was studying her intently, looking panicked, almost as if she could hear the coroner's words for herself.

'What drugs?'

But Lloyd knew. She knew before the coroner said it.

'One was perampanel. The other was—'

'Oxcarbazepine. Used to treat epilepsy. And not a common combination.'

'How on earth did you know that?'

'Because you just confirmed something I really didn't want to believe.'

Lloyd thanked her and ended the call. She pocketed her phone and allowed her hand to linger by her hip. She was wearing one of her formless grey trouser suits and clipped to her waist was a can of CS spray. She pushed back the tails of her suit jacket and unclipped the leather strap holding the spray in place.

'Melanie didn't die in that fire,' Lloyd said. 'She wasn't shot and killed. Your sister was. I believe that and I'm sorry for it. But Melanie got away, somehow. The girl who perished was Anna Brooks.'

Lloyd felt an itch in her fingers, the desire to take out the spray and aim it. But she held her nerve. Held on.

'You left a link to the truth, Fiona. You didn't shred every copy of the records. Nick faked his daughter's death, using the body of a teen runaway. I guess his friends and contacts at the path labs and the coroner's office helped him to get away with it. I bet if I look I'll find that he worked with them on plenty of cases. Or maybe he bribed them. Doesn't matter, either way. The part I'd really like to know is when did *you* know, Fiona? Was it before you cried in my arms, here in this room, or was it afterwards? Was it all just an act?'

Fiona stumbled backwards, grasping for the backrest of a kitchen chair.

'Tell me the truth right now or so help me I'll call Manchester CID and you can explain it all to them under caution. You can start right from the beginning. You can incriminate yourself a hundred different ways.'

Fiona turned her head slowly and stared at the suitcase down on the floor.

'Tell me now. I'll help you if I can. I *want* to be able to help you.'

'It was that night,' she said quietly. 'The night of the fire.'

She looked off towards the kitchen window, staring blindly out at the straggly woods and the void in space and time where her sister's house had once stood.

'I heard the shots. A scream. My sister's voice. Then I saw the flames and I knew. I knew they'd been taken from me.

'I went out into the garden and I stood there, looking. And then there she was. A miracle. Melanie, running towards me, covered in soot and grime. And Nick, just behind. A man had come into their house. Melanie had heard him shoot Sarah. She'd heard her scream. Then he'd rushed upstairs and shot Anna, in the darkness on the landing outside Mel's bedroom. They looked similar, you know, Melanie and Anna. Both had brown hair, both sixteen. The killer made a mistake. He didn't search the house for anyone else. Melanie hid in the bathroom. Then the fire started. The flames became too much. So she climbed out of a window and there was Nick, below her, yelling at her to jump, leading her off through the woods to me.'

'Why was Anna even there?'

Fiona blinked, as though coming round from a daze.

'She visited sometimes to hang out with Melanie. To watch movies. To sleep over. It wasn't supposed to be like that. Sarah wasn't supposed to allow it. But sometimes she turned a blind eye.'

'And Nick?'

'He reached the house too late. There was nothing he could do. The place was an inferno by then. The killer had used something to speed the fire. Nick tried to get inside the house and he couldn't. He saw Sarah dead on the floor, the flames taking her. Then he looked up and saw Melanie. Alive.'

The fire inspector's report into the blaze had identified the accelerant as lighter fuel. Lloyd had wasted countless hours trying to find a local shop that might have sold some to Nick in the build-up to that night.

'Nick made us come in here and he started telling us what we needed to do. He saw it all right away – before the police and the fire service and the ambulance showed up – and he swore me to secrecy. That sickened me. I hated him for it. He was trying to protect Melanie. He was scared for her. I can see that now. But back then I was angry. With him, and with myself. I should have stopped him. I should have said no to what he had in mind.'

'Telling the world that Melanie was the dead girl.'

'It was the fire. The fire made it all possible. He said it would . . . conceal what needed to be concealed.'

'And the rest?'

'He had friends, like you said. Someone at the hospital. The coroner. They'd helped Nick with hiding people before. Officially. This time, they agreed to hide Melanie for him.'

'Because Anna was disposable. Because she was just a runaway. You people.' Lloyd did nothing to temper the revulsion she was feeling. 'How do you think Sarah would have felt about that? Some legacy.'

Fiona shook her head, bewildered, unable to confront it.

'I visited Anna's parents just yesterday,' Lloyd continued. 'Good people. They still live for the day they'll see their daughter again. They still hope. And now I'm going to have to end that for them. I'm going to have to tell them Anna died four years ago. That her remains were cremated. That they'll never get to say goodbye.'

Fiona clutched at her chest, tugging on her blouse.

'Don't you think I hate myself for it? Hate what was done?'

'I'm not sure that matters, Fiona. I don't think that counts for anything right now.'

'I hated Nick for it. I hated being a part of it. *That's* why I was so angry with him. Why I said such wicked things to you. I kept thinking about the fire. About those flames. How he turned them to his advantage so quickly.'

She shuddered, and her voice became small and hollow.

'Part of me wanted you to find the truth. Part of me dreaded it. That's why I requested the records.'

'You could have given them to me, shown them to me.'

'No, I couldn't, because there was nothing to show. The coroner, McGuintyre, he came here, to my house. He told me there were no records any more. They were already gone. He'd dealt with it. There was nothing to worry about.'

Lloyd held up the counterfeit passport in front of Fiona's face. She'd curled it in her hand, bending it into a tube.

'So where are you going, Fiona? Where are you running to?'

'It doesn't matter any more. None of it does.'

'Where's Nick? Where's Melanie?'

'I don't know.'

But she did know. She had to. Lloyd shook her head, disgusted, and looked about the room, trying to calm her rage, to think, to see.

And then, quite suddenly, she did.

She moved towards the fridge, extending her hand, ripping the little magnetised frame free and tearing off the backing, removing the pretty Alpine scene.

Fiona had lied about that, too. The image hadn't come free with a magazine. It was a postcard.

Lloyd flipped it over. There was no message on the back. It was blank aside from Fiona's address and a stamp and a postmark. The stamp was Swiss. The postmark was dated nine months ago. A line of printed text at the bottom of the card told Lloyd that the image was of a place called Brienzersee, a lake in central Switzerland.

Chapter Sixty-Four

'Say something.'

Kate wouldn't speak. Perhaps there wasn't anything to be said. Miller knew that what he'd done was terrible, shameful, but he'd wanted to be honest with her, to have her try to understand.

'Please say something.'

But she didn't. Or couldn't.

'I'm sorry for it,' he told her. 'You have to believe that. But you asked me for the truth, and honestly, I'd do it all again tomorrow if I had to. You know now what Lane is capable of. You've seen it for yourself. I wanted my daughter safe.'

Kate took a step back and looked up to where the dirty grey clouds were drifting down over the high mountain peaks.

'Melanie hates me for it. I thought I was saving her and now she'll barely talk to me. But she's safe. She's alive. I have that for Melanie, and I have it for you, too. And all right, maybe I'm stupid to want more. Maybe I can't ever be allowed it. But I want it, Kate. I want a future with you. With Melanie. That's why I brought you here. That's why I told you. I saw something in Prague. Something that made me understand that there can't be any secrets between us if we want a real chance for whatever we have together to truly begin.'

Kate wiped at her face with the back of her wrist, smearing her eyes. She was sniffing, her breathing irregular, her chest hitching and falling.

'I won't do it,' she said. 'I can't.'

Miller felt his heart lurch.

'I know I'm asking a lot. I know that, Kate. But I'm going to ask it all the same.'

She smiled through her tears, as though he'd somehow misunderstood her; as if his confusion only made it worse.

'What is it? Tell me.'

She shook her head some more, drawing in a deep breath and summoning enough composure to steady herself. Then she sighed and fixed her gaze on Miller, speaking with a fragile calm.

'Is she close? Is Melanie here?'

Miller raised an arm and pointed up the mountainside, beyond the village.

'See the chalet all on its own in the clearing? She lives with a man and his children. His name is Timo. A good man. A widower. Timo, Nico and Mia. They're Melanie's family now.'

But as Miller was talking, Kate had started shaking her head, lifting her hands, backing away. What was it she was saying to him? He couldn't make it out. Her eyes seemed to be searching him, pleading with him.

He finished talking, and Kate stood still for a long second.

I'm sorry.

That was what she'd been saying. And now she was repeating it, mouthing it over and over as she reached up to the side of her head and plucked free an earpiece connected to a flesh-coloured wire. Miller, numbed, felt his whole world tip on its axis, everything thrown upside down and falling around him as she unzipped her hooded top and rolled up her white T-shirt and showed him the radio transmitter that was strapped to her chest.

352

Half a mile away, Mike Renner lowered the two-way radio he'd been talking to Kate on and turned to Aaron Wade. Both men had headphones covering their ears. Both men had been listening to every word Nick Adams had had to say. They shared a look. It was a look of shock and concern and confusion. And on Wade's bruised and grazed face Renner caught something else.

Fear.

His lips and mouth were still swollen, an after-effect of whatever drug Nick Adams had disabled him with, but the tightness that gripped hold of his features was unmistakable all the same.

He had good reason to be afraid. Connor Lane did not tolerate mistakes, least of all where his younger brother was concerned. But this mistake affected them both, and it had happened on Renner's watch.

Anna Brooks had been dead all this time. Melanie Adams was still alive. Which put a whole new dimension on the situation, though the ultimate outcome would have to be the same.

Wade reached up to remove his headphones. Renner did likewise.

'Are you going to tell him?' Wade asked.

Renner didn't know. He hadn't made up his mind just yet.

'No, and neither are you,' he said. 'This doesn't change anything for us. Or for them.'

Renner looked into the dimmed rear of the van, locking eyes with the overweight soap actress who was tied up next to the weedy black kid. He glanced at the wounded father and the scared little girl and the dirty rag doll she clenched in her lap.

Then he turned his head and traded a new look with Wade. It was a look that spoke of tough choices and hard resolve. And, on Wade's face, something else – an animal hunger.

Renner cupped an earphone to the side of his head, but all he could hear now was the whine and hiss of static. He gazed out the windscreen and lifted the binoculars off the dash, looking through the magnified lenses towards the turbulent waters out on the lake. In the foreground, he could see Adams leaning into Kate's face, trailing the wire from the radio transmitter in his fist.

'Get it over with,' he said to Wade. 'And try to keep it clean.'

He didn't lower the binoculars. He didn't want to see the eagerness on Wade's face as he clambered into the rear of the van. But he couldn't avoid hearing Becca's muffled scream as Wade closed in on her and slapped her, and he couldn't block out Emily's distressed cries as Wade began shouting questions about the location of the chalet and the man called Timo and the obstacles they might face.

Chapter Sixty-Five

Miller tore along the steep mountain track in his rental SUV, gravel and loose mud clattering against the chassis.

Kate braced a hand on the dash as Miller braked sharply for a hairpin bend, wrenching the wheel around, stamping on the gas. He was driving like he was having a fight.

Which he was.

With her.

She said, 'I didn't have a choice. You have to understand that.'

'Oh, I understand.'

'They have Becca and Hanson. They have Pete and Emily. They told me they'd kill them. They said they'd start with Emily.'

'And you believed them.'

She glared across at him. 'They killed Christine. They killed Clive.'

'So maybe you really didn't have a choice.'

'Hey.' Kate dug her nails into his arm. 'They killed your wife too, remember? Or was that another lie?'

He stared out through the mud-smeared windscreen at the raking incline ahead. They were spearing through an area of woodland, pines on either side of them. He was angry with Kate. Angry with Lane. But mostly he was angry with himself. He'd let Melanie down. He'd failed her. Again.

And why? Because he'd put himself first. He'd tried to let Kate into his life.

The SUV thumped over a pothole, the steering wheel bucking wildly in his hand.

'Sarah's dead. Lane took her from me.'

'Then you know, don't you? You know I had no choice.'

He did know. And he also knew that it had been his mistake. His error. Even without baring his soul to Kate, the outcome would have been much the same. Hanson knew where Melanie was living. Becca had visited the village with him before. Renner could have extracted the information from either of them. He'd be pressing them for details now.

So the truth was he wasn't angered by what Kate had done. He was bothered most of all because he'd been played. Because they'd used his feelings for Kate to manipulate him. Because he'd allowed them to. And, to top it all, because he'd been so caught up in what he was sharing with Kate, in his need to confide, that he hadn't taken the time to act on his instincts when he'd sensed that something was wrong.

It was also his own stupid fault that they'd been tracked in the first place. He should never have sent Kate to Arles. He should never have let any of them go into the village and approach the house. Kate had told him that Renner and Wade had caught up to them only a few hours earlier. Hanson had pulled into a deserted rest stop just beyond Bern because Emily had been feeling travel-sick. She'd needed some air. A white van had roared up behind them and Renner and Wade had leapt out. They'd been armed. They'd been rough.

And they'd been clever. Back in Arles, Pete had followed Miller's instructions and prepared a go-bag for himself and

Emily. Becca had tossed it into the back of his car before she knew that Renner was there. It had only taken Renner a second to slip a GPS transmitter and a radio bug inside the bag.

Wade must have flown in to join Renner somewhere on his route. It worried Miller to think how angry Wade would be after Prague, and he feared the revenge he might exact.

'We should have looked for them in the village,' Kate said.

Renner hadn't wanted Kate to know where they'd be watching her from after she'd been shoved out of the van. He hadn't wanted her to be able to signal to Miller in some way.

'You said they were armed, Kate. What would you have had me do? Throw rocks?'

'They'll still be armed if they find us up here. Down there, they might have held back. They would have been concerned about police, about witnesses.'

'Like they were concerned in Arles? Or at that rest stop?'

'Still.' She shrugged. 'I guess we'll be OK. Plenty of rocks to throw up here.'

Miller looked across at her, gauging her attitude. She was acting tough, but it wasn't a hard act to see through.

'Timo is Swiss.'

'Terrific. I hear they have an excellent reputation for fighting.'

'They also have compulsory national service. Timo has army training. When he completed his service, he had a legal right to buy his assault rifle. He keeps a hunting rifle, too. I've seen them both, in a small barn near his chalet.'

'Well, OK then.' She nodded. 'Go Switzerland. Why didn't you say so sooner?'

They burst out of the tree cover, speeding between pastures

and meadows. Cows grazed around them, bells clanging from their necks, several of them lying down. There was a rickety chalet up ahead, a water trough out front. Two goats were drinking from it and they raised their heads as the SUV rumbled by.

A dark shadow rushed across the fields, the storm clouds skimming low and bringing with them the first hard spatters of rain. Miller flicked on the SUV's headlamps and hit the wiper blades. They beat side to side, smearing mud, until a sudden squall struck so hard that the wipers were over-whelmed. Miller switched them to full speed, the mechanism whining, the deluge blurring the way ahead.

'How far?' Kate shouted, over the din of water on metal.

'We're a way off yet.'

'Can we make it in this storm?'

'No choice. We have to.'

But Miller cut his speed a little, straining against the misty sight from his swollen eye. The track climbed onwards, rising steeply, curving wildly. He thought of the yellow lights that had been flashing around the lake, of the warning they'd given and all the warnings he'd missed.

*

Miller had visited the chalet many times before, nearly always without Melanie or Timo being aware of his presence. It was situated in a grassy clearing, close to a wood and an over-hanging rock outcrop cluttered with trees that looked down, on a good day, over the valley and the village, the crystal-clear lake and the majestic Alps beyond. But not today, because the clouds and the rain had closed in around them, making it feel as if Miller was sliding the SUV to a halt next to a rugged and drenched ledge in the middle of a desolate wasteland.

He cut the engine and pulled on the handbrake, parking in the middle of the road, blocking access to a handful of even higher and more isolated shacks. He killed the headlamps, leaving the keys in the ignition. The wiper blades had stopped on a slant.

Miller could feel the hard journey in his jangled nerves and aching backside and in the tenderness of his bandaged palm. He checked the time. Gone 3 p.m. Ordinarily he might have expected Renner and Wade to wait for nightfall, but with the storm raging and the sky leaden, it was possible they'd come sooner.

'Melanie really lives here?' Kate asked him.

'Timo keeps cattle and goats. They have electricity. Water. They grow a few vegetables.'

'"Remote" isn't the word.'

Miller didn't say anything to that. He knew how it looked and how it was. Melanie had shut herself off from the rest of the world.

'I guess it doesn't get much safer than this.'

'It didn't. Until today.'

The chalet was squat and leaning to one side, the timber boards weathered and grey. Oblongs of yellow light shone through the recessed windows against the dreary afternoon light. A rusted flatbed truck was beached at the side of the chalet.

'What are you going to say to them?'

'Damned if I know.'

359

He pushed open his door, holding on to it against the wind.

'I'm leaving the keys here,' he shouted back. 'In case one of us needs to get out of here in a hurry.'

Then, fastening his coat and turning up his collar, he slammed the door closed behind him, ducked his head and ran.

The loamy scent of the meadow was strong in his nostrils and the air felt damp and abrasive as the frenzied rain pummelled his head and face.

The meadow fell away from him into a shallow compression and as he rushed down, his legs feeling heavy and drained, a sudden violent crack and a low bass rumble pierced the sky all around.

He turned to see Kate stumbling behind him, picking her way through the grass and mud, her arms out at her sides for balance. A brilliant flash of lightning seemed to freeze her for an instant.

He waved and beckoned her on, turning back to the chalet, racing for the porch, leaping up on to the spattered boards, then pausing to contemplate the rough plank door. They must have seen his approach. They must have noticed the lancing beams of the SUV, at least. But they hadn't come outside. They hadn't welcomed him here.

So he held off on knocking and he waited for Kate to catch up to him. She peered at him, lips parted, frowning, her expression seeming to ask what he was waiting for exactly.

He didn't know, but he waited all the same, until finally he raised his flattened hand to beat on the timber, only for the door to open in front of him.

Chapter Sixty-Six

Melanie didn't act surprised. She showed hardly any emotion at all. Her attention was drawn for a moment to the damage to his face, the bulging swell around his eye, and her lips parted with a small puff of air. She turned her head slowly and glanced at Kate. She didn't say a word.

And neither did Miller.

The thunder came again. Then the lightning.

He thought of where to begin, of what he might say. It seemed like he never had the right words to say any more.

Miller sensed Kate looking between them. He could tell she was growing restless and that she'd feel the need to intervene before long.

So he went ahead and came right out with it.

'You have to leave, Mel. All of you. I'm sorry, but we have to get you away from here.'

The rain was swirling past him and in through the door, wetting Melanie's thick woollen socks. She had on a knitted jumper over frayed grey jeans. Her hair was long and dark, parted above one eye. She looked so much like Sarah in that moment that it stilled the air in Miller's lungs.

Then her face hardened and she curled her lip and moved back as if to swing the door closed, but Timo appeared at her shoulder before she could. He clutched the door and gazed squarely at Miller.

Timo was tall and powerfully built with short sandy hair and a full beard. Farm work might have given him the body of a wrestler but the solitude of the mountains had gifted him an aura of calm assurance and control. Miller had watched him often from the cover of the dense pines that bordered the edge of the meadow. He'd seen how much Timo cared for Melanie and the children. He knew he had to have been wounded deeply by the slow, cruel death of his wife – just as Miller had been wounded by the brutal loss of Sarah – but he believed him to be a good and caring man. He'd always felt that Melanie was safe with him.

So it was to Timo that he appealed.

'I wouldn't be here unless I had to be. Please. You both know that. We don't have a lot of time.'

Timo weighed his words in silence. He was almost as tall as Miller, nearly as broad, but he looked ten times as healthy. In the winter months, he worked as a ski instructor. During the summer, when he could find someone to watch over the animals, he liked to rock climb or hunt. There probably hadn't been a day in his adult life where he hadn't engaged in some kind of strenuous physical activity.

'This is our home.'

'I know. And I want you to be able to come back here. Which is why I'll stay after you leave. I'm going to end the threat. I'm going to stop it here for good.'

'What have you done?' Melanie asked. 'What's happening?'

'It's Lane. It was always going to be Lane.'

Melanie stared at him, becoming gaunt, a desperate pleading creeping into her eyes, as though she hoped he might tell her it was all a terrible mistake.

'Let us in. Please. I already told you, we don't have long.'

Renner had Wade handle the driving. It was partly because he was tired from the long motorway miles he'd negotiated on his own and partly because he wanted Wade up front, away from the four figures huddled together in the back. But mostly it was because his injured shin was hot and painful, the tissue swollen, the broken skin rimed with green pus.

Renner clicked on the dome light overhead and studied the map Wade had fetched from the tourist office in Brienz. He'd had Hanson use a pencil to mark the correct location of the chalet and he was confident he hadn't been misled. If Hanson was as good as Renner had been told, he'd know that very few people had ever lied to him and survived the experience. Still, Renner was a man who liked to erase doubt wherever possible, and he'd allowed Wade a few minutes to make the consequences of attempting to trick them abundantly clear. They would keep their guests alive long enough to correct any misdirections they'd been foolish enough to give.

Renner's problem now was comparing the detail on the map to the terrain they were passing through. The storm was raging, the light poor, and visibility was terrible. The tyres on the van were old, the treads worn way down. They kept sliding, the engine revving wildly, hopelessly.

Renner clutched the grab handle above his seat, his mind racing with the implications of what they were speeding towards. This entire mess had started out with two bungled hits, four years apart. It was maddening to think things had gone so wrong four years ago, and that he was only finding out about it today.

363

Those two errors – neither of them his fault directly – had spiralled into something much more complex and demanding but potentially more conclusive, too. He had the opportunity now to end every threat to Russell in one go by taking out Kate and Melanie, and as an added bonus, he could finally rid himself of the inconvenience of Nick Adams.

Which should have been a good thing, except Renner's confidence was shaken – in Wade, as well as in himself – and he was becoming less and less certain that they'd be able to drive up close to the chalet. Supposing he was reading the map even halfway right, hiking from anywhere near their current position would take an hour, maybe two, and then the same again back, which was something he wasn't sure his leg could bear.

He craned his neck and gazed up at the grisly sky, then down at the shirt, trousers and loafers he had on.

He tensed his left leg, lifted it gently, and felt the savage ache and the sting. If the van made it no further, he might have to let Wade go on alone. In a twisted way, he supposed it was fitting, but it was a prospect that filled him with dread.

Chapter Sixty-Seven

Inside the chalet, a place Miller had never ventured into before, the bare wood had been varnished in honey tones and the floorboards were waxed and buffed. The modest downstairs functioned as a kitchen and living space combined. It was neat and orderly – the complete opposite of the bedroom Melanie had kept as a teenager.

There was a log fire in the middle of the lounge area and Nico and Mia were sprawled on a rug in front of it, playing a board game with dice and counters. They were lean and rangy kids, a touch feral, aged eight and six, with curly white-blonde hair and startling blue eyes. They lifted their heads when Miller and Kate came in but they didn't smile or wave. They looked to their father for an explanation instead. Miller guessed that visitors had to be rare at the chalet, particularly walking inside looking bedraggled in soaked clothes and muddy boots in the middle of a mountain storm.

Timo spoke to Nico and Mia in a hushed but stern burst of Swiss-German, and Miller watched as the kids glanced at him accusingly, then got to their feet and left the room, stomping hard on the wooden treads that led to the bedrooms above.

He stepped around the plaid sofa and stood in front of the fire, feeling the heat on his face and hands. His jacket was steaming, water dripping from his clothes. He waited until he heard bedsprings overhead and was sure the children weren't eavesdropping before he began.

'There are two men coming here. They have guns. They also have Hanson and Becca and two of my clients held captive in the back of their van. One of them is a child. A four-year-old girl.'

Miller didn't look at Melanie or Timo or Kate. He stared into the flames, thinking of the fire that had burned down his home and had seemed, for just a little while, to offer Melanie a way out. But it hadn't saved her for him.

He wanted to turn and take her in his arms. He wanted to hug her and stroke her hair, to whisper in her ear how sorry he was for all that had happened and for everything since.

But Melanie was keeping her distance. She was clinging to Timo, her fists knotted in the fleece sweater he had on.

'We have radio here,' Timo said. 'I can contact the police.'

'No police.'

'Miller.' Kate was at his side. 'Maybe he's right. Maybe we should consider it.'

'He's not. And we shouldn't.'

Miller pulled away and moved over to the tiny window in the front wall of the chalet. He tugged the gingham curtain aside and looked across the meadow through the slanted rain-fall at the lone SUV and the storm skies twitching in the east.

'All of you need this over with. I need this over with.'

He glanced at Kate, who'd dropped on to the couch, her hands clasped together in her lap.

'Contact the police and it all starts again. It just begins some-where else.'

'You're talking about killing these men?' Timo asked him.

'I'm talking about ending a threat.'

'What if they kill you first?'

'I won't let that happen. You want to hold on to your life here, don't you? Your home? Your kids? My daughter?'

Miller sneaked a look at Melanie. How long was it since he'd been able to look at her this close? He'd tried to visit often. He'd tried to stay a part of her life. But Melanie had been angry with him; was angry still. She resented him because she hadn't been able to say goodbye to her mother. She hated how he'd seized on Anna's death to protect her.

'Why now?' She shook her head at him, as though warning him not to look at her that way. 'What changed?' She flicked her eyes at Kate. 'And who is she?'

'We don't have time to go into it now.'

'No, you have time and you'll tell me. This time, I need to know why. It's my life, isn't it? That's what we're talking about here.'

Thunder detonated in the sky above, rumbling through the chalet, and Miller looked towards the window again. A flare of light bathed the side of his face.

'Tell them,' Kate said. 'Melanie's right, they deserve it.'

So he did. He told them about the trial Russell faced for the murder of Helen Knight and how Kate had been due to test-ify. He told them he'd saved Kate from an attempt on her life but that things had started to go wrong soon afterwards. He told them how his network of clients had begun to fracture and collapse, leading Connor Lane's men to Switzerland, client by client, link by link. He told them people had been killed, others badly injured.

He didn't tell them how Kate had been a part of it at the

end. He didn't tell them about the wire that had been concealed beneath her clothes, or how his need to confide in her had led them here.

Timo and Melanie didn't interrupt him as he talked. They didn't sit down. They just stood and listened and clung to each other as if they were standing out in the storm, huddling against the worst of the wind and the rain.

Finally, when he was done, Miller looked at Melanie again. Really looked this time, searching for some level of understanding or forgiveness. But she wouldn't give it to him.

'So you'll wait for them to come and you'll kill them. With Nico and Mia in the house. That's your big plan, knowing what they did to us before? Have you learned nothing?'

'No,' Miller told her. 'I want you and Timo and the kids out of here. I want you to get as far away as you can.'

'And me?' Kate asked him.

'Stay with Melanie for now. Help her to get the kids ready.' He looked at Timo. 'You come to the barn with me. Bring the keys to your rifle cabinet.'

Chapter Sixty-Eight

The barn was hunkered down at the bottom of the sloping meadow, overhung by the sodden limbs of the pines at the edge of the bordering wood. Miller had sheltered behind it many times when he was watching over Melanie from a distance. In truth, it was little more than a decrepit shed with a lean-to shelter attached to one flank. Chopped logs had been stacked beneath the shelter, packed tightly into every available crevice. The blade of an axe was resting in a split log, its handle sticking out.

The window at the front of the shed was dark and grimy, clotted with spider webs, cracked through the pane. Miller hurried after Timo to the door on the far side, the grass tangling round his ankles, his boots and socks soaked through with cold damp.

Timo was wearing a red outdoor coat over black waterproof trousers, and rain drummed off his jacket and the peaked hood he'd pulled over his head as he swung back the door.

Miller stepped inside to darkness and the smell of damp timber and mud and old cut grass. He crossed towards the window, the toe of his boot clanging off something metal and hollow-sounding, then stared back towards the chalet.

Beneath the heavy cloud cover, the light was prematurely dim, like a false dusk, and the chalet looked desolate and beaten down at the top of the rise. He could see the silhouette of

Melanie or Kate standing next to a lighted upstairs window.

There was a dry click from behind and Miller turned to see Timo banging a torch against his palm, the bulb flickering to life, the beam weak and hazy. He aimed the torch at a metal cabinet on the wall and fitted a key in the lock.

Miller stepped closer as Timo opened the cabinet and cast the torch over an upright hunting rifle and the yellowing threads of some decaying cobwebs. The rifle stock was nicked and gouged, the barrel scratched and dinged. It had a bolt-action slide. Two wilted boxes of cartridges were stacked at the bottom of the cabinet.

'Where's your assault rifle?' Miller asked him.

'I sold it.' Timo cast the torch beam over the space the rifle had recently occupied. 'We needed money.'

He wouldn't look at Miller as he said it, and Miller guessed it was because he was embarrassed for both of them. Melanie had refused to accept any money from Miller after he'd first set her up in Switzerland, preferring to finance herself. He knew her reasons and he supposed it was noble of her, though it had cost them the assault rifle he'd been relying on.

He felt a tacky dryness in his mouth, the thump of fear in his chest.

'OK.' He claimed the torch for himself and sprayed the beam around. 'What else do we have in here?'

The object he'd kicked with his toe turned out to be an old oil drum with a chainsaw and a toolbox resting alongside it. A collection of garden tools were fitted to the wall: a rusted hoe; a shovel and a pickaxe; a fork and a scythe. Closer still, a tangle of rope was hanging down in front of Miller's face. He aimed the beam upwards and saw that a plastic helmet and the rest of

Timo's climbing equipment had been slung over some rafters.

Timo was watching him in silence. Miller handed him the torch.

'Take this. Aim it up here.'

'I can stay. I can help you.'

'You are helping me. You're keeping my daughter safe. Your children, too. You know these mountains. In this weather, they'll need you with them.'

'You said there are two men.'

'Kate will stay with me. She can handle it.'

The batteries in Timo's torch were failing, the bulb growing weaker. He backed away and held the door open against the wind, grey light bleeding in.

'What if she can't handle it? What if these men kill you?'

'They won't.'

'But if they do?'

'Then you run, Timo. You find someplace new and you start again. Melanie can show you how.' Miller dragged down a heavy coil of rope amid a haze of dust, thrusting it into Timo's chest. 'But remember, I'm not going to let that happen. And once you're on your own with Melanie and the kids, you're not going to let them out of your sight, no matter what you hear down here. Understand?'

Slowly, Timo nodded, the hood of his outdoor jacket swishing, water trickling into his eyes. 'I have radios. When this is over, you'll call me.'

'Absolutely. When it's over.'

*

371

Kate stood next to the window of Melanie and Timo's bedroom, watching as Melanie dressed the children in their warmest clothes before pulling them in for a hug. She told them they were heading out on a secret adventure and that they might even camp for the night in the woods. Nico cooed and punched the air in excitement, but Mia shivered and looked over at Kate, unsettled by her presence, shaken by the storm outside.

'Are you coming with us?' she asked Melanie.

'Yes, I'm coming.'

'And Papa, too?'

'Of course Papa too.'

Melanie hitched an eyebrow at Kate from over Mia's head, as if daring her to say otherwise. But the scenario was fine by Kate. Yes, she was scared, and she hated the idea of waiting here for Renner and Wade to come, but she feared being asked to go with Melanie and shepherd the children to safety even more. She'd failed once already with Emily. She didn't know the mountain terrain. It was better for everyone if Timo went and Kate was the one who stayed behind.

'Now go on downstairs,' Melanie told the kids. 'Put on your coats and boots. Wait for me by the door.'

Nico raced off, thundering down the treads. Mia took more persuading. Another hug. A rub on the back and a kiss on the head. By the time they were downstairs, they were laughing and squabbling.

Listening to their playful bickering, Kate found herself pining after her own lost childhood with Richard. It was the smallest things they'd missed out on. Precious things. Like the chance to laugh and horse around together.

She cupped her hand to the window glass and squinted out

at the barn, unable to spot Miller, then looked towards the SUV. The sheeting downpour was backed by a misty haze. She wondered if Renner and Wade were close.

Turning, she found Melanie standing on the end of the bed, reaching up for a rucksack that was tucked away on top of a rustic wardrobe.

It felt peculiar to be alone with her. *We're ghosts.* That's what Miller had said to her at the very beginning, but right now she felt as if she was looking at a ghost for real – a dead girl, brought back to life.

Kate was having a hard time adjusting to this strange new reality, but her overall emotion was one of sadness. She felt sad for Anna Brooks and her family. Sad for Miller and Melanie and the damage to their relationship. Sad for herself.

Miller had deceived her, and she understood why, but some of her trust in him, and yes, even some of her attraction to him, had been spurred by his loss and his pain, by the bond they shared of an absent family. Maybe that said something bad about her. It probably did. But it was honest and true, whereas a portion of Miller's grief had been fabricated, and now Kate's feelings for him felt diminished, even tarnished.

Her eyes drifted towards a framed photograph on one of the bedside tables, where a beautiful woman was smiling to camera, her face lifted towards the sun. Her hairstyle and clothes were dated and she was holding a young Melanie in her arms. They looked alike. Sarah, Kate guessed. She was heartbreakingly alive in the image. Achingly content.

Melanie stepped down from the bed with the rucksack in her hands and caught Kate staring at the picture. She measured her for a long moment.

'Is it true what Dad told us about Russell? Did he really kill this Helen girl?'

'Why would your father lie to you?'

Melanie scoffed and threw back the lid of the rucksack, checking its contents, pulling a compressed sleeping bag half out and pushing it back in again.

'Because he'd say or do anything to protect me and make me leave here. He'd lie if he thought it was in my best interests. He'd do the same to you, too.'

'I was going to be testifying at Russell's trial. I wouldn't have agreed to do that – I wouldn't be here right now – if I didn't believe that I'd witnessed something important. I was the last one to see Helen alive. I saw her with Russell, down by the boathouse on the Lane estate. They were arguing. Helen's body was found washed up on the lake shore not far from there.'

'The boathouse?'

'Yes. Does it mean something to you?'

'Not really. Russell used to talk about taking me there one day. He mentioned it a couple of times.'

'Did he say why?'

'Never.'

'And you didn't go?'

'Anna told me not to. She said he was creepy. At the time, I thought she was just jealous. I thought she wanted Russell for herself. She could be like that. For a while, part of me even wondered if she invented the rape because he wasn't interested in a relationship with her. As an attention thing. But if what you say about Russell is true, then I guess he really is a monster. I guess Anna was telling the truth all along.'

'Unlike your father, according to you. Perhaps you've made a mistake with him, too?'

'Seriously? You're telling me he hasn't lied to you about *any-thing*? I'm sorry, but you're either painfully naive or you're choosing to ignore it. He lied to you about me, didn't he?'

'He had his reasons.'

'Reasons. Right.'

'He's been protecting you. Protecting me.'

Melanie looked at her again. Really looked at her this time.

'Tell me something – did he explain to you how he funds his little programme?'

Kate faltered. She didn't like where this was going. She didn't like Melanie's tone.

'He mentioned a benefactor.'

'But he didn't tell you who that benefactor is, did he?'

This is day one for you, Kate. Trust me, you'll learn more when it's safe.

'He will.'

'Huh. Well, I hate to break it to you but he hasn't been exactly truthful with you there. His mystery "benefactor" is the guy who tried to kill us both. Dad's been blackmailing Connor Lane. He gets Hanson to send anonymous threats about knowing where Anna is. Hanson filters the payments so they can't be traced. You remember dead Anna? The one who was killed instead of me?'

Kate felt herself sway. She fought the temptation to sit down, to look back over to the photograph of Sarah and Melanie together, caught in a moment in time before everything became corrupted so badly.

'*Now* you begin to see it. That's why Connor has been so

motivated to burn through Dad's network to get to Anna. It hasn't just been about protecting Russell. It's been about saving himself cash. A lot of cash.'

She turned to go, swinging the backpack on to her shoulder, snatching up the photograph of her mother and stuffing it into her bag.

'You like him, don't you? Did he tell you he feels the same way? I wonder if he was telling the truth about that.' She paused and shook her head. 'You two would be good together, I think. You both seem kind of alike. But you should forget about ever testifying against Russell. Dad'll never allow you to do it. He'll never let you go back.'

Chapter Sixty-Nine

Miller stepped up on to the porch of the chalet through the curtain of rainwater dribbling down from the swamped gutters just as Melanie bundled the kids through the front door. Kate came out behind them, buttoning a huge suede overcoat that looked as if it belonged to Timo. The shoulders dwarfed her own and the sleeves hung down over her hands. She cast a surly look Miller's way, her lips pressed into a thin line.

'We need to talk,' she told him.

He glanced at Melanie, who glared back defiantly. It wasn't difficult to imagine the kind of things she might have said. 'We will. But can it wait? At least for a little while?'

Miller set down the axe he was carrying and held the rifle out to Kate. His hand and the rifle were dripping and slick with moisture. She debated a moment, then reached out and took it from him.

'You've fired one of these before?' he asked.

'Something similar. Not for a long time.'

'Why don't you head into the meadow and take some shots at the log pile? We have plenty of shells.'

'Aren't you afraid they'll hear me?'

'They might not over this storm. Besides, they're coming regardless. And I think we'll both be happier once we know you're comfortable shooting that thing.'

He freed a box of cartridges from his pocket and held them

out to Kate. She waited a moment, then took them, stuffing them into the pocket of her new overcoat, turning to go.

Miller grabbed her arm.

'We will talk. Trust me.'

She nodded sharply and walked away, head bowed against the deluge, carrying the rifle at her side. Miller felt a tugging on his trouser leg and looked down to see Nico beaming up at him, his eyes crazed with the strange adventure of it all. He ruffled his hair.

'All set?'

Nico nodded eagerly.

'And you, Mia? Will you be warm enough? You're going to get wet.'

She stared shyly, unsure what to say, hiding behind Melanie's legs. Melanie rested a hand on her, watching Timo step up on to the porch next to Miller. He was weighed down with the sodden ropes and climbing equipment that were slung across his torso and neck.

'We should go,' she said to him.

Timo didn't respond right away and Miller could see the fear take hold of Melanie. The muscles in her jaw tensed and bunched. The wind was gusting and her hair was getting in her eyes, but she did nothing to clear it.

'You go on ahead,' Timo told her. 'I'll catch you up.'

'You promised me.'

Timo ducked his head, dropping the climbing gear in a heap as thunder tore through the mountain skies and lightning stuttered brightly. Mia shrieked and clutched at Melanie. Timo nodded at the quad bike.

'Go to Levin's hut. You can shelter behind it. I'll be there soon. I'll hike up in thirty minutes from now.'

'You swore you wouldn't do this.'

'It's my fault,' Miller put in.

'I don't have any doubt about that.'

'I need his help,' Miller explained. 'But not for long. I won't let him stay. You have my word on that.'

'Your word.' Melanie lifted her chin towards Kate, down in the meadow. 'Why don't you go and tell her what your word is worth?'

'I'll find you,' Timo said again. 'Thirty minutes. I promise.'

Mia broke away from Melanie and rushed forwards to clamp herself to Timo's legs.

'Come with us, Papa,' she pleaded.

'Soon, sweet one.' He hoisted her up in his arms. 'Now kiss me and go. Hold on to Melanie. Be brave. Stick close to her in this storm.'

He knelt down to lower her to her feet, pulling Nico into him, too. He kissed their heads, then released them back to Melanie.

Miller looked across at his daughter, who scowled at him, shaking her head. Then she turned and led Nico and Mia away in the direction of the quad bike.

'Who is that man?' Mia asked, glancing back over her shoulder.

'Nobody,' came Melanie's reply, in a tone as bleak as any Miller had ever known. 'He's no one at all.'

*

Mike Renner winced at the pitched whine of the van's engine. Wade had slowed for a hairpin corner, then found he had no

379

traction to accelerate out of it. The track was mud-slicked. Too many storms had washed the gravel away. Wade was revving so hard that the engine cover was shaking, plumes of blue smoke rising up from the tyres and the exhaust.

'You'll have to get out and push,' Wade said through his teeth, his knuckles white on the steering wheel.

Renner looked out at the pelting rain and the wind. He thought of his ruined shin. There was no way he was putting his body behind the weight of the van. If it slipped backwards, he could be crushed.

Hanson and Pete were in the back, but their ankles and wrists were bound. Releasing them would take time. Plus there was the danger that one of them might be foolish enough to try something.

'Let it go,' Renner said. 'It's not far from here.'

Wade shook his head, gunned the engine and attacked the slope once more, but it made no difference. The tyres scrabbled and spun.

'Pull over.' Renner reached across and grabbed Wade's fore-arm. It was almost wider than the span of his hand. 'It's done. Pull over. Here is good.'

There was a single-storey mountain chalet in the crook of the hairpin, a couple of goats nearby. The place was all boarded up, the grass grown long around it.

Wade cursed and let his foot off the gas, compressing the clutch, whipping the steering wheel to the left on full lock as the van raced backwards in a lurching arc. Renner rocked side-ways, his shin striking the centre console. He heard the slap of limbs and a concussion of bodies in the back.

Wade stomped on the brakes and the van tore two deep

gouges in the sodden grass before coming to a grinding halt. He cut the engine, cranked on the handbrake. Rain drummed off the metal overhead.

'Can you even walk?'

Renner had to fight against the urge to cuff him. Wade could be unpredictable at the best of times, and up here on the mountain, in a storm, they were a long way from that.

'Adams is already there by now,' Wade pressed. 'You get that, right? The longer we take, the longer he has to get the girl away.'

'They can't go far in this storm. And besides, I don't think he'll be going anywhere. I think he wants us to come to him. He needs to end this somewhere.' Renner craned his neck, looking up at the sky. 'Pull your gear together. Make sure they know not to try anything in the back. We'll give it five minutes. See if this storm eases off at all. Then we go. OK?'

Wade took a look at the conditions for himself, humming doubtfully.

'Whatever you say, Boss.'

Chapter Seventy

'I don't like this twilight. It's bad for visibility.'

'They'll come soon. They have to.'

'Another hour and it'll be completely dark. And I can't shoot what I can't see, Miller.'

'Works both ways. Neither can they.'

Kate pressed her face to the barn window. It had a crumbling timber frame and was divided into four glass panels. She'd knocked out the bottom two panels with the butt of the rifle before stepping inside and now the damp, misty breeze was eddying around the opening where she'd propped the barrel of the rifle on the base of the frame.

'How are you feeling?' Miller asked her.

'Cold. Wet. Scared. Pissed off.'

'At least the storm cleared through. Has to be good for your aim.'

Kate didn't know which of them he was trying to reassure, but there was some truth to what he'd said. She could still hear the distant boom of thunder far away across the Alps and glimpse the muted stutter of lightning. The worst of the wind and rain had passed on more than half an hour ago, and the sky had brightened for a spell. Now, though, dusk had drawn in and it would be night before long. In the mountains, the blackness would be absolute.

It was so still and quiet that Kate could hear muffled drips from the pine boughs hanging over the barn roof. The air she inhaled seemed somehow cleaner and fresher than any she'd ever breathed before. Maybe terror could do that to a person – make them focus intensely on the simplest things, like the breath in their lungs – though she guessed it also had to do with the passing of the storm and the altitude.

'Do you see anything?' she asked, trying to hide the strain in her voice.

'Nothing.'

Kate slid her thumb off the two-way radio. Her fingers were cramped, beginning to numb. She wished she had gloves to go with the black beanie hat she'd found in a pocket of Timo's coat.

More than that, though, she wished that she was with Miller inside the chalet. She could see the logic in his plan. He'd been right to say that Renner and Wade might overlook the rickety barn, and though her line of sight was compromised by the distance between them, by the grainy half-light and the faint ribbons of dewy mist, stationing her out here with the rifle seemed like a reasonable strategy. Reasonable enough, in any case, that she hadn't been able to think of a good reason to argue against it.

But right now she didn't care very much about good reasons. She was cold and afraid and alone, still reeling from meeting Melanie, still adjusting to the idea that she was alive. And then there were the things she'd said to her.

Kate pressed the talk button on the radio again.

'Melanie told me about your benefactor, by the way.'

She heard Miller exhale. Could picture him shaking his head.

'And I was mad at you. For all of five minutes. But then I started to think, Screw it. Lane's the reason I'm freezing my backside off out here. He tried to get me killed. I say take the bastard for everything he has.'

'Did I mention how much I like you?'

'I am pretty great. But since we're just waiting right now, is there anything else you want to say to me?'

'So much. Believe me. But I think it's best we save it for when we're alone again. Or at least until we're not on a radio channel that Timo can listen in on.'

Kate smiled briefly and set the radio to one side. In the silence that followed, she thought again of the woods that bordered the meadow, unable to escape the sensation that they were crowding in on her. Miller was basing his strategy on the assumption that Renner and Wade would approach the chalet along the mountain track. But what if they circled round and came through the pines? What if they sneaked up on her from behind?

She shuddered, drawing her hands up into the sleeves of the musty overcoat. The suede was heavy on her shoulders, swamping her arms and restricting her movements. Which was not great for a sniper. But the cold had already weaved its way into her toes and was gnawing at her fingers. If she took the coat off, her shivers would be uncontrollable. Her aim would be wrecked.

She bent at the hip and crouched over the rifle, resting the stock against her shoulder. The stance conjured memories of accompanying her adoptive father on dawn grouse hunts in matted Cotswold fields. Of frost, and tension, and the harrowing fear of the kill.

Miller's radio beeped once and fuzzed static in the stolen silence of the chalet. Timber boards groaned and settled all around him. Pipes creaked. He clicked the radio twice in response – the signal they'd agreed on – and his speaker crackled to life.

'If you've moved to the kids' bedroom, I can still see you.'

Miller hung his head. 'OK, so the lights are no good. I'll cut them.'

'Are you sure?'

'No. But I don't want them shooting at me from outside. I want them to try and find a way in.'

'That's going to be a problem once it's fully dark. No ambient light means no targets.'

Miller lowered the radio for moment, thinking it through.

'Like I said before: works both ways.'

He let go of the talk button and heard the muffled click of Kate doing the same thing, then took his axe and the radio and went room to room on his way downstairs. He found the fuse box in a kitchen cupboard and removed the light fuse. It was the same technique the man Lane had sent to kill Kate had used on the Isle of Man, and he supposed that was a bad omen.

The fire was still burning in the hearth. Miller stepped closer to it, the light of the flames flickering and drifting across his hands and face, shadows playing around the walls and against the floorboards.

Standing in the chalet, he found himself drawn back to that other fire, the one that had led him here. He could still feel the strange intensity of it; the awful fury and peculiar lure of the flames. Some days it felt to Miller as if the fire that had torn through his home had consumed him, too. Some days it felt like it had burned out his heart.

Slowly now, he lifted the axe on to his shoulder and crossed to the window to peek out through the curtains. He peered at the twilit meadow and the trees; the barn and the SUV; the mist and the dwindling track.

Inside his head, the terrible fire raged on.

Chapter Seventy-One

Renner and Wade sheltered beneath a group of pines. The trek had been brutal on Renner. The ascent had been steep and the mountain air thin. They'd strayed from the path to avoid being spotted and the terrain had been boggy and uneven.

Pain skittered across his shin and there was no longer any flex in his lower leg. The swelling had got so bad that his hobble had turned into a semi-crawl and he'd been pulling himself over soaked mounds and ridges, his hands clawed into sods of dank grass. In the end, he'd had to suffer the indignity of leaning on Wade, but soon even that had become too much. Wade had as good as carried him for the last hundred or more metres, like he was a wounded soldier being dragged across a battlefield.

The rain had petered out to little more than a faint damp-ness on the air but both men were drenched, their clothes pasted to their bodies, and the map Renner had tucked under his shirt had been reduced to a sodden mush of papier mâché.

Not that they needed it any more. He could glimpse the SUV Adams had driven off in through a break in the trees. It was parked in the middle of the track, blocking the way ahead. Off to the right was an unlit chalet, smoke weaving upwards from a crooked chimney.

'How do you want to do this?' Wade asked. 'You want me to go in alone?'

Renner had been asking himself the same thing. It was probably the sensible play but it wasn't one he could contemplate.

'You can rest here,' Wade went on. 'What do you say?'

'I'm thinking.'

'Is that what it is? I thought maybe you were getting ready to pass out.'

Renner stared ahead through the tree cover. There was something about the set-up he didn't like. The stillness of the chalet, maybe. Or perhaps it was just the distraction of his shin. He was worried about the wound getting infected. He hated the idea of running a fever. Once they were done up here, they'd need to leave Switzerland in a hurry. They couldn't afford delays.

'If you stay hidden in these woods,' Wade said, 'you can watch for anyone who tries to make a break for it.'

'No. We go in together.'

'And how do we do that? I can't carry you through the entire house.'

Renner dug a hand into his pocket for his pistol, biting down against an agonising surge in his leg.

'Just get me closer. Help me behind that vehicle. We'll assess things from there.'

Wade wrapped a thick arm around Renner's back, shaking his head as he lifted him. 'You're handicapping both of us.'

'I'm guaranteeing there are no mistakes. Not this time. You don't have to like it, but this is how it's going to be.'

*

Kate's father had owned many sporting rifles, nearly all of them Brownings. It was a brand he trusted for its safety and accuracy, and it was the only make of rifle he'd ever allowed Kate to shoot. Timo's rifle was a Ruger, though the basics were the same.

The Hawkeye was a single-shot bolt-action sporting rifle with a walnut stock, some checkering on the grip, and a blued finish on the barrel. It was chambered for .223 Remington-calibre cartridges with an internal magazine that could hold five rounds. Timo had added a scope to make aiming the rifle a lot easier.

Which it would have been, during the day, but right now the sky had bloomed a deep indigo grey, bleeding to black, the light fading all the while. Kate guessed that in a little over ten minutes, she wouldn't be able to see a thing.

She blew on her hands, shoulders huddled for warmth. It was five minutes since she'd last talked on the radio with Miller, almost fifteen since he'd killed the lights in the chalet. She felt alone and badly out of her depth.

A gust of wind streaked through the window, rocking the Ruger, and Kate crouched and returned her eye to the scope. She blinked as her lashes brushed the curved glass lens and the rickety porch ballooned in her straining vision.

She leaned back a little and worked a kink out of her neck, then settled herself over the rifle once more, cushioning the recoil pad in her shoulder, hooking a finger on the trigger guard and easing the muzzle to the left. The scope swooped down off the porch and across the hazy meadow towards the SUV.

Kate exhaled gently and the scope trembled, making the wet metal of the SUV appear to ripple.

She swept the scope left, then right, then left again.

And that was when she saw them. Just barely.

Two greyish blobs, blurred, almost spectral, in the very centre of her vision. The scope made the men appear close enough for Kate to waft a hand in front of her face and swipe them away.

One of them was limping badly, leaning on the other. Both were stooped at the waist, hurrying towards the SUV, looking as if they might fall.

Kate snatched the rifle off the windowsill and adopted a crouched firing stance. The men had moved ahead of the scope for just a second but she tracked them again and peered hard, centring them in the fish-eye glare.

Then she waited. Not because she wanted the perfect shot but because shooting a man required more than simply pulling a trigger. It was a totally different prospect from firing at a mechanical target during a pentathlon event or at a field of grouse during hunting season. And this time, she had to kill. Too often in the past she'd made a conscious decision to miss her prey.

'Bad luck,' her father would say. 'Better shooting next time.'

But Kate hadn't ever been unlucky. She'd made a choice.

Her pulse beat in her throat and the tip of her finger. She clamped the rifle tight but still the scope quivered.

Freeing her hand, she worked a little of the tension from it, then clicked the safety switch to the fire position and hooked her finger around the trigger.

She watched one of the men stumble, his outstretched hand and his knee striking the ground. The other man pulled him up and they lumbered on.

They were five metres from the flank of the SUV.

Four metres.

Three.

Kate sucked in a halting breath, held it, and fired.

*

Something *thunk*ed into the rear quarter of the SUV, throwing up sparks in the dim. Then a window exploded and Wade heard the clap of gunfire for the first time. He heaved Renner after him, diving for the cover of the vehicle as a third bullet whined overhead. He hit the ground, face pressed into gravel, and looked under the chassis. There was a spark way off in the meadow. The sound of drilled metal close by.

'Are you hit?'

Renner was toppled on to his side behind the rear wheel, looking fat and useless. Wade cursed himself for not leaving him in the woods. He should have come at the house clockwise through the tree cover. His instincts had been right. Renner wasn't just holding him back. He might cost him his life.

And now he was fumbling with his pistol, as if that could help. He hadn't even spotted the shooter.

Wade reached above his head from his prone position and tried the handle on the SUV. The door clicked open, a dome light shining down.

'What are you doing?' Renner snapped. 'They'll see us.'

'Who do you think they're shooting at?'

Dipshit. That's what he wanted to add. But something stopped him even now. The burden of his past mistake, perhaps.

Keeping low, he pulled himself into the footwell of the SUV and peered at the underside of the steering column. He knew how to hotwire a car. The benefits of a misspent youth. But the keys were there in front of him, dangling from the ignition.

A fifth round blew out another side window, drilling into the roof. Wade ducked back out and opened the rear door. Renner was still pinned and sheltering with his hands over his head. Wade grabbed him by the collar of his drenched shirt and heaved him on to the back seat.

'Are you crazy?' Renner tucked himself into a ball. 'They're shooting at us.'

'You want to sit here and be killed?'

Wade didn't wait for an answer. He clambered into the front seat, his head down, and turned over the ignition. The engine fired, the headlights bloomed. He threw the gearbox into first, turning hard to the right and plunging down a drainage trench into the meadow.

The rear door slammed shut on Renner as the SUV hit the first big rut and rose high at the front like it was riding a wave.

It was a Japanese model with chunky tyres and a high ground clearance. The torque felt mighty. The engine was a beast.

Leaning way down to his right, peeping up over the dash, Wade flicked the headlamps to full beam and the meadow sprang into greyscale relief. The chalet was to his left. A door flew open at the front and he saw Adams step out with an axe in his hands. Dead ahead was a small timber building at the edge of the trees. Something glinted from a window. The glinting thing sparked.

A round thumped into the engine block. Then another punctured the windscreen.

'What are you waiting for?' Renner shouted. 'Get us out of here.'

But Wade had never run from anything in his life. He was all about confrontation. His natural inclination was to go at a problem head on.

Which had to be better than rolling around on the back seat like a coward.

The big engine pushed the vehicle on. They were gaining speed. Gaining momentum.

The shooter wasn't giving up. Rounds were still peppering the SUV, hitting every time.

Which was something Wade could appreciate. Because just like the shooter, he'd zeroed in on a target. He had a fixed trajectory.

Reaching up now, he grabbed for his seatbelt, whipping it across his chest, clicking it home. He raised his eyes one last time and saw the shooter, saw Kate, swinging away from the rifle in the glare of his headlamps, turning to run.

He didn't stamp on the brake. He didn't slow at all. He just lifted his hands from the wheel and covered his face, shouting a late warning to Renner as the SUV pitched up at the front and catapulted into a hail of timber and glass.

Chapter Seventy-Two

It was dark and cold and terrifying in the windowless rear of the van. Now that the storm had passed on, Becca was tormented by the eerie stillness outside, punctured only by the distant thud of what might have been gunfire. She kept listening for the footsteps she felt sure would come at any moment. Renner and Wade would return, they would open the doors and they would kill them. It was difficult to foresee another outcome.

Emily had toppled into Pete's lap and fallen asleep a little while ago, which was a relief because her distressed mewling had been amplified by the van's metal sidings, making their plight feel so much worse. Pete was resting with his head against the back of the driver's seat. Hanson was closer, his chest lashed to a metal upright, his head bowed.

Unlike Hanson and Pete, Becca hadn't been tied to anything. When Wade had finished threatening her, and Renner had extracted all the information he needed from Hanson, Wade had simply dropped her to the ground and moved off. Her hands were secured together behind her back, the skin twisted and chafed by the duct tape that had been wound round her wrists. Her knees and ankles were also bound and a swatch of tape had been pressed over her mouth, the top edge ruffling as she breathed through her nose.

Becca had worked at the gag for close to an hour before she'd managed to loosen it. Her tongue ached from the prodding and strain. She only had the slightest corner of it poked free, towards the upper left of her mouth, but it had been enough for her to talk and try to reassure Emily that everything would be OK.

She hated the gag most of all. She was a loudmouth, a performer, and she definitely liked the sound of her own voice, but Becca's deepest, most primal fear was suffocating. She'd swallowed a boiled sweet once as a kid. She'd tripped on the stairs, rushing to see her parents, who were fetching down Christmas decorations from the loft. The sweet had lodged deep in her throat and shut off her breathing with the abruptness of a valve. Becca had hammered on the attic ladder and pointed to her mouth until her father rushed down and tried hooking the sweet out with his finger, lodging it even worse. He'd slapped her back. Then, in desperation, he'd swooped her up by the knees, turned her upside down and shaken her as hard as he could.

And the sweet had popped out, just like that. But the sensation of it stuck there, swelling her windpipe, had stayed with her ever since.

Which was why she'd flailed so wildly when Wade had applied the gag and most likely why he hadn't pressed the tape down as well as he should have.

A mistake. A small one. And up until now, it had seemed like all it had given her was some reprieve from her panic and an opportunity to soothe a scared little girl.

But maybe, just maybe, it could give her something else, too.

Becca rolled on to her side, her chin striking the moulded metal floor. Her legs were half numbed, riddled with pins and needles. She tucked them beneath her and hobbled on to her knees towards Hanson.

He lifted his head to watch her approach, blinking darkly from behind his specs.

'Take off your glasses,' she puffed, through the slit in the tape.

He didn't move.

'Please. Trust me.'

He shook his head, mumbling from behind his gag. Becca could sympathise because she knew he was almost blind without them.

'I think I can get us out of here.'

She didn't know if she believed it. She didn't know if Hanson did, either. But something about the way she looked at him, pleaded with him, made him begin to relent.

After a moment more of watching her, and glancing across at Pete and Emily, Hanson breathed out through his nose and let his shoulders drop, then he pitched his head forwards and shook it roughly until his spectacles slid down his nose, came loose from his ears and fell into his lap.

His eyes looked much bigger without his glasses, the skin around them swollen and pouched.

'Move your glasses towards me. On to the floor.'

He wriggled his legs until the spectacles clattered to the ground.

'Perfect.'

Becca turned sideways, twisting her neck and gazing over her shoulder until she had them lined up just right. She looked at Hanson one last time, then she lifted her big, sweet ass in the air and rocked backwards until she heard a crack.

The ground rushed up to meet Kate. She'd tripped and fallen into dirt and mulch. She pushed herself to her feet and stumbled into the woods, clutching at her side, branches swiping her face.

The barn was gone. It had been blown to matchsticks. The SUV had punched right through it, landed hard, then thumped into a tree.

The SUV's bonnet was crumpled. The front doors were buckled. Airbags had deployed at the front and Wade's face was buried in one of them. She couldn't see Renner.

She kept running until she was forty or fifty metres away, hidden beneath the trees, then dropped to one knee and peered out from behind a thicket of underbrush.

Brake lights glowed fiercely at the back of the SUV. A tiny bulb was hanging down on a wire from the roof, lighting the splintered windscreen. Smoke drifted up from the engine. Something was ticking or dripping. Something was hissing.

Nobody moved.

Kate waited and watched for several long minutes. Beyond the SUV, the last vestiges of twilight faded away, the darkness closing in relentlessly, encroaching upon the wrecked vehicle as if it was a softly lit prop on a theatre stage.

Then Kate heard a pained groan and one of the airbags plumped and shifted around against the remains of the windscreen. There was a repeated thumping before the driver's door was forced open and Wade staggered out into the smoking gloom. He swayed and cursed, the heel of one hand clasped to his forehead, a pistol swinging carelessly in the other. There was glass in his hair.

He peered into the trees. Had he seen her run? Could he see her now?

She wished she had the rifle still. She wished she hadn't abandoned it as she'd turned to leap clear of the barn. Even with her chest hitching, even with the hot ache in her side, she could have made the shot.

Wade bent at the hip and looked under the SUV, searching, Kate guessed, for her body. Then he straightened again and weaved groggily before turning and breaking into a halting jog, heading across the meadow in the direction of the chalet.

The blackness ate him up.

There was still no sign of Renner. There was no movement from the SUV at all.

Kate crept out from behind the brush and walked forwards very slowly. The area where the barn had stood looked like the site of a small aeroplane crash. The air reeked of hot metal, of burnt plastic and diesel and something chemical that clawed at her throat. She moved closer. Still the only movement was the swinging and slanting of the cabin bulb and the drifts of steam. Had Wade really gone or was he watching for her? Was he waiting her out?

Keeping low, she approached the open door and pushed an airbag to one side. And that was when she saw Renner, his head and shoulders wedged between the two front seats, his face glazed in blood, his mouth parted to reveal a jaw full of broken teeth. His eyes were closed. He was motionless.

His right arm was crooked and extended beyond his head, the wrist bent back by the swell of the airbag and the blown plastic of the dash. His fingers were resting on an automatic pistol.

Kate crouched, watching, but he didn't rear up. Not even his eyelids flickered.

She reached in for the pistol. She lifted it carefully.

It was heavy. It was loaded.

Still Renner didn't stir.

Kate backed away, heels digging into mud and debris, and looked into the blackness towards the chalet. The plan was never for her to go there. The plan was for her to stick to her strengths. Shooting. Running.

Miller had wanted them to come to him. Alone.

She turned with the gun in her fist and shed the big, clumsy overcoat as she sprinted for the mountain track.

Chapter Seventy-Three

Miller had broken away from the plan he'd agreed with Kate the moment he'd stepped outside the chalet. He'd heard the shots. He'd seen the collision. Then he'd stood in stunned silence, unsure what to do next.

His first instinct had been to rush over. He was afraid for Kate. He was sure she'd been hit. But then he'd glimpsed her through the scarlet wash of the SUV's brake lights, scurrying into the woods.

It had seemed for many minutes afterwards as if the crash had been fatal, until Wade staggered out of the SUV with a gun in his hand. He'd peered into the darkness that had draped itself over the chalet and the meadow – straight at Miller, it had felt like – and had started to run.

Miller waited for Kate to shoot Wade in the back, but the shot never came. He was sixty, maybe seventy metres away when he vanished from the halo of dim red light surrounding the outer limits of the crash site.

Miller held the axe down by his side. Close range, in the chalet, it could be devastating. But out here it was useless.

He looked once more for Kate, squinting hard towards the glow and the wreckage at the bottom of the field, then ducked and stepped inside and locked the door behind him. It would have been dark as a cave without the flicker of the fire. Where to go? Upstairs or down? He knew he had to keep away from windows and doors. He knew to stay low. Should he hide and wait for Wade to find him, or should he guess where he'd come at him from?

There was a front and a back door to the chalet. There was also an external stone staircase that connected with an upstairs entrance.

Wade was brash and confident but he wasn't stupid. So Miller guessed the front door was out. Wade would anticipate that Miller would have the front entrance secured, which he did, in a fashion, with a rope he'd strung up crossways at head height. Or throat height, if he was lucky.

Miller contemplated the stairs. There were six-inch nails poking up through the treads, hammered through from the crawl space beneath. The nails were spaced randomly, two or three to a tread. If Miller had to go up in a hurry, he had a gauntlet to run. If Wade tried the same thing, he'd likely pin his foot.

Miller was hoping Wade would come in from above. He wanted him to stalk around the bedrooms, find them empty, and be lured down on to the nails by the firelight. If he stepped on a nail, he might drop his gun, which was a big problem otherwise.

Miller needed Wade close to him – close enough for a swing of his axe. If Wade saw him first, he could shoot from distance. And although Timo had armed Miller with a hunting knife, it wasn't something he could throw. The chances of him missing were too high.

So Wade had a major advantage.

If he saw Miller.

If he came inside.

Where was he now? Did he know Melanie was already gone? Had he doubled back in search of Kate?

Miller felt the urge to look out of a window, but knew he'd regret it if Wade was on the other side of the glass.

He closed his eyes and tried to think. He still had his eyes shut a second later when a window in the kitchen exploded inwards and a hand raked away the remaining glass fragments with the barrel of an automatic pistol. The pistol was waved around the room. It was followed by an elbow and an arm.

Miller dropped behind the couch before Wade's head appeared. He listened to him squeezing through the opening, grunting, sweeping crockery and a toaster off the kitchen counter on to the floor.

He'd be encouraged by the fire. The logs were a long way from burned through. But he had to suspect some kind of ambush. He'd be busy asking himself what Miller's move would be.

Miller's move was to stay still and hide with the axe gripped tightly in front of him. He listened hard to the stillness in the room, to the breeze through the busted window, to the crackle of the logs in the grate. He heard the scrape of Wade's boots against the floorboards. Heard the boards deflect under his weight.

The large rug in front of the fire was thin and frayed. It was ruffled in the middle. Miller wanted very much for Wade to come at him that way.

And he did, to begin with. His steps became muffled, the vibrations getting closer. Any second now and he'd pass right in front of the fire.

Except he didn't, because there was a long pause, and then

more vibrations and more clomping footsteps and it dawned on Miller that Wade was retracing his steps, heading back to the kitchen. Which was an outcome he couldn't accept.

'Hey!'

Miller shouted and sprang up from behind the couch and Wade spun very fast, raising his gun in the air. Wade flinched, as if perplexed, then advanced on Miller, closing the distance between them. A smile split his face and he twisted his arm a quarter turn until he was aiming the pistol at Miller sideways on.

Miller stepped out from behind the couch with the axe held in a two-handed grip, his bandaged left hand below the right, the blade above his shoulder by his ear, the flames glimmering in the corner of his vision.

'You're kidding me. An axe? What are you going to do, chop through my first six bullets, then come at me while I reload?'

Wade's movements were loose and easy, despite the ugly welt on his forehead. He was pacing across the floorboards in his soaked tracksuit, mud and grass coating his white training shoes.

He stepped off the floorboards on to the rug. Took another step. One more.

Then stopped.

'Why are you even doing this?' Miller asked him. 'What's in it for you?'

'Don't start that crap.' Wade extended his arm until his elbow was locked, one eye closed in a squint. 'Although I guess you could say I'm making amends. Fixing an error I made before Mr Lane ever finds out about it.'

The pistol was centred on Miller's chest and he could feel

his skin tighten; could anticipate the impact, the bullet ripping through his lungs.

Wade relaxed a fraction more. He smiled a little wider.

'Do you want to know what I had your wife say to me before I shot her?'

Miller's stomach dropped. Suddenly, the axe seemed almost too heavy for him to hold.

'I had her beg. I made her say "please".'

There was a faint whistling in Miller's ears. He wanted to launch himself at Wade, swing the axe and take off his head at his shoulders. But he held back. Held on.

'And now I'd like you to say it, too. Say "please".'

Miller swallowed, and when he spoke, his voice was pitchy and wayward.

'Why don't you come nearer? Let me whisper it in your ear.'

Wade smiled some more.

'You'll say "please".' He lowered his gun and aimed at Miller's knee. 'But first, you're going to tell me where your daughter is. I want to make sure I kill her right this time.'

He took another step forwards, into the centre of the rug, where his shin snagged a very fine wire. The rug seemed to shrink rapidly in the middle, the material rushing in from the edges to wrap around his foot. His leg jerked up and he jerked with it, the momentum twirling him round and off the ground.

The spring snare Timo had rigged up was locked on his lower leg, hoisting him off the floor until he was suspended upside down, legs thrashing, arms windmilling, letting a shot off into the ceiling.

Miller ducked and surged forwards, allowing the axe handle to drop through his hands, changing his grip, buzzing the thick wooden handle through the air and beating hard on Wade's wrist until he heard a violent crack and the gun clattered on to the floorboards.

Wade yelled and snatched his hand to his body, bending at the waist, reaching up with his good hand to try and loosen the climbing rope that was tightened off around his ankle. The rug was getting in his way. It was blocking him.

Miller had to fight hard against the urge to strike down again with the axe handle on to Wade's head. He could have bludgeoned him ferociously, vented all his fury.

But his eyes were drawn to the burning logs instead.

Chapter Seventy-Four

The pitted mountain track fell away beneath Kate's feet. She was running into the black at a fast tempo, the ache in her side beginning to fade, her knees jarring on the uneven path. She pumped her arms with the gun in her fist and inhaled the misted air through her nostrils.

She worried about leaving Miller to defend himself against Wade and it was hard not to turn back. She kept running because of Emily, most of all. She couldn't bear to think of what she was going through.

Miller's instructions had been simple. If Renner and Wade made it inside the chalet, her job was to search for the van. They had to have driven up the mountain in it and logic suggested they wouldn't have had time to find anywhere else to contain Hanson and Becca, Pete and Emily, whether they were dead or alive.

So now all Kate had to do was find the van and confront whatever was waiting for her there.

She ran for ten minutes, building her pace, lengthening her stride, fighting to control the fear and tension that were gripping hold of her. She was beginning to suspect Miller had been wrong and that they hadn't driven up here in the van at all. Or maybe she'd missed it in the dark. Part of her was already preparing to run back up the hill, trying to plot a safe approach to the chalet, when she saw it beached on a short grassy shelf in front of a tumbledown chalet. The windows were wet with condensation. The interior was unlit.

Kate slowed, resting her hands on her waist as she caught her breath. She approached the front passenger window, smeared a circle with her palm and peered inside. But she couldn't make out anything other than the blur of the dash and the seats.

She backed off and moved carefully around to the rear, the gun held out in front of her. She was just reaching for the latch on the doors when one of them flew open and Becca stumbled out, coughing and spluttering.

*

Miller and Timo had made multiple trips between the barn and the chalet while they were gathering equipment. On one of the trips they'd worked together to carry the old oil drum on to the porch, where Miller had used the chainsaw to cut the top off. The drum was almost empty but the insides were lined with a thick, gloopy residue of settled oil. Miller had siphoned some fuel from Timo's truck and added it to the mix, and now he was wondering if he should have added a little more.

He'd rolled the drum across from where it had been stashed behind the kitchen door, positioning it directly beneath Wade. Wade was spinning above it, flailing his arms, kicking his feet. His chin was tucked into his chest to stop his head from tangling with the jagged metal edge the chainsaw had left behind.

Miller held the pistol in one fist, the axe in the other, and he watched Wade struggle for a few seconds, making sure he had the drum in the perfect spot. Then he crossed to the fire and tapped the blade of the axe into a charred log.

Sparks and cinders showered down as he lifted the axe and very carefully, very deliberately, carried the log towards Wade, who finally caught up to what was happening and became oddly still. His eyes flitted between the shimmering log and the oil drum. He opened his mouth to speak.

'Was this how it was with Clive?' Miller asked him. 'How about Patrick or Darren? How about my wife?'

Miller swept the log closer, a haze of vibrant ash spiralling down. It would be so easy to drop it in the drum. So simple to end things that way. There was a synchronicity to it. The closing of a circle. Perhaps even a way for him to move on.

*

Kate worked with Becca to help free Emily first, then she tackled Pete's restraints while Becca carried the girl outside and hugged and consoled her in the mountain dark. Emily seemed beyond scared. She was rocking in Becca's arms, not saying a word.

That changed a little once Pete was free. He shook some feeling into his arms, groaning pitifully, then clambered down from the van and cradled Emily, whispering in her ear. Emily began to cry. Her chest shuddered, her face buried in her father's shoulder, her little hands balled into fists.

Hanson was last out and Kate guided him carefully towards a mound of soaked grass, where he sat holding his head, squinting and blinking, testing the movement of his jaw.

Kate watched over him a moment, wondering what to do next. She wanted to return to the chalet. She had to know if Miller was OK.

Then she heard a door slam. The van's suspension compressed and the rear lights flashed red, staining the faces all around her.

She didn't pause to think. She didn't hesitate. She ran towards the front of the van as the engine fired and the headlamps switched to full beam, lighting her up.

She shielded her eyes with one hand and aimed the pistol blindly with the other. The engine revved. The van strained against the clutch. Kate lowered the pistol and fired a single round into the engine block, then raised her aim back up again.

Stalemate.

She took a step nearer, eyes streaming in the glare as she peered through the window and glimpsed Renner behind the wheel. He was breathing raggedly, his head lolling, his shattered teeth framing a ghoulish, desperate grimace.

*

Miller almost dropped the log. He could so easily picture the flames swirling up and engulfing Wade. He wanted it that way.

But something stopped him.

Maybe, when it came to it, he wasn't able to be quite as bad as he needed to be.

Or maybe he was something even worse.

'Let me down.' Wade's face was puce. It could have been from terror, but Miller thought it was more likely because of all the blood rushing to his head. 'I'll give you something on Lane. I have information you can use against him. That's what you want, right? That's what you really need?'

Miller paused, thinking it over, then he shrugged his

shoulders and tossed the axe and the log away into the grate.

'Good decision. Great. Now get me down first.'

Wade reached up to the noose around his ankles, waiting for Miller's help. Miller raised a hand and saw the hope flare in his Wade's wide-apart eyes, then extinguish just as quickly as he pushed him back down and jammed the muzzle of the pistol against the underside of his jaw.

'I'd like you to do a little something for my wife. I'd like you to say "please".'

*

Kate heard the gunshot on the wind. It was muted by distance but unmistakable all the same.

She whipped her head towards the chalet, lowering her gun hand by a fraction, and in almost the same instant she heard the sudden roar of the van's engine, the spin of its tyres.

The van slithered forwards, surging towards her, and she dived to her right, banging her hip, jarring her elbow, letting go of the pistol. The van swooped by, the back doors flapping, the rear fishtailing, then straightening up and streaking away. By the time she'd scrabbled forwards and felt for the gun and turned to shoot, she was too late. The van had plunged down a dip and lurched round a curve and sped away.

Renner was gone.

Chapter Seventy-Five

Mid-morning the following day found Kate drained and disoriented. The sky was a brilliant, unblemished blue, the sun high and blazing down over the jagged mountain peaks and dirty glaciers of the Eiger, Mönch and Jungfrau.

She squinted against the wet glimmer of the dewed meadow, sitting in the load bed of Timo's crappy pickup truck with Miller on one side of her and Hanson on the other, his eyes closed and his face tilted towards the sun. Becca was across from her, leaning back with her arms outstretched, her legs tangled with Kate's own. Pete and Emily were huddled together in the front cab, talking in hushed tones.

Away across the meadow, Kate watched Nico and Mia running in crazed circles, edging ever closer to the forbidden temptations of the wrecked SUV and the splintered remains of the barn. On the porch of the chalet, Timo was holding Melanie's face in his hands, kissing her forehead, looking into her eyes.

The dank smell of drying clothes, of sweat and mud, was all around Kate, but it clung to Miller most of all. He'd walked into the woods with Timo a little over an hour ago to dig a hole big enough for Wade's corpse. He hadn't spoken of it since, though there was a weary gloom about him every time he looked down at his earth-stained hands.

Kate had found him dragging Wade's body through the

soaked grass towards the trees the previous night. He hadn't heard her approach, and when she'd called out his name and he'd turned to her, letting go of Wade's wrists, the broken expression on his worn face had stopped her from coming any closer. Even in the dark, with the terrible bruising to his eye, she could see that he was crying. All the hurt and emotion of the past four years seemed to be leaching out of him, reducing him, leaving him spent and stooped.

She'd had to tell him that Renner had got away. She'd had to watch him sag just a little more.

Thinking of it now, she reached down and lifted his bandaged hand, running her thumb over the crusted mud, seeing the soil and dirt jammed beneath his fingernails. She kissed his knuckles and rested her cheek on his fist.

Tiredness pressed down on her, slackening her muscles, slowing her thoughts. She was hungry and thirsty. She craved a clean hotel room, a hot shower, food and drink, and an opportunity to pretend, at least for a little while, that life could be normal again.

'What happens now?' she asked.

'Hard to say.' Even Miller's voice sounded beaten down. 'The only thing I know for sure is this isn't over. Men like Wade are disposable to Connor Lane. They're replaceable.' He nodded across the meadow, towards the chalet. 'And Renner knows about Melanie. I can't allow that.'

'Do I testify against Russell?'

'Maybe. If you still want to. If we can keep you safe. But Connor is separate to all that. For me, anyway. For you, too, now, I think.'

Kate brushed his knuckles with her lips again.

'You're talking about killing him.'

'I'm talking about protecting my daughter. About protecting you.'

'Honey,' Becca told her, 'it's really not such a terrible idea.'

'It's a terrific idea,' Hanson said.

'But what if there was another way?' Kate asked them. 'What if we found something to hurt Connor with? Something he couldn't ignore.'

Miller frowned. 'Like what?'

'I don't know yet. Not for sure. But I have an inkling, I think, and I'll tell you about it, so long as you do something for me first.'

His swollen eye was puckered, the flesh bruised and grazed. His good eye was reddened and yellowed with stress and fatigue. It searched her face.

'This is no time for games, Kate.'

'It's not a game.'

She reached across him, slipping her hand into his trouser pocket.

'Get a room,' Becca muttered.

Kate flashed her a tired smile as she plucked free Miller's wallet. She parted it carefully and slipped out the folded drawing that was tucked inside, holding the square of paper between her finger and thumb in front of his face.

'I want you to go over and talk to Melanie about this drawing. I want you to ask her what it means.'

He shook his head and pushed the drawing away, glancing towards Melanie for a sad moment, then down at his hands.

'It's a bad idea.'

'Yeah, well, maybe all you have left to you now is bad ideas.'

He didn't even smile.

'She doesn't want to talk with me. She's mad with me about what happened here. She hates that they have to pack up and take the kids away, that I can't tell her when she can come back – if she even can.'

'She's your daughter. She loves you. And maybe she is angry with you. Maybe she has every right to be. But you need this. So go and ask her about it. Do it now before it's too late.'

'She's right,' Becca told him, quietly.

'Totally,' Hanson chipped in. 'I think I speak for all of us when I say that we're fed up of seeing you torturing yourself about it.'

'Go.' Kate shoved him forwards. 'Timo's coming now. You don't have long. And if you won't ask her, I will. Believe me.'

He gave her a dubious look, but she prodded him until he got to his feet, then opened his hand and pressed the drawing into his palm.

'This is a mistake.'

'The mistake would be not doing this. Trust me. Go.'

He looked round once more, delaying, and this time they all shouted at him, barracking him until he climbed down off the truck and crossed the meadow, offering Timo a cursory wave as he passed him by.

'That was a nice thing you just did,' Becca told Kate, smiling in lazy approval.

'Yeah.' Hanson nudged her with his elbow. 'And since we're all about closure just now, it so happens I have something to tell you.'

Kate glanced at him briefly, but her attention swung back to Miller, who was tramping on past Nico and Mia, opening out the drawing in his hands. Melanie was watching him approach from the chalet porch, her arms folded tightly across her chest. She was wearing a long cardigan over a patterned summer dress with wellington boots on bare legs.

'There could be better times,' Hanson was saying. 'I know that. But Kate? It's about your brother.'

She stilled and turned. Hanson was smiling shyly, his bleary eyes not focussed quite right on her face.

'I found him for you.'

Kate didn't move. She couldn't, somehow. Her throat closed up. She felt a stinging in her eyes.

'Take it easy, OK? It was no big deal once I figured a couple of things out. Benefits of being able to hack into any system I like.' Hanson shrugged uncomfortably. 'He lives in Bristol, Kate. He works as a lawyer, just like you. I had a photo of him on my laptop and I would have shown it to you if Renner hadn't driven off with it.' He pointed to his eyes. 'Once I can see properly again, and we can get to a computer, I can find it for you. I can help you contact him, if you like.'

Kate knew she should thank him. She knew she should tell him all that it meant to her. But she could barely breathe, let alone speak. A photo of her brother. The chance to get in touch with him, at last. How could she possibly put what it meant to her into words? How could she begin to believe it was true?

She could feel the tears on her cheeks, the shakes in her hands. She didn't move for several moments more, trapped in her strange emotional paralysis, until she broke free and launched herself at him, crushing him in her arms.

'Easy.' He was squirming, blushing. 'Easy, OK? Miller's

coming back now. I don't want him to get the wrong idea.'

Kate laughed through her tears, but she didn't let go. She couldn't just yet. And so, holding him tight, she smiled at Timo as he climbed into the cab and turned the engine over, the load bed shaking, and she blinked at Miller coming towards them across the field, Melanie watching after him, the drawing held limply in her hands.

Kate waited until Miller had clambered into the back of the truck, standing there, looking down at them all.

'Well?' She sniffed, wiping at her eyes. She felt light-headed, addled with disbelief and hope. 'What's the verdict? Were you coming home, or going away?'

Miller shrugged his big shoulders and showed them his dirtied palms.

'She has no idea. She says she can't remember drawing it. She was only eight years old, so what did I expect?'

'That's too bad,' Becca told him.

He said nothing as he stepped between their legs, smiling feebly at Kate, touching the crown of her head, then crouching behind the cab and banging a fist on the window glass, signalling for Timo to drive. Timo slipped the clutch into gear and revved the engine but he didn't pull off right away. He'd seen something Miller hadn't. Melanie was sprinting across the meadow towards them.

She ran with the drawing flapping in her hand, stumbling in her rubber boots, her hair tumbling behind her, Nico and Mia scampering in her wake.

'Wait,' she called. 'Wait.'

Kate saw Miller turn. She saw him rise to his feet and stand there tensed and uncertain.

He stepped stiffly towards the back of the load bed, lowering his hand to lift Melanie up. She leapt from the ground and hugged him, her boots in the air, her face mashed into his neck.

'Coming home,' she told him. 'Of course you were coming home, Dad. I love you. All I ever wanted was for you to come home to me and Mum.'

PART VIII

Lake Windermere, England

Chapter Seventy-Six

One Week Later

Lloyd stepped away from her car in front of the wrought-iron gates at the entrance to the Lane estate. It was late in the evening, a chill in the air. She turned up the collar of her jacket and leaned a finger on the intercom.

'Yes?'

'Mr Lane? It's your pen pal . . . DS Lloyd. You sent me a photograph of a mutual acquaintance of ours a little while ago. I think it's time we talked.'

There was no response. She raised her face to the camera fitted above the gates and stared directly into the lens.

'There's something I need to tell you, Mr Lane. Mike, too. I saw him drive in just now. Better you both hear it from me tonight than from an arresting officer in the morning.'

Nothing further was said but the gate mechanism buzzed and the latch released and the gates started to swing open. Lloyd lingered, still staring into the security camera, then finally broke away and returned to her car, tilting her rear-view mirror to take a look at herself, weighing again the significance of what she was about to do.

It wasn't that any one thing in particular was different about her; it was simply that everything was. She could see it most of all in her eyes – in the restless unease beneath the surface. All the old certainties and absolutes of her life had been stripped away to be replaced with self-doubt and loathing and the burning need to secure some measure of justice, no matter the risks involved.

She shoved the mirror away and slipped the car into gear. The magnificence of the house didn't surprise her when she reached it but its stately elegance did. She'd pictured crass extensions and ugly add-ons, but she'd been wrong about that, as with so many things recently, and it made her worry again about what she was doing here.

She almost turned back. She almost pulled the car around in a fast circle and sped away. But an inner resolve she couldn't quite fathom or shake made her rush out and hurry towards the open front door.

Mike Renner monitored her approach from the top of a flight of stone steps, sucking some kind of protein shake through a plastic straw.

Lloyd felt a flutter of nervous excitement in her throat; the sudden thrill of acting on the fly. The notion crept into her talk.

'Something happened to your face, Mike? You look like you've been in a brawl.'

There were butterfly stitches across his forehead and nose, and his bottom lip was fat and swollen. He was tilted to one side, favouring his right leg, as if he'd injured the left.

When he swallowed and pulled the drinking straw away from his mouth, Lloyd noticed that his teeth were strikingly white.

'You shouldn't have come here. You're making a big mistake.'

He had a slight lisp as he talked. Lloyd's grandmother had

been just the same when she'd first had dentures fitted.

'Oh, Mike.' She flattened her hand on his chest as she passed him by. 'This is just the latest in a long list of mistakes I've been making recently.'

Connor Lane was waiting in his study but he didn't turn to greet Lloyd when she entered the room. He was facing a large picture window with his legs parted and his hands in the pockets of the well-tailored trousers he had on. His shirt was white and fitted and looked to have been designed for an Italian male model twenty years his junior. Lloyd had seen photographs before but just a glimpse of his profile made her realise how much more handsome and powerful he appeared in the flesh.

'DS Lloyd. How very plucky of you to come here alone.'

There was a slyness to his disregard for her that pierced Lloyd. His gaze was fixed beyond the window and the lawn, as though he was searching for something out on the lake, yet he seemed aware of her every movement.

She thrust her hands into her pockets and squeezed her squash ball. It felt to her as if he knew exactly what she was doing.

She said, 'I came here tonight because there are some things I need to tell you.'

'Such as?'

'Such as that I know Nadine Foster is your source inside the Protected Persons Service, Mr Lane. I know she has been for some time. Tomorrow, my superiors will know it too. Unless for some reason I delete the email I have queued on my laptop to send.'

'I haven't the first idea what you're babbling about.'

But he did. He was too dismissive, too nonchalant, and it just made the sting of Foster's betrayal all the sharper for Lloyd. She'd confided in Foster. She'd trusted her. And look where it had got her.

It was the trip that Foster and John Young had taken to talk with Lane and his lawyer that had first triggered Lloyd's misgivings. Outwardly, the visit had seemed pointless. So why had they come?

Her suspicions had been focussed on Young to begin with. She'd watched him log in and out of his computer enough times to learn his password. She knew his routines. Three days ago, she'd let herself in to the incident room in the middle of the night and had accessed his computer terminal. She'd searched for anything out of the ordinary and had found nothing at all.

Then she'd tried Foster's desktop. She'd memorised her password, too. And it had told her everything she needed, and really hadn't wanted, to know.

She said, 'Foster is the information gatherer for our team. It's her job to pull together the data that streams into our system for any ongoing investigation. She received border-control flags against Mike's name, and also a known associate of yours called Aaron Wade. The flags showed that both men flew into Hamburg on the same flight shortly before Nick Adams and Kate Sutherland arrived in the city. A more recent alert tells me Mike flew back to Manchester out of Switzerland. Alone.'

'So I took a break.' Renner came around from behind her to perch on the armrest of a wingback chair. He slurped his drink. 'Big deal.'

'It is a big deal because Foster deleted those alerts from our system. She buried them without passing them along. I'm guessing our tech team will also be able to prove that she went into our system back before all this mess started to find that Kate Sutherland had been relocated to the Isle of Man. She sold you that information, Mr Lane. It's what enabled you to send a man to kill Kate. Or try, at least.'

'What a fascinating theory, DS Lloyd. But it sounds to me as if all you have is evidence that one of your colleagues has acted improperly. I don't believe you can link her behaviour to me.'

Lloyd knew he was probably right. Lane was too careful to leave a trail that would lead to him directly. She guessed that he'd paid Foster in cash or in kind. That could account for Foster's fine clothes, her nice handbags and jewellery. It would also explain why she'd been prepared to make the trip to the Lake District with Young. She'd had intel to pass on and a payment to collect.

She turned to face Renner. If Lane wouldn't look at her, she'd make certain that he would.

'I know why you were in Switzerland, Mike. And I'm guessing by your appearance that it didn't go as well as you'd planned. I hope not, anyway.'

'My holiday you mean?'

'Holiday. Right. So what's with the injuries? Why the new teeth?'

'I was in a car accident. A stupid prang.'

'Did you report it?'

'Didn't see the need. I was the only one hurt.'

'What about Wade? Didn't he make it back with you?'

'How would I know? He had holiday plans of his own.'

Lane turned his head slightly, though only for an instant.

His gaze drifted over her, dismissed her, returned to the view.

'Was there anything else before you leave, DS Lloyd?'

'Just one thing,' Lloyd told him. 'In my time with the force, I've always believed in following the rules. I've been a stickler for procedure and it's isolated me from my colleagues. But lately, I've started to think I've been wrong. Maybe following procedures is what allows men like you to thrive, Mr Lane. And maybe I hid behind those rules and procedures because it was the safe and easy thing to do. Maybe it stopped me from doing what is right.'

'Men like me.'

'Exactly.'

'I do hate to be tiresome, DS Lloyd, but is that some kind of threat?'

'No threat. It's really more of a personal revelation.'

'I see. And what exactly am I supposed to take from this . . . epiphany of yours?'

'Nothing. Or something, if you choose to. That's entirely up to you. But it was important for me to come here and tell you. And that's it, really. That's all. Except to say that I'll be watching you from now on. You too, Mike.'

She waited a moment more, then turned to leave. She thought they might stop her, or call after her, but they simply let her go, as if her visit had been of no consequence whatsoever.

And perhaps it hadn't been. Stepping out the front door, she couldn't tell if what she'd said had been enough, for her or for Lane. So why had she come, exactly? Because, she realised now, she'd had a need to confront the beast at the end of her quest in the hope she'd see something in his eyes that would tell her what it was she was really searching for. But Connor Lane hadn't allowed her even that satisfaction. His eyes had belonged to the lake.

Letting go of her squash ball, fumbling for her keys, she rushed towards her car, suddenly paranoid that the gates wouldn't open when she reached the bottom of the driveway, that somehow she might never leave.

But as she opened her door, her thoughts turned to the argument Kate Sutherland claimed to have witnessed between Helen Knight and Russell, down by the old boathouse, and she looked off along the sloping lawns towards the gleaming black caul of the lake, spying, in that instant, what she supposed had fascinated Connor Lane so.

Down by the water's edge, near a small outcrop of trees, was the flash and bob of torchlight.

Chapter Seventy-Seven

The old boathouse looked close to collapse. The roof was sagged, the timber bowed and flaking, the foundations sinking into a boggy inlet at the edge of the lake and the base of a rolling mound of lawn.

Miller passed his torch to Kate while he removed a set of bolt cutters from his backpack. He fitted the jaws around a corroded padlock and hasp and snipped the lock free. The boathouse doors had dropped on their hinges and wouldn't budge to begin with, so Miller cleared away a compacted ridge of mud and leaves with the toe of his boot, then worked his fingers into the gap beneath one door and lifted and pulled until it wrenched open, releasing a swampy aroma of stagnant water and rotted algae.

Kate went in ahead of him, spraying the torch around. There wasn't a lot to see. Fishing nets and oars were hanging among the decaying joists in the roof space and a vast old sideboard was butted up against the back wall, the timber bare and marked by scratches and dings. Miller watched as Kate crept closer and slid open the drawers, freeing clouds of dust.

'Crap.' She reared back, wafting her hand in front of her face. 'There's nothing here.' She coughed. 'I was wrong, Miller. I'm sorry.'

Miller didn't reply. He was crouched low, smearing his

fingers through the dirt and grime that coated the cement floor.

'I don't understand it.' Kate turned around, the torch beam whirling with her. 'I was sure there had to be something about this place.'

'Maybe there is. Point that torch over here.'

Kate stepped closer and centred the beam on the area of muddy ground around Miller's hand.

'Look.'

There was a gouge in the concrete, approximately half a metre in length, extending in a shallow arc from just in front of one leg of the sideboard. Kate pointed the torch towards the leg at the opposite end and found a matching groove.

'Help me to move this thing.'

Kate tried, but the sideboard was a mighty piece of furniture and she couldn't shift it at all. It was different for Miller. He spread his feet wide and strained his back and managed to shunt the sideboard a short distance out from the wall.

'I don't have the strength,' Kate told him.

So he came around and used the same technique and moved the sideboard about the same distance. He kept switching ends, pulling and pushing, shunting the unit in small increments.

He straightened, stretching his back, then ducked and felt around in the space behind the sideboard while Kate cast the torch beam from left to right.

'There,' she said, and pointed the beam at the outline of a crude hatch cut low in the wall.

There was no handle or latch. Miller tried pressing the panel, thinking it might pop open. It didn't, but he spied an area of peeled and grazed wood to one side and reached into his backpack for a hunting knife. He unsheathed the blade, wedging it into the crack, wiggling it sideways, forcing the hatch open on concealed hinges.

A smell of mud and stale air wafted out. Miller took the torch from Kate and aimed it along the opening, lighting up a cramped makeshift tunnel carved into damp earth, supported by timber joists and beams. It was just about big enough for him to crawl along, maybe.

'Gross.' Kate nudged him aside and grabbed the torch to take a look for herself. 'Why wasn't this found before? The police must have searched this place after Helen's body washed up.'

'Depends who searched. Depends who Lane paid off.'

'Or threatened,' came a voice from behind.

There was the scuff and scrape of footsteps, then a sudden dry click and a new torch bloomed in the fuggy darkness. Miller and Kate snatched their heads up from behind the sideboard. For a moment, all Miller could see was the white dazzle of the beam. Then the torch was lowered and his sight began to clear and he glimpsed a face he recognised. Unfortunately.

'Kate, meet DS Lloyd. She's the one who's been looking for us both. She's the one who believes I killed Sarah and Melanie.'

'Not Melanie.' Lloyd took a step closer. 'Anna Brooks, maybe.' She flashed the torch in his eyes again. 'What happened to your face? Not a car accident in Switzerland, I hope.'

Miller didn't say anything. He was thinking of the tunnel behind him and of the secrets it might contain. He was thinking of how close he'd got to them. And he was thinking of the knife in his hand.

'So what's down the spooky hole?'

'That's what we're here to find out.'

'Well, don't let me stop you. Let's all take a look.'

The tunnel wasn't long. Five metres, maybe less. Miller was first through, followed by Kate. Lloyd came last but the chamber the shaft opened up in was too cramped to contain the three of them, so she remained prone on her stomach and elbows, peeking out from the mouth of the tunnel at the tiny dome that had been carved from the compacted mud and clay all around.

The earth in the middle of the space had been formed into two long mounds, ringed with pebbles. A handwritten plaque was nailed to the wooden struts behind each mound. The first read: LARRY LANE. The second read: TO A DEAR AND CHERISHED MOTHER, DIANE LANE.

A wooden cross and a crinkled laminated photograph of the couple had been pressed into the clay above the graves. Unlit votive candles were propped in tiny crevices.

'Connor and Russell's parents.' Kate said, and Miller looked up at her colourless face in the torchlight. He was stooped with his back against the dank mud wall, wetness soaking through to his skin. 'Do you think Russell did this?'

'He must have,' Lloyd put in, angling her own torch to see more clearly, her cheek grazed with mud. 'But what does it mean?'

'Problems for Connor,' Miller told them. 'Problems that have been lurking here and troubling him for years. Problems that begin again as soon as we get out of here and Lloyd calls this in.'

But Miller was only halfway right.

The problems did begin immediately, but not for Connor

Lane. They began for Lloyd and Kate and Miller when they crawled back through the tunnel to find that Connor was waiting for them with a torch of his own, and that Mike Renner was flanking him with a revolver clenched in his fist.

Chapter Seventy-Eight

'So you've uncovered our family's grubby little secret. Good for you. Or not, as it happens.'

Connor shone his torch into Lloyd's face, then Kate's. They lowered their heads, raising their hands. But Miller wouldn't allow him that satisfaction. He stared into the harsh white light with a burning intensity of his own.

'Please, you can give the attitude a rest. And get against the wall. All three of you.'

Connor lowered the torch and Miller blinked hard against the translucent shapes floating before his eyes, looking towards his backpack, which he'd left close to the tunnel opening. He was thinking of the SIG he had inside. Of the bolt cutters he might use. He still had the knife in the back pocket of his jeans. Maybe he could reach for it.

'You.' Connor fixed the torch on Kate. 'Throw that backpack over to me. Slowly. Good. Now step back in line with the others. I want you all to hold hands.'

Miller was in the middle and he felt Kate's fingers squirm inside his right hand as Lloyd fumbled for his left. It felt oddly intimate to be holding hands with Lloyd, after she'd been searching for him for so long.

'You have a choice, Detective Sergeant.' Connor swung the torch beam towards her. 'You could step over to this side of the room, behind Mike. We could talk about your possible role in the most favourable outcome from this situation.'

'Tell me about the family secret.' Lloyd was acting as if she was the one with the gun. Which was impressive, because Miller could feel her hand shaking. 'Russell killed your parents, didn't he?'

'Hmm. How best to answer that? Or should I even care? None of you can leave here alive, if I do. You understand that, don't you?'

Miller squeezed Kate's hand. He wanted to let her know Connor was wrong. He wanted to signal that he had a way out. But he wasn't sure that he did. He couldn't get to his knife without letting go. And once he let go, Renner might shoot.

'But, as it happens, I'm going to have to explain things to Mike here, anyway.' Connor hitched his shoulders, grimacing at Renner. 'It's a shame you had to find out like this, Mike. I don't believe Russell ever told you, did he? I know the two of you are close, though perhaps not as close as you imagined.'

Renner's pupils were pinpoints of darkness in the dazzle of the torch. He was breathing hard through his nose, his free hand balled into a tight fist, the revolver pointed towards Miller.

'Russell is burdened by guilt, if that helps,' Connor went on. 'It's his cross to bear. He was the one who found Mum and Dad down on Dad's boat. They were yelling and screaming, out of control. He rushed to the house to get me and I ran back with him. Dad was raging at Mum, calling her all kinds of things. He said she was having an affair. Did you know that, Mike?'

Renner shook his head dumbly, transfixed by Connor. Miller began to wonder if he might have an opportunity to try something after all.

'Dad said he could prove it. He said she'd been cheating for years, he was getting a divorce and she'd get nothing from him. Mum saw us watching and it seemed to change something in her. She told him she was glad it was over. That she didn't love him any more. That she hated what he'd become. We were on the bank when Dad first struck her. He'd hit her before, hit us, too, so neither of us moved to begin with. But this time he didn't stop. He pummelled her face and he kept hitting her when she fell on to the deck. Then he strangled her.'

Renner peered at Connor, his face slackening. He took a half-step towards him, faltered.

Miller was fixed on his revolver, willing him to shift his aim. He was readying himself to burst forwards and make a grab for the gun.

Connor shook his head, as if the memory confounded him. 'Russell got away from me and raced along the pontoon. I tried to catch up to him but by then he'd grabbed an oar and swung it at the back of Dad's head. One strike, and Dad was gone.' He paused and raised his eyes to the rafters, as if communing with the stars beyond. Then he looked back at Renner, a grim expression on his face. 'We had a mess to clean up. I know Russell always thought it might have been different if he hadn't run back to get me. If he'd fetched you instead, Mike.'

Renner lifted his gun to his face, mashing the cold metal against his cheek.

Was this Miller's moment? He tried loosening his hand from Lloyd's grip but she squeezed his fingers tight.

'So you hid their bodies here,' she put in, snagging Connor's attention. 'You buried them together.'

'Russell insisted on it. He was always the sentimental type. I

435

would have dumped them in the water. It was all they deserved, frankly. And it would have fitted with the rumours that went round after they vanished. But Russell wouldn't agree to it. Here he was, having just killed Dad, babbling on about needing somewhere to visit him. I had to make a decision. I had to contain the situation.'

There was a splash of water and the flap of wings out on the lake. Connor whirled towards the blackened waters.

'What happened next?' Lloyd asked him. Her tone was tough and demanding, almost as if Connor was in an interview room with her at the local station.

'Oh,' he said, waving a hand, 'I sent Russell in here to find something to cover Mum and Dad with. No real need. It was dark and we were hardly overlooked. But I thought it would give him time to calm down so I might convince him to ditch them overboard. He came up with the idea of putting them in here instead. Of building his stupid shrine. You'd taught him to build dens, hadn't you, Mike? He worked at this one for days.'

Renner steadily lowered the gun from his face. 'I can't believe you never told me.'

'But look at you now, Mike. This was years ago and see how it's affecting you. It was already difficult enough for me to stop Russell from handing himself in to the police. If he'd seen the look you have in your eyes now . . .' Connor shook his head. 'Sorry, but it had to be this way. And I had to let Russell bury them here. I shouldn't have agreed to it, but I did. Because it was Russell. Because he was special. Because we'd always indulged him and it was what he expected in life. What he expects still.'

'But it bothered him, didn't it?' Miller put in. 'It ate away at him.'

Miller had some understanding of how it would work. He was a man who knew what it was like to have a burden of guilt gnaw at you for years.

Connor sneered, pinning him with the torch beam again.

'Russell was weak. He felt the need to confide in someone. He thought it would lessen his guilt. He even asked for therapy, though naturally I said no. I didn't know what he might say. I think you know yourself by now that the truth is an infection. It spreads, no matter what you do. Better never to let the infection out, wouldn't you agree?'

He held the torch on Miller's face for several seconds more.

'I'd very much like to get back all the money you've extorted from me. But I suppose I'm going to have to settle for killing you instead, then finding and killing your precious Melanie.'

He smiled thinly before glancing at Renner once again. 'You should probably know, Mike, that Russell asked me right at the beginning if we could tell you. Can you imagine? I told him he was insane.'

'You could have trusted me.'

'No, I don't think so. You were loyal to Dad. You would have walked out on us and thrown us to the wolves. We needed you then, Mike. Just like we need you today. And, over time, I think, you've come to respect me perhaps even more than Dad. Look at what we've built together.' He shrugged. 'Plus, I don't think I need to remind you that there are things I know about you, Mike. So many unpleasant tasks you've helped take care of over the years.'

'Like killing my wife,' Miller said. 'Like killing Anna Brooks.'

'And trying to kill me,' Kate added.

'Oh, don't hold that against Mike.' Lane rolled the hand

with the torch in it, whipping the beam around. 'Or me, for that matter. It was Russell again. His stupid need to offload. First, there was Anna. I know he told her about Mum and Dad because she came to me for money. And I paid her a little, at first. But then she got greedy and I refused to pay any more, and all of a sudden, she accused Russell of rape. She tried to apply pressure. Too much pressure, for her.'

'And Helen Knight?' Kate asked. 'I saw her here with Russell. That's why they were arguing, wasn't it? He showed her this place. He told her what he'd done. And she can't have reacted the way he wanted. She wouldn't absolve him. I knew Helen. She'd have told him to tell the police. So he killed her.'

'Well, now.' Connor weaved the torch through the air some more, looping spirals in the dark. 'That's not *quite* how it happened. Young Helen came to me, too, you see. She approached me first.'

'Helen wouldn't blackmail anyone. She wasn't like that.'

'No, she wasn't. She came to tell me that Russell needed to own up to what had happened. That she was going to help him.' Connor twirled his finger next to his temple. 'Loopy. You'll appreciate there was no way I could allow it. Not after all this time.'

He flicked the torch beam at Kate, seeming to enjoy the disgust on her face.

'*You* killed Helen.'

'There we go. You cracked the big mystery. But really, she as good as killed herself, the poor girl.'

And right then, Miller understood it fully for the first time. He understood why Lane had sent Wade to kill his wife and daughter. He knew why he'd set Renner and Wade on Kate

438

and why he'd had them pursue the ghost of Anna Brooks throughout Europe. It wasn't only about protecting Russell. It wasn't even about the money Miller had been taking him for. It was also about eradicating anyone Russell might have confided in. It was about burying the truth.

'You sicken me,' Kate told him.

'Oh, I sicken myself. Quite regularly. But I get over it. I'm sorry to say you won't have that opportunity.'

Lloyd was growing tired of Connor's performance. She swore under her breath.

'Problem, DS Lloyd?'

'Yes, I have a problem. If what you say about your brother is even halfway true, it was an accident when he killed your father. He didn't have intent to murder. He hit him once. A single blow. To protect your mother. Even hiding the bodies, concealing what had happened . . . It never warranted this. Not all of it.'

'See?' Lane wagged a finger. 'An infection. The truth begins to spread. But I can tell you the rest now, I suppose, because then Mike will shoot you, and you'll have no way to spread the disease. The lake will swallow it up. I've learned from the mistakes I made with Helen's body.'

'It was you.' Miller felt even more certain the moment the words were spoken. 'You killed your parents. It wasn't Russell at all.'

Connor's eyes glinted. 'You expect me to tell you that?'

'We deserve the truth,' Kate said. 'Helen deserved the truth.'

'You deserve nothing. And neither did she. But Mike? Well, Mike should probably know it all. So, look, Dad was dead, and that was all on Russell I'm afraid, but Mum wasn't . . . *quite*. But she was so nearly gone already and she'd seen Russell hit Dad. She would have told someone about it. You know that, Mike. She was weak, like him. And she was the one who'd cheated. She was the one to blame. So I told Russell to run in here and I finished it. Finished her.' He shone the torchlight on his hand, as if marvelling at what it was capable of. 'I had to smother the infection before it could begin. You'll understand that better than anyone, Mike. You're the best I know at containing a situation. Tell me you wouldn't have done the same thing if you'd been there.'

But he wouldn't have. Miller could see that, even if Connor couldn't. Because Renner was blinking, lips twitching, looking blearily around the boathouse and out towards the lake, as if he was caught in a trap he couldn't see a way out of. The wash of light from Connor's torch was dim at the edges, but Miller could glimpse the dampness in his eyes. He could read the emotion in his face.

It wasn't rage or anger or disgust. It was something Miller recognised because he'd suffered from it himself for so long. It was heartache. It was grief.

It was love.

But not for Connor. Not any more.

'No,' Renner muttered, lifting his gun. 'No, see, that's where you're wrong.'

And he shot Connor in the side of the head.

*

For the first time in his life, Mike Renner didn't make any effort to cover up a crime. He didn't attempt to run or to silence the witnesses. He let go of his revolver as soon as Connor fell, his sole focus being on grabbing the torch that was tumbling from Connor's hand, ducking behind the sideboard and scrabbling into the tunnel.

Alone in the musty silence, the din of the gunshot reverberating in his head, the torch beam slanted across the ground, he reached out his hand to the mound of earth where Diane was buried.

Finally, Renner had his answer. He'd found the woman he'd loved.

And with Connor dead, it would all unravel now anyway. He had so many crimes to answer for. So many offences that went far beyond betraying his best friend by falling for his wife.

*

'What do we do?' Kate whispered. She was backing away from Connor's body, blocking the sight of his bloodied head with her splayed fingers.

Miller didn't answer. He was busy crabbing sideways, snatching up his backpack.

Lloyd had been quick to make a grab for Renner's gun and now she was holding it in a two-handed grip with the muzzle pointed towards the hole he'd crawled through. She looked as if she knew what she was doing. She looked as if she'd shoot if she had to.

Kate stooped for Miller's torch, throwing light on the tunnel opening, the beam trembling against the timber planks.

'I'll call it in.' Lloyd reached into her jacket, removing her phone. But she didn't begin to dial. Not yet. 'I have to get a team here. We'll have to sift through everything Lane said. It changes things for his brother. Changes a hell of a lot of things, really.'

'For us, too?' Kate asked.

Miller tugged on her arm, trying to drag her away, but Kate resisted.

'Maybe. It's too early to say.'

'We're leaving,' Miller told her. 'There's nothing for us here now.'

'No, you'll wait.' Lloyd swung the revolver towards them, her arm extended, a sweaty gleam on her face. 'You'll have to run through it all. You'll have to give statements. You know I can't leave you out of it.'

'So don't. But we won't be here.'

'I have a gun.'

'So do I.' He withdrew the SIG from his backpack, turning it in his fist as if he hadn't the faintest clue how it had got there. 'But I don't plan to use it and you really don't want to shoot us. Right now, you're a winner. You have a big success on your hands. We led you to this. We're giving it to you. The truth, all wrapped up. It's what you wanted, isn't it?'

Lloyd wet her lip. She glanced back towards the tunnel opening.

Was Renner weeping in there? It sounded that way to Miller.

'Two questions,' Lloyd said. 'Will you answer them for me?'

'Depends on what they are.'

'The fire at your house – I want to know, did you find your wife and Anna dead and see it as an opportunity? Were you the one who set the blaze?'

'You honestly believe I'm capable of that?'

'I've wondered.'

'Then stop. The fire was already raging. Wade set it. Wade

442

killed them. I couldn't get in the house. I tried. I tried everything I could. Believe me.'

Lloyd watched him carefully, weighing his words. Maybe she did believe him. It was hard to tell from her reaction. But then she sighed and shook her head and beckoned to Kate.

'Give me that torch. I'm going to need it if I'm sticking around here on my own.'

Kate hesitated, looking between Miller and Lloyd until Miller snatched the torch from her and stepped forwards to pass it across. He held Lloyd's eye for a beat, then turned and caught Kate's hand and guided her towards the open door and the waiting lake.

Kate was almost outside ahead of him when he paused and looked back, tugging on her arm. Lloyd was switching her attention between Miller and the tunnel opening, the torch clamped beneath her elbow, tapping the lighted display of her phone with her thumb.

'What was the other question?' he asked her. 'You said there were two.'

'Melanie.' Lloyd's thumb hovered over the phone. 'How is she? Is she well?'

'She's alive.'

'And happy?'

Miller considered it.

'She will be. She's been lost a long time. Both of us have been. I'm hoping now this is over we can find our way back to each other again.'

'So go to her.' Lloyd made the call and raised the phone to her ear. 'Get away from here and hide. It's what you do best, I think.'

PART IX

Epilogue

Five Months Later

Eight a.m. in London and Jennifer Lloyd buttoned her silk blouse, tucking it into the waistband of her fitted skirt. She checked her make-up in the mirror, patted her hair. The style was softer than she was used to. Longer than before, swept back around her shoulders and tinted. She liked it, and so did a lot of other people judging by the compliments she was receiving from colleagues and friends. Colleagues who *were* friends. That was something new. Lloyd had become part of a team in a very real way.

Her life had changed, so it seemed only fitting that her view had, too. She'd invested in a two-bed apartment in a water-side complex next to the Thames. It was a modern place with a curved glass balcony that offered her a glimpse of Tower Bridge and, on a clear day, the dome of St Paul's. But not this morning, because Lloyd was in a hurry, swallowing the last of her tea and popping her mug in the dishwasher before locking her apartment and pressing the call button for the elevator.

The doors parted and a silver-haired professional in a tailored suit flashed her a wolfish grin as she stepped inside. Which amused her, though not because she was attracted to him. The fact was Lloyd was seeing someone. It wasn't a regular thing, and it was long-distance, but she had a feeling it might develop into something more. Julia Summerhayes was ten years her senior, but she was a remarkable woman: intelligent, kind, funny, but most of all, wise. It was Julia who'd helped Lloyd to understand how her perceptions had changed.

The fallout from events at the Lane estate had been complex and frenetic. They'd led to the arrest of Mike Renner on multiple serious charges, to the release of Russell Lane from prison, to the formal burials of Larry and Diane Lane in a local churchyard, and to the cremation of their son Connor, whose ashes, despite the wishes plainly expressed in his will, had been scattered by Russell from the side of a small boat over the deepest, darkest waters of Windermere.

An investigation had been launched into the failures and oversights of the UK Protected Persons Service, during which Nadine Foster had been found guilty of gross misconduct and dismissed from her role with the National Crime Agency. Foster would never work as a police officer again, but that was the least of her worries, since the Crown Prosecution Service were still considering the criminal charges she would face.

Lloyd had been called to give evidence in front of a six-person investigatory board that counted Commissioner Bennett among its members. Bennett had smiled knowingly when she'd taken her seat in the faceless meeting room in Whitehall. This was the moment he'd been waiting for; a chance for Lloyd to give voice to the many doubts and concerns they shared, not just about the way the Protected Persons Service was being run, but about its very existence in the first place.

And yet, by the time Lloyd found herself clearing her throat and leaning towards the microphone in front of her, she'd come to realise something. Yes, there were flaws in the way the service was being operated, but when she thought of everything she'd experienced in the wake of Kate Sutherland's disappearance, when her mind turned to the murders of Sarah Adams and Anna Brooks, to the repercussions of Connor Lane's actions throughout Europe, and to the desperate measures Nick Adams had taken to safeguard his daughter, she had to state for the record, in clear, concise terms, that the Protected Persons Service was a highly valuable programme that did important work and that its future had to be secured, no matter the difficulties involved.

And then – to hell with the inappropriateness of the setting, or to the unmistakable distaste she could see spreading across Bennett's skeletal face – she made a pitch to play an integral role in the future of the programme, to help guide it and shape it, with the aim of making it the best, most comprehensive scheme of its kind anywhere in the world.

Which was a little over the top, she had to admit, but her passion had impressed enough key members of the board that her proposals were taken forward for further discussion despite Commissioner Bennett's complaints. Not long afterwards, she'd been promoted to the rank of DI and placed on permanent assignment to the National Crime Agency, with special responsibility to develop and implement a new set of rules and procedures for the handling of protected persons.

Lloyd lived for the role. She had a fresh hunger for her job, and for her life outside it. Yet there wasn't a day that went by when she didn't think of Nick Adams and Kate Sutherland, and wonder where they might be or what they might be doing.

The elevator dinged, the doors slid open and the silver-haired man in the expensive suit motioned for Lloyd to step out ahead of him. She crossed the foyer towards a bank of mail-boxes to retrieve her post and found there was only one item waiting for her.

It was a postcard.

*

Six days previously, Miller sat in a canvas restaurant chair beneath a parasol, his arm resting on Kate's freckled shoulder. He was wearing mirrored sunglasses and a short-sleeved shirt over linen trousers. The remains of an octopus salad were on the table in front of him, next to an empty bottle of Sauvignon blanc.

Across the table, Becca smiled lazily from behind her Jackie O shades, her bosom straining against the material of the pat-terned sundress she had on. Hanson was bent forwards over the last of his lobster dish. He looked different with his new con-tact lenses. Younger, if that was possible, though perhaps Miller was swayed by the pink polo shirt and skinny shorts he was wearing.

The early-afternoon heat was intense, even in the shade of the restaurant terrace, and the tourists ambling along the lime-stone esplanade seemed wearied by the ceaseless sun. Miller could feel the warmth of Kate's skin through the thin cotton of the pink vest top she had on. He could smell the sea and he could hear the wheeling gulls. He felt drowsy from the wine and the heat. He was relaxed and content.

'It's been so good seeing you both.' Kate reached across the table to squeeze Becca's hand.

'You too, sweetie.'

'Really good,' Hanson added, sucking lobster juices from his fingers. 'So what's next for you? Have you decided?'

Miller felt the muscles ripple and tighten across Kate's back.

'We've been talking,' she said, glancing at him. 'And I think I should go back to the UK. It's safe for me now with Connor gone. And I'd like to meet my brother. Or try to, at least. Thanks to you.'

She kicked Hanson's feet under the table, and he smiled broadly, his lips shimmering with grease.

Becca pushed her sunglasses down on her nose, staring at Miller over the frames as if she expected him to intervene.

But Miller had already talked with Kate. They'd discussed it many times. *There's no going back.* That's what he'd told her right at the beginning. And maybe he'd been wrong where Kate was concerned, but he'd been right about himself. There were crimes he'd have to answer for, decisions that held consequences he'd be required to face. Lloyd might have allowed him to run once, but if he tried to go home for good, she couldn't ignore what he'd done. He'd conspired to fake his daughter's death by concealing the murder of Anna Brooks. He'd broken the law countless ways to identify and protect his clients. And besides, people were reliant on him. There were Pete and Emily to think about. There was Darren and Agata. There was Melanie, Timo, Nico and Mia.

Becca kept staring, hitching her eyebrows, and when he remained motionless, she sighed and shook her head.

'Honey,' she told Kate, 'you know there's something else you can do. Miller will never ask you, or tell you that it's what he really wants, so I guess it's down to me. You can stay and work with us. You can help us to carry on with what we do. We have people who need us. People to look after. And you can bet there'll be more of them soon.'

'We could definitely use you,' Hanson added. 'You've proved that already.'

'Plus, we love you, sweetie. And Miller loves you – in a different, down-and-dirty kind of way. You're good for him.'

'You *humanise* him.'

'Hey.' Miller raised a hand, sneaking a look at Kate. A lop-sided grin tugged at the corner of his mouth. 'Well?' he asked her. 'What do you say?'

'I don't know.' She half smiled, half winced. 'Maybe. I want to say yes. I do. But there's my brother to think about. I want to try and meet him. I need it.'

'Yeah, about that.' Hanson dabbed at his lips with a cotton napkin. 'We're great at hiding people, Kate. And we'd be better at it with you, no question. But don't ever forget we're also pretty great at finding people.'

He nodded to a point somewhere behind Kate, winking encouragement when she still didn't turn. Miller lowered his hand from her shoulder and swivelled with her, looking along the sunlit esplanade, lined with seventeenth-century stone buildings, towards a tall bell tower and a giant, ornate brick fountain.

A red-haired man was standing at the base of the domed fountain in a white button-down shirt and beige chinos with a travel bag slung over his shoulder. He was shading his eyes with one hand, scanning the plaza.

Kate pushed back her chair, the metal legs scraping on the flagstones.

'You didn't.'

452

'Trust me. It's Richard.'

'Hanson.' She shook her head as she rose slowly to her feet. 'I am seriously impressed by you right now. But don't think I don't know what this is really about. I get what you've done here. Because how could I possibly say no to working with you guys after this?'

She smiled against the tears in her eyes and started towards her brother, one hand trailing in her wake, fingers spread, beckoning to Miller.

'You go with her,' he said to Becca and Hanson. 'See that she's OK.'

'You should come too.'

'I will. Soon. I just have one thing to do first.'

He laid down enough cash to cover their bill, then glanced over at Kate, who was stepping towards her brother hesitantly, accepting his outstretched hand, the two of them shaking formally before her brother laughed and dropped his bag, opening his arms, pulling her close.

Miller watched them a moment more, then nodded once at Hanson and crossed the street, passing through the blazing sunshine into the shade beneath an arched colonnade, where he contemplated the display of postcards outside a souvenir shop.

*

Lloyd stared at the postcard for a long moment, her heart clenching, her vision seeming to throb.

The image was a view of a sun-bathed harbour. She saw azure waters, a dun-coloured citadel, moored yachts, and a cascade of white houses with terracotta roofing tiles.

453

Slowly, she flipped the card over. Dubrovnik. It was post-marked six days ago, addressed to her in a slanted biro scrawl.

Dear Jennifer

You were right in what you said to me. This is what I'm best at. Please don't look for us in Croatia. We'll have moved on by the time you get this. But as Kate tells me now, even the best runners eventually tire. Every now and again you have to stop and catch your breath. So that's what we're going to do. We're catching our breath. At least for a short while.

The card wasn't signed. Lloyd glanced up and turned it over, weighing it in her hand, imagining Nick Adams writing his message in a seafront hotel room; thinking of him picking up his luggage and strolling away hand-in-hand with Kate to post the card before moving on.

She checked her watch. She was running a little late. She had a packed schedule of meetings ahead of her and a new case file to oversee. She should go. She should hurry outside and catch her bus.

But instead she walked back to the waiting elevator, hit the button for her floor and returned to her apartment. She entered her kitchen, took a magnet from a drawer and stuck the postcard to her fridge. Then she stepped back with her arms folded and lost herself in the blazing sunshine and turquoise waters of Dubrovnik. For a few precious minutes, she caught her breath.

Acknowledgements

As ever, this book only exists because of the support and hard work of a lot of fine people. Huge thanks to my agent, Vivien Green, and the teams at Sheil Land Associates, Georges Borchardt Inc. and the RWSG Literary Agency.

To my editors, Katherine Armstrong and Angus Cargill, along with everyone at Faber & Faber.

To Louisa Kermeen (of the Milan Veterinary Practice, Douglas, Isle of Man); Gill Young, Sabine Lemmer-Brust, Dr Lucy Hanington and Dr Saleel Chandratre.

To Hart Hanson and Andrew Miller, for trusting me with their names (the fools . . .).

To Mum, Dad and Allie.

And to my wife Jo, my junior editor Jessica, and Maisie.

Also by Chris Ewan

Safe House

When there's nowhere else to hide

A MISSING WOMAN

When Rob Hale wakes up in hospital afer a motorcycle crash he is
told that Lena, the woman he claims was travelling with him, doesn't
exist. But has he really only imagined her?

A SEARCH FOR THE TRUTH

Convinced that Lena is real and that she needs his help, Rob sets
out to find her. He's assisted by Rebecca Lewis, a PI who's also been
investigating his sister's death. But is there more to Rebecca
than meets the eye?

NOWHERE TO HIDE

Together Rob and Rebecca follow the clues to discover Lena's fate. In
doing so they discover a conspiracy that goes much deeper and spreads
far wider than either of them could have imagined. They also realise
that sometimes your best option isn't to hide, but to stay and fight.

'An exciting, well-crafted thriller.' **S. J. Bolton**

'Chris Ewan is an author to watch – and enjoy.' **Andrew Taylor**

'A high-octane thriller . . . Proceeding at warp speed with plenty
of twists and excellent use of its setting . . . a terrific holiday read.'
Laura Wilson, *Guardian*

ff

Dead Line

She's gone and time is running out . . .

When hostage negotiator Daniel Trent's fiancée, Aimée, goes
missing without a trace, he does everything he can to find her.

Suspecting shady businessman Jérôme Moreau had something
to do with her disappearance, Trent plans to abduct and
interrogate him. But when Moreau is kidnapped, Trent must
get him back quickly – and alive – before time runs out.

'An intense, rapid-fire thriller with plenty of twists and turns from a
rising star of the genre.' **Simon Kernick**

'This is a compulsive against-the-clock thriller that cleverly turns the
kidnap plot on its head. Great stuff!' **Robert Goddard**

ff

Dark Tides

One night. Six friends. One deadly dare.

From the bestselling author of *Safe House* comes a story about
friendship, family, secrets, lies and the things we do for love.

When Claire Cooper was eight, her mother disappeared
during Hop-tu-naa, the Manx Halloween.

Ten years later Claire and her friends took part in a
Hop-tu-naa dare that went desperately wrong.

Now she is in her early twenties and a police officer, and
what happened that Hop-tu-naa night has come back
to haunt them all. Claire must confront her deepest
fears in order to stop a killer from striking again.

'Ewan has become a master storyteller.' **Ann Cleeves**

'A truly atmospheric thriller that's impossible to put down.'
Daily Express

'A clever, gripping blend of thriller and detective-story elements.'
Sunday Times